LOOSE LIPS

Books by Kemper Donovan

THE BUSY BODY

LOOSE LIPS

LOOSE LIPS

kemper donovan

JOHN SCOGNAMIGLIO BOOKS
KENSINGTON PUBLISHING CORP.
www.kensingtonbooks.com

JOHN SCOGNAMIGLIO BOOKS are published by

Kensington Publishing Corp.
900 Third Avenue
New York, NY 10022

All Kensington titles, imprints and distributed lines are available at special quantity discounts for bulk purchases for sales promotion, premiums, fund-raising, educational or institutional use.

Special book excerpts or customized printings can also be created to fit specific needs. For details, write or phone the office of the Kensington Special Sales Manager: Kensington Publishing Corp., 900 Third Avenue, New York, NY, 10022. Attn. Special Sales Department. Phone: 1-800-221-2647.

Library of Congress Control Number: 2024934944

ISBN: 978-1-4967-4454-8
First Kensington Hardcover Edition: February 2025

ISBN: 978-1-4967-4460-9 (e-book)

10 9 8 7 6 5 4 3 2 1

Printed in the United States of America

To my loving parents, Daniel and Maureen Donovan, both of them a lifelong inspiration in more ways than I can list here . . . and neither of whom would ever dream of setting foot on a cruise.

Part One
Departure

CHAPTER 1

Cruises are a love-it-or-hate-it proposition. There's no middle ground on the matter, and from the moment I'd become aware that voluntarily imprisoning oneself at great personal expense on a slow-moving island of "fun" was a thing, I vowed never—ever—to take part in a cruise. But such promises are made to be broken, which was how I found myself watching forlornly as Slip 90 of the Cape Liberty Cruise Port in beautiful Bayonne, New Jersey, shrank into the distance.

The Manhattan skyline was too blurry to make much of an impression on this cloudy, late January morning. Just as well. I rarely think about 9/11 when I'm in the city, going about my day. But it's impossible not to conjure those two towers when viewing downtown from a distance. They've officially become the world's most distressing set of ghost twins (sorry, *Shining* gals; you've been unseated). It was windy out on the harbor—cold enough for gloves, a hat, and a scarf. Not that I minded. The winter had been so warm, I'd hardly been able to use such accessories till now. For me, winter clothes are a sneaky means of cosplaying as a fancy lady from days of yore, the only time I get to wear a hat and gloves without looking like an eccentric. As for scarves, I always have grand plans to wear them in temperate weather the way French people do, but then I always chicken out. The one I had on now was a behomoth: eggshell-white with an inky-red design blooming across its surface like creamer spreading through coffee, and long enough for me to wrap several times in loose, luxurious loops. I burrowed my face into it now, warming the tip of my nose.

There were only a handful of people on the upper deck with me, watching the departure. I was a little surprised by this—not that I expected the crowds of people you see in old black-and-white footage waving hankies from ships with so many tiers, they look more like stadiums. For one thing, there were no tiers, just the one deck exposed to the elements. There was also no one to wave at on the shore. People don't gather to see off ships anymore, especially not puny ones like ours: a white dwarf compared to the red giant of a *Queen Mary* or *QE 2*, or any of the old trans-Atlantic steamers, which have themselves been dwarfed by the hulking supernovae to come out of the Royal Caribbean/Costa/Carnival fleets in recent years. Cruise ships put the "big" in "big business" these days.

The people who'd come to Slip 90 had all boarded the ship. There were a little over two hundred of them, the majority now snug in their cabins, unpacking their suitcases like sensible souls. My own little wheeled number stood beside me, upright like a dog on hind legs. I patted it with a gloved palm, thinking fondly of the various gels, liquids, pastes, and creams inside it, almost all of them larger than the four ounces we're reduced to traveling with by air (speaking of 9/11 . . .). I'd chosen to re-main outside, both as a means of staving off motion sickness and from a masochistic impulse to watch my beloved isle of Manhattan slip away from me.

And yet I couldn't help feeling hopeful as the skyline re-ceded, fool that I was—seduced by the common fallacy that a temporary location change would make a meaningful differ-ence in my life. Little did I know, as I closed one eye and blot-ted out the Statue of Liberty with the thumb of my glove, that for once the fallacy would hold true. This cruise would change my life. Permanently.

Would it have been preferable for this magical transformation not to have involved a triple homicide on the open seas? (That's right: triple. There will be *three* dead bodies on this boat before you or I are done with it.) Sure. But *c'est la vie*.

Or *la mort*, as the case may be.

CHAPTER 2

In the same way luxury liners departing from the English coast would cross the Channel and make a final stop in Cherbourg, France, before traversing the Atlantic, we docked in the Clifton neighborhood of Staten Island to bring another eighty people on board. I could make a joke about how uncouth this rabble was compared to those posh, fin-de-siècle crowds. But for all their bustle skirts and bowler hats, people back then were undoubtedly sicker and dirtier than the well-to-do travelers I saw bounding up the gangway, Athleta gear peeking from underneath their North Face jackets. These sybarites were propelled by an energy that requires heaps of leisure time and the disposable cash with which to enjoy it. No one gets on a boat these days unless they want to.

Unless someone is paying them to be there, of course.

Can you guess which category I fell into?

The Get Lit Cruise had been arranged for passionate (read: rich) fans of literature, who would be attending a one-week series of lectures while the ship ambled eastward into the North Atlantic and then turned around at some indeterminate point, shuffling its way back to New York. Like many cruises, it was all about the journey, not the destination. And that journey was officially starting now, as the ship pulled away from the dock and headed for the open seas.

I was standing in the back of the ship (the stern, I should say), in an area raised half a staircase above everything else. The floor consisted of wide wooden planks that contrasted with the poured cement covering the rest of the deck. My guess was that in warmer weather, people sunbathed here. There would be no sunbathing today, or any of the seven days allotted for our outing—no chance of the air temperature budging north of forty. I didn't mind this. Warmth demands enjoyment; we're expected to capitalize on a warm and sunny day, whereas appreciation of cold or otherwise "bad" weather is attainable on its own terms.

It struck me that a ship is one of the few places where people live out their lives according to the sort of rigid hierarchy ubiquitous a hundred years ago: the "help" toiling away unseen in support of the moneyed class of paying passengers. I was just about to formulate some deep thoughts on this topic when a seagull swooped so low, its talon nearly grazed my forehead. Seriously—this thing came so close, the force of its body whipping through the air blew actual wind onto my face.

"Is your shampoo potato-chip-scented?" asked the woman beside me after I ducked theatrically, checking myself over for blood. I suppose she had to say something.

She was wearing a trench coat, which is one of those articles of clothing that resides in Frumpsville unless all the details are just right. All the details on this trench were just right, nothing loose or baggy about it, its top half fitting her like a second skin, a horizontal stitch under the bust reminiscent of those Empire-waisted dresses we all love staring at in Jane Austen adaptations. There were epaulets on the shoulders, and an olive-green trim on the cuffs and belt, the latter of which she'd knotted to one side, showing off her lean figure. Her gray hair was frizzy and untended, but I guessed this was a choice, and that she made a practice of avoiding the chemicals found in dyes and gels and other such products. An absence of makeup was doing her face no favors in the dull yet luminous sunlight seeping through the clouds, but I could only hope my skin looked so good at her age, which I guessed to be mid-sixties or thereabouts. Her wrinkles were so fine, they gave her cheeks a feathered softness that was nothing like the dewiness of youth, but which served as a testament to a youth spent wisely. Like so many on this ship, she exuded good health. No question that inside her oversized shoulder bag was a reusable water bottle she drained several times a day.

"I'd totally use potato-chip-scented shampoo if it existed."

She laughed—more enthusiastically than my response warranted.

"Now which one did you sign up for?" she demanded. "I'm doing personal essay. With Payton."

"None of them," I replied, enjoying her momentary confusion. "I'm an instructor."

"Oh! Which one? No wait, let me guess."

I waited, letting her guess.

"Poetry?"

I shook my head: *no.*

"Young adult?"

She laughed when I crossed my arms into an *X.*

"It can't be romance, can it?"

I didn't know whether to be flattered or offended.

"Not romance," I assured her.

"So that leaves . . . Oh! It's mystery, isn't it?"

It was most assuredly mystery. As you may know, I wrote a mystery novel based on real events that took place up in Maine a while back. This book got me some attention. Before then, I'd earned my proverbial bread by way of ghostwriting other people's memoirs—celebrity memoirs, mainly. For all intents and purposes I was *still* a ghostwriter, though I hadn't booked a gig in some time.

"That makes you Belle Currer!"

"Belle Currer" was the pen name I'd used for my mystery. Do you see what I did there? I didn't want to use my real name, which occasionally graced the covers (more often, the acknowledgments pages) of my ghostwritten books. And I didn't mind that "Belle Currer" was what most people were in the habit of calling me now—even my agent, Rhonda. Beyond the Brontë of it all, it helped that Belle was easily my favorite Disney princess. Anyone whose constant refrain has to do with how bored she is, *and* who can negotiate a crowded street with her head buried in a book is okay by me. I told Rhonda I wanted to print up business cards with my new name on one side, and on the other: THERE MUST BE MORE THAN THIS PROVINCIAL LIFE.

She said if I did, she'd fire me.

"I'm Geraldine Forrest." The woman held out her hand. "But please, call me Gerry."

We shook. I leaned over the railing again, and so did she. Staten Island was already long gone, little more than a strip of land surrounded by water, and a few minutes later the strip was gone too. There was nothing but sky and water now. We were officially out on the ocean. I couldn't believe how quickly this had happened, and a pang of alarm hit me—something halfway between a throb of the heart and a sob in the back of my throat, a spasm of remorse for dry land, which I knew I wouldn't see for one full week. This current view was it: there would be nothing but endless blue on endless blue, though at the moment it was endless gray on endless blue.

Gerry breathed in deeply. "Smell that gorgeous ocean air," she murmured. We were standing close enough that I could sense her head turning toward me not by sight, but by feel, a shift in the air. "You must know Payton really well then?"

"Oh yes." I took a deep breath of my own. "I know Payton well."

"I just *love* her," said Gerry.

That's because you don't know her, I thought.

Payton Garrett was the mastermind behind the Get Lit Cruise, and there's a good chance you've heard her name before. She's a famous writer, but her fame is of that specifically twenty-first century, social-media-infused variety that's more about engaging with readers than writing something and stepping back to allow the work to speak for itself. There was no stepping back where Payton Garrett was concerned.

Her first book was called *A Rising Tide*. A meditation on her claustrophobic Christian upbringing, it straddled the boundary between memoir and self-help, Payton explaining how she'd managed to transcend her background without rejecting it wholesale—a nuanced playbook she invited the reader to apply to her own life. It did extremely well, and deservedly so. Payton Garrett was a damn good writer. She was also a savvy entrepreneur who maintained a death grip on the buzz her book generated, using it to build a robust presence on all forms of social media, and to launch a hit podcast called *Girls Will Be Girls* in which she shared her life wisdom in conversation with pretty much any celebrity guest she wanted, so massive was her audience. Other books followed: another memoir, a collection of essays culled from her many think-pieces scattered across the Internet, and most recently, a sprawling novel set in the nineteenth century, fictionalizing the life of Augusta Leigh, Lord Byron's somewhat notorious half-sister. Payton Garrett was an established brand now, an *influencer*. And if that meant she had to hawk teeth whiteners and food delivery programs from time to time, then more power to her because that's the way business gets done these days.

I couldn't help comparing myself with her because we'd known each other for ages, having gotten our MFAs together at an embarrassingly third-tier program in the backwoods of southern Illinois. (Those woods are metaphorical, by the way; I would have killed for some trees in that flat-ass, *Children of the Corn*–addled wasteland.) Her memoir had come out around the same time as my first—and until my mystery, my only—novel, and I think I did a decent job of pretending to be happy for her as she shot off into the stratosphere and I remained earthbound, with my lukewarm reviews and nonexistent sales. But then I began building my career as a ghostwriter, and I was savvy enough to keep in touch with her, if only sporadically. From time to time I'd ask her for career advice, which she never failed to give. That was the thing about Payton Garrett: she *loved* to help. It made her feel like a good person while simultaneously proving she had the upper hand.

I'm being petty. I realize this. But to give you a sense of what she was like, *and* of how desperate I was to have taken her up on her offer to join this wackadoodle cruise, behold the subject heading of the first e-mail she sent me on the topic: "Pretty Cool Opportunity for a Kickass Writer Lady Like Yourself Unless You're Too Busy BELIEVE ME I GET IT 😂😂😂."

Jesus retched.

"Payton is amazing," I said to Gerry.

Not a lie. Whatsoever.

I leaned farther over the railing, taking great gulps of the ocean air and enjoying the salty prickle on my soft palate. The air smelled of ice itself, which made me think of snow and glaciers and old-school adventurers like Ernest Shackleton and Edmund Hillary. My remorse turned to excitement, and I leaned out farther. The sides of the ship were painted a bright, hospital white that would be blinding when the sun came out. It must have been painted recently, as the vessel wasn't brand-new, though it wasn't ancient either. (It was eight years old, and yes, I'd looked this up. Eight years felt like a nice Goldilocks number for a boat: fully vetted, and yet by no means rickety.) There was a blue design just below the railing—a squarish, geometric pattern that wouldn't have looked out of place on a Grecian urn. This same blue was repeated in a thick band at the bottom of the boat, just above the water line. And above that in a lighter blue was the name of the ship: *Merman Rivera*, the *M* and *R* with long curlicue tails wrapping around their respective words.

The name was a partial nod to the dual nature of the ship, which was large enough for ocean voyages, but small enough to traverse rivers as well. I found it to be smaller than expected, but then, what isn't? If I hadn't known its capacity was three hundred, I would have guessed one hundred at most. It's easy to pack people onto ships, though. Today was Sunday, and classes would take place Monday through Friday, the ship docking again on Saturday afternoon. This meant that for one whole week there was nowhere to go outside of the 300-by-50-foot dimensions of this floating hulk of metal. The panic returned, leapfrogging up my gut and through my throat in a hideous sort of reverse peristalsis, landing in the back of my mouth, my tongue quivering sickly. Suddenly I felt like I was going to vomit and I whipped myself upright, managing to collide with Gerry.

"Sorry!"

We said this in unison.

"Well aren't we a pathetic pair of over-apologizing women?"

She gave me a saucy look as she said this, which was the moment I decided I liked her. Joviality pairs well with me, so long as it isn't inane. It helps balance out my phlegmatic tendencies.

"Do you want to go inside?" I asked. "It's getting cold."

And I don't want to throw up in front of you, I added to myself.

"Yes, please!"

The doorway leading to the stairwell had a sizable lip at the bottom, no doubt to prevent any water on the deck from flooding inward. It had the look and feel of a porthole, and despite the awkwardness of having to lift my suitcase over it, I experienced a thrill upon stepping into this enclosed space and hearing a far-off groan of metal, the boat creaking around us. I loved knowing that everyone could feel the same motion: that we were together, en masse, aboard this ship. It was the same collectivist spirit that sent me running to Twitter whenever I was in LA and an earthquake happened, no matter how minor. (Yes, I know technically it's "X" now. But eff that noise. Sorry/not sorry, Elon.) For all my misanthropic ways, I enjoy feeling like I'm a part of something bigger. It's an ancient, animal instinct, and whenever it recurs I find it both comforting and exhilarating, which shouldn't be possible, yet somehow it is. Here we all were, three hundred strong embarking on a journey together—embarking literally, as the original definition of "embark" is to board a ship, or "bark." (Per Shakespeare, love is "the star to every wand'ring bark.") Looking back, I wish I'd appreciated this moment more, when everything was still ahead of us. Before long we'd be underway, then half finished, then back in this very spot—except the boat would be facing the other direction and it would all be ending. Time screws us over in this way again and again, and yet we never learn.

We never appreciate the beginnings enough.

Gerry and I descended to the second deck, where all the public rooms were situated: lounge, ballroom, dining room, and five—count 'em, five!—auditoriums of varying sizes. People on cruises love their musical theater, and according to its rather paltry Wikipedia page, the *Merman Rivera* had been built as an "intimate show ship," which was another reason for its curious, bifurcated name. As many of you are no doubt aware (let's not pretend there isn't a higher proportion of women and gay men reading this than in the general population), *Merman Rivera* was a reference to the late, great songstress Ethel Merman, and the one and only Chita Rivera, a legendary performer who departed this world fairly recently—much to the world's desolation. I have no doubt that on previous outings, these theaters had been used not just for musicals and other vocal performances but for all sorts of shows—a cringeworthy stand-up comedy routine here, a downtrodden magic act there, maybe even a mime show or two (though I hope not). We'd be using these spaces to conduct lectures: to lead group discussions pertaining to the art of the personal essay, poetry, young adult fiction, romance, and mystery. But not yet. The only event planned for tonight was a drinks reception followed by dinner. And so Gerry and I bypassed the second deck, clanking our way down the metal stairs toward the lower levels.

"Did you travel far to get here?" I asked politely. The darkness of the stairwell was having a soothing effect on my nausea.

"Not *too* far. I live in the Bay Area, out in Northern California."

This tracked. She had a NorCal vitality to her—a hale, peppy energy.

"Are you here on your own?"

"I sure am!" she said. "Footloose and fancy-free, just the way I like it! Me, I live a simple life. No partner, no children, not even many friends except for the few who count. Got to be your own best friend, I find."

I paused in the middle of the stairwell to throw her an appreciative glance.

"Good for you," I said, hoping this wouldn't come across as patronizing.

"It *is* good for me!"

Her eyes were too shiny, her smile too wide—more of a rictus, really. I should have known something was wrong. But I was too focused on finding my room, too stressed with the uncertainty over what exactly I was supposed to teach these freaky rich people for five whole days.

It's a shame, because if I *had* noticed, if I'd stopped her right there on the stairs to ask what was the matter, she very well may have told me.

And then maybe all the bad things that were yet to happen could have been prevented.

CHAPTER 3

Gerry's room was on the third deck and mine was on the fourth, these two decks being devoted to en suite passenger cabins arranged in a bewildering labyrinth of hallways. We parted in the stairwell, promising to meet up at the welcome drinks in an hour. My room number was 69, and if that made you snicker then congratulations, you are as immature as I am. Upon boarding the boat I'd been given an actual key to open my door, which felt like a quaint touch in this modern age of key cards and fingerprint scans and other "smart," high-tech means of entry. I located my room eventually, the ship bobbing as I slid the bolt back and the door swung inward. Suddenly my nausea returned tenfold—the motion sickness I've been prone to since childhood kicking into overdrive.

The room wasn't much bigger than the full-size bed it contained, with a tiny closet and a chest of drawers on one side and a desk on the other, all accessible while sitting on the bed. I wasn't fazed by this; such is the power of living in various minuscule Manhattan studio apartments for most of my adult life. Everything was bolted to the ground: a precaution in case of stormy weather. Above my bed was an honest-to-goodness porthole, adorably small and perfectly circular. I slipped off my boots and stood on the bed to gaze out of it, getting a repeat view of sky meeting water, except that it was darker now, and the grayness of the sky had overtaken the water: iron on iron.

The bathroom was a little horrifying. It was the size of a shower stall because it *was* a shower stall, in addition to being a water closet, one of those two-for-one deals you get sometimes on a train (and apparently also on a boat), the shower-head positioned directly above the toilet with a drain in the middle of the floor. Whenever I showered, I could see that the water was going to splash everywhere—on the sink, the mirror, the toilet. (As it turned out, I'd even have to shut the door to make sure I didn't get the bedroom wet.) And yet I should have been counting my blessings I wasn't swabbing decks, consigned to one of the steerage-like rooms reserved for the crew. If a ship's hierarchy is as rigid as in days of yore, there was no denying my position was somewhere in the middle. I wasn't a paying guest, but I wasn't a crew member, either. Come to think of it, I was a little like the governess. Was I one of the servants, or one of the family?

A PA system turned on. The hollow drone and vibrating hum of feedback triggered an echoic memory, catapulting me back to high school in Mesa, Arizona. I found myself anticipating the nasal tones of Miss Peabody, the school secretary. Instead, it was a husky voice—rich and low, honed over hundreds of podcast episodes—a voice made for TED Talks and viral graduation speeches.

"Laaadies!" began Payton, conveying with this silky exclamation that: *yes, this was cheesy, but it was also fun and what was wrong with fun?* "We are thirty minutes away from our first round of cocktails in the main lounge. So powder your noses, your wigs, and your privates if that's your thing."

I heard titters through the door, and rolled my eyes fruitlessly.

"Don't use talcum powder though. It's been proven to cause lung and ovarian cancer. I mean it! See you soon."

The PA system cut out. I should probably mention that one

of the biggest selling points of the cruise was that it consisted entirely of women. It was ingenious of Payton to spin gold out of the straw reality that almost everyone who bothers to show up to bookish events is a woman. Every single one of the 275 passengers, all five instructors, the cleaning staff, the technical crew: women, all of them. Even the ship's captain was a woman, which was quite a feat. Did you know that only three percent of all sea captains are women? *Three percent!* That's as heinously skewed as it is for music conductors. What these two professions have in common is that they involve ordering people around, and since men don't like women ordering them around, women are averse to doing these jobs in the first place, and so the snowball accumulates, the feedback loop perpetuates, and the song never ends, yes it goes on and on my friend. . . .

But I suppose some progress has been made. Women used to be banned *altogether* from maritime vessels. We were deemed "bad luck" on the open seas, the only female allowed being the boat itself, on whose back these intrepid men rode from coast to coast.

This time, at least, the *Merman Rivera* would have plenty of female companionship.

CHAPTER 4

I threw up in the toilet.

Near the toilet, I should say. Good thing there was a showerhead directly above it. I cleaned the area while still in the blessed afterglow of having evacuated one's stomach, when it feels as though nausea has been permanently conquered. Of course, I knew the motion sickness would return—and soon.

By this point a change of clothes was in order, so I shimmied into my favorite black dress: long-sleeved, cocktail-length, and made of a rayon-cotton blend that was stretchy and structured without looking cheap. There was still a half hour before the reception began, so I decided to seek out the ship's doctor, using the excellent Wi-Fi at my disposal to figure out where to go. (It was a little depressing how good the Wi-Fi was, actually. Weren't we supposed to be getting away from it all? At least there was no cell service.)

The medical bay was on the fifth deck, which made it the sole reason any passenger would venture down there. This was the lowest level, which contained all the ship's utilitarian machinery (an engine room, a sewage treatment facility, air conditioning units, fuel bunkers, water tanks, plumbing pipes, fans, etc.) in addition to the dorm-style bedrooms of the ship's crew. Contrary to expectations, this level was no more hot or humid than the rest of the ship. But the ceilings were lower, and I couldn't help feeling like I was in a basement, knowing that most of this floor fell below the water line, meaning I was surrounded on all sides by the abyss of the ocean. . . . Unlike the third and fourth decks, it was easy to find one's way on the fifth deck, because it was accessible by only one stairwell: the main one in the center of the boat, which ran alongside an elevator I had no idea existed till now. (If I had, I wouldn't have lugged my suitcase down three flights of stairs.)

I had emerged from the elevator into a tiny, fluorescent-lit lobby. To the left and right were doors marked CREW ONLY with windows in them, through which I could spy long, industrial-looking hallways lit with the same harsh, flat light. In front of me was the medical bay, unmissable with its illuminated red "plus" sign. The entryway was a pair of extra-wide doors, both of which had been thrown open.

Before I entered, I could see a woman in a long white coat reading something on her phone. When I took a step toward her she looked up, stuffing the phone in one of the coat's deep front pockets.

"My first patient!"

She threw up her hands the way you do when presented with a tasty meal you're about to devour.

Naturally, the ship's doctor was a woman too.

"What ails you?"

"I'm a little seasick." I rubbed my stomach for effect. "I just threw up, actually."

"*Ex*cellent," she said. "I stocked up on so much Dramamine, I was getting worried I overdid it. With any luck you'll be miserable all week."

I laughed, more out of surprise than anything. Medical people aren't usually so effervescent.

"My name's Dr. Chen, by the way. But you can call me Joan."

Dr. Joan Chen was petite, her personality easily outweighing her slender frame. She wore more eye liner than I expected a doctor to, especially while on the clock, and her black hair had purple streaks in it. But the streaks were tastefully done.

She administered my first dose of Dramamine, a pill I swallowed with a paper cup's worth of water.

"Might make you a little sleepy, but it doesn't have that effect on everyone. You can take it with or without food, doesn't matter. You're not supposed to take it with alcohol, so just do me a favor and don't be a *total* boozehound, okay? I do realize we're on a cruise ship here."

"Not a problem," I said. "This is a working gig for me."

"Uh, I'm aware. It isn't every day a bestselling mystery novelist comes hobbling through my door."

"You're a mystery fan?" I asked, flustered to have been recognized. Flustered, and wildly delighted.

"Industrial strength," she averred. "Golden Age, contemporary, even the earlier Victorian stuff like Poe, Collins, Doyle—you name it, I've read it. The only reason I became a doctor is that I had a biology professor in college who compared it to being a detective of the body. Well, that, plus it was one of very few parent-approved professions."

"Who's your favorite mystery author?"

"Josephine Tey."

She said this without hesitating.

"Good answer," I replied.

"Thank you! I apologize for all the e-mails, by the way."

There had indeed been a flurry of e-mails in the days leading up to the cruise, from Payton and her staff in preparation for the trip. Dr. Chen had sent her share, including a few jokey ones that made more sense now. It figured that even the medical assistance on Payton's fabulous cruise would be fabulous.

"Not at all," I assured her. "I enjoyed them. Do you write yourself?"

"I dabble, but I've never finished anything. My problem is

coming up with a mystery plot that's good enough. What happened to you is basically my dream—to *live* through the solving of a mystery? And then be able to write about it? Hey! Maybe someone will get murdered on the ship and we can solve it together!"

"Bite your tongue," I said laughingly.

This wasn't the first time someone had said something like this to me since I'd published my first mystery novel.

But it was the first time such a jest would turn out to be prophetic.

"Do you like other genres besides mystery?" I asked her.

"I like *anything.*" She pointed at herself. "Big reader. It's how I made it through my childhood."

We nodded at each other conspiratorially, two fellow survivors.

"Lost my mind when I scored an invite to this thing," she continued. "Not that I'd ever have been able to afford it."

Payton had sent out a first wave of five hundred invitations to a random smattering of her newsletter subscribers—not entirely random, as she sent them to women only, but then, women made up the bulk of her subscribers anyway. Each invitation had a QR code that could be scanned for purposes of registration. The price tag for this weeklong experience was upwards of five thousand dollars per person, which meant a good number were expected to decline. As it turned out, many of these five hundred women responded positively. They also took advantage of the fact that the QR code on each invitation wasn't unique, and began passing these golden tickets among their friends, which resulted in a feeding frenzy featured on many an Instagram story and TikTok account, followed by a series of impassioned pleas from Payton not to game the system. The whole debacle even got some traditional media coverage, and much of it negative. There were many who decried the Get Lit Cruise as being both sexist *and* elitist. But negative press is still press, and Payton was able to parry a backlash to the backlash on the grounds that people are quick to condemn such female-driven endeavors. It took just two more waves of invitations for the cruise to sell out.

As usual, she knew exactly what she was doing.

"Good thing I'm used to making my own luck," continued Joan. "I got in touch with Payton directly and offered my services as locum doc."

"Locum doc?"

"The doctor on a ship's called the 'locum physician.' Just a fancy way of saying the post is temporary, for as long as the cruise lasts. This way I get *paid* to hobnob, maybe even sit in on a few lectures if no one's dying. Hey, maybe I can take a peek at yours?"

"I'd love that," I said. "Anything to beef up my numbers."

Of the 275 passengers, only twenty-five had opted to enroll in my mystery course.

"Don't you have anyone to help you?" I asked. "A nurse or something?"

She screwed up her mouth to one side. "I *did*. She came down with a bug. *Last night*. No time to replace her."

"Seriously?"

"Yeah, but she wasn't making it up. I could hear her retching in the room next to mine. We got on the boat a few days early to get ourselves organized. Poor thing had to abandon ship before we even set sail."

"Oof, I'm sorry. Well, thanks for seeing me, Dr. Chen."

"Stop! And I told you, it's Joan. Dr. Chen is my father." She paused. "*And* my mother. Mom and Dad were both overachievers. First-generation immigrants, all that jazz."

"They must be proud of you," I said politely.

"Ha! Spoken like one who doesn't have first-generation immigrant parents." She folded her arms over her white coat. "I run my department at UCSF, and have a four-year-old daughter who's currently being spoiled rotten by my parents. They adore her, and vice versa. And do you know what they remind me of, every chance they get?"

I shook my head.

"That the man I almost married, who cheated on me *one month* before our wedding, now has four beautiful kids with his beautiful wife. Natural birth beats artificial insemination, four beats one, married beats single. Boom! Which makes me a failure."

"Wow, that's brutal."

"Eh, it was a gift to get knocked off the good girl path a bit." She lifted one hand, cupping her hair with a curved palm. "Never would've gotten these rad highlights, for instance. I'm thinking of going rainbow next time, my daughter'll lose her shit. In a good way for once. You know I actually miss her?"

I made a noise intended to convey interest, which didn't fool either of us.

"Hey, are you going to this welcome drinks?" she asked.

"I am, do you want to go together?"

Between Joan and Gerry, I wasn't doing half bad: two cruise friends in under an hour.

"Yep, let me just take off my doctor costume."

She peeled off her white coat, revealing a shirt that was off-the-shoulder in a vintage eighties way, with a splotched, piebald pattern in black and white. Her skirt was burgundy—sleek and hip-hugging.

"When people see the white jacket they start asking me to look at moles, and whether coffee or red wine or whatever is really as good or bad for them as they've read." She pointed a finger at me. "So *don't* blow my cover. This is my one chance to mingle unmolested."

"I won't," I promised her.

She crooked her elbow into mine, and we walked like this up the three flights of stairs to the second deck. I'd suggested we take the elevator, but Joan (already she was "Joan," not Dr. Chen) wasn't having it.

"Good for the heart," she said, before adding, "Sorry. As a doctor I'm obligated to say crap like that from time to time."

The cacophony of many people talking at once grew stronger the higher we climbed. As I mentioned, these were the main stairs, which were nicer than the ones Gerry and I had used earlier. They were wider, and had carpeting; there were even white nautical symbols spray-painted onto the wall beside the access door for each floor. These images were artful and modernistic, one symbol per floor: a ship's wheel on 5, an anchor on 4, a compass on 3, and a life preserver on 2, which was where we stopped. (Of course Deck 1 had no symbol, since it was open to the air.)

On the second deck, three corridors branched off from the stairs, lit by a series of rather tacky wall sconces made to look like candelabras: a plasticized version of the freaky ones featured so famously in Cocteau's *Beauty and the Beast* (more Belle on the brain). Signs affixed to the walls told us what lay in each direction. THEATERS 1–3 could be accessed by going right, while the BLACK BOX THEATER, GYMNASIUM & POOL were to the left. Straight ahead, we'd find the DINING ROOM, LOUNGE & BALLROOM. Judging by the noise, it was obvious our destination lay straight ahead.

This middle corridor widened into a high-ceilinged anteroom where little throngs of women were holding animated conversations, the air crackling with an anticipatory buzz. In front of us was the ballroom, which I couldn't see properly yet, though I caught glimpses of a shiny parquet floor and a chandelier fit for the Phantom himself. People kept drifting toward this room the way water does in a river as it gathers momentum: hurtling ever forward and succumbing eventually, inevitably, to the crash and chaos of the great cataract beyond.

Women, women, everywhere! And not a one to silence. Short women, tall women, skinny women, fat women, women dressed to the nines, women in their pajamas, women with a ton of friends, women flying solo, a woman with confidence here, a woman with a complex there. Here a woman, there a woman, everywhere a woman woman. So many varieties, though most of them were white, cis, and older. Also, they were rich— or knew someone who was rich, since they'd been able to pay for this cruise.

"Here goes," whispered Joan as we promenaded into the fray.

If women on a boat were considered bad luck, then we were all in deep, *deep* trouble.

CHAPTER 5

The ballroom was so enormous, walking into it felt like walking outside. I could see now why the noise of the crowd had traveled so far. There was nothing to absorb it: no furniture, nothing on the walls, just that chandelier hanging from a domed ceiling made of the same cloudy-white, translucent material through which a PI might spy the silhouette of a femme fatale seeking his services. It was a colossus of a chandelier, with great looping strands of crystal beads that tinkled against each other regularly, the loops swaying in rhythm with the ship—a movement that had already become as indistinguishable to me as the movement of the Earth itself. Just a few hours in, and I'd gotten my sea legs.

In the center of the room was a circular bar being manned by a single bartender—woman-ed, I should say, since it was a female bartender, of course. I knew from the tag clipped to her shirt that her name was Sandra, but I know now her full name is Sandra Gutierrez, the first person to sign a book deal off the mayhem that took place aboard the *Merman Rivera*. (The book's working title as announced on Publishers Marketplace was literally *Murder & Mayhem on the Merman Rivera*. I was approached for ghostwriting duties, but declined due to a competing work—i.e., this one.) Sandra was wearing black pants and a white shirt, an outfit calculated to be unremarkable. I could say the same about her makeup and hair, and yet her foundation was pancaked onto her face, and there was an overabundance of gel glistening in her dark, slicked-back hair. She was clearly not a person who half-assed any task put before her, which was fortunate, because bartending solo for 275 ladies looking to get their "drink on" was no small task. (This was my first inkling of the extreme staffing shortage on the Get Lit Cruise.) The passengers were enjoying an open bar, which is what a price tag north of $5K will get you. We lowly staff members, on the other hand, had to use one of a dozen "coupons" allotted each of us. Joan gave me a knowing look as she forked over her first coupon. "Now I know how Lily Bart felt when she had to write letters for Judy Trenor while all the legit house guests were sleeping."

"So soulmates *do* exist," I said dreamily.

I decided I was in the mood for something dry, given all the water surrounding us, and ordered a Pinot Gris. I almost always go for white wine, as it sums me up so well: I'm white, and I have a tendency to whine. In truth, I wasn't too far off this cruise's target demo, though I was a good ten, fifteen years below the median age of the ladies milling around me. To the left of the entrance we'd walked through, I spied Gerry Forrest. We waved at each other.

"Who's that?" asked Joan while I was still waving.

"A passenger I met on the top deck. Name's Gerry Forrest."

"Do you know many people here?" she asked.

"Not at all, other than Payton. And now you."

We cheers-ed to this. Her drink was an amaretto sour, I noted with chagrin, debasing my PG by clinking it.

Joan wagged her head at my glass. "Pairs nicely with dimenhydrinate."

"I'm going to assume that's the active drug in Dramamine."

"You assume correctly." Something caught her eye, and she ducked her head. "Uh-oh," she whispered into her glass.

"What?" I whispered back.

"Incoming. And she means business."

I looked up, gaining fresh sympathy for how a mouse must feel when a hawk or eagle is bearing down on it. The person in question had broken away from the main crowd and was already halfway toward us, her eyes trained unmistakably on . . . me.

"Good luck!" chirped Joan, abandoning me with glee and walking farther into the room, toward the windows overlooking the ocean.

The girl's hair was orange, and I don't mean it was red, or auburn, or strawberry blond, or any of the other hues we're used to seeing on gingers. No: this was an unnatural, carroty shade the exact color of turmeric powder. I associated it with the Russian biddies who loved to walk slowly in front of me on the sidewalk when I lived in Queens, in Astoria, except their hair was shoulder-length at most and had the consistency of straw. This girl's was long and lush, undulating like a mermaid's. Her complexion was dark—what some might call olive, her skin tone accentuating the artificiality of her dyed hair, as did a good half-inch of black roots.

I called her a girl because she was so young. If I were fifteen years younger than the average passenger, she had to be at least fifteen years younger than I was: twenty-five at the outside. Her beauty was classical in that her face exhibited perfect vertical symmetry (rarer than you think), and everything was in proportion to everything else, except for her eyes, which were massive and too far apart. They gave her an otherworldly appearance, as did their color—a mint-jelly green practically radioactive in its brilliance, and as outrageously phony as her orange hair. She must have been wearing colored contact lenses, which was curious because she was *also* wearing glasses: fashionably oversized ones, with clear plastic frames.

When people look this strange, the big question for me is whether their appearance is a calculated effort to convey eccentricity, or a symptom of genuine weirdness. My gut was telling me this person was one of the few who fell in the latter category, a veritable weirdo.

She reminded me of an exotic fish, or one of those alluring aliens deployed in old-school science fiction, who draw in the unsuspecting (male) humans, before their uglier (male) compatriots bust out the probes. (Internalized homophobia knows no bounds when it comes to genre.) I can't remember what clothes she was wearing because they were unremarkable by comparison. It was her face that demanded attention.

I watched helplessly as she drew nearer, invading the space Joan had vacated.

"You *are* Belle Currer?" she demanded.

"That's my pseudonym," I said. "Feel free to wear it out."

"Ha."

She said this flatly: an acknowledgment that I'd made a joke, that she'd understood the joke, and that she refused to engage with said joke any further.

"My name is Helen Sanchez. I'm a writer and I'm in your class."

"It's nice to meet you," I lied.

"I've wanted to be a writer ever since I was seven years old and wrote my first story. Books are everything to me. Mysteries especially."

This was becoming a running theme. Not that I minded.

"What was your first story about?" I asked.

"My father. He died."

"I'm sorry to hear that."

She batted away my condolence with a shake of her head.

"Heart condition. Nothing mysterious about it. But it's why I turned to mysteries. The only thing that made me feel better after he died was *The Westing Game*." She paused. "I used to read *The Westing Game* a lot."

"You read *The Westing Game* when you were seven years old?"
The Westing Game was one of my favorites too. It's the rare children's mystery that features a legitimately complex, yet solvable puzzle. But I was twelve when I first read it.

She nodded.

"So you're a smarty-pants."

She shook this off just as she had my condolence, which was interesting. Ninety-nine out of a hundred people are pleased when told they're smart. (I am among the ninety-nine, no shame.)

"I'm struggling with what I'm writing now. I'd love to ask you a few—"

"Helen." I cut her off. "We have plenty of time to talk shop. Starting tomorrow."

"We have five days."

She said this the way the crew of the doomed spacecraft announces how much time they have left before the ship explodes, a klaxon alarm blaring in the background along with pre-recorded evacuation instructions.

"Exactly! Plenty of time. Can I get you a drink?"

"I don't drink."

"Not even water?"

Her eyelids drooped. Was this how Helen Sanchez smiled?

"I'll get you a seltzer," I said. "Bubbles! It'll be fun."

I spent as long as possible ordering our drinks. (Sandra didn't ask me for a coupon for my second white wine, and I didn't give her one.) In fact, I was still facing the bar when someone sang into my ear:

"Well, well, well!"

I knew that voice. I'd already heard it once today over the PA system. Before I turned, I prepared my face, which isn't to say I put on a fake smile. What I did was to steel it by way of "delight" and "animation" so there was no way of penetrating the veneer and accessing anything real. Exposing oneself to

Payton Garrett was dangerous; there was no telling what she might do with an honest, unfettered emotion.

"I made it!" I said jauntily. "Barely, though. Seasickness has *set. In.*"

Behind her, Helen Sanchez receded into the crowd from whence she'd come. So much for bubbles. She reminded me of one of those unlucky mortals of Greek myth, obliterated upon finding themselves in proximity to a goddess.

Not that Payton Garrett *looked* like a goddess. I'll say this about her: she never used her appearance to get ahead, or at least, not in the conventional sense. She was no clotheshorse, for instance, and I guessed the slacks and suit jacket she had on came as a set, since they were the same neutral shade of beige or taupe or tan. If you saw her on the street you wouldn't look twice at this nice, middle-aged white lady, with her ash-blond hair tied up in an afterthought of a ponytail. The most interesting thing about her face was the way her eyes curved downwards at the outer edges, which gave her every expression a beseeching quality. People opened up to Payton easily, disarmed by her appearance, and celebrities loved to be photographed alongside her, glittering more brightly for the contrast.

If ever a spider figured out how to look this benign, it could have all the flies it desired. . . .

"Oh, girl, you need some Dramamine. Let me hook you up with Joan, she's our cruise-ship doctor and she's the *best*. I know she's around here somewhere."

"Already hooked," I said. "Dramamine downed, and Joan and I are officially besties. I mean, she's a mystery freak *and* can do deep cuts of *The House of Mirth* off the cuff, how could I resist?"

"Now see, that's what I love about you. You know how to take care of yourself. And then some."

I raised PG number two with a smirk.

Ugh, how I hated all this. It was like bantering with the most popular girl in school, and even though you didn't buy into the fallacy of popularity—even though you prided yourself on resisting such nonsense, you couldn't help caring about her reaction, and whether you were acquitting yourself well. Taxing *and* shameful: a lose-lose.

On the plus side, my nausea was gone. I chugged half my wine.

"Joan was one of my greatest finds," said Payton, adding a fatuous little sigh that sent me over the edge.

"Oh, but I thought she reached out to you?"

Payton's eyes narrowed—still managing to retain their winsome lilt.

"She *did*. And then I chose to hire her, hence her being one of my greatest finds."

"I see. Got it."

This time my smirk was real. Two minutes in, and I'd gotten a rise out of her. Having known each other in our early twenties, Payton and I occasionally squabbled in this sibling-adjacent way—despite her charm, and my reserve. I did this with no one else in the world, which was the best proof of how close we were.

She leaned in confidentially. If she'd been drinking, I would have been able to smell the liquor on her breath, but like a drug dealer who never uses, Payton Garrett was too smart to drink on her own booze cruise. No question she'd be stone-cold sober for the duration of the trip.

"I'm so glad you agreed to do this. I know it isn't your thing."

"My pleasure," I said.

"Liar."

"Manipulator."

Something real rippled between us. Is it possible to both love and hate a person—*passionately*—who doesn't figure into your life on a regular basis?

Anything is possible, duh.

A hush fell over the room, like when a performance is about to begin. And then a voice rang out from within the sea of people: deep, rich, and deliberate, a round tone for each and every syllable. A voice that demanded attention.

"For seven days, we come together,
Seven days to work, to weather
The storm that creativity brings.
Glorious storm, this maelstrom that rings
With the thunder of curiosity, and of dreams.
For we women, three hundred strong:
How often are we told no? That we are wrong
To question, to fight, to long
For that which resides in our hearts
And remains unwritten.
I say we are wronged, not wrong.

And so we gather forces here
On this boat, raise our voices, make it clear
We will question. We will fight. We will long.
We take this journey today
Because we are not going anywhere.

There is strength in numbers,
But also is there strength in the blunders
We make when we engage in the art
That fuels us, when we take part
In the creative process without judgment.
It has been said a rising tide lifts all boats.
So let this one rise, and rise, and rise—
And toast with me now to productivity.
And joy. And possibility.
To a week of strength. And boundless positivity."

By the time she finished, she'd waded through the crowd of attendees, the sea parting for her as she came to stand before me and Payton.

Nicole Root had made a big splash a few years ago with a fiery poem she'd composed and recited for the opening session of Congress. It had been a fraught moment in politics—more fraught than usual—and she'd tapped into the discontent so many were feeling about the current president. Both the poem and her performance had gone viral, and it wasn't long before she was a guest on Payton's podcast, where the two of them hit it off. *Really* hit it off. One year later, Payton had divorced her husband and she and Nicole were getting hitched in a star-studded affair on Martha's Vineyard.

Nicole was leading the poetry course on the cruise and, wifey or not, her presence was a coup. She was easily the most famous poet in the country. (Can *you* name another living poet? I sure can't.) On the line "So let this one rise, and rise, and rise," she'd raised her shallow, bowl-shaped champagne glass, and now she tipped it downward, not so much sipping from it as receiving its golden liquid in her upturned mouth.

The rest of us settled for sipping, including Payton, who'd acquired a virgin frozen strawberry daiquiri from a server just in time. Frozen strawberry daiquiris had always been her go-to drink, I remembered, though back in the day they definitely weren't virgins.

"That was beautiful, babe." Payton raised her voice, projecting into the vast room. "I especially love how you shoehorned *A Rising Tide* in there. Don't think that was lost on me."

Nicole let loose a whopper of a smile. "I never did."

They smacked lips, a few scattered titters erupting from the crowd. I don't think anyone in that room had a problem watching two ladies kiss, but I was sure there were at least a few among them who *prided* themselves on not having a problem watching two ladies kiss. I was equally sure Payton knew it.

You're expecting me to make fun of Nicole's poem, aren't you? It's not gonna happen. First, the written version doesn't do justice to her delivery, which was superb. Second, when it comes to poetry I have no authority upon which to criticize. I simply don't get it. Never have.

I'd also never met Nicole Root before. (My sporadic contact with Payton didn't come close to clearing the bar for a wedding invite, alas.) So this was my first good look at her.

I may as well acknowledge that white women like me can get into trouble describing Black women like her. But I'll venture to say she was ill-suited to her name. "Nic Root," as she was often called, has such a guttural ring to it, whereas everything about the woman towering over me was high-flown and flowing. She was wearing a velvet cape made of alternating peach and fuchsia panels, and this cape was so long, it trailed behind her in a train. Her eye shadow and hoop earrings were both golden, with beads of the same color interspersed throughout a braided updo held in place by a royal-blue crown. In my wildest dreams I couldn't have pulled off anything so dramatic, however much I wanted to. (And for the record, I very much wanted to.) Underneath the cape she wore a satiny, cream-colored jumpsuit with heels to match, though the heels were unnecessary. She must have been close to six feet with nothing on.

The passengers had all begun to talk amongst themselves again. (Linda Richman from that old SNL skit, "Coffee Talk," would have been pleased. There was a fair chance Linda Richman was *there*, actually.) Many of them were two if not three drinks deep at this point, and the frenetic energy that alcohol whips up among a crowd was palpable, the air thick with the noise of three hundred mouths' worth of fevered chatter.

"Come meet one of my oldest friends." Payton skipped over to me, taking Nicole along with her. "It's *bananas* you two haven't met yet."

Up close, Nicole Root was even more intimidating. When she turned her eyes onto mine, her gaze was so intense I had to stop myself from cringing or turning away. This happens sometimes with fellow writers, who tend to be sponges—absorbing everything that comes within their orbit, storing away every detail, no matter how minute. It wasn't so much that she could see through me or into my soul, as that she would remember every word I said, every gesture I made. Her eyes were dark brown, but what they reminded me of was the unblinking, remorseless red light of a camera lens set to record.

"I've heard a lot about you," she said. "Payton's told me stories."

"I'll bet," I replied. "I've also heard a lot about you, though more from the *New York Times* than Payton."

"More's the pity. Payton's stories are much more entertaining than anything you'll find in *that* rag."

We laughed. She was as good at deflecting compliments as I was.

Nicole turned to Payton, bending slightly to reach her ear. "Was it all right?" she asked in a low voice. "You know I pulled that thing out of my ass this morning."

A man dressed in a pale, dove-gray suit sidled up to us before Payton could answer. I had been under the impression there were zero men on board, but every rule has its exception, and I'd met him earlier in the day, albeit briefly. He'd been in charge of passenger check-in, and I knew he was Payton's personal assistant, though I hadn't learned his name. At the moment, his arm was linked through Joan Chen's. (Apparently arm-linking was her thing. *Hmph*.)

"You knocked it out of the park," Payton assured her wife.

"Ugh," said the man. "We get it, Payton, you're a dyke now. You don't have to use sports metaphors to prove it."

Payton rolled her eyes at me. "I don't believe you've met my outrageously gay assistant, Jackson Richards."

"Not properly," I said.

"Duh, Payton, I checked everybody in, don't you remember? You sure that lemon daiquiri is a virgin?"

"First of all, it's strawberry, are you blind? Second of all, I can't believe I thought it was a good idea to make you the first person every passenger saw," his boss retorted. "I'm surprised no one asked for their money back."

Jackson was tall and fit—so fit, he was in danger of hulking out of his tailored suit, which I suspected he'd bought at least one size too small for this effect. There was no doubt many people would have found him handsome—gorgeous, even. But for my taste his perfect skin was too tan, his perfect teeth too white, his perfect hair too shiny.

He looked me up and down, plainly liking what he saw as little as I did.

No one deserves to be reduced to a stereotype, and every cliché is in the eye of the beholder. I felt sure he was sizing me up with my black dress, dark-framed glasses, and lack of makeup as another female frump, a sad/serious denizen of the book world. (Guilty as charged!) The thing is—and I speak from experience here—when *every* aspect of a person's appearance seems calculated to confirm a stereotype, it begins to feel as though they're wearing a costume. I knew *I* was harboring a secret or two, and I wondered what unmentionables Jackson Richards might be concealing—though I suspected a drug habit was one of them. He had the sweaty sheen and hyperactive manner of a man who likes his uppers: Adderall, or Ritalin, or maybe something more lethal.

Nicole waggled a long, elegant finger at him. "'Dyke' is not a word you have the authority to use, Jackson."

"Go fuck yourself, cunt."

Nicole's smile grew wider as Payton bit her lip, trying not to laugh. But Joan recoiled, her arm falling through his. He regarded her with surprise.

"Come on, Joanie, we've grown so close during our time together on this floating prison, don't turn on me now. Aren't you from Frisco? I can't be the first bitchy fag you've come across."

"True." Joan had recovered by now. "But you know, no one calls it 'Frisco' who actually lives there."

"Nice!" Payton held up her hand, which Joan gamely smacked.

"Didn't you live there, though?" Nicole asked him.

"I did. It was Payton who dragged me away with the job offer of a lifetime." He raised his nose in the air with a mock show of dignity. "Guess I never got the memo about 'Frisco.' "

"Well"—Joan patted him on the shoulder—"if you ever come back, I'll show you the ropes."

"Please, I'm done with that place for a good while. Already screwed my way from one end to the other. Which didn't take long, it's so tiny. Gotta wait at least a good five years for a new crop of fresh meat. You know what they used to call me, back in the Castro?"

"I'm honestly afraid to hear this," said Payton.

"Loose Lips. On account of the fact that I'm a big old gossip, and give *amazing* head."

We laughed gamely at this. There was no other choice.

"Well in that case," said Nicole, "you're a dangerous man to—"

"Yeah yeah, loose lips sink ships, we get it. Next!"

Nicole smiled at him benevolently. She was trying so hard not to convey even a scintilla of annoyance, which was why I was convinced she hated him.

I can't say I blamed her.

"And on that note . . ." Payton began tapping the side of her glass with a metal cocktail stirrer. "We need to shut down this open bar anyway," she half-whispered as the crowd began to quiet down. "You wouldn't believe how much these fuckers drink in an hour."

The cacophony dissipated much faster than I expected.

"Heyyyy, ladies! First off, kudos to my wife, the insanely talented Nic Root, for kicking things off *right* with that original poem of hers she wrote *today*, if you can believe it."

Murmurs of appreciation rippled through the sea.

"We'll go into dinner in just a sec, but I wanted to say how effing thrilled—that's right, *effing* thrilled!—I am you're all here. It's going to be an amazing, *life-changing* week!"

The women whooped and hollered like they were at a pep rally. Which I suppose they were.

"As my brilliant wife said, we are three hundred women strong on this cruise, with *zero* men aboard either to help *or* hinder us!"

Behind her, once the latest round of applause had died down, Jackson cleared his throat theatrically.

"Of course, there are exceptions to every rule. My *fabulous* assistant here, Jackson, is one of them."

Scattered applause for Jackson, who waved at the crowd like a beauty queen, elbow ratcheting back and forth while his cupped hand merely rotated.

"*Also* on board is our Michelin-starred chef Pierre Gascoigne, who will be preparing *all* our dinners!"

There were legitimate gasps at this. I'm not much of a foodie, and even I had heard the name Pierre Gascoigne. He was in that upper echelon of chefs whose name meant enough to be attached to multiple restaurants dotting the globe, and whose reputation was so stellar, his numerous appearances on reality television had done little to dilute his brand. How on earth had Payton managed to snag him?

"No problem with a man or two serving *us*, am I right, ladies?"

Predictably, this got a big round of applause. I stole a glance at Jackson. He had spackled his face with an oversize grin, and was clapping as loudly as anyone. (His clapping was manic, like all his gestures.) But it was easy for me to imagine the resentment lurking under the surface.

Just under the surface, then. When he noticed me looking, he gave me the finger on the sly. I looked away immediately.

"All right." Payton motioned good-naturedly for everyone to stop clapping. "And now let's—"

She broke off: not with a shriek or anything so dramatic, though her silence was just as effective because Jackson filled it now with his own over-the-top reaction.

"Oh. My. *God.*"

A woman had appeared on the edge of the crowd. A woman who had no business being there. A woman who had managed, somehow, to Trojan-horse her way aboard—perhaps in a literal wooden horse, because if Payton or Nicole or even I had seen her while we were still docked, there was no question we wouldn't have left shore till she'd been escorted off the boat.

Payton continued to stare, as did everyone in our vicinity. It would have been eerily silent if half the room hadn't been unable to see what was going on. Already I could hear people murmuring impatiently behind us.

"What's happening?" Joan whispered.

"Just watch," Jackson whispered back. "This is going to be good."

In the end, it was Nicole who found her voice first.

"What on earth are you doing here, Flora?"

CHAPTER 6

Flora Fortescue is going to require some backstory, I'm afraid.

Luckily I'm the perfect person to provide it. Flora attended the same crappy MFA program that Payton and I did, you see—the one in southern Illinois. And for the two years it lasted, we were something of a trio. Not that I want to over-state matters: this was grad school, not high school. There were no cliques, and no one cared that we hung out as much as we did. Many of our classmates already had spouses, and more than a few of them had children, which was one reason we three single ladies gravitated toward each other.

Payton informed us early on that we were all going to be friends, and I saw immediately there was no refusing her—not without a fight. For her part, Flora proved to be one of those submissive types, happy to latch on to an alpha personality and go along for the ride. That sounds dismissive, but I promise I don't mean it that way. There's a surprising amount of power behind the ability to cling: a drive and determination that oth-ers underestimate at their peril. Payton may have been vocal about her ambition, but Flora was just as intent on going places.

Since Payton had been the one to bring us together, she was the focal point of our group, which made Flora and me friends-in-law rather than proper friends. For all the time the three of us spent together, I can't remember ever hanging out with Flora one-on-one. But I do remember lots of joint writing sessions that turned into the sort of long, lingering meals you have on a regular basis when you're in your twenties, during which we'd agonize over our writing, gossip about our classmates and teachers, and just generally support each other. For me, this was a big deal. My default state was (is!) that of a lone wolf—drooly fangs/bristly hackles and all. This was the only period during my adult life when I could truthfully say I wasn't alone.

It helped that we were interested in the same thing. Writing ruled us, and we talked about it the same way our high school counterparts would have obsessed over matters of the heart. The funny thing was that Flora, for all her meekness, was the insider. She came from a patrician family who'd lived on the Upper East Side for generations. Her father was a semi-successful novelist, her mother an extremely successful editor for a major publishing house. In a few years, her brother would become one of the most sought-after literary agents in the industry. This meant that Flora was slumming it in Illinois. Her parents could have paid for much fancier graduate programs where they doubtless had connections, but she hadn't gotten into any of them. She'd tanked her writing samples (she admitted this readily, and often), getting rejected everywhere other than our downtrodden little school. She was obsessed with becoming a writer because it was *expected* of her, whereas for me, it was something I barely dared to dream.

Payton's situation was more extreme than mine. Her evangelical family had done everything they could to prevent her education from advancing past middle school. Of course, it was their resistance that spurred her to greater heights, ever since she was a small child (see chapters 2–6 of *A Rising Tide*). By the time she was in graduate school, Payton Garrett was an unstoppable machine, full to the brim of a potent brew of ambition, talent, and discipline.

Once we graduated and Payton became famous almost immediately, I'd allowed her to drift out of my friend orbit without a fight. (She certainly hadn't fought to stay in touch with *me*.) But Flora had done the opposite, clinging ever more fiercely as the years went by. She managed to finagle her way into a top-tier writers' group with Payton, despite not having published a word herself. For years, Flora plugged away at a fictional account of the scandalous intrigue surrounding Lord Byron and his half sister, Augusta Leigh. Oh, does that ring a bell? *Ding ding ding*: Payton's recently published novel was on the same subject, and there was no denying she'd read many excerpts from Flora's work-in-progress over the years.

Payton claimed the book simply flowed out of her (it took her less than six months to write: an extra twist of the knife), and while she admitted the subject matter came by way of Flora, it wasn't as though anyone owned the real-life Augusta Leigh. Did I mention Payton's novel was short-listed for the Booker? It really was a wonderful book. Part of what made it so compelling was the existence of a frame story in which a present-day female author was attempting to write the Augusta Leigh–focused novel. The author was spoiled and lazy, and the perfect foil to the bright, vivacious Augusta. The author character grew to hate her subject, and tried to contort Augusta's story as a form of revenge. Payton's novel was lauded as a sly meta-commentary on the art of storytelling itself. In this way, it managed to straddle the discrete realms of critical *and* commercial acclaim.

Can you blame Flora Fortescue for being jealous? Furious, even? The mouse turned into a lion, and Flora did what most Americans do at some point in their lives.

She sued.

The lawsuit became a cause célèbre in the literary world, spawning a piece in *The New Yorker* that went viral, particularly on Twitter—that cesspool where such viruses propagate. Payton had tried multiple times to settle, just to make it go away, but Flora refused. She said she wanted a written apology that included an acknowledgment that Payton had plagiarized her, that she had done something morally reprehensible. Apparently, there were a few passages close enough in wording to Flora's unpublished manuscript that the suit couldn't be dismissed out of hand, even though Payton said she hadn't copied a word, and that any resemblance must have been coincidental or unconscious. I believed Payton, but I also understood Flora's rage.

It was a perfect Internet debate because it was easy to flip-flop from one side to another, and there was no element of "punching down," given the wealth and privilege of the warring parties. An aspiring "BookTuber" (kill me) had even created a weekly show centered on the feud called *Isn't It Byronic? Garrett v. Fortescue.* The last time I checked, each episode was getting several hundred thousand views.

All of which is to say that Nicole's question had been a fair one:

What on earth was Flora doing on Payton's cruise?

"Hello, my *darling* friend," Flora said to Payton, ignoring Nicole, and me, and all the other hundreds of people assembled in the ballroom. She curled her fingers onto her palm in a cutesy parody of a wave, sipping champagne from a glass whose stem she held between her thumb and index finger, as though she were about to twirl it. Enveloping her skinny frame—a much skinnier frame than the last time I'd seen her—was a lavender gown made of chiffon, high-necked and long-sleeved. Back in our MFA days, Flora wore all-black outfits with a pair of black-and-white Converse so old, they were held together with duct tape. Despite her mousy demeanor, she'd had a sense of fashion at a time when I was still figuring out my own. I remember admiring her understated makeup, and the way she rocked her short, mussed-up hairdo straight out of bed, not bothering to style it. With her dark features and pale skin, she reminded me of Winona Ryder in her pixie prime—not that she was anywhere near as pretty as Noni. (Who is?) But she was my first taste of the effortlessly chic style of the native New Yorker.

Now, apparently, she was all about the effort. She'd grown her hair out, though I suspected she was using a hairpiece to achieve the elaborately coiled, shiny monstrosity resting on the crown of her head like a jumbo Cinnabon. There was blush splashed across her cheekbones, and I could see the demarcation between her lipliner and lipstick. Also, she was wearing false eyelashes worthy of a drag queen: four bristly caterpillars I swore I could hear grating against each other every time she blinked.

"Check out Little Miss Sunshine," marveled Jackson.

Payton turned to him. "Why didn't you tell me she was here?" she asked him quietly.

His eyes widened in protest. "I had no clue! Crazy bitch must have disguised herself when she checked in."

"Whatever," sighed Payton, as though her main reaction to Flora's presence was one of disappointment. She sauntered to the door, taking all the tension with her. "Dinnertime, ladies!"

The crowd began moving with her as one, the cacophony of voices swelling instantly. But Flora didn't move a muscle other than to push her lower jaw to one side. All the passengers gave her a wide berth, I noticed, flowing around her the way any liquid entity does upon encountering a solid obstruction.

I watched as she downed the rest of her champagne and deposited the glass on a waitress's passing tray. There was something else about her that was different—something beyond the clothes, the hair, the makeup, and the fifteen-ish pounds she'd shed. When she allowed herself to be swept up in the current and began moving toward the door, I realized what it was. Her posture. The Flora I'd known was a huncher; she used to hold herself in a concave manner—chest sheltered, never on display. But now she'd gone convex: shoulders thrown back, chin thrust out so far, I could see her neck muscles straining. She was ready for a fight, and even though I found this shtick of hers sad and ridiculous, there was no denying she'd never looked more magnificent.

I had to swim through the crowd to reach her. By the time I did, we were back in the anteroom heading rightward, toward the dining room.

"Oh, hey, *Belle*," she purred.

"So I'm getting the Joan Collins treatment too," I observed. "What'd *I* ever do to you?"

"You agreed to be a part of this cruise."

"Like you wouldn't have if you were me."

"But I'm not you."

Our eyes met. We were much nearer to each other in motion than we would have been at rest, and a throb of fear, a primordial warning bell I could remember from my playground days sounded in me now: *This person is dangerous.*

"*I'm* the friend whose lifework was ruined and who became a punchline over *pommes frites* at Balthazar."

She pronounced *pommes frites* with the perfect degree of Frenchified accent—so light, it was barely there. I'd have either said it with no accent, which would have sounded wrong, or gone so heavy as to invite ridicule. Flora's genteel upbringing flashed out this way from time to time, and back in our MFA days I had looked forward to being as polished as she was in the not-too-distant future. Since then, I've come to accept that such polish comes from its unthinking, ingrained quality, and that there's no amount of effort that will produce it. Buff a cheap slab of pinewood as much as you want; it's never going to shine like old mahogany. In fact, all you'll end up doing is wearing it out that much more quickly.

"Fair enough," I said lightly. "So how *did* you get in here?"

"What do you mean? I got one of those little invitations in the mail like everyone else did. With the QR code. It had my name on it and everything."

"You subscribe to Payton's newsletter?"

"Of course I do. I was the first one to sign up for her Substack when she started it, loyal friend that I am. I was a little surprised when I got an invite, but I went online first thing and signed up."

"With your real name?"

"I played fair," said Flora. "Payton was put on notice I'd be in attendance. Or at least she should have been, if she'd been paying attention."

It wasn't lost on me that this was not a direct answer to my question.

Even before she'd morphed into whatever this new version of herself was, Flora had a stubborn streak—the dogged persistence of the hanger-on. I could see she was going to stick to her story no matter what, so I dropped it. But as it turned out, this was an error on my part.

Because the riddle of how Flora gained entry to this cruise was very much at the heart of the murder mystery yet to come.

CHAPTER 7

The dining room was easily the biggest room on the ship—much grander than the ballroom, with a peaked roof instead of a dome (Gothic beats Romanesque). This roof was made mostly of glass, which meant for breakfast and lunch it was filled with natural light. But for dinner?

The stars came out.

You have to remember: I live in New York City, where the sky acquires a pinkish haze in the dead of night from all the light pollution. This is all we get. But out here at sea, there was no artificial light other than the little that came from the boat itself. And inside the dining room, the interior lights had been dimmed for maximum effect—an effect I took in now, craning my neck upward.

The clouds from the afternoon were gone, making for a breathtaking view, and I do mean that literally, my breath catching in my throat as I gazed upon the myriad points of light. Were all these stars up there all the time, hiding? They didn't dot the firmament so much as blanket it: great, winking swirls of luminescence. No wonder ancient civilizations spent so much time making up stories about what they saw up there—

"Careful, you'll tweak your neck." Flora was regarding me

with a bemused expression. "Having one of our nature reveries, are we?" She made her way toward a long side-table with hundreds of name cards lined up on it. I followed her dumbly. "I still say you missed your calling. You should be Rachel Carson by now. Or Annie Dillard."

"I wish," I said lightly.

It was true that I was prone to mooning over such rustic tableaux. But it was jarring to be with someone who knew me so well. I didn't like it.

"You've got to admit," I continued, "Payton picked a good boat."

"Payton is good at *everything* she does. Especially plagiarism."

"Welcome," said a crew member whose name I can't remember, though I do remember her name tag included the title First Mate. Also, her accent and Aryan looks marked her out as Nordic. "Please find your name card. It will have your table number on it. This will be your table for the duration of the journey. You may sit anywhere at the table that you like."

Now that we were closer, I could see the cards had been arranged in alphabetical order by last name. Flora plucked hers out and flashed it at me: AUGUSTA LEIGH. Oh, Lord. If Payton had been reviewing her guests' names herself, surely she would have flagged this one. Her team of lackeys must have failed to note its significance.

"Tootles," she purred.

Tootles? She may as well have been clutching a cigarette holder in one hand and a lap dog in the other. For all I knew, she'd trot out these accessories later. I watched her flounce away in the direction of one of four narrow, banquet-size tables that ran the length of the room. Each of these was long enough to seat seventy-five people, which meant among the four of them they took care of all the passengers. Naturally, I likened them to the Hogwarts tables, even though they had individual chairs rather than benches. When Gerry sat down at the leftmost one (we waved at each other again), I designated it Ravenclaw, which as everyone knows is the best house. Flora 2.0 sat at the table all the way on the right, a few seats down from Helen Sanchez.

Slytherin, obviously.

The kitchen, or "galley," to use the seafaring lingo, was to the left of the dining room, as evidenced by two swinging doors communicating between the rooms. Every now and then a waitress dressed in a white shirt and black pants would bustle through one of them, using the force of her body to push the panel in whatever direction she was walking. Already they were depositing bread rolls on tiny plates, and individual medallions of butter. I guessed the bread had been warmed and the butter chilled, and looked on with envy as the famished passengers downed great slathered-up hunks without chewing.

My card said I was at Table 2, which was located on a raised platform at the front of the room. This was where the adult witches and wizards sat, but instead of one long high table, our dais featured two small, square tables, each with four place settings. By the time I reached Table 2, all but one of the seats had been taken, which meant I could sit without delay.

Across from me was Joan Chen, chugging the glass of white wine that had been poured for each place setting before we sat down. (Booze with dinner was gratis.) I followed her example. Ugh: a Chardonnay, and a bad one at that. If I *must* with Chards, I prefer them buttery, but this one was watery. You get what you pay for, I suppose. (You want me to stop talking about white wine, don't you? Noted.)

"It's awful, isn't it?" whispered the woman to my right.

I nodded, agreeing.

She had a small, freckly face dominated by orangey-red lipstick—a hideous shade of apricot I guessed had been chosen not for aesthetic reasons, but for its ability to stand out. On her head was a brightly colored scarf knotted under one ear like a Halloween pirate, the scarf's tail trailing down her chest. She leaned forward, turning one hand sideways and raising it a few inches—still well below her mouth, but recognizable as a vestigial gesture meant to convey the imparting of a confidence.

"I hear the guests get a *much* better table wine," she hissed. "I would have thought Payton—"

She cut herself off.

"What?" I asked curiously. "You would have thought Payton what?"

She hesitated.

"I'm sorry to have to ask this, but are you recording this conversation?"

The hell?

"No!"

"Don't be offended," said Joan, who was watching us with amusement. "She asked me the same thing."

"It's just you never know these days with smartphones," the woman fretted, her dangly earrings swinging against her neck as she turned to Joan and then back to me. "Before you know it, you're an upload away from an awkward post that can derail you for days. And that's a best-case scenario."

"Ah," I said, "so you're Talia Simmons."

Talia Simmons was a YA author. As you probably know, YA is short for Young Adult, a subset of literature that has eclipsed its adult counterpart in recent years. These days, every genre of adult fiction exists within the YA sphere (YA Mystery, YA Romance, YA Sci-Fi, etc.). Talia did YA Fantasy, which was a world I knew nothing about, other than if you hit in it, you hit big.

Talia had hit big.

She held out a hand with at least one ring on each finger, including the thumb. When we shook, her half-dozen bracelets jangled against each other. With the scarf and the jewelry and the outlandish lipstick, she looked like a local librarian who'd been put in charge of the fortune teller tent at the village fair, and taken the role a little too far. . . . Unlike in the case of Helen Sanchez, I felt sure her getup was a pose.

"I don't know how you live like that," marveled Joan. "*Je cannot* with the Internet."

"I'm sure the royalty checks don't hurt," I observed.

"They don't," she admitted with a simper. Her face grew serious again. "Not that I do it for the money. I'd still write if I got nothing for it. I'd *pay* to do it!"

My eyes skidded over Joan's, widening slightly. We both reached for our wineglasses. Clearly Talia Simmons was in the habit of being "on" every waking moment of her life. Maybe every sleeping moment, too. (Is there an app for accessing people's dreams yet? Give it time.)

Up to this point I hadn't heard a peep from the fourth member of our table, who had a mousey-colored bob and wore glasses so thick, they reminded me of the ones Marcie wears in the *Peanuts* comic strip. Come to think of it, her disengagement was rather Marcie-like too: she wasn't doing much, other than staring into the middle distance. There was no need to ask who she was, however. Her all-white uniform—including her cap with braided trim—marked her out as the ship's captain.

For once, I opted to be the breaker of the proverbial ice. I held out my hand, introducing myself.

"Ellen McDwight," she responded, crushing my hand in her viselike grip. "Ship's captain," she added unnecessarily.

I soon learned that the only way to draw out Captain Marcie was to talk about her boat.

"She's on the smaller side, it's true, but that means she can ride at a pretty fast clip, long as the wind doesn't work against us. Steady, too, for one so petite. Almost no rocking to speak of."

"I didn't think people still called ships 'she,'" I said. "It seems so old-fashioned."

"It's tradition," said the captain—as though this refuted what I'd said, rather than confirming it.

"Jackson's decided the *Merman Rivera* is a gay male ship, which isn't as big of a leap as it would be for other boats," said Joan. "But the sort of gay man who's happy to go by 'she,' so it works out."

Joan and I laughed at this; even Talia let out a giggle. But Captain Marcie looked at us quizzically, pulling her head back the way people do when trying to get a better view of something they can't fully see. She was, for lack of a better word, a nerd: a person consumed by a singular pursuit, which in her case was nautical navigation. I tend to like nerds, because I am one. Often you can learn a lot from them, and they're rarely cruel. Few people were tormented by a nerd in high school, though they probably weren't saved by one either, as much as popular fiction likes to pretend otherwise. A true nerd is too busy pursuing her passion to involve herself in the emotional lives of others—absent any extenuating circumstances, of course.

"You and Jackson seem to be fast friends," I observed to Joan.

"He kept me entertained while we were docked and prepping for the cruise," she said. "He's a lot, but in a vacuum, that's an asset."

Joan's eyes strayed in the direction of Captain Marcie, and I understood her meaning. It must have been slim pickings those first few days.

"Are you a fan of Payton's too?" I asked the captain, partly to deflect from this derisive moment that had played out in front of her, partly out of genuine curiosity.

"I've never read anything of hers," she replied neutrally. "But we knew each other when we were children."

"Really?" This was interesting. "What was she like back then?"

"I didn't know her well. Her family was very religious. Mine wasn't."

"But you kept in touch over the years?" I pressed her.

"No. It was a coincidence when she reached out about the cruise." The captain paused. "She didn't even remember we grew up together. Till I reminded her."

Was that a hint of resentment I detected in Captain Marcie's tone?

"Well, now that we're all here, should we raise a toast to Table Number Two?" proposed Joan. "I mean, it's only appropriate, given how shitty this wine is."

Only Joan and I laughed this time, but we were loud enough that the occupants of Table 1 took notice. This table consisted of Payton, with Nicole to her right and Jackson to her left. At least, Jackson *had* been sitting to her left. I scanned the room, surprised to see him chatting with none other than my new friend Gerry, though their conversation was short-lived. While I was still watching, he came bounding up the dais, throwing himself into his chair. When he tried to speak to Payton, she made a point of turning away from him. *Still angry over Flora*, I guessed. Instead, he settled for a chat with the fourth member of the table, a woman whose back was to me, and whom I hadn't met yet. I knew by process of elimination that she had to be the romance novelist, Jessamine LaBouchère. Even from behind she looked the part, with her moussed crest of platinum hair.

I locked eyes with Payton, raising my glass a little higher. She raised hers back. I wondered whether she'd come up with a plan yet to deal with the Flora situation.

Knowing Payton, she had.

CHAPTER 8

The food was good. As I mentioned, I'm not much of a foodie, but Talia proved to be a finicky eater, the kind of person who has to know every detail about each morsel to pass her lips. I learned from her that our crispy sea bass came from the very waters we were floating in, and that a thin layer of shaved truffles had been added to each filet, complementing the dish's delicate umami. There was a period a few years back when *everything* had truffles on it (or at least truffle oil), and I thought I'd passed the point of no return with truffles. But I hadn't—at least not when I was in the superior hands of Chef Gasçoigne. Also, he didn't skimp on portions, which I appreciated that evening in particular. The Dramamine had begun to feel lonesome inside my recently evacuated stomach, and I was happy to give it some company.

One disappointment: there weren't enough servers to go through the charade of arranging the food on individual dome-covered trays and removing the domes at the same time, like a magic trick. In fact, there were hardly any servers at all. Each of the Hogwarts tables had just one waitress (Sandra the bartender had been assigned Slytherin, poor woman), and a fifth was in charge of the two tables up on the dais. Her name tag said she was Kendall, and I suppose she was lucky to be re-

sponsible for eight people rather than seventy-five, but I thought
she looked stressed. I wondered if being assigned the dais was
a big deal.

Kendall's skin was so pale, I'd say it was like porcelain if that
comparison didn't make me gag. Also, there was nothing delicate about her. She was tiny—barely clearing five feet—though
I would never have called her petite. She had a compact, muscular frame easily capable of supporting the giant tray she was
carting to and from the kitchen. I put her at thirtysomething,
with light brown eyes that reminded me of a bird's the way
they darted here, there, and everywhere, taking in everything.
And yet there was a hardness to her expression: especially in
the way she held her mouth in a grim, compressed line. She
was all business, balancing her tray on her shoulder and neck
with one hand, while with the other she held one of those collapsible serving stands that looked a lot like the luggage rack
my suitcase was resting on back in my room. I watched as she
used gravity to flip the stand open, sliding the tray into place.

When I was fifteen, I worked at a terrible "family-style"
Mexican restaurant one summer, and I can still remember the
neck burns I got from the rims of the plates sitting on just such
a tray, held in just such a way. It's a wonder I can remember
anything from the experience. I got fired my fourth day on the
job after accidentally serving a frozen margarita to an eight-
year-old whose parents had ordered her a "virgin." (The eight-
year-old was fine. Unless my blunder was the inciting incident
on a long and tortured journey ending in alcoholism and sub-
stance abuse. I guess I'll never know.) And yet I draw on this
experience every time I interact with a server of any kind. I
think everyone should be required to work at some point in
their lives as a waiter or barista or dishwasher, or something
else menial in the food services industry. It would make fewer
of us such high-maintenance assholes.

I doubted Talia Simmons had ever been a waitress. While

serving us our dessert, Kendall had to field various questions from her, such as whether sugar had been added while preparing our tapioca pudding (yes, but only organic cane sugar, no high fructose corn syrup), how much trans fat was in it (trace amounts), whether the tapioca root used was GMO (no), and where it came from (Brazil).

"I've committed myself to cutting out foods from countries that are known to exploit their native populations," Talia explained to us—which only accounted for her last question, but no one mentioned this as we nodded along.

By the time Kendall was collecting our dessert plates (best tapioca pudding evah), her blond ponytail was plastered to the back of her shirt. She had the sort of straight yet coarse hair with natural highlights that many would have killed for, myself included. My own monochrome and lanky brown locks were shoulder-length at the moment, which was as long as they could get before edging into stringiness. But her hair was gloriously thick, and she had piles of it—an abundance of hair, a follicular cornucopia. And yet I couldn't help thinking how heavy it looked, one more thing for this harried woman to carry around with her. While she was pouring me some water, the glass nearly slipped from her grip, her hands were so sweaty, and when she put the glass down, they were visibly shaking.

"Are you feeling okay?" Joan asked gently.

Kendall nodded a few times in quick succession: a rapid, nervy gesture that reminded me of a bird that's alighted on a branch for a quick moment. It was the second time she'd reminded me of a bird, and the comparison was apt. We like to pretend birds are cuddly and delicate; we talk about people cooing; we say someone eats "like a bird" when she eats barely anything, whereas in reality, birds are bad-asses with beaks more than capable of drawing blood and a metabolism that forces them to eat a sizable fraction of their body weight each day.

"You let me know if you need anything, okay?" said Joan. "You're as much my concern as any of the paying passengers. Remember that."

Kendall nodded once more before darting away, the bird lifting off its branch.

Joan caught my eye across the table as she picked up her wineglass. "We day laborers have to stick together."

By the end of the meal, I realized I was exhausted, though I had nothing like Kendall's excuse.

"Cocktails in the lounge?" suggested Joan.

"Not for me." I stifled a yawn.

"That's the Dramamine talking."

"Well worth the drowsiness." I stood up. "My bed is calling me."

After saying my goodbyes I exited swiftly, descending from the dais and barreling through the gen pop by way of the wan smile and middle-distance gaze I've deployed in countless crowds to ward off those around me. I find neutrality is superior to antagonism in such scenarios, as the latter may be interpreted as a challenge, and offer up unintentional enticement. The only person I regretted blowing off was Gerry, who I hadn't managed to speak to that evening. But there would be plenty of time for chatting in the future.

I didn't go straight to my room. I wanted a little air before sealing myself inside my narrow box for the night, so I went upstairs, to the observation deck. Without thinking about it, I returned to the stern of the ship, leaning over the railing to look out on the water.

The ocean was so black, I wouldn't have been able to distinguish it from the sky if it weren't for the stars. My God, those stars. . . . They were even brighter without the filter of a glass roof. For the first time, it was obvious to me why the ancients named our corner of the universe the Milky Way. I'd always thought of stars as pinpoints of light, but like one of those paintings by Seurat or Van Gogh where you stand back and the dots coalesce, a white cloud with purple shadows had appeared in the middle of the sky—a bulging ripple spilling from the upper left to lower right of my field of vision, a diagonal crack in the heavens themselves. It looked like the freeze-frame of an explosion mid-billow, and put me in mind of the original explosion, the supposed Big Bang, which has never satisfied me as an answer to the question of how everything started. Often when I contemplate the night sky, I can't help airing such weighty, philosophical concerns. It all seems so random: this void inside of which we're so hopelessly lost. . . . But the Milky Way was something to hold on to—a presence mighty and beautiful enough to make the void feel a little less empty.

Fortunately, there was no moon in the sky, as the moonlight would have overpowered the dimmer stars. I stood leaning against the railing for some time—longer than I meant to, given that I didn't have a coat on, though my long-sleeved dress was very warm. When I lifted my arms to blow into my hands, I saw to my delight that the starlight was so bright, my arms cast a fuzzy shadow on the railing's white surface.

"Well, look what the Leach's petrel dragged in."

Before I turned around, I remember thinking: *Of course. Of course he's here.*

"Oh hell no," I said. "What are you doing here? Also, did you just say a leach dragged me in?"

"A Leach's *petrel*, you philistine."

"Fuck off," I replied sweetly.

He stepped closer. Unlike me, he was wearing a coat—a black woolen number that went well past his knees, accentuating his willowy frame and making him look taller than he was, not that he wasn't tall. His name was Gideon Pereira, and most people would have identified his profusion of chestnut curls as his most prominent feature. They were worthy of a Botticelli angel, and had clearly never seen a comb in their freewheeling existence. It was a good thing Gideon was so thin, as any facial pudge would have edged him into cherub territory. He was downright gaunt, in fact, with a long, bony nose and cheeks so sunken, he appeared to be perpetually sucking them in. But I eschewed all this and fixated instead on his full, cherry-red lips. I knew from past experience that his lips always looked a little chapped, but never more so than on this night.

Gideon was Payton's ex-husband.

"A petrel is a bird often found in this part of the Atlantic."

He was also a bird-watching enthusiast, or "birder" (ugh). *And* a writer (surprise!), a journalist who freelanced for only the highest-profile magazines—one of the few among his endangered breed with enough clout to be picky about the stories he wrote.

He sauntered up to the railing, leaning on it as I'd been doing. I leaned with him.

"There've been petrels flying all over the place today," he said. "Not that anyone cares."

"Ah, but *you* care. Because you're special."

He grinned without showing his teeth, those pin-cushion lips of his expanding easily to accommodate the gesture.

"It's not that I'm special, it's just that everyone else is so *un*-special."

This made me laugh aloud. He laughed too, leaning farther over the railing, his bony rump sticking out of the slit in the back of his coat. Even though I was many inches shorter than him, there was a fair chance I weighed more, and I found myself wondering whether I could pin his arms down while lying on top of him.

Hm. Interesting.

"What the hell are you doing here?" I asked him again.

"Payton asked me to write a story about the cruise." He shrugged. "You know how difficult it is to say no to Payton."

Gideon and Payton had gotten together when they were still in their mid-twenties. Like me, Payton had moved to New York after our MFA program ended—the obvious destination for every wannabe twit of a writer. Back then Gideon had a position at a respectable magazine procured by way of a fancy undergraduate degree. They were a good match in terms of ambition. Both were on the rise, and I always thought of their union as a modern-day marriage of convenience in that it allowed them to amplify their circle of influence—like joining a minor Habsburg to a member of the House of Saxe-Coburg and Gotha. (I *was* invited to their wedding, where I got magnificently drunk.) And they really did flourish. Gideon's career took off the same time Payton's did, and you'd better believe an invite to one of their Chelsea dinner parties was a ticket you didn't pass up. Unless you were me. (I was invited to one early on, begged off, and never got invited again.) You can also imagine the shock, and glee, that reverberated throughout the literary community when Payton's affair with Nicole Root became public, and she and Gideon split up.

I'll say this for him: he handled it well. They had two kids, which meant they were motivated to keep things friendly—or at least, friendly seeming. I'd never heard of any friction between him and Payton, or him and Nicole. While my contact with Payton over the years had been sparing, I ran into Gideon somewhat regularly. A lot of journalists freelance on the side as ghostwriters, and while he didn't, it meant we knew the same people and often found ourselves at the same obligatory parties, where catching up with each other was easily the best half hour spent in an otherwise dreary evening. Post-divorce, we'd fallen into the habit of engaging in a low-grade flirty banter whenever we met—like Hepburn and Tracy, except no one was watching, or cared, and we never actually did anything.

I liked Gideon. For all his arrogance, there was none of the territorial male about him. Whether this was because he was truly evolved or merely good at faking it, I wasn't sure. But the older I get, the less I mind the gap between appearance and reality anyway.

And yet I couldn't make sense of his presence here. Over the years he'd acquired a reputation as the kind of journalist who never lets his subjects off the hook.

"Isn't she worried you're going to rake the whole 'Get Lit' thing over the coals?"

He grasped the railing with both hands and pushed himself up till his arms were straight, as if performing a diagonal pushup. His hands were as thin and elegant as his body—not feminine, but prettily masculine, if that makes sense.

It made sense to me.

"She is." He lowered himself onto the railing again. "But she also knows that whatever I write, it'll get a ton of eyeballs."

"I think what I value most about you is your modesty."

"Please, I meant because I'm her ex and people will love reading between the lines. I can see the subreddit now." He shook his head, one of his little curls flopping onto his forehead. "She also knows if I make fun of her, and all this, *I'm* the one who'll get raked over the coals."

"Because it'll come across as misogynistic," I said. "And you're not a misogynist."

He grinned. "I'd say I'm as much of a misogynist as you are."

"Well then God help us all."

While we chuckled over this, I thought about how Gideon Pereira was the perfect person to write a buzzy think-piece about the Get Lit Cruise. The chatter over whether he had the ability to be objective would only heighten the article's profile. God, she was good at this.

He turned to me, all that glorious starlight shining from within his dark eyes.

"I guess I'm going to have to keep an open mind."

"First time for everything," I replied.

When he sidled a few inches closer to me, I didn't sidle away. I could smell his expensive cologne, which was too floral for my taste. But there was a whiff of whiskey underneath it that was much more to my liking.

"Where'd you eat?" I asked him. "In your room?"

He nodded. "My choice."

Payton hadn't mentioned him when she announced the presence of Jackson and the chef, however. It was one thing to have a male assistant and cook on board an all-female cruise. Gideon's presence was awkward, and I guessed Payton would do her best to avoid acknowledging him.

"So how does it feel to be one of three men on a ship full of ladies?"

"Three?" he repeated in surprise. "I know Gasçoigne's here, who's the other?"

"Jackson."

He grimaced. "Oh. That guy."

"Can't say I was too enamored of him myself."

If this had been one of our party chats, we'd have moved on to another topic, or one of us would have moved on from the other person altogether. But we were stuck on this boat for six more days. Our options were limited.

"You know my ten-year-old, Clyde?"

I nodded, though I hadn't remembered Clyde's age, or name. I knew Gideon and Payton had two children, a boy and a girl, both of whom were in that prolonged hazy period during which they were no longer babies and not yet teenagers.

"I picked him up from Payton's one day, and I could tell he was upset. Took a while to get it out of him. Apparently Jackson's in the habit of watching gay porn in his office, which is right next to the playroom. Kid said he could *see* it every time he passed the door. So I called Jackson and told him to stop watching porn around my kids. You know what he told me?"

"That you were being homophobic?"

"How did you—"

"Oh God, did he actually say that? I was joking."

"Obviously the fact that it was *gay* porn didn't matter. I would've been just as upset if it'd been straight porn." He considered a beat. "Maybe *more* upset."

"Watch out, you're treading on thin ice there," I teased him.

He pitched his body sideways into mine and then stood up, stretching his catlike torso to its utmost extent. When he motioned me with his head to follow him, I realized something was happening between us—if I wanted it to happen. I watched as he sauntered down the half flight of stairs connecting the raised platform to the rest of the deck, and then followed him as he doubled back to a narrow, semicircular ledge that ran around the platform we'd just been standing on. A series of benches had been bolted to the floor every few feet along this horseshoe-shaped viewing shelf, all of them facing the ocean—a sort of "Lovers' Point," which was how I came to think of this area from then on.

We aimed for the bench at the top of the horseshoe, so to speak—at the tip of the rounded stern, thereby maximizing our ocean view. When we sat, we did so at the same time, our legs touching, knee to thigh. Even so, I began shivering upon contact with the icy metal slats supporting us. I pride myself on my ability to withstand the cold, but it was January, and nighttime in the northern Atlantic, and I'd been outside for many minutes by this point.

"Here—"

He slipped one arm out of his coat, which was wide enough to wrap around my back and fasten around the two of us in the front.

I'm not going to lie: it was a bold move, and smoothly executed. Also smooth? His face, which had no five o'clock shadow, despite the fact that it was nearly ten. *He must have shaved before dinner*, I thought to myself idly, while relaxing my body against his. Now I was close enough to smell his aftershave too, which had a hint of crème de menthe in it.

The truth is that a cruise ship is a pretty safe place for a one-night stand. It's much more difficult to dispose of a body on a boat than on dry land, plus people will notice quickly that you've gone missing. Also, the close quarters mean that if you scream, you're likely to be heard.

But then I'm just a romantic at heart.

"You're a comfy pillow," I murmured.

"Yes, my concave chest is the perfect shape for lounging," he remarked.

"Stop fishing for compliments."

"Aye aye, Cap'n."

I turned my face upward. I could have touched his chin with my tongue if I wanted to. "Actually, have you met her yet? The captain? She's a piece of work."

"Takes one to know one."

"Right back at you," I murmured.

I could feel the laughter rumbling inside him. Was it possible the stars had gotten brighter? It was like being sheltered under a canopy. . . . I raised my hand, brushing it against his cheek. His skin was even softer than I'd imagined.

He pressed his face into my palm. "I thought you'd never ask."

Part Two
First Murder

CHAPTER 9

Sex with Gideon was exactly what I needed it to be: good enough for a diversion, not so good that it would become a distraction. I returned to my cabin afterward, which meant I was able to begin Monday morning on my own terms, with a clear head. In keeping with my routine, I spent the first ninety minutes of the day in bed on my laptop, sawing away at a short story I'd started a few days earlier. I like writing short stories from time to time, and fantasizing about publishing them in high-end journals like *The Atlantic*, or *Granta*. Sometimes I even submit to these places, though I never tell my agent Rhonda when I do. They've become a guilty pleasure of mine, and it's important to have a guilty pleasure when you're a working writer. I also journaled about the events of the day before, as I make a point of keeping a chronicle of my activities whenever I'm on a job. It helped that even though I'd accessed the ship's Wi-Fi on my phone, I'd willfully forgotten the password so that I couldn't connect to the Internet on my laptop. Such little tricks do wonders for my productivity.

When I emerged from my room, it was still early enough that the boat felt empty, and I could feel virtuous about having been productive. I passed Kendall, our waitress from the night before, in one of the hallways on the fourth deck. Apparently she had housekeeping duties in addition to food service, which I intuited by the stack of fluffy white towels covering the lower half of her face. This allowed me to pretend she returned my smile, even when my "good morning" went unreciprocated.

Breakfast in the dining room was served buffet-style, so I inhaled a bowl of cornflakes and made a coffee to go, nodding at Sandra as she lugged a silver vat of what I guessed were scrambled eggs or bacon from the galley. (I don't really do hot or hearty breakfasts, unless I'm eating them for dinner.) It was time to prep my classroom. They'd put me in the black box theater, which was next to the dining room, though I had to go back to the lobby area in front of the elevator and then down the hallway to the left, which also led to the gym and pool beyond the theater—neither of which I had any plans to visit.

True to its name, the black box theater was a windowless box painted entirely black: floor, walls, ceiling. There were no permanent seats, just a few rows of folding chairs. The space was smaller than I expected (see? happens every time), and I hadn't been expecting much. But I also wasn't going to obsess over the fact my class of twenty-five was the smallest of the bunch. (Payton had nearly a hundred students, while Poetry, YA, and Romance each had around fifty.) This occasional ability of mine not to take such slights personally is one of the happier outcomes of a hard-won lesson—that the world doesn't revolve around me.

I sat on one of the folding chairs. It was hot in there, and it smelled of paint and sawdust with a hint of body odor—acrid scents that kicked my nervous system into overdrive, not that my nerves needed much revving up. Through the wall, I could hear a spin class taking place in the gym: an electro-funk version of some peppy pop song, an automated instructor's high-pitched exhortations punctuating it at regular intervals. I was glad to be sitting where I was, motionless, save for the guzzling of my coffee.

I'd decided when I took this job that I wouldn't plan for it. Teaching was about inspiration, right? (Stop laughing, teachers. I can hear you.) But now I wished I had a lesson plan, something to grab on to as my first two-hour block of time drew closer: an abyss I had no idea how I was going to cross.

What the hell was I going to *do* with these people?

The purpose of a black box theater is to blur the line between audience and performer, so I decided to lean into this blurriness. To start, I collapsed all the folding chairs, propping them against the wall. I put a rickety lectern and whiteboard-on-wheels in the corner (it's not like they were Baby or anything). I scrounged up a "meditation" playlist I'd assembled years earlier on Spotify, and blasted it through my smartphone. Somehow it was almost ten by this point, so I plopped down on the floor in the center of the room and affixed a hideously fake smile to my face, hoping it would come across as welcoming rather than demented.

Two women appeared in the doorway.

"Come sit!" I cried, patting the floor. "We're forming a circle."

This was the sort of thing I would have rolled my eyes at if I were in their position. But they popped a squat without hesitating, mirroring my jack o' lantern leer. The next five who came in did the same. I think it helped that they were all dressed as if for a yoga class, in leggings and stretchy tops. Judging by the aroma a few of them brought with them, they may have come straight from the spin class next door, which had just ended.

"I won't be doing that," declared a woman who had just walked in. She was easily among the oldest on the boat—well north of eighty—with orthopedic shoes and a walking stick. And yet there was no hunch to her back or shoulders, and she held up her head like a much younger person, chin raised. I could easily picture her in her twenties, and I know I'm supposed to add something about how beautiful she must have been back then, but I'm not sure she ever was beautiful. Unless vitality is its own form of beauty.

"Once I go down that low"—she tapped the floor with her cane's rubber tip—"I don't come back up without a song-and-dance number. Not a pretty one, either."

"Of course." I scrambled off the floor and retrieved one of the folding chairs from the wall, popping it open.

"Thanks, doll. Name's June, by the way. Don't need to ask you yours, do I?"

Not a Baby June, I said to myself, determined to remember as many of their names as possible.

Two more opted for folding chairs once they saw they had the option, while a third woman named Phyllis asked if she could lie flat on her back with her legs resting on an empty seat.

"I've got a bad back and varicose veins," she explained. "I know it's unorthodox, but it would be heaven if you're okay with it."

"I'm all about heterodoxy," I assured her, garnering a few nervous laughs.

Phyllis on the flooris, Phyllis on the flooris.

Helen Sanchez took the spot everyone else had been avoiding, immediately to my right. She sank down in one fluid motion, arranging her legs crisscross applesauce. (Her mnemonic was obvious: *Helen of Troy*, though I had no need for it.) I envied the way her back remained straight throughout this maneuver, her core locked and loaded. Have you ever watched a toddler squat? Their form is perfect, their knees never straying past their toes. Most of us lose this innate grace by the time we've stopped shitting ourselves, but it's one of the reasons aspiring ballerinas are advised to start as early as possible. I wondered if she'd been a dancer in her formative years. It would have helped shape the iron discipline I suspected she brought to her every endeavor. In her lap lay a worn Moleskine journal open to a fresh page, her uncapped pen hovering above it, ready to pounce. No one else had thought to bring note-taking materials, and I caught a few of her classmates throwing nervous looks her way.

Most of these women were fiftyish, give or take: ladies who loved or at least *really liked* literature, and had the cash to pursue their inclination. But they were all pleasant people. The rich almost always are. Everyone wants them to be cruel, or contemptuous, or at the very least aloof, but as one who's spent years around wealthy people telling their stories, I can attest to the fallacy of this pipe dream. Money may not buy you happiness, but it buys you ease, and comfort—a layer of emotional cushioning that allows you to be nice to those around you. The well-to-do have the *wherewithal* for kindness, and while that may not be fair, it doesn't change the fact that they're usually pretty great company.

I waited until 10:10, by which point sixteen of the twenty-five people I'd been expecting had arrived. It seemed that nine of my students had ditched me. (I'd learn later that seven of them chose to sit in on Payton's course, despite the fact it was full. The other two had jumped ship—an intra-ship jump—to Nicole.) This is going to make me sound more confident than I am, but whenever I experience a setback that's imposed on me by other people, as opposed to the mind games I play with myself, I take satisfaction in meeting these challenges head on and conquering them. So what if I had only sixteen people in my class? I'd turn it into a seminar, or a workshop. Those nine idiots would have no idea what they were missing. This was the inverse of the dark, doubting moments we all endure late at night when we're utterly alone in the world, no matter who might be sleeping beside us or in the other room. Here, on a Monday morning with thirty-two eyes trained on me; here, stuck on an effing *cruise ship* in the middle of the North Atlantic, I felt both capable and competent—more than equal to the task before me.

Wonders never cease.

We went around the circle clockwise, doing introductions. It's interesting what information people choose to include in a byte-size autobiography of themselves. Most of them started off with their relationship status: proudly married for however many years, or just as proudly divorced. (I started things off by saying I was "proudly single," which got the amused reaction I intended.) Many of them mentioned children. June said she had three, who'd given her eight grandchildren. "So the gamble paid off!" she added, to a hurricane of laughter.

Phyllis had to crane her neck so that she was looking at us upside-down as she spoke about the autoimmune condition that necessitated such contortions—a smorgasbord of woes many doctors and so-called friends of hers thought she was making up, or exaggerating. "My back is the tip of the iceberg, which is probably a metaphor I shouldn't be using on a cruise ship in the winter. Most of my other symptoms can't be discussed in polite company. Makes my life hell," she said cheerfully. "Which is why I do fun stuff like this from time to time, when I can." She too was married, with a grown daughter.

Jobs were a popular topic, though many of them were of the cushy, philanthropic variety. But there was one woman named Theresa who was a corporate lawyer. She had the sort of glossy ringlets I associated with child pageant performers rather than mature women, though hers were raven black, not blond, and shot through with streaks of silver. (*Theresa with therrific hair.*) Judging by her modish glasses and designer outfit, she was a good lawyer.

"I haven't taken a vacation in six years," she said. "This is my big splurge."

I found myself hoping fervently I was up to the task of justifying Theresa's big splurge. When I'd accepted Payton's offer, I hadn't considered the people I'd be teaching. Now that they were here, in front of me, I wanted to make good on the promise that I would be teaching them something useful about mysteries.

Helen went last, clipping her pen to her notebook before speaking.

"I'm a writer. It's all I've ever been, and all I ever want to be."

Ugh. And yet a part of me was moved by the rawness of her ambition, and the unvarnished way she was willing to share it. There was an innocence about her that I hadn't appreciated the night before. Why was I so desperate for her to dissemble like everyone else? Or at any rate, like me?

"You weren't ever a dancer?" I asked her.

Her wide and lovely eyes opened a little wider behind her glasses. She'd left out the colored contact lenses today, I noticed. Her real eyes were so dark, they were nearly as black as her pupils, which made them fathomless and lent her an air of mystery. Someone needed to tell her to ditch the contacts permanently.

"How did you—"

"Elementary, my dear Helen." God, I was laying it on thick. "Your posture."

She made a little doffing-the-hat gesture that endeared her to me more than anything she'd said thus far.

"There's your first lesson." I looked round the circle. "On the power of observation. One of the most important tools a writer has. *Especially* a mystery writer."

If the student version of me hadn't been rolling her eyes before, she would have been looking directly at her brain by this point. And yet they oohed and aahed over this, while Helen scribbled away.

"Okay, let's cover some basics. This is going to sound obvious because it *is*, but at the heart of every murder mystery is a murder. Now my first piece of advice to you is to *start* with that murder and build the story out from there. Because if the murder isn't both convincing *and* compelling, the story surrounding it will fall like a house of cards."

"Ooh, I just loved that show," Phyllis told the ceiling.

"You and me both, doll," said June. "Except that last season. Where it was just the wife? What was with that? Terrible."

"Oh, he got MeToo'ed," said Theresa.

"Isn't he gay though?" asked Phyllis. "He sure was on the show."

"You can still get MeToo'ed when you're gay," explained Theresa.

This went on for a while. I decided to let it play out, because they were the ones paying for their time. I wasn't their schoolteacher, and it's not like they had a standardized test to take at the end of the week. I was under no social obligation to teach them anything.

But I sympathized with Helen, who sat there with her arms crossed like a big sister annoyed with her siblings for not following the rules clearly printed on the board game's instruction manual. When she began throwing me imploring looks, I took pity on her and clapped my hands, calling them to order.

"As I was saying, at the heart of every murder mystery is a murder you as the writer have to account for. There are a lot of ways to do this, but I like to think about how a prosecutor would go about proving the culprit did it, so I can be sure all the pieces are there. Now what are the three criteria for proving someone committed a crime?"

Helen spoke first, as I knew she would. Come to think of it, *Hermione Helen* was a better mnemonic than *Helen of Troy*.

"Motive, means, and opportunity."

"Thank you, Helen. That's correct. And how many times have we heard this, right? Motive, means, and opportunity. It's *Law and Order*, Agatha Christie 101 type stuff. And yet I posit to you that one among these three criteria is consistently underestimated."

"Well it sure isn't motive."

"You're right, June. No shortage of ink has been spilled about motive in the annals of detective fiction. Or noir. Or any of the other subgenres of mystery. Motive is the *why* of murder, and it's crucial. But we all knew that already."

"I suppose alibis are used in defense of . . ." Theresa paused, considering. I pictured her in some light-filled corner office, patiently scanning a contract on her screen. "An alibi would negate a person's opportunity, wouldn't it?"

"*Very* good, Theresa. Opportunity is the *how* of murder. Was this person in the area? Can their whereabouts during the relevant window of time be accounted for in a reliable manner? Et cetera. It's about whether the culprit had the *situational* ability to do the deed. But here's the thing."

If I'd been standing, I would have begun to move around a little. Since we were all sitting in a circle, I settled for leaning forward.

"Means is also about the *how* of murder. But in a more indirect way. Did this person have the ability to commit the crime? Maybe the culprit had to have been short, or strong, or left-handed. All that goes to means. Anyone who doesn't qualify can be removed from the suspect list. Nine times out of ten, means is used negatively, as a tool for elimination. A sort of background supplement to opportunity. But in some of the best mysteries, it's deployed proactively."

I did get up now, wheeling the whiteboard from its corner and into the center of the room. With a blue marker, I wrote in big capital letters that I wished were a little neater: ACCESS.

"Access goes to means," I said. "And to the heart of credibility. If it's easier for a person to insert himself into the environment where the murder took place, regardless of logistics or any of the situational specifics covered by opportunity, then it's that much easier to believe he did it. A mystery writer ignores this at her peril."

I paused to catch my breath. Helen was writing so hard, her notebook was in danger of catching fire by way of friction. Theresa, June, and Phyllis seemed to be following along, but everyone else was regarding me with that unfocused stare I remembered so well from the faces of my childhood classmates. I felt a pang of remorse for all the nasty things I'd ever said about my public schoolteachers. Faced with that glazed look day after day, I'd have given up a lot sooner than they did.

Maybe if I brought up *House of Cards* again I could get them back? If it had been possible to wheel out a TV on a cart and pop in a VHS tape of that show or anything else, I would have done it. And yet the two-hour session was well past the halfway mark by this point.

Thank goodness for Hermione Helen, who raised her hand for a follow-up. Aided by her along with my semi-engaged trio, together we lurched our way to the end of the two-hour session and broke for lunch. I had survived my first lesson.

CHAPTER 10

I'd been planning on eating lunch with my students. Tables 1 and 2 were used for dinner only, and I wanted to make a point about being accessible. (I wasn't a regular teacher; I was a *cool* teacher!) But Flora accosted me as soon as I entered the dining room.

She'd toned down for daytime: two-thirds less makeup, and no false eyelashes, thank the Lord. The hairpiece was also gone. Her dark, shoulder-length hair had been pulled into a wincingly tight ponytail. She must have used hairspray because there was nary a strand or wisp to be seen. She looked like she was about to go horseback riding, or engage in some similarly uptight/upscale pursuit. I suppose her khaki slacks and lilac sweater were an improvement over the monstrous gown from the night before, but since when had she gotten so preppy? I missed the old Flora, with her taped-up shoes and baggy black trousers cinched at the waist with a safety pin. Again, I was struck by how thin she was, and not in a good way. Her clavicle was so prominent, it was staring me down.

"Can we talk?" she asked. "Alone?"

"As long as we're eating."

Two hours' worth of extroversion had taken its toll. I was ravenous. Like breakfast, lunch was served buffet-style, though unlike breakfast it was a cold buffet, consisting of a salad bar and sandwich-making station. (Payton had blown her meal budget on Pierre Gasçoigne, which meant that while dinner would always be a showstopper, breakfast and lunch were more modest affairs.) Happily, I slapped together a PB&J on rye—one of my favorite meals, bar none—and poured myself a tall glass of milk using one of those metal-knobbed dispensers I remembered from my college days. You know: the ones you have to lift *up* to make the milk come out of that fat plastic tube that looks not unlike a cow's udder?

"Let's go to the lounge," said Flora. "It's more private there."

She'd deposited two slices of cheese on a plate and was clutching a bottle of Poland Spring—the barest pretense of a meal.

"Is that all you're eating?"

I wouldn't usually ask such an intrusive question, but Flora and I had known each other since we were in our twenties, when such intrusions were still on the table. That's the joy, and danger, of old friendships. You can always revert to that former version of yourself, no matter how much time has passed.

She grabbed a monster of a chocolate-chip cookie (surface area of a CD, girth of a hockey puck). It was sheathed in plastic, and when she threw it on top of the cheese it slid a little, the orange slices already beginning to sweat. "Better?"

"Much," I said. "As long as you're sharing."

The lounge smelled of booze. The break between the morning and afternoon sessions was three hours long, and many of the passengers were filling this gap with copious day-drinking. We were the only ones who'd brought food in here, and I hesitated in the doorway, feeling embarrassed to be carting my milk and sandwich in front of a crowd. This was exactly the sort of social diffidence à la Laura-from-*The-Glass-Menagerie* the old Flora would have shared, and yet she sallied forth with her unholy plate of cheese and cookie, plonking it down on a glass coffee table in the least populated corner of the room. I watched as she sank onto a white leather couch, waving me over imperiously. Was the old Flora still in there somewhere? The tricky thing about assuming a new personality is that unlike a suit of armor, the more time that passes, the harder it is to remove the façade and revert to your former self.

I would know.

I threaded my way through the many tables and the much larger obstruction of a white baby-grand piano playing music by itself. The mechanism was digital rather than a roll of paper, making it the slinky, futuristic version of a saloon piano. At the moment it was churning out some anodyne Chopin, but all I could focus on when I looked at it was the timer counting down the song, rather than the music itself.

Finally I reached Flora, and sat down. This part of the lounge was the least populated because it was bathed in the direct sunlight of high noon. The ocean sparkled in the windows behind us, intensifying the glare. The effect was overwhelming, but not unpleasant, the combination of sun, sea, and diffuse conversational hum making for a holiday feel. If I hadn't been working, I would have ordered a cocktail myself.

Flora produced a pair of sunglasses from a small and no doubt expensive purse she'd been carrying on one shoulder. Sometimes I feel as though there are two types of people in the world: (1) those who have sunglasses on them when needed, and (2) those who do not. There's no question which category I fall into.

I angled my body away from the windows to keep my squint to a minimum. Flora held up her bottle of water.

"Do you mind opening this for me?"

She tapped the cap with a long, manicured nail. *For fuck's sake.* My disdain for long nails is one of the few personality traits I've preserved since my early adolescence. More proof that Flora had changed for the worse.

I accepted the bottle from her, crushing the top half of it in my rushed attempt to twist off the cap. This mistake is easily made with the squishy plastic of a Poland Spring bottle—more so than any other brand. But I blamed Flora, who was watching my every move with a smirk.

"What's going on with you?" I asked, handing back the mangled bottle.

She took a long sip before answering me.

"Is this an intervention? *I* asked to talk to you, remember?"

"Okay, so what did you want to talk about?"

"I wanted to see where you stand," she said. "So I know whose side you're on."

"Isn't it a little childish to be talking about sides?"

"You're right, it is childish. Because children haven't learned to lie to themselves or each other yet. So which is it? Are you on the side of good? With me? Or of evil with Payton?"

I took a bite of my PB&J because I didn't know what else to do. (Also: hunger.) The sunlight was so strong, I could see her eyes through her tinted glasses. They were glued to mine, waiting for an answer.

I swallowed. "Come on. Payton isn't evil. What happened between you two was unfortunate—"

"I'd been working on that book for *fourteen years.*"

I winced. I couldn't help it.

"You're a writer," she continued. "Of a kind."

Oh, fuck you, Flora.

"You know what it's like when you've been working on something for way too long."

I did. One of my favorite aspects of ghostwriting is that it involves external deadlines. It means you can't obsess over every little thing, which means you can't let the writing process get to that horrible point wherein you lose perspective on what's good and what's not, and the words *congeal*, the sentences refusing to flow or even to make sense. Suddenly, your favorite thing in the world—this little treasure you've been honing, perfecting—becomes despicable, a source of shame. It's like the love of your life morphs into your mortal enemy, and you're the purveyor of the black magic that did it: a self-hating, talentless little witch. And while it's possible to recover from this affliction, to claw your way back to sanity, it isn't easy. I know there are many aspects of life that are hard, many of them more deserving of sympathy than such patrician plights of the creative class. But in its unique way, writing can be so, so awful.

"She knew I was in a state of agony over it," Flora went on. "She'd ask me about it all the time, and I thought she was being a good friend, checking in with me, letting me vent so I'd feel less alone. But she was storing it up for herself. I could've gotten over the fact that she stole Augusta Leigh from me."

No you couldn't.

"I obviously understand you can't own a subject."

No you don't.

"But I'll never get over the way she stole my experience as a writer. Never. It's like she figured out how to humiliate me in every way a person can be humiliated. It was so . . . cruel. She may as well have cut off my hand. Or killed my mother."

"I completely understand why you're upset, but—" I stopped, struggling for the words. "It's done. Payton's book is out. I'll bet you could easily get a bunch of publishers interested in yours now—"

"Oh, no." She inched the cookie out of its wrapper, tearing off the exposed edge. "My book's dead. It's never seeing the light of day. If it did, it'd just be another way for people to make fun of me." She shoved the cookie shard into her mouth, jaws snapping.

"Then what do you *want?*"

"What everybody wants when they've been wronged. Revenge."

This would have been a more effectively dramatic declaration if her mouth hadn't been full of cookie when she said it. I felt the urge to laugh at her, but I was afraid of what she'd do to me. Also, it wasn't funny, not really. She was in pain. That was obvious.

"So you're just, what? Going to keep following her around? Is that your plan? Play the Goddess of Discord and mess up her life as much as possible?"

"Good comp," said Flora approvingly. "I'd make a good Eris. Do you think I should start throwing down an apple whenever I enter a room?"

She grinned, and the old Flora flashed out at me, the one who had a lively sense of humor. She'd been a classics major in college, I remembered now. It figured she would appreciate the mythological reference.

"Didn't you ever wonder what Eris did *after* she ruined the wedding she wasn't invited to?" I asked her.

"Cackled with glee?"

"At first, sure. But you can only cackle for so long. I think there was even an *Austin Powers* joke about that. Eventually, she's got to go home."

"Point being?"

She already knew what my point was.

"It just seems like a lonely existence."

"Are *you* seriously trying to lecture *me* about not cutting myself off from people?"

"Takes a self-*saboteuse* to know a self-*saboteuse*," I said lightly. "Come on, Flor. It's not like all this anger is helping you. You know you're going to have to move past it eventually."

"You sound like my therapist. Who I fired. Everyone's so afraid of anger these days, but I've decided to embrace my anger. So far it feels amazing. Also? It's Flor-*ah*. I refuse to answer to 'Flor' anymore. It's honestly too perfect that that's what you and Payton used to call me. I'm done being a doormat."

She beckoned to a server nearby who was carrying a tray full of drinks. Surprise: it was Kendall again. Flitting between the bar and various parts of the room with her birdlike energy, she was handing out drinks with a towel over one arm.

"Could you clear this?"

Flora gestured to her sad cheese plate and the rest of her cookie. Somehow, Kendall made room for it on her tray, moving away so quickly it was more like she ricocheted off the coffee table toward another part of the room.

"Oh no!" cried Flora. "I forgot, didn't you want some of that?"

"It's all right—"

"Excuse me! Miss?"

"You don't—"

"Miss! Ex-*cuse* me!" Flora trilled.

Half the lounge was looking at us now, among them Gerry Forrest, who was playing what looked to be a game of bridge with three elderly companions. We made eye contact, exchanging rueful smiles.

Kendall was already some distance away. But she turned, letting out a sigh I could see rather than hear, her vest rising and then falling to its previous position.

"We need the cookie back!" cried Flora across the room. "We changed our minds, sorry!"

Kendall backtracked, handing Flora her damn cookie, the pad of her thumb getting smeared in the process with a half-melted chocolate chip. Her hands weren't sweaty today, but they were looking rather flushed. She rubbed her thumb on the towel over her arm, making it redder.

"Thank you *so* much." Flora paused, and she and Kendall stared at each other. "Aren't you going to ask me if I need anything?" she asked finally.

I watched the thin, compressed line of Kendall's mouth grow thinner, her lips turning white.

"That *is* your job, isn't it?"

"Would you like something else?" asked Kendall.

She managed to say this in a neutral tone of voice, which I found impressive.

"You know what, now that you ask . . . a French 75 would be lovely. Thank you *so* much."

The old Flora was the type of person who gladly accepted the wrong order at a restaurant rather than make a fuss. Flora 2.0 was meant to be an upgrade: an empowered Flora, a Flora who'd "found her voice." But I found this derivative, "rich bitch" act of hers downright repulsive.

She broke off another piece of the cookie. "I will *never* let Payton forget what she did to me. It's become my life's mission. I don't care if you or anyone else thinks that's sad."

We ate in silence for a minute or two.

"For the record, I *do* think it's sad, though the irrelevance of my opinion is noted," I said. "I think you're wasting your life."

"Yes, I'm clearly such a great talent."

"You *are* talented," I insisted.

"Please stop," she snorted, breaking off yet another hunk of cookie and shoving it into her mouth. "Do you know what that little assistant of hers said to me last night?" I shook my head while she swallowed noisily. "Right here after dinner. He said a lack of talent is no reason to persecute another person. He said I was being a sadist. *He's* the sadist! But then, he's learned from the best."

"Jackson seems . . . challenging," I acknowledged.

"He's a monster. But don't worry, I've got something planned for him."

"What?" I asked uneasily.

"I'd tell you if you were on my side."

"I'm not on *anyone's* side," I insisted.

"Well, now, that I'll believe."

"What's that supposed to mean?"

"That you've *never* been on anyone's side. Other than your own. You've always been like that. Payton and I used to talk about it all the time." More cookie in mouth. "What a selfish bitch you were."

"You know, it's such a shame we never hung out more, just the two of us, Flora. I can't imagine why that never happened."

"I can. You and I both know the real reason we never hung out is that we were too similar. You hated yourself so much, you couldn't help hating me too, and I was too shy to do anything about it. Back then we were both sheep in wolves' clothing."

"Don't you—"

"No, I've got it the right way around. We were both so *desperate* to prove how serious we were. Smart women with something to say, watch out, world! Nothing more dangerous than that! But that's who *Payton* was. Not us. All we ever wanted was to be praised and loved. We were just too chicken-shit to admit it."

"And now you don't want to be praised and loved?" I asked skeptically. "You've moved on to a higher plane?"

"Who said anything about a higher plane? I've just stopped caring what other people think. But you haven't. That's obvious. You pretend you have, with your black clothes and big glasses. All your homespun snark. But you're still a sheep."

She tossed the remains of the cookie into my lap.

"Whereas I'm *all* wolf now. So I have no problem telling you to go fuck yourself, *Belle*. You do realize the only reason Payton invited you on this cruise is that she doesn't see you as a threat, right? She pities you, as do I, and anyone else who knew you back when we did. You had such big dreams then. And now you ghostwrite celebrity trash, and I guess write cute cozy mysteries on the side? Not exactly the brilliant literary career you were hoping for, is it?" She stood up, pointing at the quarter or so of cookie lying in my lap. "That was revolting, by the way. But you go ahead and enjoy your little treat."

Flora stormed out of the lounge, whipping past Kendall, who had just returned with her French 75.

"I'll take that," I said, reaching for it.

I downed it in three gulps. I could feel the gin and champagne mixing with the milk that was already coating my mouth, throat, and stomach. I stared at the floor, fighting the impulse to vomit—not wanting to embarrass myself any further than Flora already had.

"Are you all right?"

Gerry was wearing a gauzy scarf today, knotted at the neck like a flight attendant. It was turquoise, and made her eyes pop even more than they had yesterday.

"I'm fine," I said. "Don't miss out on your game, I don't want to spoil it any more than I already have."

She waved a hand in the air. "Oh, don't worry about that! I'm dummy this round, I've got nothing to do for a while."

"Okay."

I paused. Was the alcohol actually curdling the milk in my stomach now? Clearly the best thing to do was to add cookie to the mix. I broke the quarter into eighths, offering one to Gerry.

She declined. Smart woman. I downed both pieces, mashing them into oblivion.

"How much of that did you hear?" I asked her.

"Oh! I'm pretty sure the entire lounge heard all of it," she replied with brutal honesty. "Her voice carries, doesn't it? She's a very unpleasant person. So negative."

I knew Gerry was trying to help, but I don't like using "negative" as an insult. Often enough, negativity is an appropriate response to the world. And nine times out of ten, the person labeled "negative" is female. It's the same impulse that results in women being told to smile by strangers on the street.

"Flora is going through a lot," I said.

"She sure is! You'd better believe I know all about it, it's all anyone's talking about. You know she heckled Payton today, during her first lecture?"

"Really?"

Gerry nodded cheerfully. "Every time Payton tried to say something, that woman would start talking over her with her own lecture about plagiarism. She'd written out what she was going to say on notecards. When she was done with a card, she'd fling it onto the stage. We had to end early."

"Yikes."

It looked like Payton hadn't figured out the Flora situation yet.

"Yikes is right! You know, I also have to tell you, I spoke to Payton last night, after dinner." Gerry smiled. "Managed to elbow my way into the fray. And I told her I'd met you. Do you know what she said?"

"Do I want to know?" I asked.

"You certainly do, that's why I'm telling you! She said you're one of the smartest people she knows, and the real writing expert on this cruise. She was positively *gushing* about you."

I wish I could say this meant nothing to me—that Flora was wrong about my wanting to be praised and loved. . . .

"Well, she had to say that to you."

Gerry shook her head. "No! She really meant it, I could tell. I just wanted you to know because I, well, I heard what that woman said just now—"

"I understand," I said hurriedly. "Thank you, Gerry. I appreciate that."

"Would you like another drink?"

"Better not, I'm still on the clock. But do you want to grab one after dinner? I'm sure I could use another cocktail by then."

"I would love that!"

Alas, it would be the second evening in a row my plans with Gerry didn't pan out. In my defense, I'm not normally such a flake. But the entire ship was in such upheaval by then, drinks were out of the question.

CHAPTER 11

I'd given my students an assignment to complete during their three-hour break, dour schoolmarm that I am. Since the only way to learn about writing is to write (are you bored yet?), I tasked them with creating a protagonist for a mystery of their own. This meant we'd spend the afternoon session, from three to four, workshopping their responses to my prompt.

I told them to keep it short—a few hundred words at most. I didn't want the assignment to be onerous, and I wasn't interested in listening to the spontaneous tome Helen would have no doubt produced if given free rein. Still, I was curious to see how they might surprise me.

Six of the sixteen people who had made an appearance at my morning session surprised me by not bothering to show up. I guessed they were downing their fourth white wine spritzer in the lounge, or else "resting" in their cabins. Among the remaining ten, many of whom were visibly drunk, only four had done the assignment: June, Phyllis, Theresa, and of course, Helen. There's a reason these four are the only students I named; those other losers don't deserve the distinction. (I'd been aiming for Robin Williams from *Dead Poets Society*, and before the first day was over I'd turned into Viola Swamp from *Miss Nelson Is Missing!*) Both June and Phyllis had chosen a police officer: fairly ho-hum, though June's was male while Phyllis's was female, which showed some progress from one generation to the next. I'm not sure what I'd been hoping for from Theresa, but when she announced her protagonist was a "PI," I had to stop myself from growling:

A PI? In a mystery? Groundbreaking.

"What did you land on, Helen?"

At this point I would have gladly listened to her recite *The Odyssey*, *Clarissa*, *Infinite Jest*—or anything of commensurate horrifying length.

But Helen didn't recite anything. She put aside her notebook and sat on her hands, rocking a little from side to side.

"So there's this pregnant woman, and it's her first child, and she's really nervous about it. Not just the health of the child, but how she's going to handle everything, because her life is about to change so drastically, right? She's single, by the way, lives alone, though we don't know why or how she came to be pregnant. We'll learn that later, I guess. So sometimes, when you're pregnant—this is an actual thing—your sense of smell is heightened. And for her it's a problem because there are certain foods she used to like she can't eat anymore. Because the smell of them overwhelms her. And one day she smells something in the courtyard of the apartment complex where she lives, and it's terrible, it's driving her crazy even though no one else can smell it. Like she asks people about it and everyone thinks she's crazy. And so one night, when she can't sleep because she's so uncomfortable anyway, she takes out a shovel and starts digging in the dirt where the smell is strongest, and she finds—"

She dislodged one of her hands, throwing out her arm to indicate the obviousness of what came next.

"—a dead body."

We made genuine noises of appreciation—the few of us who were listening. Phyllis was literally sitting on the edge of her seat, I noticed. (She was upright for this session, having announced when she arrived that two gin-and-tonics had done "wonders" for her back.)

"That *exact* thing used to happen to me, doll," said June. "When I was pregnant with my three. A banana would get even *close* to ripe, I'd have to throw it out. Nauseating."

"Really?" Helen smiled: a real smile, like a drawbridge breaking free from the fortress, making contact with the outside world. "That's amazing!"

If I'd seen this version of her at a party, I would have latched on to her immediately—not for her pretty-princess face, but because there was obviously so much going on in the beating brain behind it. For once she didn't look preoccupied, or forbidding. She'd be all right once she got past her psychotic twenties, I decided, resolving in this moment to help her however I could.

"Do you mind if I use that?" she asked June, taking up her notebook. "The detail about the bananas?"

"You go right ahead," said June. "I don't think my Officer Preston will be getting pregnant anytime soon," she added with a wink. "Besides being a man, he's well past sixty!"

"Really?" I said, turning to her eagerly. "I hadn't realized he was older."

June nodded. "He's got one last case before he retires."

Oy.

Class was dismissed at 4:00. There were three hours till dinner: plenty of time for some early evening drinking to complement the day drinking everyone had already embraced. Payton had confided in me that the biggest expense on a cruise like this was the booze—bigger than the chef, or even the teachers' salaries. (We'd been haggling over my fee when she told me this. It was one of the reasons she barely moved up from her initial offer. But we'd both known if I was considering the gig, this meant I was desperate, and had zero leverage. Rhonda scolded me later for not leaving the negotiations to her.) Everyone hustled out of the classroom with a spring in their step I tried not to find insulting—even Phyllis, no doubt off to her next gin and tonic.

Only Helen held back. Suddenly I felt like I was in one of those Wild West barrooms where the rabble have cleared out, leaving the two opposing gunslingers to face off. Her eyes never left mine as she reached wordlessly into her backpack, producing a sheaf of papers fat as a brick, neatly bound with three brass "brads" (those wiry, flexible nails) jammed through the looseleaf holes on the left side. It was a manuscript, obviously, and already she'd made two missteps. First, you're never supposed to fill the middle hole with a brad. It's just not done. Second, she shouldn't have revealed the thing this way, without preamble, because once it came into view, I knew what she wanted.

She wanted me to read it.

I do realize I'd just resolved to help Helen however I could. But I'd been contemplating a kind word, a supportive chat, a list of book recommendations. I stared in horror at this behemoth, pondering the least confrontational way to avoid having anything to do with it.

"Don't worry, this isn't my first novel," she said. "It's my sixth."

"How old are you?" I asked incredulously.

"Twenty-four," she said. "I wrote the first one when I was twelve, so it doesn't really count. Neither do the second or third ones, they were so bad. The fourth was less bad, and the fifth one was okay. But I think this one is good. Would you read it? Please? It would mean so much."

I feel petty saying this, but I could have used a little more caveat-ing, an apologia of some sort for such a big ask on the second day of our acquaintance. It's what I would have done if I were in her shoes. Because reading an unpublished manuscript *is* a big ask. It takes a lot of time—and energy—if you're going to do it right, and provide useful feedback.

One thing was certain: there was no way I was reading her manuscript while we were on this cruise together.

"I can't read it now," I told her. "And I don't want to make any promises I can't keep, so I won't promise I'll read it later, either. But let's keep in touch after the class ends. I'll give you my e-mail and we can talk, okay?"

A reasonable and generous response, no? Especially when what I really wanted to do was channel my inner Amy March and watch that brick *burn* to ashes. (#Neverforget; Jo should have let the little brat perish under the ice.)

"Oh." She hitched up one shoulder, flipping her mermaid hair onto her back: an impatient gesture, as evidenced by what came next. "I was hoping you could read it in a day or two, and we could discuss it."

Was she for real? I'm about as interested in ranting about the entitlement of Gen Zers as you are in hearing said rant, so let's skip it. Ten years earlier, I would have caved. I would have accepted the manuscript and taken forever to read it, complaining to anyone who'd listen about what an imposition it was. But forty-something me had no problem saying no. Also, I could intuit with my decades of acquired wisdom that passive aggression would never work with Helen Sanchez. If I accepted the manuscript, she'd follow up with me every day—multiple times a day.

"If you have any questions about specific issues you're having, I encourage you to bring them up in class. Or if you want to use parts of your manuscript during our afternoon workshops, you're welcome to do so. But I won't be reading your manuscript this week," I said firmly. "I've got to get going now."

She didn't move. Her eyes were doing that manic quivery thing—switching focus from my left eye to my right eye and back again, over and over. (Try it on yourself in the mirror if you don't know what I'm talking about. It's weird. And unsettling.) She was *angry*. But my fight-or-flight instinct had kicked in, and for once, I'd chosen fight.

"I know you're passionate about writing," I said with a kindness I didn't feel. "You're impatient to get going. Believe me, I understand the feeling. And I know it seems like it's never going to happen. But, Helen, you have *so much* time."

"I could die tonight," she said matter-of-factly. "So could you. Or any of us."

Was that a threat? But I dismissed the thought as soon as I had it.

"That's . . . true," I said. "But why worry about improbabilities? It's not a way to live your life."

Helen stuffed the brick o' pages into her backpack and walked to the door, clutching her bag to her chest the way a child holds a toy or other cherished item. My shoulders sagged in relief, but when she stopped and turned around, they went up again. *What now?* I thought. But she didn't say anything. She just nodded at me and I nodded back, even though I knew it wasn't a nod of thanks.

She was putting me on notice that this wasn't over.

CHAPTER 12

I knew that if I stayed in my cabin there was a good chance I'd pass out for hours, and run the risk of missing not just dinner but a scheduled tryst with Gideon at six o'clock. I had about an hour and a half to kill before I met up with him, so I grabbed my coat and winter accessories and went up to the observation deck. It was nearly empty on what had turned out to be a fairly frigid day, the temperature never rising much above freezing. And with a fierce wind whipping unimpeded across the open sea, I had to make a cocoon of my billowy scarf before I could return to Lovers' Point—that line of benches curving around the stern of the ship where Gideon and I had sat the night before.

There was no one there, and in a matter of minutes I gave up, too frozen to enjoy the view. The middle of the deck was shielded from the elements by a sail-like canopy, so I sought shelter there. Throw rugs littered this area, with wicker chairs and sofas arranged on top of them in cozy groupings, the furniture capacious and cushioned for maximum comfort. There were even potted plants to give it more of a "living room" feel. The sideways light of late afternoon had rendered this canopy vestigial, and the absence of obstructions on the horizon meant I'd get every last drop of orangey goodness before darkness took over for the night. This time, I didn't mind not having my sunglasses, and chose the port side of the ship to get the best view of the coming show.

There weren't as many people here as I thought there would be, given the outdoor heaters that had been installed on the underside of the canopy and placed at strategic intervals to ward off the cold, The air temperature was tolerable, if not comfortable, and I relaxed my body as I crossed from the starboard to the port side under this protective covering. A tableful of ladies on the starboard side were maintaining a steady burble of conversation, accompanied by the gentle tinkling of ice against glass. They must have carried their drinks up from the lounge, flouting the No GLASS OUTSIDE rule so clearly stated on a sign in a clear plastic holder on their, and every, table. I smiled warmly at them, on my best behavior as a quasi–authority figure. They smiled in return; one of them even waved. I resolved inwardly to be a more friendly person, as I invariably do in the first flush of such positive interactions—even though I find this resolution impossible to keep.

And yet for once, my bluff was immediately called.

On the port side sat the romance novelist, Jessamine LaBou-chère, who I'd seen from behind the night before, at dinner. There was no mistaking that white hair of hers—so white, it almost had a fluorescent glow to it—styled into a giant wave that reminded me of a rooster's comb, or the way toothpaste is made to sit atop toothbrushes in television commercials. The white was obviously a dye job, but it gave her a hip, fashion-forward vibe that didn't come across as desperate the way a darker or more forthrightly blond hue would have done. She was older than I'd been expecting (somewhere in her seventies, I guessed), not that it was a conscious expectation on my part. But there's no question I registered the deep lines across her forehead and the curved grooves around her mouth with surprise. I suppose I've been trained to equate fashionability with youth, and I suspected Jessamine was doing what she could to militate against this ageist proposition. She had on both lipstick (pale pink) and mascara, but no foundation, no attempt to smooth out or otherwise mask her furrowed—even mottled—complexion. I got the feeling that if there were a socially acceptable way to draw circles around her wrinkles and arrows pointing to her age spots, she would have done it.

I'd dismissed her the night before as looking every inch the stereotypical romance novelist, but now I wasn't so sure. She was wearing wide-legged linen trousers with an untucked, pin-striped dress shirt whose front tails were so long, they extended past her lap. Her boots were ankle-length and made of white leather (or some material made to resemble leather), and on her shoulders she'd draped a cardigan that was technically pink, but a pink so dusty and muted, it was almost gray. I would have worn it myself.

"We meet at last," she called out to me. "Come over."

She was knitting, which as an activity for a solitary individual is similar to smoking in that it prevents a person from looking lonely or otherwise pitiful. I'd never thought to equate the two until this moment—knitting is so uncool, so earnest, whereas smoking *still* has an air of chic detachment to it, despite the fact we all know it's poisonous to air of any kind. Somehow, Jessamine was making knitting look cool. Or at least, less uncool than it usually did.

She inclined her head toward the sofa across from hers, on the other side of a wicker coffee table that featured, in addition to the No Glass Outside sign, a medley of succulent plants including one enterprising "string-of-pearls" that had crept its way over the table's edge, making a run for the floor. The rug marking out this space was so thick, I stumbled onto it in my rush to obey her summons, landing heavily, and noisily, on the wicker sofa.

"Pretty empty up here, isn't it?" I observed.

"Payton and Nicole are holding a special talk about juggling the personal and professional. Wives and Writers, I believe it's called."

She unspooled a few inches of gray yarn with her free hand, looking up at me as she tossed the yarn up and over whatever it was she was making—a jaunty gesture. Sassy, even.

"You can roll your eyes now if you'd like."

I laughed, and so did she—a soft chuckle that sprang easily from her throat, as though she'd been holding it there, ready-formed.

"What are you knitting?"

"Nothing." She looked up at me, eyes full of mischief. (I can't remember what color they were; doesn't eye color bore you sometimes?) "Prepare to be annoyed. I'm not knitting, I'm *crocheting*."

"Ah."

She held up her single, oversized needle the way a teacher would brandish a piece of chalk while delivering a lesson. It consisted of two pieces: a handle made of a honey-colored wood that was the same width and overall shape as a Sharpie marker, and a much narrower metal hook that came out of the handle, curving inward at the end. The initials "JL" had been engraved in the lower end of the wooden handle. Clearly the woman took her craft seriously.

"Knitting is with two, crocheting is with one. Not all the time. But most of the time."

"I see. So what are you crocheting?"

She held up the mass of yarn that had been sitting in her lap. I could see now it was L-shaped: like a sock, or maybe a Christmas stocking. If a gray Christmas stocking were a thing?

"A gun cozy. But it's not what you think," she added, before I had a chance to think it. "We give the cozies to gun owners as a way to encourage them to store their firearms properly. A gimmick, but at this point I'll try anything. These cozies are a *hit* on Instagram, there's no question about it."

She punctured the mass of yarn with her needle again.

"How did your afternoon session go?" she asked.

I groaned, the wicker sofa harmonizing with me while I tried to find a more comfortable position. The seat cushion was surprisingly thin. I told her about my less-than-stellar workshopping session.

"Well, I applaud you. All I did was show the first half of *Love Story*. Most of them slept through it, which was the best thing for them, poor things."

"I guess babysitting a bunch of drunk ladies with disposable income on a cruise in the North Atlantic means never having to say you're sorry."

Her soft chuckle made a second appearance.

"Why did you agree to do this cruise?" I asked her. "If you don't mind my asking?"

"I don't mind whatsoever. Payton and I are on the board of Read It and Reap, a charity devoted to eradicating illiteracy."

"Good name."

"*Memorable* name, which is all it needs to be. I've been on the board for decades. Payton joined six months ago, and in that time she's revolutionized what we do. She's a wonder."

"She really is," I said glumly.

Jessamine chuckled again. "Yes, yes. But she's done a great deal of good."

"I'm sure she has."

"*Such* a work ethic," she said admiringly.

I have a good work ethic too; I pride myself on it. But Payton's is better. I've always known this.

"So when she invited me to go on this cruise," continued Jessamine, "I was inclined to say yes, despite the disruption it would mean to my production schedule."

"That's right. You're pretty prolific, aren't you?"

I'd Googled Jessamine LaBouchère before boarding the ship, so I already knew the answer to this question.

"We romance novelists have to be. Did you know the average romance reader finishes three point five novels per month?"

"They're not really finishing that last book, are they, if they only read point five of it?"

"You joke, but you'd be surprised how many people misinterpret that statistic in exactly that way."

"No, I wouldn't," I replied airily. "So how many books have you published?"

"The current count is seventy-eight," she said. "But I'll hit eighty by the end of this year."

"That's amazing."

"No, it's just a lot of hard work. And there are many others who have written much, much more."

"I can only imagine," I said. "I've only published one mystery."

"I know, and it's quite good. You'll publish more." She paused to perform what I assumed was a tricky stitch, her brows puckered in concentration, the vertical crease between her eyes approaching the depths of a crevasse.

"You can ask me, you know," she said without looking up from her work.

"Oh, I'm fine using your pen name," I said. "It's only fair, since I force everyone to call me Belle Currer."

The soft chuckle made an encore appearance. "Not what I meant. Though I don't mind telling you my real name is Janet Levine, which wouldn't look nearly as good on a cover." She pointed to the handle of her crochet hook. "Same initials though. Did you know 'La Bouchère' means 'The Butcher'? I didn't, when I chose it." She shook her head at her youthful folly. "One of many mistakes I made early on. I suppose I should have been writing mysteries after all."

I was inclined to ask her what other mistakes she'd made so I could avoid them, but I didn't want to come on too strong.

"What was it you were thinking I wanted to ask you, then? I honestly have no idea."

"Why I write such tripe, given what an obviously smart person I am."

My laughter came as easily as hers.

"You needn't pretend to admire my output when I imagine that for you, as with most literary types, you see it as a sign of quantity over quality."

She said this sweetly, with zero rancor, and I had no idea how to react. She was right, of course. Anyone who writes more than one book every few years is in danger of entering "hack" territory. Even Joyce Carol Oates seems to have damaged her reputation not by a degradation in the quality of her output, but ironically, by the consistency of her output, averaging a book a year for over half a century. (Her Twitter account isn't doing her any favors, either.)

"I have no illusions about the way I'm perceived," continued Jessamine. "You're going to have to get used to it too. The mystery and romance genres are sisters, you know. Mystery readers are nearly as voracious as romance readers. Perhaps that's an overstatement, but not by much!"

I immediately wanted to deny the connection, or to clarify that it was *cozy* mysteries that had a lot in common with romances. But wouldn't I be playing into the hands of people like Flora, who had called my mystery novel a "cozy" by way of an insult? Was it really so far off to call *The Busy Body* a cozy? And why did this question bother me so much? Did I think so little of romances, and cozies, that I couldn't bear to be lumped together with them? Sure, I wasn't a romance reader, but I'm not into science fiction either, and I can't bear literary theory of any kind. There's no question I wouldn't have felt the same way if Jessamine had grouped me in with sci fi or lit crit.

"People are always willing to shit on work that women do,

especially if other women tend to be the ones who enjoy it," I said, neglecting to point out that I was one of the shitters. "It's why noirs have always gotten so much respect."

"Well, there's no equivalent to noir in the romance genre. If there was, it might be all I wrote!"

Jessamine laid down her half-finished gun cozy. (A Mad Libs sentence, if ever I've written one.)

"I'm going to hazard a guess you aren't a romance reader."

I shook my head: *no.*

"Then you probably don't know that the statistic I quoted you of three point five books a month is conservative. I've known many readers to get through multiple books a *day.* And several books a week is by no means uncommon."

She paused to gather her words.

"I like to think of my work as sustenance. A special type of food that has to pass a certain threshold of quality to sustain my readers. To nourish them. And to do that, I don't have to serve them gourmet-quality fare. Actually, if it *was* gourmet, it wouldn't do its job nearly as well. In the same way you can't eat rich or fancy dishes other than occasionally. Do you see what I mean?"

I nodded: *yes.*

She picked up her hook and ball of yarn, siccing her fingers on them.

"No one thinks less of a farmer for the mass production of crops. They don't think less of the crops, either. But then"— her fingers froze and she looked up at me, eyes twinkling— "most farmers are men, and the men of the world need their food. *My* food is consumed almost exclusively by women. And as you so astutely pointed out, we're easily dismissed." Her fingers began moving faster. "I think the world of my readers. Harried mothers in need of a break. Busy career women desperate to let off a little steam. There are a million and one reasons to want to escape from the rigors of reality and indulge in

the world of romance. But most men don't get it. Is it any wonder my product gets so little respect?"

I shook my head: *no*. I'd never thought about romance novels this way.

"So is this the sort of thing you talked about with your students this morning?" I asked.

"Hardly!" She waved her cozy at me, which looked like it
was nearly finished. The woman was fast at everything. "With
them it was all muses and passion and catharsis. You've got to
keep up the façade, my dear."

No problem there, I thought. My façade's so thick, it has its
own façade.

We lapsed into a comfortable silence, Jessamine crocheting
as I contemplated the sun, the orb of which had begun to dip
below the horizon, meaning I could sneak direct glances at it
every now and then. For once I could see this celestial object
for what it was: an enormous ball of roiling fire, its surface ever
churning. . . . Did you ever notice how big the sun or moon
looks when it's on the horizon, or near it? The weird thing is
that it's not actually any bigger, not taking up more space than
it does higher up in the sky, which you'll realize if you take a
photo of it. The "oversized" effect disappears in the photo-
graph, which doesn't have our sense of perspective. There are
a few explanations for this phenomenon, but the one I find
most convincing is that it's an optical illusion due to the fact
that we imagine the dome of the sky to be longer than it is
higher. So when we see something at the horizon and it's the
same size as it is way up in the sky, our dumb brains think:
*Wow, this must be even bigger now, since it hasn't gotten any
smaller.*

Makes you wonder how else we unknowingly distort our reality as we go about our day, doesn't it?

"So is this whole endeavor what you thought it would be?" I
asked. "The cruise?"

I watched as the ball of yarn tumbled this way and that, steadily shrinking.

"I can see that you're looking for me to complain," she said.

"So that we can commiserate together—"

I tried to protest, but she waved me off.

"It's all right, I'm not averse to that sort of thing every now and then."

She completed a few more stitches while I waited.

"This cruise *is* what I thought it would be," she said eventually. "And that's the problem." This time when she looked up, her hands didn't stop moving. "I was hoping it would surprise me."

The sun had almost disappeared, sinking below the horizon with a rapidity I never fail to underestimate, no matter how many times I witness it. The ladies on the starboard side had left, and it was almost time to meet Gideon. I was freezing by this point anyway—despite the heaters above us, or the fact that Jessamine was doing fine in her skimpy cardigan. (I learned later she was from Chicago, which made sense on a number of levels.) I was about to announce my departure when a pair of passengers burst out of the nearest stairwell and raced past us, giggling loudly. They were two of the younger passengers on the cruise—not Helen-level young, but somewhere in their early to mid thirties, I guessed. Jessamine and I watched, bemused, as they hurtled past us toward the front of the ship, one of them carrying what looked to be a step stool. *Huh?*

Past the middle of the deck was a glass-enclosed space called the "bridge," just like the bridge of the *Starship Enterprise*: the command center inside of which the crew controlled the ship. These passengers skirted round the bridge now, heading for the bow of the ship, which also had a railing around it.

Unlike the railing around the raised deck in the stern— which, except for Lovers' Point, went to the very end of the ship's body—the railing in the bow blocked off a large triangular area, the ship coming to a point beyond it. The flooring there was a rougher, popcorned concrete, with boxy metallic protrusions I imagined held various nautical gear. It was obviously off limits for passengers, but just in case, a large metal sign affixed to the railing blared: CREW ONLY. PASSENGERS KEEP OUT.

You may well know where this is going, or rather, where *they* were going. The two ladies hoisted themselves up and over the railing, and continued onward. I stood up in alarm.

"Where are they—oh, no."

"Oh yes," said Jessamine, whose fingers hadn't missed a stitch. Her ball had officially dwindled into a long string. "It's happening."

"No!" I wailed. "It's only day two! I had day five!"

I craned my neck. They'd reached the edge of the ship, where there was an additional rail to keep any crew members from falling over. They were just standing there, peering over the edge.

"Maybe they won't go through with it."

"They will," said Jessamine with cool certainty.

One of the women climbed onto this railing—high enough to position herself in front of a rigging cable that stretched diagonally from the bridge to the bow. Resting her back against this cable with her arms crossed in front of her like a mummy, she waited for her companion to place the stool on top of one of the metal protrusions on the ground. In this way, the second woman could support the woman leaning against the cable from behind.

"You're right," I said resignedly. "They will."

The woman in front stretched her arms out wide, while the woman in back steadied her. It looked as though the one in front was about to jump, or submit to being pushed. I turned away, unable to stomach it.

"I can't look," I moaned.

"I'm flying!" cried the one in front. "Jack, I'm flying!"

"Wooooo! I'm the king of the world!" cried the other.

"Damn it," I muttered, sinking onto the uncomfortable wicker sofa again. "Which day did you have?"

"I already lost, dear. I thought someone would do it before the ship moved. But that's the difference between my generation and yours." She waited for me to look at her. When I did, her eyes were dancing. "You've managed to retain a speck of faith in humanity."

The pool had been Joan Chen's idea, conducted over e-mail in the days leading up to the launch. How long would it take before one of the passengers reenacted the scene at the bow of the ship from *Titanic*? If I remembered correctly, it was Payton who'd guessed day two.

Figures, I thought.

CHAPTER 13

I went down to my room to discard my winter things before meeting up with Gideon. Also, I had a vague intention of "freshening up" for him. This vanished in the face of what I found lying in the center of my bed.

There was no mistaking that fat sheaf of pages, or the three shiny brads holding them together. Somehow, Helen Sanchez had gained entry to my room—my *locked* room—and left her manuscript there for me. I tiptoed toward it, as if it were a baby I dared not rouse. She'd stuck a blue Post-it on the cover page: *Please*, it read, with two underlines for good measure.

Well, so long as she was being polite about it.

I went in search of Payton's room, which I knew from an extremely funny *1984* joke Joan had made in one of her whimsical e-mails was Room 101. If it hadn't been for the signs indicating which range of numbers lay in which direction, I would have gotten lost in the warren of passageways. The halls on Decks 3 and 4 were also illuminated by wall sconces, but unlike the candelabras on Deck 2, these were muted affairs—small semi-globes set a few inches below the ceiling, which emitted a soft light that felt designed to create shadow rather than illumination. In contrast to the stark, echoey hallways on the public-facing deck above, here there was wallpaper on the walls (dark mauve stripes separated by narrower bands of emerald green), and the floor was carpeted in a speckled gray-and-tan design that did a good job of hiding dirt and other blemishes. The idea must have been to make these bedroom hallways more of a cozy, domestic space, but all it did for me was to muddle them into a maze. Even with the aid of the signs, I had to backtrack a few times.

In my defense, it was difficult to concentrate on anything other than my smoldering rage. Helen Sanchez would have to be ejected from my class, if not the ship. Maybe she could be made to walk the plank? Were planks still a thing? If not, it was time they made a comeback.

At last I found Room 101, which was on the third deck and located almost directly across from the elevator. This would make it easy to find again, if ever I had reason to go to it. I rapped sharply on the door. No answer. Was she still doing that stupid lecture with her stupid wife? I knocked again—louder. Still no answer, but this time I sensed movement. After a third knock I'm embarrassed to admit was more of a pound-ing with the side of my fist, the door opened.

Nicole was shrugging on a robe that looked to be made of gold lamé. Her hair was up the same way it had been at the re-ception the night before, though without a crown, and she wasn't wearing any makeup. She looked confused, which was a more effective rebuke than fury or irritation. *Why is someone being so rude as to bang on my door?* her expression asked. *Surely there must be a reasonable explanation for such inappro-priate behavior.*

"Who is it?" asked Payton from the unseen depths of a room I could already sense was much bigger than mine.

"It's me," I said ungrammatically.

"Get in here!" she cried.

Nicole stepped aside and I moved past her—which was how

I came to be confronted with Payton Garrett's fully naked body reclining on a king-sized bed.

"Oh!" I turned away. "I'll just—"

"Are you *embarrassed*?"

She was smirking. I couldn't see the smirk, obviously, but I could hear it in her voice. I'd heard that smirk many times before, in our MFA days. Usually when gossiping about our classmates.

"Girl. We saw each other naked *tons* of times, back in the day."

"Why would we ever have seen each other naked?" I asked the wall.

Their cabin had artwork in it: a cheap reproduction of one of Degas's ballerinas, but still.

"Why not? Nudity is amazing. When you do it on your own terms, you get to be both vulnerable *and* empowered. Actually, I need to write that down."

I heard the rapid-fire clicking of a smartphone's miniature keyboard. Nicole gave me a conspiratorial look while retrieving a towel from the top drawer of a dresser to my right, which, like every item of furniture in this room, was a larger version of what I had in mine. She crossed behind me.

"Everyone deserves to have their boundaries respected," Nicole counseled like a woke Mary Poppins, presumably handing her wife the towel.

"Fair," admitted Payton. "Are boobies okay?"

I turned, relieved to see her mid-region was now covered.

"Boobies I can handle," I assured her.

Now that I didn't have to avert my eyes, I got a proper look at their room, which was enormous—at least four or five times the size of mine, with three portholes in the far wall, a seating area that included a full-length sofa and reclining armchair, a kitchenette, and a floor-to-ceiling entertainment center with a big-screen TV in the center of it.

"Wow," I said.

"I'm going to assume that's a reaction to the room. I'm aware my breasts are nothing special." She looked down. "Sorry, guys."

"Your breasts are male?"

"'Course they are! There's a reason the French noun for them is masculine. The room was the captain's, but she begged us to take it. She said she prefers smaller, enclosed spaces. You know I knew her, when we were kids? Total coincidence I hired her, I don't know if I'd even have remembered her if she hadn't brought it up. My bad, cuz she stood out back then as much as she does now. I should've remembered her right away."

"She mentioned she knew you, at dinner last night," I said. "It sounds like you two ran in different circles."

"You can say that again. She was an outcast." Payton let out a fatuous sigh, which was meant as a joke though I wasn't buying it. "I was one of the cool kids."

"You were super religious though, right?"

"Yeah, which made me one of the cool kids. Rules were reversed in rural Iowa. Ellie's parents were, like, hippie atheists who lived off the land or something. Total freaks for that time and place. Honestly? I could've been nicer to her. I was a real bitch before I figured my shit out."

"Yes," I said dryly. "You're an angel now."

This got a laugh from Nicole—a real one, straight from the belly—so loud that I couldn't help joining in.

"So you two are going to gang up on me, are you? I see, I see. Whatever, it didn't matter. Ellie was always too far along the spectrum to care about all that cliquey stuff."

This sounded like a convenient theory for a (semi-)reformed mean girl. . . .

"What?" asked Payton, picking up on my hesitation. "It's okay, you can still say 'on the spectrum.' It's 'Asperger's' that isn't kosher. Because Asperger was a big ol' Nazi. We can stick to 'neurodivergent,' if that makes you more comfortable."

"I like 'neurodivergent,' " I said.

The truth is, I'm pretty sure I fall somewhere within the large swath of shade this umbrella term provides. As do so many of us—though if I had to choose one person among my acquaintance who *didn't*, it would be the socially savvy Payton Garrett.

"Sorry we didn't answer the door right away but we were in the throes of passion." She tossed her phone aside. "All the adrenaline from public speaking's got to go somewhere, right?"

Nicole perched on the edge of the bed, cupping Payton's calf fondly. "Darling, if your intention is to make your friend uncomfortable, I think you're succeeding."

"Don't worry about Belle here, she's no prude. Actually, don't you have a nooner of your own to get to?"

Payton reached for her phone again, touching the screen to check the time, which I could see from where I was standing was 5:46.

"Eh, you're okay," she added. "Still got fourteen minutes."

Gideon, she mouthed to Nicole.

I don't know why I was surprised. It's not like I'd sworn Gideon to secrecy. And I already knew he and Payton talked constantly.

"I didn't think it was a big deal," I said.

"Aren't we worldly?"

"What, was I supposed to ask your permission first?" I snapped at her.

This was Flora all over again; it was so easy to regress in Payton's company, to become the most immature version of myself. It was a version that was always lurking under the surface. But usually, I had the wherewithal to keep it at bay.

"Oh, come on, I'm just messing with you. And hey, enjoy his enormous penis. It's why we lasted as long as we did."

Nicole rose from the bed, sweeping past me toward the

bathroom. I caught a whiff of her body lotion, which smelled (deliciously) of orange blossoms and cinnamon.

"Ba-abe!" Payton called from the bed.

Nicole spun around. "Forgive me if I sit out the portion of the conversation surrounding your ex-husband's genitalia."

"Hey, it's a gherkin compared to your strap-on; you have *nothing* to be jealous of."

Nicole glowered at her. "Now you're making *me* uncomfortable."

Payton got up, holding the towel around her waist. "You're right," she said in a conciliatory tone. "That was bad form. I'm sorry." She turned to me. "You should be flattered. Nic only gets flustered in front of people whose opinion she cares about."

They exchanged a peck, and then Payton whisked past us, slamming the bathroom door behind her.

Nicole turned to me. "I'd explain how she's a handful. But I don't have to, do I?"

"I heard that!" Payton hollered through the door.

We shook our heads at each other, lapsing into silence.

"I love your necklace," I said, overstating my regard out of a desire to keep the silence from turning awkward. I gestured to a large pendant nestled deep in the V of her shiny robe. It was amber in color, and about the size of a half-dollar. More than anything it looked heavy. If I were to lift it from off her chest, I could easily imagine there might be a half-dollar-sized welt beneath it.

"Thank you." She caressed it: Gollum doting on his *preciousssss*. "Do you see the little slip of paper inside?"

I squinted. There *was* something suspended in the amber, like the mosquito trapped in that walking stick from *Jurassic Park*. I never would have been able to guess what it was on my own, but now that she'd said it, I could see a little piece of paper folded over and over again.

"Here we go," muttered Payton as she exited the bathroom wearing a robe of her own, white and waffle-patterned, the kind you might get in a spa. (No way their showerhead was positioned over the toilet. They probably had their own steam room in there.)

"Hush." Nicole turned to me, compelling eye contact in her intense way. "Printed on this paper is the password to a digital wallet that contains hundreds of bitcoin. Five hundred bitcoin, to be precise. Technically it's a 'seed phrase,' not a password, but we don't need to get into all of that. The only way the digital wallet can be accessed is here"—she tapped the pendant—"through this piece of paper."

"You own five hundred bitcoin?"

I was impressed. Horrified, but impressed.

"I do *not*," she said triumphantly. "The digital wallet belongs to . . ." She paused, searching for the name.

"Some crypto bro douchebag," supplied Payton, "who cheated on his wife. Remember, we're not supposed to say his name."

"You're right, thank you." She turned back to me. "This philandering man's ex-wife stole the slip of paper before she left him. The paper was then sealed inside the necklace, which we bought at a charity auction, anonymously, for an eye-wateringly unreasonable amount of money. All we have to do is contact this—"

"Crypto bro douchebag," offered Payton once more.

"—and he'll pay me what I paid for the necklace. And then some."

She stroked the necklace again. "But I never will."

"Isn't it so fucking perfect?" remarked Payton. "Rendering a crypto bro and all his precious bitcoin impotent, just by wearing a kick-ass piece of jewelry."

"I like it," I said. Though did I? Aren't we supposed to learn

around age five that two wrongs don't make a right? The necklace felt a bit mean-spirited to me.

"So you're walking around with a piece of jewelry worth
tens of millions of dollars to some guy who's desperate to get it
back?"

"Till crypto goes bust and it becomes worthless again," said
Payton. "And believe me, he's doing fine."

"Have you ever heard the song 'The Best Things in Life Are
Free'?" Nicole asked.

"Yes," I said with some surprise. "I love that song."

"So do I. But I think what it's really getting at is that the best
things in life can't be *used*. Nature. Love. Beauty."

"Um, beauty can be used," said Payton.

"Of course it can," Nicole replied. "So can love. And nature. Anything can be sacrificed on the altar of capitalism. But
when we do, we degrade it. We lose something by subjecting
these qualities to the transactional sphere."

"I feel you, babe."

Nicole stroked her necklace again. "This is my way of evening the score a little. I'm working on a poem about it, actually."

"Oh really?" I tried to keep the alarm out of my voice.

Payton laughed. She knew me too well. "Belle here doesn't
do poetry."

"Aha." Nicole crossed her arms, appraising me with a smile
I couldn't help finding infectious.

"I fully recognize *I'm* the problem," I said.

"Let me guess, it either makes you cringe, or it makes no
sense to you?"

"Correct."

"Well, I have a week to work on you. We'll see what we
can do."

Payton turned to me, clutching my arm. "Well now I *know*
she cares about your opinion. Be afraid. Be very afraid."

LOOSE LIPS / 117

For one lovely moment, we three basked in the knowledge that for whatever reason, Nicole and I liked each other, and Payton cared enough about both of us to be delighted by this state of affairs.

"To be continued." Nicole took off her necklace. "I've got to put this back in its resting place, since I never wear it out." She glided inside the closet I was sure was a walk-in, as opposed to the shallow, poky space allotted regular cabins like mine.

Payton turned to me. "Hey, I'm sorry I was weird about you and Gid, I seriously don't care." She eyed me the way a cat eyes a mouse before toying with it. "You'd actually be a great stepmom, my kids would *love* you. They go apeshit over anyone who plays hard to get. You hate kids, right?"

"I don't hate kids!" I exclaimed. Maybe a little too forcefully.

She cackled. "Hey, I'm one of those moms whose kids make me realize how much I hate every other kid in existence. No, thank you. By the way have you spoken to Flora at all?"

"We had lunch," I said archly.

"*Good*, I was hoping you could give me some intel. What did she say? What's her angle?"

"Revenge." I raised my eyebrows as high as they would go, knowing Payton would take this as a tacit acknowledgment that Flora was being absurd. I did this because as Flora herself had pointed out, I am a sheep at heart—a people-pleaser who likes to give others what they want and expect.

"Jesus H. Christ, she's such a baby. Does she really not know everything is copy? Has she never seen that Nora Ephron doc?"

I laughed—not because I felt like laughing, but again, because it was expected of me. Flora was right. I liked to pretend I was all about rocking the boat, when really I did all in my power to absorb these blows, to keep the boat nice and steady.

"At least she didn't do anything during the talk Nic and I gave just now. I don't even think she was there. Maybe she's having second thoughts."

"I wouldn't bet on it."

"Neither would I. Ugh, when exactly am I supposed to make time to coddle her ass? Every freaking moment of this cruise is scheduled out, and speaking of"—she drew her phone out of the pocket of her robe—"you've got to get going, you've get less than five minutes! Believe me, Giddy-boy does *not* appreciate tardiness."

It was only after I left that I remembered what had brought me to Room 101 in the first place. I stopped in the main stairwell, contemplating the circular compass spray-painted onto the wall, noticing for the first time all the elaborate hash marks and concentric circles drawn inside of it—as though it were the titular Golden Compass from the Philip Pullman series (the antidote to C. S. Lewis's Narnia books, and yet I love them both). For a moment I considered going back. But then I'd be egregiously late. I began hurrying down the stairs.

This was what happened when you tangled with the likes of Payton Garrett, whose presence was all-consuming.

Helen Sanchez had managed to buy herself a little more time.

CHAPTER 14

I got lost on the way to Gideon's room. The bad news: it was ten past six when I finally got there. The good news: he was in such a state of agitation, he had no idea I was late. I found him pacing from one end of his cabin to the other—a slightly larger space than mine, but nothing like Room 101, and easily small enough to give the repetitive motion a trapped, rodent-like feel.

"Are you okay?" I made for the bed, slipping off my shoes and drawing my legs up after me so as not to collide with him.

"Am I okay? No, I'm not okay. I took a little visit to the engine room after lunch. And the kitchen."

"Don't you mean the galley?"

"Have you been there yet?"

I shook my head.

"It's bigger than the kitchens in most restaurants. I don't think you have to say galley."

"Sorry, my reference point for ship terminology is the *Dawn Treader* from book three of *The Chronicles of Narnia*," I replied, having just conjured up this series in the stairwell. "I'm pretty sure the ship doesn't have hanging lanterns or a dragon's head for a bow, either."

If he'd been in a better mood, this would have made him smile, but he waved my joke aside.

"I'm making a point of seeing all the places people ignore when they're on a cruise."

This made sense. Gideon Pereira was not the sort of writer whose long-form think piece about an exclusive literary cruise would neglect the workers behind the scenes. There was a decent chance one or more of these workers would become his focus.

"And what did I see there?" he continued, flicking the glass of his porthole in a furious manner before turning around and retracing his steps. "A hellscape."

"Is it because they're understaffed?" I asked. "I don't know about the technical crew, but I think Payton must have skimped when she was hiring the kitchen and cleaning people. No question she has them doubling up. I've seen the woman who waits on our table all over the place."

He pulled up short, stopping in front of me. I could see the sweat glistening on his brow, and there were stains under the arms of his baggy dress shirt. He didn't smell, though. He was in fact the rare man I couldn't imagine having any sort of body odor, good or bad.

"What? No, they seemed fine, I guess. It's the bilge-water tank in the engine room that did me in."

"What exactly *is* bilge water?" I asked him.

He regarded me impatiently—and bear with me a moment, but this impatience was proof of his value. Most men would be delighted to discover their female companion was more ignorant than they, but my cluelessness was merely frustrating to him. A wave of affection swelled inside me, and I listened with something approaching fondness as he began his harangue.

"Bilge water is water mixed with engine oil and all the other crap that's required to keep this gas-guzzling RV camper of a boat zipping through the water while all the Karens up there"— he thrust his thumb toward the ceiling—"sip their sugary cocktails and argue over which Brontë is the best Brontë."

I nodded dumbly, hoping he'd stop talking about bilge water. (Also: Charlotte. There's no question. Come at me; I dare you.)

He began moving again. "And then I got to see a nice big juicy tank of *gray* water in the kitchen. Gray water is all the runoff from sinks and dishwashers. Showers and toilets, too. Goes right in the ocean, not a single law to prevent it from happening once you're in international waters." He was back at the porthole now, and this time he jammed his index finger against it—so forcefully that I winced on his behalf. "It's a fucking free-for-all out there! Do you know how many other types of hazardous waste we'll be dumping in the ocean this week?"

"No, but I think I'm about to."

He began ticking them off with his fingers, which is something I thought people only did while making speeches.

"One! Black water, more commonly known as shit and piss."

I'll admit I'd been hoping for slightly sexier foreplay.

"Two! Ballast water, which is water taken *from* the ocean to stabilize the ship until it's dumped elsewhere, disrupting multiple ecosystems in the process. Three! Solid waste like all those plastic bottles holding all that tasty booze getting glug-glug-glugged up in the lounge. That all gets burnt into toxic soot and ash and tossed directly in the water. And finally, drum-roll please! Four! An oldie but a goodie, hazardous waste like cleaning fluids, paint flakes, and other chemical garbage that's supposed to be sealed aboard the ship and disposed of properly when it docks, but in reality seeps its way, you guessed it, directly into the ocean."

He stopped in front of me. Now he was panting, his curly hair alternately flopping over and sticking out at various angles. It was how I wanted him to look, but for a reason that involved a lot more enjoyment on both our ends—ends that were not just figurative, if you know what I mean (and of course you do). What could I say to salvage our sexy times without seeming like a ditz or a jerk?

"Well . . . why don't you write about it? Use it as a frame, or an underpinning, something you come back to again and again? The world of the ocean surrounding this world of people who are obsessing over another world entirely, of literary endeavor. I've never seen that before. I think it'd be fascinating."

Fascinating? *Please.* I was trying too hard. But would he buy it?

"Huh."

He stood there, thinking. I held my breath.

"I don't hate it."

Score! I scooted to the edge of the bed, my face inches away from his crotch. As expected, he took the hint, bending down and kissing me, during which embrace I leaned back, bringing his body down on top of mine.

When we had (both) finished, there was still enough time before dinner to lounge. Lying flushed and naked on the rumpled sheets of his bed like the heroine from one of those romance novels I'd never read, I found it impossible not to think of Payton and Nicole in their own post-coital glow.

"Did you know about Nicole's necklace? With the password embedded in it?"

He didn't answer. He was busily typing on his phone—making notes for his piece, I guessed.

"She showed it to me today," I nattered on. "I know it's supposed to be making this grand statement, but it's all a little facile, if you ask me."

He hadn't. And yet there was an intimacy to my babbling and his typing, and I couldn't resist imagining us in bed like this night after night. I'd casually use words like "facile," and he'd have to look up from his damn phone eventually. I don't engage in these sorts of what-if scenarios often; I enjoy my un-encumbered life. But we humans aren't renowned for our con-sistency, and every now and then I catch myself fantasizing about the addition of a cumber or two to my freewheeling ex-istence.

"I wonder how much she actually paid for it?" I persisted.

He looked up from his phone.

"The crypto thing? Half a mil."

"*Seriously?*"

He nodded, resting his phone on the taut surface of his stomach. Stretched out flat he was too skinny, but in a seated position bent at the waist, his body was at its best advantage. I wish I could say the same for me. My body needed all the stretching it could get.

"It's not a password, it's a seed phrase."

"I know that," I snapped at him. (I'm still not sure what a seed phrase is, but what I'm sure about is that I don't care.)

"Payton bought it for her. Right after the Spotify deal went through for the podcast. Nicole does well for a poet, but it's nothing compared to Payton. She's rolling in it," he said dole-fully. "I remember when that auction happened, there was a big spread about it in Sunday Styles. No one's supposed to know Payton and Nic were the ones to buy it, but everybody does. *Un secret de Polichinelle.*" His French accent was heavier than Flora's, but still enviable. "That's a—"

"A French phrase for an open secret. Yes, I'm aware," I said, unwilling to endure another lecture after the one I'd got-ten on cruise ship pollution, and then the one I'd narrowly avoided on seed phrases. If I was going to be stuck on a boat with three hundred women, my ordeal at the very least should be light on mansplaining.

"That's why she never wears it in public," he said. "How'd you manage to get a glimpse?"

Leaving out the part about Payton's post-coital nudity, I told him about going to Room 101 to complain about Helen, and getting waylaid by the necklace.

"Did Payton say anything about me?"

He sounded like an anxious middle-schooler asking about the coolest girl in school.

"No," I lied.

"Really? We got in a big fight this morning, so I would've expected her to say something nice. Makes her seem like the bigger person since she knows you'll pass it along. That's the way it works with our kids, anyway. Keeps me from talking shit about her to them. Not that I would," he added hastily—and unconvincingly.

"No, she didn't say anything."

I glanced apologetically at his penis, which was no longer so gargantuan in its coiled, resting state. (So I guess not everything is smaller than expected.) Even so, it was doing well for itself. I mean, it was coiled, which is more than most penises at rest can manage.

I laid my hand on his arm. "Please feel free to talk shit about her to me, though."

I don't think Gideon would have opened up if we hadn't been naked. But as one of the foremost writers of the digital age once said, when you engage in nudity on your own terms, you get to be both vulnerable *and* empowered. He turned to me.

"She is the most self-centered person I know. And that includes my father, who was diagnosed with narcissistic personality disorder. Payton makes him look like Gandhi."

I made a noise calibrated to be both sympathetic and encouraging.

"You remember what I told you about Jackson? Watching porn in front of our kids? You know what *her* response was when I told her about it?"

"I'm going to guess it wasn't that you were being homophobic."

"That I shouldn't have spoken to Jackson directly. I was undermining *her* authority." He shook his head. "Fucking Payton. She had no idea what was happening since she's never around. She's either traveling, or on the off-chance she's in the house, working behind a closed door."

Hm, sounded to me like many a blameless father who's existed down the ages. . . .

"She has a whole fleet of nannies though, doesn't she?" I asked.

"She has no dearth of help, that's correct. Not that I begrudge her that," he added, realizing how this sounded. "If I had them all week I'd need help too. But she takes it too far. She takes *everything* too far." He sat up, imparting what he said next with a palpable urgency. "The truth is, we would've broken up anyway, even if Nicole hadn't come along. No one believes me, but I'm *grateful* to Nic. She was my exit ramp without having to be the jerk who left, the deadbeat dad. I can't even *imagine* the field day Payton would have had if I'd left her. Gives me chills to think about it."

"Why?" I asked. (I knew why. I was goading him.)

"Because she would've figured out a way to destroy my career without seeming like she had anything to do with it. She's an incredibly vindictive person. Devious too."

"I'm sorry."

"I wouldn't give a damn if it didn't affect our kids. The fight this morning was about Lola, one of the *three* nannies she employs, who I know for a fact shoves screens in their faces when she has them. Woman doesn't even try. But Payton refuses to fire her. Lola's Latina, and a Dreamer, and Payton says it wouldn't be a 'good look' to let her go. Yet another instance of choosing herself over Clyde and Hazel."

He fidgeted, his phone falling off his stomach into the nest of sheets.

"She's a bad mother. There, I said it. I wish I could just get sole custody and be done with it. The stupid thing is she'd be fine seeing them once a week. She goes way longer than that when she's on her tours, or doing bullshit like this." He swept his hand across the room. "But she'll never let it happen, for the same reason she won't fire the nanny. Image killer."

"Isn't that what lawyers and family court were made for?"

"Are you kidding? *No one* is willing to cut out the mom. Unless she's a drug addict, or worse. Plus it's *Payton*. She can command any room she walks into if that's what she wants to do. It's what I used to love about her."

He flopped around some more—curls, penis, and all.

"Courtroom would be just another room for her to conquer." He sighed. "So we hash it out between ourselves. But it's getting worse, not better. I don't know what to do about it."

There was a lot to unpack here, but will you think less of me if I admit my overriding reaction was careering toward the giddy smugness I tend to feel whenever I hear about couples— even ex-couples—behaving badly? Such stories validate my single status, and we all like to be validated. I arranged my face into a frown.

"I'm sorry," I said again. "I know how challenging Payton can be."

He pulled the sheet over the lower half of his body. When he retrieved his phone, he grimaced at the time. "You should probably get going if you want to make it to dinner."

I took the hint—always searching, as I am, for such hints. Sometimes it feels like my life is one big stakeout for hints I'm no longer wanted. That sounds sad, but my horror of overstaying my welcome has less to do with feelings of inferiority and more with a hypervigilance surrounding others' cues. I'd hate to be one of those myopic people who have to be bombarded with such hints. And so I act on them quickly. Maybe a little *too* quickly.

"You're eating in here again?" I asked him while throwing on my clothes.

He nodded.

"Do you just get your food straight from the kitchen?"

He nodded again. "Gasçoigne's got me covered. I think you're right about the short staffing, he seems to be doing everything himself other than serving. God knows how Payton got him to agree to it."

I zipped up my boots. "I think we've established that Payton is very persuasive."

He snorted. "Last night I got my food before everyone sat down, but I think tonight I'll go after. Got some light reading to do first."

He reached for a book on his nightstand, holding it up: *All She Ever Wanted*, by Jessamine LaBouchère.

"For background. No way I'll get through it though. Trash."

He let the book fall to the bed.

"Maybe it's not written for you," I said, thinking back to my conversation with Jessamine.

"It's *definitely* not written for me."

"Then why pass judgment on it?"

He looked at me incredulously. "Please tell me you don't read this drivel."

I was fully clothed now, which helped. I stood up.

"I don't," I said. "But I also don't dismiss it out of hand."

"It's *objectively* bad. Do you need me to read you a few sentences?"

"Nope."

He grinned. "That's what I thought."

He was so sure of himself, so convinced his point of view was the correct one, the only one that mattered. Let's see. How else can I put this?

He was a man.

Poor Payton.

This wasn't a phrase that came to me often. But as it turned out, this wouldn't be the last time it occurred to me on that day.

CHAPTER 15

The main course on the menu that night was Lobster Thermidor. This had been a great topic of conversation among my students during those chatty interstitial periods I glossed over in the recounting of my lessons earlier in the day. Apparently, Lobster Thermidor was a Pierre Gasçoigne specialty. I knew before I sat down to dinner that he used a combination of three different cheeses no one else did, which smothered the lobster. It sounded delicious, but like one of those dishes that inspires people to become vegetarians—not due to health or environmental concerns, but on the principle that killing animals is cruel. From what I understood, the meat was ripped from the lobster's body and then cooked in a butter-and-brandy sauce before being stuffed *back into* the animal's carcass, its shell serving as a gruesome container in which the meat was topped with that special three-cheese combo and then browned in the oven.

I mean, the witch in "Hansel and Gretel" wishes she could have thought up something so depraved, especially where a creature as intelligent as the lobster is concerned. While the notion that lobsters mate for life has been debunked, it's been proven that lobsters, crabs, shrimp, squids, octopuses (*not* octopi), and crayfish (aka crawdads, just please God don't let them sing) are all sentient creatures, capable of feeling complex emotions. So perhaps it was a blessing that the Lobster Thermidor was not to be. Not for me, anyway.

I arrived late, having stopped off at my cabin for a quick shower after my rendezvous with Gideon. Hurrying through the little antechamber that led to the dining room, I nearly collided with Jackson Richards, who was hurrying in the opposite direction.

"Hey *you*," he said accusingly.

Today he was wearing a suit of light blue plaid with no tie, though he had a frilly pocket handkerchief peeking out of his top pocket that reminded me of the way Easter eggs look when they're stained for decorative purposes: a watery, marbleized blue. He would have looked dapper if he weren't so sweaty. His collar had a dark ring around it, and droplets of moisture were gathering forces on his forehead, preparatory to making a run down his face. I took a closer look at him. His pupils *did* look rather big. . . .

"Where are you off to?" I asked him. "Aren't you eating?"

"As soon as Payton lets me," he remarked acidly. "I've been tasked with getting Her Royal Highness a drink from the lounge."

"Another daiquiri?" I said sympathetically.

"The daiquiri I got for Her Majesty when the afternoon session ended was not to her liking," he said. "Now she's requesting a cranberry and soda. Maybe she has a UTI?"

As much as I would have loved to extend this conversation, I was relieved when he brushed past me, leaving me free to enter the dining room.

The first course was a salad, and quite a hearty one for a dish that featured greens with no add-ins: nary a ring of onion nor slice of cucumber, not even a single cherry tomato. But there *was* red in it by way of the radicchio and red oak leaf mixed in with the arugula, endive, butter lettuce, and mizuna. There was also kale, of course (forgetting the kale in a salad these days is like forgetting the Cool Whip in a "salad" made in 1972). And finally, there was spinach, because every salad has to have a base. Thank goodness for spinach, a basic bitch if ever there was one. After all, it's the basic bitches who make the world go round. (Signed, a basic bitch.) There was also basil and mint to liven things up. All in all, it was an unusually flavorful collection of leaves, which is why the vinaigrette was light—little more than olive oil with the slightest hint of apple cider vinegar.

Even though I was late, the two teachers' tables hadn't been served yet. As I ascended the dais, the gen pop below me were just starting to tear into their beautiful bowls of foliage.

"Isn't there something you can do?"

Talia Simmons's hand shot out, the jangling of her bracelets underlining her appeal. I slipped into my seat, looking from her to the captain, who was sitting opposite her. Across from me, Joan raised her eyebrows in greeting.

"No," said the captain flatly. "If we had a working CCTV I could check the record, but Payton had me disable it before any passengers came on board."

"Why?" demanded Talia.

"Payton thinks video surveillance is fascist," said Joan, coming to the captain's rescue. "There was a whole disclaimer about it in the registration forms we had to sign. That and the absence of security personnel. She made a big deal out of it; I'm sure because her lawyers wanted to make sure no one would sue her."

I'd given the "terms and conditions" of the cruise the most cursory of glances, but even I had remarked on this unusual waiver. I know more about the matter now than I did then, and the truth is you *can't* have a police presence on the open seas, since no jurisdiction can assert control in international waters.

But usually there's at least an ex-cop or marshal or someone with a law enforcement background on board to keep the peace. Payton had ixnayed this, likening the Get Lit Cruise to a mobile autonomous zone: down with the patriarchy and all that jazz. The cynic in me would like to add that the corporate entity from which she leased the ship had no problem with the lack of surveillance and security, since it made the reporting of any crimes that might occur that much less likely, thereby limiting their liability. But Joan was right; we'd all given our written consent, and entered into this wackadoo situation with our eyes open.

"I guess I didn't read the fine print as closely as I should have," sulked Talia.

"I didn't realize you were such a fan of law and order," Joan replied mischievously.

Talia's apricot mouth opened wide in protest. "I'm not! I have all the empathy in the world for the victims of those institutions. It's a systemic issue, and it's up to all of us to acknowledge that, and do the work to fix the system so it isn't rigged anymore."

"Hear, hear."

Joan held up her wineglass, which Talia clinked automatically.

"What happened?" I asked.

"Talia says Flora Fortescue attacked her outside her room."

"Talia says that, because it's *what happened*," Talia hissed.

"Flora says she didn't touch her," Joan added.

I turned to Talia. "Did she ask you whose side you were on?"

Talia's hand shot out again, bracelets clanging. "You see! I'm not lying! When I told her I wasn't taking sides, she pushed me against the wall and said I was going to have to." She put her hand up to her scarf, which was yellow tonight, with blue polka dots. "Gave me a nasty bruise," she added, rubbing the back of her head gingerly.

"The ship's registered in New York, I assume?" asked Joan. The captain nodded.

"Then you could call the NYPD," she said to Talia. "You could press charges directly with them."

Talia glowered at both of them.

"I could've used you in my class today," I told Joan after ten seconds of silence that felt more like ten minutes.

"I could've used me in your class too. Busy day in the medical bay. Nothing major though. I've been putting that Dramamine to good use."

The mere mention of Dramamine made my stomach growl. I was relieved to see that Kendall had appeared at Table 1 at last, and was depositing bowls of salad there with a speedy precision. I watched as Jackson returned, handing Payton her cranberry-and-soda before putting down a cocktail of his own beside his plate. To my surprise, rather than taking his seat, he sauntered across the platform to us.

"Heyyyyyy kweens!" (It pains me to have to spell it this way, but his inflection left no room for debate.) "Sorry to interrupt, but I have a little present for my bestie here."

He laid a hand on Talia's shoulder. She tensed up immediately, and I felt sure she was fighting the urge to throw him off. Jackson's hand was probably clammy, and according to her she'd already suffered one bout of unwanted physical contact today. Slipping his other hand inside his jacket, he produced a thumb drive that he placed beside Talia's unused utensils.

"Oh!" Talia looked at it as though it were a worm or other species of vermin that had somehow found its way next to her fork.

"You. Are. Thee. *Bestest!*" Jackson gave her shoulder a vicious little squeeze before turning around to eye his table. "Ooh, looks like out salad era is upon us!" he cried. "Later!"

When he left, he crossed paths with Kendall, who looked almost as sweaty as he did. Her white gloves even had a ring of moisture around the wrist that reminded me of the ring around Jackson's collar.

"It's criminal to use the phrase 'sala era' without punning on 'salad days,' " remarked Joan before turning to Talia.

"What was all that?" she asked as Kendall began serving us.

"That was nothing," said Talia. "He wrote a YA manuscript and asked me to read it."

"You're a lot nicer than I am." I told them about Helen Sanchez, who was too far away to hear me. (I'd scoped out her location upon entering the room the way an animal does in the vicinity of a predator.) By the time I'd finished, a good quarter of an hour had gone by and we were all done with our salads.

Sometimes, when I write in public places, I listen to white noise on my headphones to keep myself from focusing too much on strangers' conversations. (You may be wondering why I don't write at home, and the answer is I usually do. But sometimes even a crotchety misanthrope like me requires evidence that other people exist in the world.) Often, this white noise takes the form of the light background patter of dishes clanking and diners chatting in a crowded restaurant or café—which means that as I sit in one eating establishment, I listen to another, more acoustically perfect eating establishment. (Modern technology has made such weirdos of us.) Anyway, the reason I prefer diffuse noise is that it's hard for anything to break through it and make itself heard.

The commotion in the dining room that night was easily ten times as loud as the white noise on my phone. Just imagine it: nearly three hundred women, many of them drunk for hours and getting drunker by the minute, tucking into dinner with old friends, new friends, but above all—drunk friends. When Joan asked me whether I found Freeman Wills Crofts to be as boring a classic mystery writer as she did (answer: *mainly*), I could barely hear her. For this reason it wasn't a scream or a cry that alerted me to the fact that something had gone wrong at Table 1. It was the sight of three chairs being pushed back more or less simultaneously—three people obeying the involuntary impulse to avoid the spray of vomit that emitted from the table's fourth occupant.

Payton Garrett.

Due to the way we were sitting, I had the best view whereas Joan had her back to them. But she could see by my reaction that something had happened. By the time she turned around, Payton had slumped forward, her face landing in her salad bowl. In another context this would have been comical: a Marx Brothers sketch, or the hijinks-y climax of a Disney movie wherein the villain gets her cartoonish comeuppance. In theory I wasn't averse to Payton being knocked down a peg or two by way of a humiliation she never seemed to suffer. But there was no humor here, no secret satisfaction.

Something was very, very wrong.

Joan sprang into action, and I mean that literally. I think she bridged the gap between the two tables in a single leap. I stood up and then I sat back down again, uncertain what to do or how to help. Joan crouched beside Payton, who by this point had at least lifted her head out of the bowl. Nicole was squatting on the other side of her, wiping dressing off her face with a cloth napkin. Jessamine was out of her chair as well, pouring a glass of water. The only person who hadn't moved was Jackson, who sat staring at his boss in horrified, slack-jawed fascination.

And then, without warning, his head jerked in *my* direction. It was like one of those jump cuts in a horror movie when a corpse comes alive, so startled was I by the spontaneous eye contact. But also, I was surprised by what I saw on his face.

Guilt. It was guilt; there was no mistaking it. But why?

It would be a long time before I had a satisfactory answer to this question.

* * *

"Oh God, I'll bet it's food poisoning." Talia pushed away her salad so forcefully, she almost knocked over her wine and water glasses. "Or maybe she's drunk?" she added hopefully.

I shook my head. "No way. She hasn't had a drop of alcohol this whole trip."

I should remind you there were nearly three hundred people below us, watching this drama play out as if they'd paid good money for their unobstructed orchestra view. Gone was the jolly cacophony, which isn't to say the vox populi was silent. Whispers were whipping through the crowd like wind through the leaves on a tree, each lady making sure her neighbor knew something was amiss, and speculating as to what was happening.

To my relief, the next time I looked at Payton she was sitting upright, answering a series of questions posed by Joan, none of which I could hear. A minute or two later, she was standing with the help of her wife, and people began clapping the way spectators do when an injured athlete is escorted off the field. She raised a hand weakly, acknowledging the applause.

The stairway leading down the platform was between the two tables, which meant Payton had to hobble in our direction before turning. I stood up, moving toward her as she faced me. It wasn't that she said anything, or made a gesture. But when she looked at me it was with a searching, unvarnished expression: *Can you believe this is happening?* It was an expression of dismay without an iota of irony or annoyance, and knowing her as well as I did, it was obvious to me how much she was hurting, and how badly she wanted me to come with her. Or maybe I just wanted to come myself. Either way, I found myself falling in behind Payton and Nicole, walking side by side with Joan as together we made our way down the platform, and through the sea of well-wishers offering words and even pats of encouragement here and there.

I only remember seeing two people within this sea. The first was Flora Fortescue, decked out for the evening in a shimmery, skintight dress with a mandarin collar. There was no triumph on her face now. Just worry. And fear. The second person was Helen Sanchez, and I couldn't tell you what she was feeling, because her head was down. But I suspect she was feeling absolutely nothing, because I kid you not:

That little sociopath was *literally* taking notes.

CHAPTER 16

It took us forever to get from the dining room to the elevator. Payton spent this time fretting about the effect her illness might have had on the paying passengers.

"Do you think I traumatized them?"

She'd already asked Nicole and Joan the same thing.

"Not at all," I assured her, echoing the others. She was embarrassed—humiliated, even—and we were all doing our best to buck her up. But wasn't it a good sign she was focusing on the social-emotional side of things? I exchanged a good-natured grimace with Nicole, who seemed to be thinking the same thing.

The elevator door dinged open. We shuffled on. The doors closed, and the elevator began moving.

Payton looked at Nicole and me.

"You two should go back, I don't want to disrupt dinner any more than I already have. Why don't you let everyone know—"

This was the moment that Payton Garrett lost consciousness, her body sagging against her wife's, its dead weight nearly bringing Nicole down with her.

"Payton, are you okay?" I asked her. It was a dumb question for two reasons: (1) she obviously could not hear me; and (2) just as obviously, she was not okay.

The elevator doors opened. We were on the fifth deck now. "Stand here," Joan commanded me, pointing at the empty space where the doors would close any second. "I'll be right back."

"Do you have any idea what happened?" I asked Nicole, who'd sunk to the floor and was cradling Payton's head in her lap. "Food poisoning?" I suggested, remembering what Talia had said. "Maybe an allergic reaction?"

Nicole didn't answer. I guessed she was too upset and disoriented to say anything. Her face was frozen in a mask of alarm, her eyes fixed on Payton's. As odd as this is to say, I was reminded of the Pietà: those sculptures and paintings of Mary cradling Jesus after he's been taken off the cross. That's how vivid Nicole's anguish was. It had its own presence, here in this cramped space.

I turned my head away to give them as much privacy as possible, which wasn't much.

The doors tried to close just once before Joan came trotting back with a gurney, its wheels rumbling in protest the way a shopping cart's do in the supermarket when you push it too quickly. The gurney was collapsible, which meant that with Joan's instruction, the three of us managed to get Payton on it with a minimum of fuss. Joan wheeled her across the lobby and into an alcove in the medical bay beside a high silver table. Picking up a pair of scissors from the table, she cut open Payton's shirt, a champagne-colored jersey that was now ruined.

"She's in cardiac arrest and even though this may not be necessary, I've got to use the AED, as scary as that's going to look."

I had no idea what she meant by AED, but I wasn't in suspense for long. AED stands for automated external defibrillator, and it's the device you've seen in countless medical dramas: the paddles that doctors in the ER rub together, shouting "Clear!" before they zap the hapless extra splayed on the bed.

"You can draw the curtain around us if you'd like," Joan said calmly as she prepped the machine.

Neither Nicole nor I moved.

Joan never yelled "Clear!" but she administered three shocks with the paddles, Payton's body twitching slightly from the electrical current (not convulsing like those hammy actors do). After each application she listened to Payton's chest while looking at a digital clock that kept time by the second. This couldn't have lasted more than a few minutes, but I won't soon forget the terror of it, the paralysis. I remember staring at all the paraphernalia attached to the wall behind the bed: a big white vacuum tube beside two valves, one for oxygen, the other for "medical air"; a clear plastic case stuffed with vinyl gloves; a panel of unused outlets for both phone/Internet and electricity; two wire baskets filled with alcohol wipes, tissues, and the tops that go on those instruments that doctors use to look in your ears and nose. There was also a whiteboard with a marker for taking notes, and one of those pain-rating scales with the androgynous face that registers mounting discomfort from 0 to 10, though I was interested to note that the "0" looked deranged, leering in ecstasy like some sort of religious zealot. My ideal face was the one associated with 2, "Hurts a Little Bit," which involved a genial-enough smile conveying: *I've got this, I'll be fine.*

After the third shock, Joan apparently liked what she heard. "Her heartbeat is stable. That's good. But it's fainter than I'd like."

She ripped the stethoscope out of her ears by pulling on the junction point above the plunging neckline of her print dress, which featured big, droopy tropical leaves and flowers drawn in primary colors: like something out of Matisse, and much too cheerful for the occasion. Not that it mattered. I was impressed with how quickly she'd snapped into professional mode—

impressed, but not surprised. "I've got to hook her up to an EKG and do an epi drip." She looked at Nicole. "Does she have any heart conditions you know of?"

Nicole shook her head.

"Verbal answers are preferred," Joan said gently, adding: "I know this is hard."

"No." Nicole's voice was raspy, but she cleared her throat. "As far as I know, she has no heart conditions."

"Great." Joan began drawing the curtain along a semicircular groove in both the floor and ceiling, which curved around the bed. She paused before closing it all the way. "I assume you're her healthcare proxy?" she asked. "If I need any permissions?"

"She's not."

We all turned. (All of us except Payton.)

Gideon was standing in the doorway hunched over and panting heavily, one hand on his knee and the other on the doorframe. If it hadn't been for the noise of the curtain, we would have heard him approaching. He'd clearly been running.

"I'm still"—he paused for a gulp of air—"her proxy. Haven't gotten around—to changing the paperwork."

Nicole drew herself up to her full height, which as I've already mentioned was impressive, roughly equal to Gideon's, especially when he was bent over like this. It was a gesture she was particularly good at pulling off.

"Let's not play *that* game, shall we? I'm her wife. You're the father of her children. I'm sure we can figure it out together."

"That sounds reasonable."

To his credit, he said this with zero hesitation.

"Great! I have work to do." Joan whisked the curtain closed.

Gideon and Nicole sat down on a bench together, much closer than I would have expected if I'd given the matter any thought beforehand.

"Her heartbeat is stable," Nicole told him. "She's getting some epinephrine now, some adrenaline, to make it stronger." He nodded.

There was no room on the bench where they were sitting, nor any chair beyond one of those backless, circular wheeled stools that's closer to a skateboard than a piece of furniture. Gideon had taken out his phone, and Nicole had reverted to her comatose state. Suddenly I felt like I was intruding.

"I'm going to see how everyone else is doing," I announced, more for my benefit than theirs. When neither of them responded, I left the room without delay.

I didn't go see how everyone else was doing.

I couldn't face the lounge again, and I had no appetite for dinner—not even for Lobster Thermidor. (Besides, I had a stash of protein bars in my suitcase, which I always bring on trips for emergencies since you can't rely on ready access to food while traveling.) It had been an exhausting day *before* dinner, and in the aftermath of whatever it was that had happened to Payton, I found myself seeking the sweet release of solitude, if only for a minute or two.

There was no reason to assume anything other than a medical emergency had befallen her. But Payton rarely fell ill, and whether it was warranted or not, I'd already made the leap to wondering who could have done this to her, and how. Along with the million-dollar question:

Why?

Flora had such an obvious reason to harm Payton; it was almost *too* obvious? My pet theory, only half-formed by this point, was that Helen Sanchez had done it for purposes of research. Her words in the black box theater came back to me now. *I could die tonight. So could you. Or any of us.* Sure, it was a ridiculous motive: the mystery writer who commits murder for purposes of achieving verisimilitude, something you might expect from a Queen of Crime, but not from reality. I knew it was insane as soon as I thought it, but then, so is murder. And why had Jackson looked so guilty when Payton became sick? And what about Nicole and Gideon? It's sad but true that when a person is harmed, the most logical suspect is their spouse if they've got one, or an ex. On this boat, Payton had both.

All these thoughts came unbidden into my head, and I did my best to push them away while trudging up the stairs from the fifth to the fourth deck and getting lost for the umpteenth time in the maze of dark, shadowy hallways.

But there was an upside to my poor sense of direction. It meant that I pretty much wandered into the hallway where my cabin was rather than walking there with purpose, which would have involved a firmer, more audible footstep. For this reason, the person who was testing the lock on my door had no idea I was watching her. This made for extremely interesting viewing, especially when she crouched down and put her eye and then her *ear* to the keyhole.

I froze—in horror and fascination.

It was Gerry. I could tell by the sprightly way she moved, and also by her oversized shoulder bag and trench coat, its olive-green trim just visible in the dim light. What the hell was she doing?

She must have sensed my presence, or maybe I made a noise because she turned around, straightening up hastily.

"Oh!" she cried when she saw me. "Thank goodness! I couldn't find you for our drink after dinner. I was worried, I thought maybe you'd been taken ill too."

"No." I walked toward her, not hiding how weirded out I was by what I'd caught her doing. "I'm fine. Were you just trying to get into my room?"

"Well, I never lock mine," she said. "I thought you might do the same, and be too sick to answer. I knocked first, of course."

Had she, though? I stared at her, and she stared right back

with those merry eyes of hers. Had I misjudged Gerry? Was she a nutjob?

"Tell me!" she said eagerly, "How is Payton?"

"She's okay." I had no idea how much I was allowed to share about Payton's medical condition, and I wasn't feeling chatty anyway, certainly not with her. "No one else got sick at dinner, did they?"

She shook her head. "Thank goodness, no."

And yet—surely this was uncharitable of me—I couldn't help feeling she was disappointed. This didn't prove anything. In times of calamity, we often get a rise out of matters going as badly as possible. Whenever I hear about the inevitable downgrading of a hurricane upon making landfall, there's a sliver of secret disappointment mixed in with my relief. This is akin to Jane Eyre wanting it to rain *harder*, the wind to moan *louder* when she's away at school, and perhaps the impulse is a sign of deep-seated issues, but murderousness needn't be one of them.

Still—the weirdness of Gerry's manner shook loose something I'd forgotten, and had been meaning to ask her.

"I saw you talking to Jackson Richards the first night of the cruise," I said. "Just before dinner. I didn't realize you knew him."

"Oh! I don't. He just checked me in when I was boarding. He checked in all the passengers."

This was true enough.

"I was holding the latest Sally Rooney, and we got to chatting about it because he was reading it too. He'd finished it since checking me in, and let me know at dinner. That's all."

This felt like a pat, prepared answer. Also, I love Sally Rooney as much as the next human, but I found it hard to believe Jackson would have sought out Gerry to discuss one of Rooney's novels. I was too tired to press her on the issue, however.

"I don't think I have it in me to do drinks tonight," I told her plainly. "I'm sorry."

"Understood! I should turn in myself. But I have to ask, does the doctor have any idea what might have caused the attack? There are people"—she paused delicately—"people are wondering if maybe she was . . . it sounds so silly to say it aloud. But could she have been poisoned?"

She had a glint in her eye, and her lips were quivering as though she were doing everything in her power to keep them from curling upwards. The day before, I'd been drawn to Gerry's sparkly demeanor. Now her cheerfulness struck me as tasteless. Ghoulish.

"No idea," I said tersely. "By the way, how did you know where my room was?"

"You mentioned it when we were trying to figure out where our rooms were! After we first boarded the ship, don't you remember?"

"No," I said honestly. "You must have a really good memory."

"I do," she said. "For better or worse!" She shook her head—so hard, it felt like she was trying to forget something. "I can't tell you how many times my son begged me not to be so exacting, remembering every little thing. 'Don't be a drag, Mom!' I should have listened to him." She shook her head again. "No, take it from an old lady like me. A good memory can be more trouble than it's worth."

Normally, I would have been intrigued by such a statement. But I was tired. And weirded out. In short: I wasn't playing. I gave her a tight smile I knew would convey my desire to be rid of her more clearly than any forthright statement or gesture.

"I'll let you go, I can see you're wiped and I completely understand. And I *am* sorry to have bothered you. I just had to know how Payton was doing. I suppose I'm nosy that way!"

My smile tightened. If I held it much longer, my cheeks would start hurting.

"I just thought—" She hesitated. "When I saw the commotion up at the table, I thought. . . ."

"You thought what?" I asked impatiently.

Looking back, I can see that she was desperate to unburden herself. Even if she wasn't willing to tell me everything quite yet.

"I thought it was fate," said Gerry. "But then I realized *she* was the one who was sick. It was all wrong." She sighed. "But I promised myself I wouldn't dwell on any of that anymore. That's what I mean by a good memory being a burden. So much easier to forget, isn't it? Well, I'm off to bed myself. What a strange evening! Let's try for that drink another time, yes?"

She bustled away without giving me the chance to ask her what the hell she was talking about. Something was off about Gerry Forrest, there was no question about it.

Another mystery, I thought to myself as I unlocked my door. They were accumulating at an alarming rate.

CHAPTER 17

Helen's manuscript stared up at me from the bed, looking somehow more sinister *and* more pathetic than before—as though it would do something cruel to me in its desperation to be read. My hand shot out, knocking it to the floor. I collapsed face down on top of the quilt, even though you're supposed to avoid contact with the topmost layer of bedding in any shared-room type of situation. (They're rarely cleaned, if ever, despite being exposed to the various shenanigans that go down in such spaces. Let's just say that viewing them under a blacklight would be an . . . illuminating experience.) I had every intention of getting up in a minute, eating a protein bar, brushing my teeth, washing my face, undressing, getting under the sheets—all those mundane tasks that are supposed to become second nature by the time we've reached adulthood, but which occasionally still elude us. Or me, at least.

I fell dead asleep.

It was hours later—just after one in the morning—when a series of urgent knocks woke me from my dead sleep. I stumbled out of the bed and opened the door.

"I need help."

Joan was still in her Matisse outfit. It had gone saggy, with dark spots under the arms, and a multitude of creases running across the middle. It seemed strange that the bright and bouncy tropical flowers themselves hadn't gone dull or droopy. Her mascara was smeared, and her hair looked in need of a wash.

"What's wrong?" I asked, and even though I was still half asleep, the memory of the night before was enough to send my eyelids shooting open like one of those window shades that works on a spring. "Is it Payton?"

Joan shook her head. "Payton's stable. It's Nicole. She came down with some of the same symptoms. Nowhere near as bad, but dizziness, nausea, some heart palpitations. It's concerning."

This meant that two of the people sitting at Table 1 had now fallen ill.

"I already checked on Jessamine, who was fine. No issues whatsoever. But when I knocked on Jackson's door I didn't get an answer. So I had to call the captain. She's coming with a master key, and I'm sorry to be waking you up, I just—it's been a long night and"—she pressed the skin between her eyebrows with her index finger, moving it slowly in circles—"I could use a friend."

"Of course," I said, checking that my key was in my pocket and then closing the door behind me. This swift transition from a sleeping to a waking state is the sole benefit of falling asleep in one's clothes. "Don't apologize, I'm glad you woke me up."

Joan seemed to have no problem negotiating the hallways on the fourth deck, or on the third, where Jackson's room was located.

"Have you been able to sleep at all?" I asked her.

She made a snuffly noise in the back of her throat. "No. It's been a busy night. Besides the two I've got in the medical bay, I had a handful of hypochondriacs who were convinced we had an outbreak of norovirus. Always a worry on a cruise ship. One woman, I think her name is June? She said she was in your class. Total character. She insisted on telling me the story of the Carnival "Poop Cruise" from a few years back, which apparently she experienced firsthand. It was like listening to some old sea dog tell me a shipwreck story."

I laughed, even though I didn't feel like laughing. I could tell Joan was in a state of high anxiety, and I understood why. There was a chance we hadn't heard from Jackson yet because he was a heavy sleeper, and simply lucky enough to be unaffected, like Jessamine. In this scenario, he was sleeping the sleep of the innocent. But there were two other possibilities, both of which seemed more likely. In the first, *he* was the one to have administered whatever it was that had made the others ill. Which meant there was a chance we were about to rouse an attempted murderer. Unless the second possibility had come to pass, in which case we weren't rousing anyone. Maybe Jackson was the unluckiest of the four.

Maybe he was dead.

Jackson's cabin lay at the end of a long hallway, which meant we had an unobstructed view of the captain standing with her back against the door. Two of her passengers were seriously ill at this point, and for this reason I would have expected her to be on the phone (Wi-Fi calls were feasible), or at the very least typing or swiping furiously. But she was standing there motionless with her arms crossed, staring into space. When she saw us, she turned, the glint of a metallic object shining from inside her hand.

"You must knock clearly at least three times," she said. "The master key is only to be used in case of emergency when a passenger is deemed to be unresponsive."

It was obvious she'd memorized this from a manual.

Joan nodded before knocking sharply on the door.

"Jackson!" She paused. "Jackson, are you in there?"

No answer. She tried the handle. Locked. She knocked again. "Jackson, are you all right?"

Still no answer.

Joan's final knock was similar to the pounding of my fist against Payton and Nicole's door. If someone was in that room, there was no way they could have missed it.

Joan slipped a small bag off her shoulder, unzipping the main compartment and producing a portable AED (the paddles I'd already seen her use on Payton). She nodded at the captain.

"We are coming in!" the captain shouted at the door panel. It felt as though she should have produced an ax now, or maybe one of those battering rams that medieval armies used on castle doors. But all she did was to slip her key in the lock and click it open.

The door swung inward. Joan entered first, and then the captain. I lingered in the doorway like the scaredy-cat I am. But Jackson's cabin was as small as mine, which meant I could already see the figure in the bed, huddled under the sheets. He was here.

Please let him be sleeping, I thought as Joan inched toward him. He was facing away from us, so she turned him—ever so gently—onto his back.

It was true that sleep had overtaken Jackson, but the special kind of sleep Hamlet refers to in his famous soliloquy: "a sleep to say we end the heartache, and the thousand natural shocks that flesh is heir to." Whatever this sleeping man's heartache, whatever his struggles with this world—all that was over.

Jackson Richards was dead.

Part Three
Second Murder

CHAPTER 18

His eyes were open, and while his face wasn't screwed up in horror like many a fictional corpse, there was a tightness to his parted lips and a flare to his nostrils that indicated the end hadn't come pleasantly.

"He must have been in a lot of pain," said Joan quietly from beside the body. She turned abruptly to the captain, who stood frozen at the foot of the bed. "You need to report this. Immediately. And turn the ship around."

I caught a flutter of movement from within the depths of her Coke-bottle glasses. "Yes. Yes. I'll turn her around. It's a good thing she's equipped with azimuth thrusters, they'll make the one-eighty—"

"We don't have time for that," Joan admonished her. "Just do it. But first, report the death. Given what took place at dinner, there's obviously a good chance he didn't die of natural causes."

"Who do I—"

"NYPD. Ask for Homicide."

Captain Marcie nodded, hurrying away. Joan watched her go, fixing me afterward with a look of wide-eyed disbelief.

"Almost makes you wish we had some washed up ex-cop on board, doesn't it?"

I signaled my assent by way of a half-strangled exclamation. I was still in the doorway, leaning back every now and then to take a gulp of air from the hallway. I have a horror of dead bodies, which is a pretty ho-hum quality except that in my case, it wasn't the generalized aversion to death so many of us share. The truth is that the body whose pajama sleeves Joan had begun rolling up was officially my *fourth* dead body. I'd encountered corpses two and three during the events related to my first mystery novel, but I was only a teenager when I became intimate for the first time with the transformation that death brings about: the suspension of animation, the dissipation of heat, the extinguishing of light—an absence made remarkable by the way we take for granted the presence of life each day. The thing you don't realize till you see death up close is that it doesn't confine itself to the body it's visited. Death hangs in the air; it pervades the room; it rubs off on you, so that you become a part of it.

People talk about how "a piece" of them dies when someone close to them passes away. But that's not quite right. It's more that death takes ahold of you, now that you've brushed against it. Death takes up residence, making you—your whole self—a little less alive than you were before, a little closer to the end that awaits us all.

Death beckons for everyone, but for those of us who have seen more of it than others, it beckons louder. . . .

"Are you just going to stand there and watch?"

Reluctantly, I took a few steps inside the room. "What are you doing?"

She held up his arm, pointing to a series of red, scabby dots on the inside crook of his elbow. "Needle marks. Not a surprise."

I agreed, telling her about how sweaty he'd been before dinner, and how I'd noticed his dilated pupils.

"I noticed that too." She drew the sheet up, letting it fall gently over his face. The body would have to stay here for now. Believe it or not, the mammoth cruise ships out there—the ones that carry thousands of passengers at a time—actually have a designated morgue. But the *Merman Rivera* was too small for such a dread facility.

On his nightstand were the usual personal effects: a smartphone, a wallet, a room key, a tin of breath mints, and what looked to be a leather-bound journal. Joan produced a pair of vinyl gloves from her bag, holding out a pair for me. I hesitated.

"Come on." She shook them at me impatiently. "You don't think the captain is going to do any investigating, do you? And Payton and Nicole are down for the count. I need to go check on them soon, which means we don't have much time." She gave the gloves another shake. "You know you want to. This is obviously cuckoo, but it's also an opportunity I have no intention of passing up. We can be like the Hardy Girls."

Could this really be happening again? Could I be so lucky as to have another murder land in my lap? Feel free to judge me for my heartlessness, but this is what ran through my head as I reached out and accepted the gloves from the mystery-loving Joan Chen, who with this gesture became my official partner in crime.

"Only if I get to be Frank."

"Hey, I'm fine being Joe. Blonds have more fun. Just as long as neither of us is Chet."

"Fuck Chet," I agreed.

Jackson's phone was passcode-protected—no surprise there. I made Joan try one-two-three-four and a few other obvious combinations, but no luck.

Joan opened up the tin, scrutinizing its contents before handing it to me.

"These don't look like Altoids, do they?"

The dozen or so pills inside were rainbow-colored, with miniature designs carved into them: a star, a smiley-face, a hand with its middle finger raised, a skull-and-crossbones. They looked like a child's stash of vitamins. If that child were a raging junkie.

"I'll bet they're curiously strong though," I said. "Ecstasy?"

"Could be. In which case there's a chance they're laced with fentanyl or something equally lethal he had no idea he was ingesting. He was the youngest and fittest of the four people sitting at that table. He probably reacted badly because of what was already pumping through his system."

We moved on to the leather-bound journal, which turned out to be nothing of the kind. Instead of paper, there was a deep pocket on the inside of each cover. The left pocket contained various unused needles, still sheathed. The right pocket held two miniature Ziploc baggies filled with white powder.

Apparently Jackson Richards had taken his drug addiction seriously.

"Well, we knew he used needles." Joan had already moved on to his wallet. "This is interesting." She held up his driver's license.

"What?"

"His legal name is *Jared* Richards."

"Understandable. Jackson's got a better ring to it."

She held up his room key. "Try this in the lock, will you? Just to make sure it's his. That's the kind of dumb assumption Japp or Lestrade would make."

"Or Charles Parker," I added, unwilling to be out-geeked.

I put the key in the lock, turning the bolt easily.

"Okay, good," said Joan. "That means he came in here and locked the room himself from the inside. And from the looks of it, got himself ready for bed and managed to lie down. Before whatever was in his system kicked in." She sucked the air through her teeth, considering. "The captain's the only other person who could have gained access to the room." She looked at me. "I don't think Captain Ellen McDwight is a psychotic murderer, do you?"

I shook my head. Captain Marcie was many things, but a murderer didn't seem to be one of them. Of course, one never knew.

A quick look through the rest of his things turned up a password-protected laptop, and a surprisingly expansive collection of suits that must have been worth tens of thousands of dollars. Where had he gotten the money for all these clothes *and* an expensive drug habit, I wondered, on an assistant's salary?

We left the room, locking the door from the outside with the key.

"This will have to do for now," she said, placing the key inside an unused glove, and putting it at the bottom of her bag. "Come on, let's poke our heads real quick into the dining room. I may as well neglect my patients a little longer."

We began walking at a fast clip.

"Why the dining room?"

"To return to the scene of the crime, *mon amie.*"

Oh, so now you're Poirot? I thought as we hurried along. Not that I have anything against the little pedant, but I was damned if I was going to play the sidekick again. This was my second outing, after all.

I could do better than Hastings.

CHAPTER 19

The dining room looked eerie in the middle of the night, the habitually bustling space devoid of humanity, imbuing it with the creepiness of an empty mall, airport, or city center—even with the lights blaring. (The lights must have been on all night. No doubt Gideon had a ready-made rant concerning the waste of electricity.) We were in zombie-apocalypse, last-man-on-earth territory, tiptoeing our way past the four long tables, every tiny noise we made echoing off the peaked ceiling above us. It was easy to pretend Joan and I were the last two survivors on this doomed ship, especially when we approached the dais and the surface of Table 1 came into view.

"I told Kendall not to touch a thing," said Joan. "Looks like she listened to me."

There were the wine and water glasses, the silverware, the white tablecloth, stained and rumpled. (There was dried vomit, too, but let's not dwell on that, shall we?) Someone must have pulled on the tablecloth in the frenzy of tending to Payton—maybe Payton herself, as it was hanging down so far on her side that on the opposite edge, where Jessamine had been sitting, the tabletop was in danger of a Janet Jackson–style exposure by way of a wardrobe malfunction (excuse me: a Justin Timberlake–style exposure by way of a wardrobe malfunction). Jessamine's salad plate had been pulled a good six inches toward the center of the table, while Payton's peered cautiously over the edge.

We walked up the steps, circling the table in silence. Three of the four people sitting here had been brought down by something that in all likelihood was still lurking within view, ripe for the finding. . . .

"Well, we know it couldn't have been in the wine," I said. "Because Payton didn't drink any."

"Neither did Nicole or Jessamine, by the looks of it." Joan pointed to their wineglasses, which were both empty. "They had cocktails, though. Looks like Jackson was the only one who was drinking the wine. *And* a cocktail."

"And it couldn't have been in the water," I continued, "because Kendall used the same jug to fill up our glasses. I saw her do it both nights."

"Right. So it's got to be the salad. Whatever it was, I'm guessing it's incredibly poisonous, so let's continue to be responsible little detectives and not touch anything with our bare hands."

She pulled out two more pairs of vinyl gloves from her bag. How many did she have in there? Even as this idle thought flitted across my consciousness, something weightier struggled beneath it, desperate to breach the surface. Who *else* had been wearing gloves recently? And why was this important?

The leaves in what was left of the salad were wilted and soggy—not just with dressing, but with the heat of a few hours' worth of decay. Still, it wasn't too difficult to identify each of them: the arugula, endive, radicchio, butter lettuce, mizuna, red oak, spinach, kale, basil, and mint. Once we did, it was clear there was one more kind of leaf among the group.

This leaf looked similar in both texture and shape to the mint, which was why I hadn't noticed it before. Both were fuzzy, and medium-sized: fairly broad-faced, neither skinny nor fat. They were different colors, however. While the mint was bright green (even with dressing smeared on it), this mystery leaf was much darker, practically black.

"Is that . . . maybe it's sage?" asked Joan doubtfully.

I Google-imaged "sage" on my phone. No way. The sage plant had a much slimmer, tapered leaf.

"Well, I'm out. Too bad I hate cooking. Can you think of any other herbs?" she asked. "Preferably deadly ones?"

And then, I had an idea. I did another Google-image search, barely managing to keep my gasp on the inside when I saw the result.

"So don't laugh at me," I began.

"Okay?"

"Maybe I've been reading too many mysteries, but . . . what about foxglove?"

"Sounds kinky. But sure, let's take a gander."

I angled my screen toward her.

"Oh, *hello.*"

There was no question.

This was our leaf.

"Foxglove," I said.

"Foxglove," she echoed, already on her phone. "A-*ha.* Or digitalis, to be more exact. That's the toxin in foxglove, and I have *definitely* heard of that. It's no joke."

Joan explained to me how digitalis acts on the heart; how for some people with certain heart conditions it's actually *helpful,* the active ingredient in lifesaving heart medication. But how when it entered an otherwise healthy person's bloodstream, it interfered with the function of this vital organ, which was when all sorts of bad things happened: dizziness, nausea, loss of consciousness. And in some cases, death.

"Just from a few leaves?" I asked.

She was still on her phone. " 'Fraid so. Sorry, texting with a colleague who does, like, chem and tox research on the side because that's her idea of a fun Friday night. She says 'ingesting a leaf or two will endanger the life of a person of average weight.' Sheesh."

"But why did they react so differently?" I asked.

Joan shrugged. "Aside from the drugs Jackson was already taking? You'd be surprised how the same drug or even infection does different things to different people. Different system, different reaction," she explained. "Also, it doesn't look like they did eat the same amount, does it?"

She was right. Jackson had practically no foxglove left on his plate: just the fragment of a single leaf, whereas Payton and Nicole had eaten a good two-thirds of their salads, a few foxglove leaves left on both their plates mixed among everything else. But the most interesting plate was Jessamine LaBouchère's. The foxglove had been sorted out and pushed to one side. They were in fact the only leaves left uneaten—six total, by my count, which meant Jackson had probably eaten five or so, Payton and Nicole something like three or four.

Joan picked up one of the offending leaves from Jessamine's plate, placing it in another makeshift "evidence bag" fashioned from an unused glove.

We were getting good at this.

CHAPTER 20

We hurried back to the medical bay so that Joan could check on her patients. Nicole lay on a second gurney beside Payton, her forehead glistening with moisture, the sheets tossed off her body into a knotted tangle at her feet. The two gurneys were actually pushed together: the way married couples did with their twin beds back in the day, when it was time to make babies. By pulling up the railing on the outside edges of both, they'd managed to make something resembling a two-person bed for themselves. This would have been a cozier setup if not for Nicole's intermittent moaning, and the fact that Payton was sitting up with her back against the wall behind her, which had all those tubes and other paraphernalia on it. She couldn't have been comfortable, which I guessed was one reason she was glaring at us.

But not the only one.

"Where have you been?" she hissed.

Joan gestured for me to answer while she slipped a stethoscope underneath Nicole's nightshirt with a practiced stealth.

I took a deep breath. "Jackson is dead."

I saw her flinch and then nod—taking this in the way a prize fighter absorbs a punch. I hadn't known Payton when she was little, but I was reasonably sure she was one of those kids who would rather have died than let anyone reduce her to tears.

"Do we know how?" she asked quietly.

"Digitalis." Joan was already done with Nicole, and was now checking the readout from one of the machines monitoring Payton. "Foxglove in the salad. In the dining room, if we want to go full-on *Clue*."

"Just our table, though?" asked Payton. "No one else was poisoned?"

"Seems that way," replied Joan. "Even though there's been wishful thinking on that front from a few people."

"Didn't it all happen kind of fast?" asked Payton. "Our reactions?"

Joan shrugged. "Not hers." She pointed to Nicole. "Her reaction was textbook. So was Jackson's, especially if his heart was already weakened from prior drug use. Yours was super quick, but sometimes the strongest constitutions react big. And fast. Like your body knew it needed to rid itself of what had just gone in it."

Payton patted herself on the arm. "Good body," she cooed. "That means whoever did this must have administered it in the kitchen, no?" She looked from one to the other of us while beside her, Nicole let out a plaintive moan.

"Probably," I said.

Payton picked up her phone, which I hadn't seen before. (I guessed Nicole had brought it down for her before she got sick herself.)

"I need to call Jackson's mother before any of this gets out, which I'm sure it will. I don't want her to hear about it from anyone but me."

"Were they close?" I asked.

She shrugged. "Not really. But he was an only child, and his father never had much to do with him. I learned all this from *her*, by the way. She went to college with my business manager. Basically browbeat me into hiring him as an assistant."

Aha: a rich and well-connected background explained Jackson's fancy clothes and expensive drug habit.

"Was he a good assistant?"

Payton lowered the outside rail of her gurney. "In some ways. He wasn't an idiot, and he was actually great with all the nitty-gritty, boring stuff. Like scheduling, phone calls. He rarely messed up when it came to that. But his attitude was . . . well, you met him. I thought he was hysterical when I first hired him, but it was wearing thin." She glanced at her wife, who'd rolled onto her side, facing away from us. "Nic hated him."

"How long had he been working for you?"

She took a moment to calculate in her head. "Three years? Maybe four? Well before Nic, which was part of the problem. I think he felt threatened by her, like she was replacing him or something." She swung her legs off the bed. "Which is insanity."

"What are you doing?" asked Joan.

"Well, first I'm going to see if the waitress who served us our salads is awake. And if she isn't, I'm going to wake her up myself so I can ask her a few questions."

"Her name is Kendall," I said.

"I'm aware of that," Payton said icily. "I hired her, remember? Then I'm going to call Cheryl, that's Jackson's mother, and *then* I'm going to find the captain to make a plan for keeping Flora-fucking-Fortescue locked up in some makeshift brig for the rest of the trip." She put her feet on the ground. "And fingers crossed, she'll stay locked up the rest of her life."

"I hate to break this to you," said Joan—looking for all appearances like the first person in the world to use this phrase and mean it—"but you're hooked up to an EKG and IV right now. Because your heart wasn't working properly a few hours ago. You need to stay here." She bent down, detaching Payton's feet from the vinyl flooring and hefting her legs back onto the gurney. "I insist. We don't need two dead people on this boat. Also, the captain's busy right now turning the ship around."

Joan ratcheted the gurney's railing back into place, punctuating her point. I expected Payton to lower it immediately, swing her legs off, but she didn't.

"The captain's turning the ship around?" she asked faintly.

"We need to get back ASAP," I explained. "So the police can get involved."

Do you ever get a rush imparting bad news to people? I know it's an ugly quality, but sometimes I can't help it. I think it's the younger sibling in me.

"I'm going to get sued, aren't I?" she said dully. "A lot."

Even my callousness has its limits. I looked to Joan for help, but she was pretending to be busy smoothing out Nicole's tangled sheets.

"Well, we all signed that waiver about having no law enforcement on board," I said, trying to be helpful.

Payton groaned, grabbing the pillow from behind her and holding it over her face. "This is such a *mess*," she wailed into it.

Beside her, Nicole lifted her head and said something unintelligible.

Payton dropped her pillow. "What?"

"She's fine," offered Joan. "Just needs more sleep."

"Go back to bed, babe."

Nicole dropped her head obligingly.

"Fucking Flora. What a loser," said Payton scornfully, nothing like the mindful, kindly presence she'd honed over many years spent in the public eye. "Bitch couldn't even kill the right person."

"You don't know that," I said. "Whoever did this could have been targeting Jackson."

"*Flora* did this," retorted Payton. "It's not a question. And don't even try to say this isn't about me." She struck the gurney's railing. "I've been *hospitalized*!"

She hadn't, technically. But I saw her point. Also, the beeps on her EKG monitor were getting noticeably faster.

"Careful," said Joan. "You don't want to overexcite yourself."

"Yeah, I'll try to be more chill about the end of my career I've spent two decades sacrificing everything to build up."

"And about Jackson," I added, unable to help myself. "You're obviously devastated about him."

She gave me the finger, thereby justifying the twisted love I harbored for her. Ninety-nine out of a hundred people would have been shamed by my comment. But not Payton.

I gave her the finger back. "You seriously think Flora is capable of murder. *Flora?*"

"You've only gotten a taste of what she's like now. That twat is off. Her. Rocker. I still have no idea whose invitation she used to get on this ship, but I'm sure it was easy enough for her to track someone down. There was all that press about people sharing invitations when we first sent them out."

"She claims she got her own invitation, sent to her real name and address," I said. "Though she admits to using a fake name when she registered."

"Augusta Leigh, I'm aware." Payton rolled her eyes. "I mean, in a perfect world the bookers I hired would've realized 'Augusta Leigh' wasn't a real person, but they made such a mess of things, I can't say I'm surprised they didn't flag it."

"Registering under a fake name doesn't make Flora a murderer."

"I'll bet she didn't mean for anyone to die. She probably just wanted to humiliate me in front of everyone, and Jackson was collateral damage."

"Actually, she didn't like Jackson either." I told them about what Flora had said in the lounge the day before: about having "something planned" for him.

"Holy crap!" cried Payton. "I just thought of something else!" She gestured at me, her IV tube flapping in the air. "Do you remember how she was always into gardening?"

With a sinking heart, I remembered as soon as she said it. How we used to make fun of Flora for living up to her name. . . .

Payton sat up straighter. "Remember how she had this plot of land outside her crappy little apartment where she'd, like, till the earth in her spare time? Who *does* that while they're getting their MFA? In their mid-twenties?"

It had been another of Flora's quirks. I wondered if she still did it, before answering my own question. There was no time for such hobbies when you were busy refashioning yourself as vengeance personified.

"Remember how her fingernails were always so dirty?" continued Payton. "Why she couldn't have worn gardening gloves like a normal person, I couldn't tell you."

I thought the dirty fingernails had gone well with the mussed-up hair and taped-up clothes, but before I could say anything about it, I remembered something else, something important. The something that had eluded me when Joan and I were investigating in the dining room.

"Wait," I said. "The waitress. Kendall. She was wearing gloves when she served dinner tonight, but she wasn't the night before." I turned to Joan. "Remember how she almost dropped the water glass on our first night? Because her hands were so sweaty?"

"Sure do," said Joan.

"You said foxglove can irritate the skin, right? And Kendall's the one who served us the salads. So what if she touched the foxglove and it irritated her hands? Maybe that's why she was wearing gloves."

"It's a possibility," Joan said slowly.

"Okay. Here's the plan." Payton picked up her phone again. "You two go and interview Kendall. She's in . . ." She fiddled with her screen, magnifying whatever was on it by spreading her thumb and middle finger apart. "Room 4. It's on this floor, just go down the hallway to your left when you're facing the elevator." She looked up. "I'm going to call Cheryl, and then the captain, to see about detaining Flora. I don't care what anyone says, it's got to be done."

She stabbed her phone with her index finger, and then held it up to her ear. I could hear the other line ringing, even though she hadn't put it on speaker. When she saw that we hadn't moved, she swept the air with her fingers, her meaning unmistakable: *Scoot!*

We scooted.

CHAPTER 21

"I know we're not supposed to use the word 'bossy' anymore." Joan opened the door marked CREW ONLY, and a flood of motion-sensitive fluorescence poured down on us. "Since it's used almost exclusively on women and all. But that is one bossy lady."

"You don't know the half of it," I assured her. "Do you think Kendall will even be awake?"

It wasn't quite four in the morning.

"If she's not, she's about to be," said Joan grimly.

We turned a corner, the light leading us toward what would have been called "steerage" a hundred years ago, and nowadays wasn't called much of anything. The corridor consisted of six dormitory-style rooms with a set of communal bathrooms. One was marked for men, the other for women: a meaningless designation on this outing, since every person who lived down here was a woman. The bathroom doors had been propped open, I guessed for better ventilation, and I was happy to see there were at least separate stalls for showers, each with its own grimy curtain. (And here I'd been complaining about the size and layout of my en suite bathroom.) There wasn't much ventilation to be had in this part of the ship, open door or not: the air felt stale, and stagnant, the way it does in a basement or attic that hasn't been opened in a while. This was where the ship's crew slept, along with the people who cleaned up for us and kept us fed. I already mentioned that a ship is a throwback to a bygone era when rigid class hierarchies were tolerated, and I couldn't help feeling like we were visiting the servants' quarters in a rambling country estate, where the have-nots were forced to live out their lives at the edges, belowstairs.

Joan stepped back, gesturing for me to knock on the door of Room 4. I held up my hand, pausing to make a face at her. She made one back in sympathy. Dreading having to knock louder, I knocked as gently as possible. To my surprise the door opened almost immediately, revealing a wide-awake Kendall in full uniform—white gloves and all.

Behind her, I could see that the room held two bunk beds and not much else besides a honeycomb of open cubbies on the wall opposite the door—in the place where the picturesque porthole window was in my room. This room didn't have a window, and by the light from the hallway I could see that the cubbies were a mess of clothes, wires, and even dirty dishware stacked here and there. If the air was stale in the hallway, it was downright fetid in here, and when I made eye contact with Kendall I registered a defensiveness I tried to pretend I hadn't noticed. I assumed a cheery expression I knew wouldn't fool her, and would succeed only in alienating her further. All this happened in approximately two seconds, but already we were off to a bad start.

Even though there was space for three roommates, she had just one: a woman in the top bunk to the right who was snoring loudly, and who I recognized as Sandra Gutierrez, the bartender of the as-yet-unrealized book deal. Sandra made a plaintive noise similar to Nicole's in the medical bay, followed by a tossing of her sheets. Kendall flapped the back of her hand at me, and when I took a few steps in reverse she followed me, turning around to shut the door behind her. This took a bit of time because she did so quietly, and it wasn't till the door was closed and she'd turned around again that she saw there were two of us. She froze.

"I didn't do anything wrong." Her eyes darted from me to Joan, and back again. She still hadn't moved, but it felt like she might rocket down the hall any moment. "I was just doing my job."

Joan stepped forward. "Of course you were. All we want is to go over what happened last night. So you can help us get to the bottom of things." She reached out, cupping Kendall's elbow with one hand. "Everything is going to be fine," she said kindly.

Kendall looked at her. I had no idea what she was thinking, but I was pretty sure she didn't believe everything was going to be fine.

We went to the lounge, which was as eerie as the dining room in the solitude of an early morning that felt like night. Even though the sky had acquired a smoky grayness portending the sun's arrival, I was glad the three (rather tacky) faux-chandeliers above us were blazing.

We sat at one of the tiny cocktail tables, in flimsy chairs made of clear plastic with glitter suspended throughout. They reminded me of those jelly watches, shoes, and phones that were so popular at one point in the nineties. (If you're too young to remember the nineties, you should be ashamed of yourself.) It felt wrong to be conducting an interview of such gravity—of *any* gravity—in chairs so clearly designed for frivolity.

I couldn't help noticing that when Kendall sat, she pressed her gloved hands between her knees, hiding them from view.

"Now Kendall and I know each other a little bit," Joan said to me, but it was obvious she was doing this for Kendall's benefit. "I did a quick consultation with each member of staff when they came on board, just to make sure everything was in working order. Which it was. Blood pressure was a little high for someone so young, but then working a cruise is stressful. You're going to make sure you keep an eye on that after you get home, yes?"

"Yes."

"Good. Now let me see if I can remember some of the vital stats, it's kind of my job to remember stuff like this. Your last name is Monteague, is that right?"

She nodded.

"And you grew up in Texas, where you still live."

Another nod.

"You have a daughter who's nine years old. Her name is . . . hold on, it'll come to me . . . Amelia! Is that right?"

I marveled at Joan's memory—and her people skills, her friendly demeanor stopping just short of condescension. And yet, at the mention of her daughter's name, Kendall's compact frame contracted further: she hunched her shoulders, doubling over at the stomach as though preparing for a physical blow.

"That's right," she said in a small voice.

Joan looked at me, tilting her head ever so slightly toward our subject. Her implication was clear: *Your turn.*

"It's nice to meet you, Kendall," I said, mimicking Joan's geniality. "Not meet you, really, we've seen each other for two days now, right?" I let loose a nervous laugh. "I guess I should say it's nice to properly *talk* to you for the first time!"

She pressed her lips together harder, staring at me with her grim matchstick of a mouth. I was reminded of the girls from my high school who worked at various recreational spots over the summer (the pool, the movies, the ice cream shop), and who I'd move heaven and earth to avoid interacting with as a customer. They were all so much cooler, and tougher, than I could ever be.

"Is this your first cruise?" I asked her.

"No. I work them whenever I can. They pay well."

I learned later that people who work on cruise ships make up to five times what they would make doing the same job on land.

"How did you find out about this one?"

"A friend of mine told me. We do them together sometimes, but she couldn't make this one."

"Why not?"

"She already had another job lined up. It wasn't a big deal. I applied on my own and got it."

"So you didn't know Payton Garrett before? Or her assistant, Jackson Richards?"

"I don't know anyone on this boat," she said.

"Until now!" chimed in Joan. "And since we've broken the ice, let's get down to why we knocked on your door at this ungodly hour. Sorry about that, by the way."

Kendall shrugged—another of her tiny, rapid-fire movements. If a bird ever shrugged, this was precisely how it would look.

"My first shift starts in half an hour," she said. "I wasn't sleeping."

"I'm glad we didn't put you out too much."

Joan paused, and something shimmied in the vicinity of my small intestine—as though my nether regions were hosting a wedding and had just busted out "the worm." It was time to get down to business.

"We noticed you started wearing gloves. Why is that?"

Kendall looked at her hands, but she didn't move them.

"Why don't you let me take a look?" Joan asked gently. "Maybe I can help."

Slowly, Kendall removed her hands from between her knees and peeled off her left glove.

I had to keep from gasping. Her hand was red and mottled,

like the surface of a pizza, and even though I didn't touch it (never would I have touched it), I could tell its texture was leathery like a pizza's, too. And it wasn't the back of her hand that was damaged, which is the part of the hand that tends to be affected when hands get chapped or otherwise irritated. It was her palms, the insides of her fingers. It looked like a rash gone wild: the skin all cracked and abraded. I even saw a few blisters on her fingertips. I wondered at the fact that she could tolerate having gloves over skin in such a condition. But then I've always had a low tolerance for pain—almost as abysmal as a man's.

"I can give you something for that," said Joan calmly. (I suppose she was used to such sights.) "Some calamine lotion at the very least. It'll get better on its own in a few days, I promise."

Kendall didn't respond. I got the sense that the alleviation of physical pain wasn't a priority for her. Not because she was impervious to it, but because she had more pressing concerns.

"How did this happen?" asked Joan. "And, please, don't pretend it was stress."

Kendall looked doubtfully from one to the other of us.

"Just tell us the truth," Joan said softly.

Her eyes landed on Joan, staying there. She puffed out her chest, and then: the little bird began to sing.

"There are shelves in the kitchen for the food we bring out to the dining room, after it's plated. Tables 1 and 2 are in the front, so it's easy to keep them straight. The plates get lined up in a row, and I put them on my tray."

Eight plates on one circular tray was a lot, but I'd already seen her do it.

"I put the four plates from Table 1 onto the tray when I realized I forgot the pepper mill."

Being offered fresh pepper with every course is a fiercely guarded right of the moneyed classes. I once saw a woman request it on a piece of tiramisu cake. I'm not joking.

"I went to get it but when I came back, I bumped against the tray with the four plates on it. They all fell onto the floor."

Up till then she'd been speaking in a low voice—so low I had to lean forward to hear her. Now her voice rose as if in protest.

"None of the food made contact with the floor."

I felt sure at least some of the salad had fallen directly on the floor.

"The plates didn't break, either. But the salad got all mixed up on the tray."

"And that's when you touched the leaves," said Joan.

"Yes."

"How quickly did you have a reaction?"

"Right away. Burning, itching, redness. It swelled up too, but that's gone now. I thought I was having an allergic reaction. I'm allergic to a lot of things."

Joan nodded. "That might explain why your reaction was as fast and extreme as it was."

"I put on gloves and finished putting the salad on the plates. And then I went out to the dining room. That's why I was late."

She stopped. Her story was over.

"Is that everything?" asked Joan.

She nodded. "I don't know anything else."

That was that, apparently.

I had a thought.

"Was there an order to the way the plates were lined up on the shelf?"

I remembered from my (short-lived) waitressing days that arranging the plates on your tray in a certain sequence— usually according to where people were sitting around the table—was the best way to ensure everyone got what they ordered without having to rely on your customers to tell you. (You'd be amazed how many idiots can't remember what they

ordered, or how annoyed people get if you dare ask them anything.)

Kendall nodded. "Mrs. Garrett's plate was always first."

"You can just call her Payton," said Joan, "I'm sure she'd
prefer it, less *Facts of Life*-y that way. But why did it matter
which plate she got? Wasn't everyone eating the same thing?"

Kendall hesitated, so I jumped in for her.

"It's a way to make sure the most important person gets a
good plate," I said. "I remember when I worked in a restaurant"—I neglected to add for how long—"I was surprised how
much the kitchen kept track of the food that was going to be
served to specific people."

The children of the man who owned the crappy Mexican
restaurant where I worked would eat there regularly, and the
head chef was always psychotic about their getting the best
version of everything. (It was in fact one of these children to
whom I accidentally served alcohol.)

"She's right," said Kendall. "Mrs. Garrett was the only person who had her own plate."

Joan and I looked at each other. Well, now *that* was interesting.

"But how could you be sure to serve it to her?" asked Joan.
"Since the food was all the same. Was the plate *itself* different?"

Kendall shook her head. "I put it in the center of the tray.
The center plate's always the first one I serve."

"But since you dropped the tray after loading it for Table 1,"
I said, trying hard to keep the excitement out of my voice, "the
salad meant for Payton got all mixed up. Right?"

"Right," she said reluctantly.

I looked at Joan. "They could have all been on her plate—"

Joan sliced the air with one hand, effectively shutting me
down.

"Who prepared the salads and put them on the plates?" she
asked.

"Chef."

"You mean Pierre Gasçoigne?"

Kendall nodded.

"Isn't that unusual?"

Another birdie shrug. "I guess. But there's hardly anyone on staff here. And some chefs like the control. They like doing everything themselves."

"Do you think he likes it?"

"No. He's been pretty grumpy the whole time."

"How long were the plates sitting out before you put them on your tray?" I asked.

"Twenty minutes. Thirty at most."

"And how many people knew about that first plate being for Payton?" asked Joan.

"Chef went over it with me, since I was the one serving her." She must have realized the implication of this, because then she added: "But it wasn't a secret. Everyone on staff knows how a kitchen works."

This made sense. The four waitresses responsible for the Hogwarts tables (Sandra plus three others) would have been aware of the practice. Which meant it wouldn't have been too hard for anyone on the ship to find out about it.

"Did you notice anyone in the kitchen last night who didn't belong there?" asked Joan.

"No," said Kendall immediately.

Joan smiled, but for the first time I could see her patience wearing thin. "You sure you don't want to think about that for a second?"

Kendall tilted her head to one side: the little birdie considering. . . . She righted her head again.

"Early on, that woman who sits at your table—"

"The captain?" I asked.

She shook her head. "The other one."

Talia Simmons, then.

"She came in to ask Chef about the menu. She did it the night before, too."

This lined up with Talia's fussiness, the way she had questioned Kendall at our table.

"I see," said Joan. "Anyone else?"

Kendall shook her head.

"You're sure?"

"Yes."

The sky had lightened during our conversation; it wasn't so much smoky as misty now—a mist I knew would dissipate the moment the sun made its appearance. One of Kendall's co-workers entered the room with a vacuum cleaner. She hesitated on the threshold, eyeing us curiously.

"It's okay!" called out Joan. "Do your thing. We're leaving."

The vacuum began whirring.

"How is Mrs. Garrett doing?" asked Kendall.

It was the first time she'd spoken voluntarily.

"She's better," Joan said cautiously. I tried catching her eye, but she refused to look my way. I could only imagine how Kendall was going to feel when she learned about Jackson Richards. It was a death she'd played a role in, however unwittingly. . . .

"I'm sorry she got sick. I never meant that to happen."

"Of course you didn't," said Joan kindly.

"I would never do anything other than what I was hired to do. All I want is to get paid, and go home."

"We understand," I said, doing my best to match Joan's tone.

Kendall turned to me. "My daughter—I'm all she has. I can't get into any trouble."

"I have a daughter too," said Joan. "And I know exactly what you're feeling. Don't worry, we'll do everything we can to keep you out of this."

I could see this brought her some relief, not that it "washed over" her, or induced her to relax in any way. She remained tightly wound, but perhaps a little further from the breaking point than she'd been at the beginning of the conversation.

"Thank you," she said.

"No, thank *you*." Joan stood up. "For your time. And your honesty."

CHAPTER 22

"Do you really think she's being honest, though?" I asked.

Kendall had gone off to the galley to help prepare the breakfast buffet, which would open for early risers at 5:30. We were both ravenous, and after running back to our respective cabins to dress for the day, we'd reconvened on one of the sofas in the lounge, waiting it out till 5:30. I'd put on the black jeans I wore the day I boarded, pairing them with a tight black turtleneck I've always thought looked slimming on me. Joan had shed the Matisse dress, and had on a pair of gray utility pants made of rough canvas, with horizontal seams above and below the knee, and a high elastic drawstring waistband that looked both stylish and comfortable. I suspected her light blue dress shirt was a man's, though if it was, it must have been extra-small because it fit her perfectly.

"She was so adamant about basically having no knowledge of anything," I continued.

"You mean, 'the lady doth protest too much, methinks.'"

"Yep. Gold star for putting the 'methinks' in the right place, by the way."

She pointed a finger gun at me, clicking through the side of her mouth. "The one thing I'll say is if she really *did* mean to poison someone, you'd think she'd have worn gloves when she touched the foxglove leaves. Unless she's an idiot. Which I don't think she is."

"Good point," I said. "That's probably what the real poisoner did."

"So you *don't* think she had anything to do with it?"

I hesitated, considering the question. "No," I said finally. "I don't. She has zero motive, unless she's lying about knowing someone on the boat. And I don't see why she *would* know anyone. I guess someone could have paid her to poison the salad."

"You think?"

"It's possible, but at that point we're getting into contract killer territory. Did she seem like a contract killer to you?"

"No," admitted Joan. "But is that sexist of us? And/or ageist?"

"Well, you know what they say. If you have to ask the question. . . ."

The woman with the vacuum cleaner came nearer. We lifted our feet off the ground, tucking our legs under us while smiling manically and doing that head bobbing thing you do when you want to be perceived as *extremely* friendly and nonthreatening.

"It's not like she had any special opportunity," I yelled into Joan's ear. "Anyone working in the galley could have tampered with Payton's plate. Including the chef."

"You think celebrity chef Pierre Gasçoigne is secretly a murderer?"

It's difficult to sound skeptical while shouting, but Joan was pulling it off.

"I mean, have you seen him?"

I shook my head. I had no idea what he looked like, but then, I couldn't pick Gordon Ramsay or Jamie Oliver out of a lineup, either. Come to think of it, the only living chef I could identify on sight was Guy Fieri, thanks to those frosted tips.

The woman moved on. We lowered our feet.

"It didn't even have to be someone who worked in the kitchen," Joan pointed out. "Anyone could have gone in there. All they had to do was put on a black shirt and pants and a white apron, and they'd blend right in. Ballsy move, but it's possible."

"Well, we know Talia didn't blend in," I said. "Maybe that speaks in her favor."

"It might. I still want to know what was going on between her and Jackson. Remember when he gave her that thumb drive at dinner? What was that about? Something was going on there, no question."

I agreed, but before I could say anything further, Flora Fortescue raced into the room.

She was in sweats and a T-shirt that was so ragged, it was almost see-through at the shoulders. Her ponytail bore no relation to the stiff and immaculate version she'd been sporting yesterday, or if it was a relation, it was a poor and downtrodden one with its low, lazy cinch. A limp curtain of hair had escaped from it on both sides, framing her unmade face. Most jarring of all: she was barefoot. It was obvious she'd rushed out of her room in her pajamas, and I found this heartening because it meant that when Flora was by herself, she still dressed like the old Flora. If Flora 2.0 were real, she would have worn a silk negligee or lace teddy, or some other frilled monstrosity, her fluffy heels positioned *just so* for slipping on the moment her feet touched the ground.

"Oh, thank God," she cried out, covering the considerable distance between us and the door in no time.

"I take it you've heard?" I asked her coolly. "About Jackson?"

"Captain Weirdo woke me up and told me."

I guessed that Payton had insisted the captain do something when they spoke, and that the captain had obeyed.

"She actually implied I had something to do with it! I

LOOSE LIPS / 183

thought she was going to lock me up or something, but I was able to get rid of her pretty easily. I called and texted you but you didn't answer."

"I have my phone on 'do not disturb.' We've been busy," I said, gesturing to include Joan, who nodded at her.

"I'm sure. When you didn't answer, I figured you might be somewhere up here." She flopped onto the white leather sofa opposite ours. "You have to talk to Payton. I'm sure this is coming from her."

"It is."

I gave her an abbreviated rundown of what Payton had said in the medical bay.

"I hope you told her she's being ridiculous!"

"Oh, but Flora, how could I possibly have done that?" I tilted my head exactly as Kendall had. "After all, I'm just a sheep in wolf's clothing. All I care about is whether people like me. *You're* the wolf. You're much better equipped for this sort of thing than I am."

I saw the despair in her eyes. I'm not lying—truly—when I say I felt sorry for her. But I suppose I felt sorrier for me.

"You said yourself, in this very room, you were out for revenge. You couldn't have been clearer about it. Also, I only ever look out for myself, right? I'm a . . . how did you put it, again? Hold on, gimme a second, it was such an artful turn of phrase. . . . A selfish bitch. That was it, wasn't it? Yeah, a selfish bitch. That's what I am."

"Please don't do this," she begged me. "I was a total asshole to you and I'm sorry. You have to know I didn't mean a word I said to you yesterday, it was all bullshit. *I'm* bullshit. I had zero plans other than to make Payton suffer in whatever stupid little ways I could figure out. And you're a great writer, everyone's always known that, I've always been so jealous of you. Payton too. She can't *stand* what a good writer you are!"

She was laying it on too thick—and yet I crossed my arms, inviting her to continue.

"You *know* me," she pleaded. "You know I would never do anything like this. I'm not a murderer! I can't believe I even have to say that to you!"

She paused. I paused longer.

"Come on, say something. Anything. Even if it's just to yell at me. Come on, get it off your chest. I deserve it. I'm listening, I promise."

I opened my mouth, as though I were about to speak. And then I counted out five seconds in my head. I'm not proud of this, but I knew a pause would make for a better dramatic effect when at long last I said my piece.

"Baaaaaaaa. Baaaaaaaa."

The thing is, I believed her. I didn't think for a second that Flora Fortescue was capable of murder. I, on the other hand, was extremely capable of sadism.

Flora tipped over at the waist, her head smashing sideways into the seat of the couch. "Payton's going to ruin me," she wailed. "She already took away my career. Now she's going to take away my *liberty*."

Oh, Lord. If only they knew how similar they were—a twin pair of drama queens. It would have been adorable if it wasn't so annoying.

"What if someone wanted to kill Jackson?" she suggested hopefully from her recumbent position. "Has anyone thought about that? He was awful too."

"As you yourself pointed out yesterday," I said. "Remember? When you said you had 'something planned' for him?"

She sat up again. "So I'm being framed either way, is that it?"

"No one is framing anyone," Joan said calmly. She'd been watching me and Flora with an anthropological fascination, and I appreciated the injection of sanity.

Unfortunately, Flora didn't seem to have heard her. She was

staring into the distance, lost in thought, and when her eyes cleared a few seconds later, she let out a gasp so loud, it made me jump.

"Of course!" she cried. "It makes perfect sense!"

"What does?" I asked her warily.

"Remember how I told you I got onto this cruise?"

"I do," I said, "because it never made sense to me. So how'd you really get on? Whose invitation did you borrow?"

She shook her head impatiently. "That's just it, I was telling you the truth. I got an invitation in the mail with my name on it. Then I signed up as 'Augusta Leigh.' I figured someone would get in touch with me, tell me my invitation was rescinded, but they never did. And then when I walked onto the ship, I wore sunglasses and a big straw hat—"

Of course you did, I thought.

"But he recognized me anyway. Jackson recognized me, I *know* he did, because he smirked at me."

"Dude smirked a lot," I pointed out.

She shook her head again. "No, he *did*, I could tell. I just figured he didn't care, or was getting a kick out of the drama of it all. But don't you see?" She stood up, drawing closer to us. "I was *lured* onto this ship. So that I could take the fall."

"And you think Jackson was involved in the luring? How would that have worked?" I asked. "Whatever was going on, it ended up killing him. Are you saying Jackson poisoned himself?"

"No, I'm saying *Payton* poisoned him."

I ventured a glance at Joan, who was regarding Flora with confusion. At this point, confusion struck me as charitable.

"Think about it," Flora continued. "It's the only way it makes sense for me to have gotten on the boat. She *had* to have seen my name at some point! And if you're planning on killing your assistant and making it look like *you* were the intended victim, I'm the perfect person to have around. I'll bet she swallowed something *else* to make her throw up like that. Just to sell it. Foxglove leaves affect your heart, right? Do they even make you throw up?"

"How did you know it was foxglove that killed him?" I asked.

"The captain told me, duh."

I'd have to check on this later. "But how do you know about the effect of foxglove?" I persisted. "Seems like pretty specialized knowledge."

"Wikipedia," she said. "I looked it up after the captain told me what was in the salad."

"I thought you said you ran straight here?"

"Ooh, you got me there. I guess I waited a minute or two to do some Googling, which means I must be the killer. Belle Currer, mistress of mystery, strikes again!"

"All right, all right," said Joan. "Settle down, children. The thing is, digitalis *can* induce vomiting. And there's no way Payton was pretending when it came to her heart symptoms. She was in legitimate distress. I would've known if she were faking it."

"That doesn't mean a little mild self-poisoning wasn't part of the plan. Maybe she just overdid it. It's *Payton*, after all."

Flora drew closer—close enough that I could smell her morning breath.

"Isn't that a thing in mysteries? Like a trope? The intended victim did it?"

"Why, though?" I asked. "Why would Payton want to kill Jackson?"

"Why not?" she shot back. "He was the worst, everyone knew it. I'll bet you he had some dirt on her and was using it to try to get ahead in publishing. He was a frustrated writer. Like all of us."

"Not me," I said lightly. "Everyone's jealous of *me*."

This merited a snort from Joan.

Wisely, Flora ignored my interruption. "You know there's been a rumor for a while that Payton's been cheating on Nicole? With a *guy*. Not a good look, right? I wouldn't put it past Jackson to get some sort of physical proof and then hold it over her. I'll bet this whole cruise was an excuse to get rid of him. If she tried something back home in New York, it would be too easy to trace it back to her."

I was by no means convinced. Just as I found it impossible to believe that Flora was a killer, I felt the same about Payton. Was I being naïve, though? Stick around long enough in this world and eventually things happen to you that you imagine happening only to "other" people. I was already intimately acquainted with death.

Was it so hard to believe I could be intimately acquainted with a murderer?

CHAPTER 23

Flora ran away soon after that, to place a call to her family's lawyer.

I told Joan about my difficulty believing either Payton or Flora could have gone through with murdering a person.

"I'm with you on Payton," she said. "Murder is stupid, and Payton doesn't do stupid. But Flora Fortescue has proven over the last two days she does lots of stupid things."

"Murder, though?"

"She might not have meant to kill anyone. Maybe she wanted to humiliate Payton, or scare her. Can't you see it? If everything at that dinner last night had gone slightly differently?"

I could—just.

"If you think about it, putting foxglove leaves in a salad feels like more of a prank than a murder plot. It's so . . . quaint."

She had a point.

"But then Kendall dropped the tray and unknowingly distributed foxglove to everyone at Table 1, and Jackson ended up dying. A series of unfortunate events Flora couldn't have predicted would happen. But it's still murder. I'm not a lawyer, but my guess is it'd be second-degree rather than first-degree. Maybe that's what she's asking her lawyer about right now."

Oh no. I had to admit this all sounded plausible. Had Flora bumbled her way into committing homicide?

We ate breakfast on the dot of 5:30. I went for oatmeal out of one of those big metal vats. Packaged cereal eaten dry would have been a safer option, but I needed something to stick to my bones, and there was no reason to think anyone's food would be tampered with again. (Looking back, I'm surprised how blasé I was about the possibility of being poisoned. I guess I really wanted that oatmeal—and the brown sugar I piled on top of it.) Joan opted for more of a traditional English breakfast of eggs, sausage, and toast. It was a shame they didn't have any of those soupy baked beans. Despite my aversion to hot breakfasts, I definitely would have gotten some of those if they'd been on offer.

We didn't talk about the case while we were eating. In fact, we didn't talk about much of anything. I was surprised by how quickly we'd graduated to the "comfortable silence" phase of our friendship, but there's nothing like the pressure cooker of a closed-circle murder to bring two strangers together. I know that people get in trouble when they compare any experience to being in combat other than *literally* being in combat, and I understand why. A soldier's experience is unique— and uniquely important—and it's offensive to pretend otherwise. And yet I couldn't help likening the two of us to comrades-in-arms fortifying ourselves for the day to come, the war raging around us. . . .

Our fortification was still in process when we were ambushed. We were sitting on the dais—at our usual table in our usual seats—which meant I was facing the side of the dining room that communicated with the galley, while Joan was facing the temporary breakfast buffet. For this reason, it was she who saw them first.

"Three weird sisters, incoming," she muttered.

I turned. My three mystery students, Phyllis, Theresa, and June, were hovering behind me. Their plates were steaming and piled high, and they each had an expectant look on their faces.

"Do you mind?" I muttered back at her.

"Not at all," she said. "I'm pretty sure I'm going to enjoy this."

I waved them over. They tramped up the steps a little self-consciously, though in Phyllis's case, her slowness was partially due to some pain she was experiencing.

"Back acting up?" I asked.

"Like you wouldn't believe," she said. "Though by all means, please *do* believe me."

"I hope we're not intruding?" asked Theresa nervously.

We assured them they weren't. It took them some time to deposit their meals on the table, since Theresa had been carrying June's plate for her, which meant she had to go back for beverages, and then leave again to get an extra chair. Once this was done, I introduced Phyllis and Theresa to Joan. (She and June had already met over their cozy chat about norovirus.) "My star students," I added.

"Not counting Helen." June's eyes twinkled above her coffee mug. "We all know Helen's the showstopper."

It had been hours since I'd thought of Helen Sanchez. I scanned the room for her, but she was nowhere to be seen. *Probably writing*, I thought with a pang. There would be no morning writing session for me today.

"I assume class is canceled?" asked Theresa. "I know the boat was already turned around."

I nodded. To be honest, the thought of conducting classes hadn't even occurred to me. "I don't think it would feel right, under the circumstances."

"Just as well," said June. "I could use the cash back, this was a pricey trip."

Oof. I did not envy the sorting of legal/ethical/reputational concerns Payton had ahead of her when it came to reimbursing—or not—the passengers of the Get Lit Cruise, which had never gotten the chance to get properly lit. (Fortunately, I'd insisted my fee be paid upfront.)

"I assume you've got your own muscle relaxers," Joan said to Phyllis, changing the conversation tactfully. "But I've got a pretty excellent heat pad you could use down in the bay if you'd like."

"I may take you up on that," said Phyllis. "Depending on how the morning shakes out."

"Bless you, doll." June reached out and patted Joan's hand. "What a godsend it is to have a capable doctor on board."

"I didn't sleep well last night," said Phyllis. "But then, did anyone?"

We all agreed we'd slept terribly, or in Joan's case, not at all.

Phyllis took another slug of coffee. "And then to wake up to this awful news about Payton's assistant!"

Up till then I hadn't been sure how much they knew. But of course they knew. Such news travels at lightning speed.

"Jackson Richards," said Theresa. "We should always name victims whenever possible. Unless they'd prefer to remain anonymous."

I was pretty sure Jackson Richards would have preferred to have his name shouted as loudly and widely as possible, but I kept this to myself.

"That's right, doll. Give the poor fellow as much respect as we can. How are the others doing?" June asked. "Do you think they'll make it, Doctor?"

"I wouldn't be very good at my job if I spoke openly about my patients' medical condition," said Joan apologetically.

"I still can't believe this happened," commented Phyllis. But the excitement in her voice far outweighed any sadness or concern.

"So!" June struck the ground lightly with her cane. "What leads have you got?"

I at least appreciated her candor. I thought back to Gerry the night before, whose excitement had so repulsed me. Maybe I hadn't been fair to her. If Payton and Flora had been strangers to me, I might have been enjoying myself too.

Theresa put down her fork. "They obviously can't tell us anything, June."

"Worth a try," June grumbled.

Theresa picked up her fork again. "I keep thinking about what you said in class."

I raised my eyebrows in a question.

"About access, and means. And how to apply it positively to figure out who was more likely to have done it."

It was the first time I'd experienced the professorial thrill of hearing a point I'd made explained back to me by someone who gets it. I can only imagine what it must be like when that someone is a child and the lesson is fundamental—about reading, or algebra, or history. I nodded, encouraging her to continue.

"The problem is that *everyone* here has access," she said. "It's not like the murder happened in a locked room or some special part of the boat that only a few people could reach."

"Well, we don't really know *where* the murder happened, do we?" asked Phyllis.

"I think we do," said Theresa. "And I know you can't tell us anything, but it's pretty obvious somebody put something in the salad."

She gestured to the table beside us, which still hadn't been touched. It remained frozen in mid-crisis, like those village scenes uncovered in Pompeii, and we all stared at it with a horrified fascination.

"Well, in that case"—Phyllis adjusted herself painfully in her seat—"any one of the three hundred people on this ship could have done it."

"The waitstaff would have had an advantage," said Theresa. "They're in the kitchen constantly."

"Why would anyone *other* than the waitstaff go in there?" I asked—more in teacher mode than detective mode. I wasn't about to invite these three into our investigation, but I was enjoying watching them think.

"*I* went in there, on the first night," said Phyllis. "To see if they had any pink Himalayan salt, which they didn't. It's anti-inflammatory," she explained. "Does wonders for my psoriasis, among other ailments. Take it from me, *anyone* could have popped into the galley a little before dinner. It's chaos in there. The chef's in a separate room and all the servers are running all over the place. It's not like anyone's keeping watch. It would be a risk, but it's doable."

"That's the other thing," said Theresa. "We all spend heaps of time alone in our cabins, which is the nature of a cruise. But it makes alibis a lot less useful than if we were going about our regular lives."

She was right. I was reminded of what Flora had said, about the advantages of being on a cruise surrounded by suspects, as opposed to on dry land, where any such opportunities for obfuscation would be thinner.

"This is all very interesting," I said. "But the captain is already in contact with the police, and we'll be back in New York by midday tomorrow. Till then, the priority is to keep everyone safe. *Not* to investigate."

"That's right," said Joan. "Any and all amateur sleuthing is strictly prohibited." She held up an admonitory index finger. "There will be no Jessica Fletcher-ing aboard this vessel, is that understood?"

"Got it, doll. As long as that rule goes for the two of you as well?"

"Of course," I said, embracing my role of gumshoe gate-keeper. Not that I was very good at it, because when I caught June's eye, her expression was unmistakable.

Sure, Jan.

Or whatever the octogenarian spin on that phrase may be.

CHAPTER 24

Pierre Gasçoigne was high on our list of people to question. Unfortunately, he was not in the galley yet, and when we asked Kendall, she said he never made an appearance till later in the morning. We took the opportunity to ask her coworkers whether they'd seen any passengers in the galley the night before, and once again, the only name that came up was Talia Simmons.

When we returned to the medical bay after breakfast, Jessamine LaBouchère was sitting on the visitors' bench. Payton was nowhere to be seen.

"She left about twenty minutes ago," explained Jessamine. Her crimson bathrobe had seen better days, but it looked comfortable. She was crocheting, of course, her metal hook flashing in the flat, fluorescent light. "Just after I arrived. She asked me to keep an eye on her." She nodded at Nicole, who was resting more peacefully than before. "I couldn't sleep after you came to check on me," she explained to Joan. "So I figured I'd come down here and check on the state of things."

Joan walked over to the EKG machine, which had been powered down. She flicked it on and then off again.

"She turned it off because when she pulled the sensors off her, it started beeping. She was worried it would wake *her* up."

196 / KEMPER DONOVAN

Jessamine gestured with her hook to Nicole. "It felt like some-one should have rushed in shouting 'Code red!' or something. I once set a novel in a hospital and followed around a doctor for a while, looking for exactly those sorts of phrases. I didn't get much. The reality was more mundane, as it so often is."

For once, Joan wasn't playing. "I should have gotten an alert when this went offline." She turned to me, holding up the slick, slightly bloody needle that lay abandoned on the bed, leaking IV fluid. "She just ripped it out of her hand, can you believe that?"

I could, actually. In our first year of grad school, Payton had come down with the flu—a rare illness for her and a true case of influenza, not just a flu-like cold. I'd gone to the hospital to hand-deliver her enormous, early-aughts laptop to her so that she could keep working. I can still see her crushing the IV bag in her free hand to get as much hydration as possible before sneak-ing away with me in much the same manner, while the nurses were busy elsewhere. I remembered giving her a Band-Aid from the first aid kit in my car to use on the back of her hand, where the IV needle had gone in. And how, rather than thanking me, she'd made fun of me for having a first aid kit in my car. . . .

Despite this memory, I shook my head. "No" was clearly the answer Joan was looking for.

She turned to Jessamine. "Do you know where she went?" For the first time since I'd known her, she sounded angry.

"She said she had a million things to do, and that if you asked, she's fine now, she couldn't lie here all day."

"Well, I'm glad she has the medical expertise to make that decision."

Just then the PA system turned on, and we froze in Pav-lovian expectation.

"Hey, ladies. This is Payton. I have an important message."

I was glad she'd identified herself, because her voice was un-recognizable. Gone was the knowing lilt, the exclamatory silkiness of her opening announcement on Sunday. She was all business now, with a clipped and brittle cadence not unlike the late Queen's.

"As many of you are no doubt aware, we lost a fellow passenger in the night. My beloved assistant Jackson Richards will be missed, and I ask on behalf of myself and his family and friends that you refrain from jumping to any conclusions about what may have caused his death. In particular, I ask that you refrain from posting anything on social media. There is no reason to assume anyone here is in any danger whatsoever, but please know the ship has already turned around, and is due to reach the Clifton dock in Staten Island in a little over a day's time. All classes and lectures have been canceled, and I encourage you to remain in your cabins, though you aren't required to do so. Should you have any questions or concerns, I ask that you use the phone number and e-mail address in your welcome packet, and I will respond to you as quickly as I can. I am so sorry this happened."

Her emotions overcame her, her voice nearly cracking. She paused to compose herself.

"I had the highest hopes for our time together. Maybe someday we can do it again, with greater success. For now let's be kind to one another, and do what we can to look out for each other and keep us all safe. We ladies have to stick together. In good times, but also in the not-so-good times. So stay safe out there, and take care."

Allow me to remind you: it wasn't quite six in the morning. But I guessed that disturbing her passengers' rest was the last thing on Payton's mind. As it was, Nicole was sleeping so deeply, she hadn't stirred.

"You two seem to have had a busy morning." Jessamine's eyes were cast downward on a fresh ball of gray yarn. She was nearly done with another gun cozy. I decided to ignore her implicit question, and ask her one of my own.

"Why did you put all those leaves to one side of your plate?"

She waited to finish whatever stitch she was doing, which gave her some time to compose an answer. When she relinquished her hook, she pulled her bathrobe more tightly around her, looking for a moment much older than her usual self—more like the septuagenarian she was.

"Were those fuzzy leaves the ones that did it?" she asked quietly.

"Seems like it," I said.

"Though nothing is confirmed," Joan hastened to add.

"Why didn't you eat them?" I asked her again. "You ate everything else."

"You'll laugh at me," she said. "But I didn't like the look of them, so I picked them out much the way my grandchildren do with their food. Drives me batty when they do it."

She was lying. Her discomfort was palpable. I felt Jessamine LaBouchère was not someone who lied often, so it made sense to me that she was doing such a poor job of it.

But the question remained: If she'd put the leaves aside because she knew they were poisoned, why would she have left them on her plate like that for anyone to find? It made no sense.

"I think I'll return to my room now." She rose with ease, looking spry and strong again. "And endeavor to get some shut-eye."

It wasn't till the elevator doors had closed on her that we realized she'd left her crochet work on the bench.

"I could go after her?" I offered. "Not that I have any idea where her room is."

"Nah, leave it here," said Joan. "That way she'll know where to find it."

"It's a little surprising she left it behind," I said. "She seems addicted to crocheting."

"Maybe she's not herself because she just murdered a man," suggested Joan brightly.

"That was weird though, right? About the leaves? Didn't you feel like she was lying to us?"

Joan nodded soberly.

"I just don't see why she'd want to kill Payton," I continued. "Or Jackson. Although, other than Flora, I could say the same for pretty much everyone on board."

"It's not enough that Jackson was a jerk?" Joan paused. "And Payton, for that matter? In her own way?"

"Not unless you go around killing every jerk you come across. If I did that I'd be a record-breaking serial killer by now. I'd also be dead because I would have killed myself ages ago."

"Same. But at the very least, it makes sense to start with the people who were also poisoned and didn't die, since it's such a good cover, you know? And where Payton's concerned, it sounds like maybe she had a good motive to kill Jackson."

"You mean"—I glanced at Nicole, making sure she was still asleep—"the cheating thing?"

Joan nodded. "It's possible."

I had another thought.

"Hold on. What if it's the other way around?"

"What do you mean?"

"Remember when Flora was saying how only someone who worked for Payton could have arranged for her to be on the ship?"

"Sure. What does that have to do with anything?"

"Well, what if *Jackson* was the one who arranged for Flora to be here? He could have done it easily." Joan was stripping Payton's gurney, and I waited till she looked up at me to continue. "What if Jackson had planned all along to kill *Payton*?"

I told her about Jackson's guilt-ridden expression when Payton had first gotten sick during dinner.

"And then, in the ultimate form of poetic justice," Joan said, working it out, "he ends up killing himself. I mean, it's possible?"

"He might not even have meant to kill her. Couldn't you see him doing it as a prank, just as easily as Flora? A way for him to get back at Payton for being a terrible boss, which I'm sure she was. He could even eat a few leaves himself, get a little sick, no harm done. He probably thought his body was a lot stronger than it was. And then he could blame it all on Flora. It tracks."

"Definitely an interesting theory," said Joan, though I could tell she was less enthused about it than I was. Just as I was about to advocate for its merits, a third voice asserted itself in the room:

"You two have all *sorts* of theories, don't you?"

Uh-oh.

How long had Nicole Root been awake?

CHAPTER 25

Nicole failed to follow up her dramatic interruption with anything explicit about what she may or may not have overheard. Instead, she focused on getting out of the medical bay as soon as possible. She insisted she was feeling better—perfect, even. After a thorough examination, Joan agreed to discharge her, though she was adamant about accompanying her to her cabin. I was pretty sure this was an excuse to confront Payton, and I tagged along to watch—also, because tagging along is what sidekicks do. The sooner I was honest with myself about my role, the better. If I was going to be Hastings, I could at least be a self-aware Hastings. And this way I could take pride in my superior taste in amateur sleuths: first Dorothy Gibson, now Joan Chen.

As I mentioned earlier, Payton and Nicole's room was across from the elevator, so we had a short walk upon reaching the third deck. Just before we got to Room 101, the door opened, and out walked Helen Sanchez.

"What are you doing here?" I demanded.

Helen opened her eyes in surprise, which gave them the effect of being wider than they already were: as wide as two eyes could go before they stopped being considered in relation to each other and became singular objects—like the way a flounder has one eye on either side of its head. Come to think of it, she didn't look unlike a flounder—or maybe the product of an unholy union between a mermaid and a flounder. A very lovely product, for all its unholiness.

"I was asking Payton for some advice," she said.

Did I detect a hint of reproach in her tone? Was she *angry* with me for not agreeing to read her manuscript? Did she *dare?*

"Advice on how to avoid a criminal prosecution for breaking and entering, I hope?"

This was nonsense; I had no intention of pressing charges against her. Given all that had happened since finding Helen's manuscript on my bed, it felt ridiculous to harp on such a minor offense. And yet she was so unrepentant, I couldn't help myself.

"Simmer down, Belle."

Payton appeared now in the doorway of Room 101. She stood behind the girl, putting her hands on her shoulders—as though *Helen* needed protecting. From me.

"Helen told me what she did. She knows she was wrong, and she's very sorry. Isn't that right, Helen?"

Helen nodded. "I'm sorry."

Her delivery was robotic. I didn't believe her for a second.

But then Nicole fell into Payton's arms, and Joan ushered them both inside, already remonstrating about the importance of following medical advice.

Helen and I were left alone in the hallway.

"How did you even know where my room was?" I asked her.

"I saw your key," she replied coolly. "In class."

It was true that each key clearly stated its room number on a circular disc that served as a key ring. *Fine.*

"But how did you get in?"

"It wasn't locked."

"Now you're lying."

I always lock my door. *Always.* I consider this practice to be fundamental to my identity, as it reflects my issues with trust and intimacy, my general state of paranoia, and my ongoing struggle with compulsive behaviors. In fact, the next time I'm asked to describe myself in as few words as possible, instead of refusing on the principle that I love words—and detest such exercises—I might answer: *Always locks door.*

"I'm not lying," said Helen.

"Even if it were unlocked," I said, "*which it wasn't,* you still shouldn't have walked into my room and left your manuscript there. It was a total violation."

"Do you remember?" she asked. "What it was like before you were published?"

Of course I did. "Of course I do. But I never broke the law."

"Do you remember how desperate you felt?"

Against my will, I nodded. A word like *desperate* is so often an exaggeration. But in the case of an unpublished writer, it's dead-on.

"I'm sorry I went into your room. But I was desperate. And when you're desperate, you'll do anything."

"I don't know if that's something I'd be telling a lot of people right now," I said. "That you'd do *anything.*"

I saw the confusion cloud her lovely eyes, and for a moment I wondered if she even knew about Jackson Richards. Was she so absorbed in her quest for publication that she wasn't aware a fellow passenger had died?

"You can't think I had anything to do with that man's death."

Never mind: she knew. She just didn't care. Unless she was lying. . . .

"I can think whatever I like," I said. "And as of now, I haven't ruled out anything."

I turned away, opening Payton's door and closing it behind me. But even as I was effecting this triumphant exit, I considered the possibility that Helen Sanchez wasn't lying about my door being open. Because if she wasn't, it meant that someone else had entered my room and left it unlocked.

But who? And why? And most crucially: *how?*

Inside Room 101, a much friendlier argument was underway. "I know, I know, I'm the worst," Payton was saying.

"I just want to be very clear that less than twelve hours ago, your heart, which is responsible for pumping all the blood, hence oxygen, to all your body's organs *including your brain*, was not doing what it was designed to do. It seems to be functioning okay now, but until you can get a proper workup it's critical that you rest."

Joan was pacing back and forth in front of the king-size bed, upon which Payton had been induced to sit with her back against the headboard, knees raised for the purpose of propping up her laptop. (I guessed from the din of rushing water coming from the bathroom that Nicole was taking a shower.)

"I promise"—Payton's phone began to ring; she paused to silence it—"I promise to rest as much as I can, trapped on a boat with a murderer on the loose and my business empire crumbling around me." Her phone rang again. "See what I mean?" She raised her screen to eye-level. "Oh hell no, no way I'm talking to *her* right now." Again she silenced it. "I am getting *destroyed* on social media, you should see some of the Tik-Toks they're *beyond* vicious. Do you know the first thing Cheryl asked me when I talked to her? Cheryl ay-kay-ay Jackson's mom?"

Joan shook her head.

"Whether I think this was a hate crime. I'm just praying she doesn't say anything like that online. She has a Twitter account but she hasn't used it in, like, two years." Payton sighed dramatically. "If I knew Flora Fortescue was under lock and key somewhere, that would definitely make me rest easier."

I stepped forward. "I'm not so sure that's going to happen."

I explained about our conversation with Flora, ending with her consultation of a lawyer.

"Wow," said Payton. "I'm almost impressed. I never thought she had all this in her."

Nicole emerged from the bathroom on a cloud of steam, like some minor goddess of lavation, one towel wrapped around her body and another on her head. Never have I seen two bath towels rocked so hard; she seriously could have been modeling them on a runway. Payton reached out for her, and Nicole came to the bed. They threaded their hands together, swinging them from side to side.

"*So* glad to have you back, babe," said Payton softly.

"And I am in awe of how you're handling all this."

"You know, I was thinking about what Meg said, the last time we were talking"—she looked around at Joan and me—"that's Meghan Markle, the Duchess of Sussex."

Oh, for fuck's sake.

"And she was talking about how you have to take challenges as they come, you can't let them overpower you. *I'm* in control of that, you know? I'm in control of what I let them do to me."

Nicole let out a corroborative murmur.

"I mean, there are so many people who've had it way harder than me. I can do this. *We* can do this."

Nicole kissed the back of Payton's hand before releasing it, and then she headed for the closet, closing the door behind her—except that before it shut all the way, it flew open again, Nicole rushing, wild-eyed, into the middle of the room.

"My necklace!" she cried. "It's gone!"

CHAPTER 26

The safe was the same as the one in my cabin—one of the few items in the palatial Room 101 that hadn't been upgraded. It was made of a black metallic alloy, and looked like a dumpy microwave or toaster oven, less than six inches in height. I'd noticed the one in my cabin because like most of the safes I've come across in the thousands of hotel rooms I've occupied over the years, the door hung open and got in the way, and even though I didn't put anything in it, I had to lock it by way of its analog dial to keep it from being a nuisance. I've always regarded these safes with disdain: the kind of thing people who want to *seem* rich and important would use, whereas truly rich and important people make other plans. Every time I see one, the same thought passes through my mind. *Who actually uses that thing?*

Now I had my answer.

The safe in Room 101 had been lifted off the shelf where it lived and thrown to the closet floor. I'm afraid the abuse didn't end there. Someone had taken a hammer to it, smashing the dial to the point where it hung off the front panel—wrenched, pummeled, all but severed into a hideous, nearly unrecognizable form. The door of it was hanging open, of course, and there were dents, scratches, and scuff marks littering its body.

If it had been made of flesh rather than metal, it would have died from blood loss—though the blunt-force trauma probably would have killed it first. The poor thing had been violated and then emptied, and now it was useless. It was officially the corpse of a safe.

In a twist that surprised no one, the captain turned out to be an amateur cryptographer. She was performing a necropsy on the corpse in the main area of Room 101, where there was more space to work. I watched along with Payton, Nicole, and Joan as she fiddled with the dial, forcibly putting it back where it belonged—like a doctor resetting a dislocated nose. She spun the dial, closed the door, and tried to open it again. It was locked now.

"This is weird," she said finally.

Which part? I thought.

"I'm nearly positive the safe was opened the normal way, and then smashed."

"How could you possibly know that?" asked Joan with interest.

"The locking mechanism is intact," she replied. "Which means it must have retracted inside the dial when the dial was smashed. If it had been engaged when the dial came off the panel, the mechanism would have been ruined, and I wouldn't have been able to relock it. What's the combination?"

"Three, thirty-one, eighteen," said Nicole.

"Our wedding date," added Payton. "Feel free to go 'awwwwwww' now."

But none of us did. We were too busy watching the captain. The safe's dial functioned like those Master Locks so many of us had in high school. First, she turned it three full rotations to the right, stopping at three. Then one full rotation to the left, stopping at thirty-one. And then a final, lightning-quick spin to eighteen. I'd forgotten how entering a combination on a Master Lock had a rhythm to it, a cadence that picked up in speed, ending in a rapid-fire flourish on that third number followed by a quick tug on the body of the lock, and the satisfying release of the horseshoe-shaped shackle. But in this case, something merely clicked inside the front panel, and the door swung open.

"Still works," said the captain. She looked up at Nicole. "I'm ninety-nine percent sure whoever stole your necklace knew the combination. Or guessed it. You shouldn't use a wedding anniversary or a birthday, you know. It's too easy."

"My fault," said Payton. "I've always been lazy about passwords. I never think people are going to actually steal my stuff. It seems so . . . clichéd."

"Was there anyone else who knew the combination?" I asked. "Other than you two?"

"Jackson knew it," said Payton. "I remember him coming in here when we were setting it. It was the first day we were on the ship, a few days before we set sail. He made fun of us for using our wedding anniversary and called us cornballs." She turned to Nicole. "Do you remember?"

"I do," said Nicole grimly. "The actual word he used was 'cheesy,' which allowed him to make a vile allusion to the female anatomy."

"Ever the charmer, that Jackson," said Payton wistfully.

"And you never opened it up in front of anyone else?"

"Never," said Nicole.

"Okay." I'd been sitting in the comfy armchair that didn't exist in my cabin, but I stood up now so that everyone could see me. "Let's try to narrow down the window of time for when this could have happened."

"Wow, someone's been getting her sleuth on," observed Payton. "Should we bust out the corkboard and thumbtacks?"

She was smiling, but her irritation was plain enough. She hated not being in control.

"I'm just trying to help, Payton."

"Never mind me," she cried, waving her hands in front of her. "I'm just a bad patient who's going stir-crazy. Go on. I'll behave. I promise."

"Now that's what I like to hear." Joan gestured for me to continue.

"Correct me if I'm wrong, but the last time Nicole wore the necklace was before dinner last night." I turned to her. "You took it off in this room, and you didn't leave the room till just before dinner. Is that right?"

"It is," said Nicole.

I turned to Payton. "When did you come back here this morning?"

"About an hour ago," she said. "First I went to the bridge to make that announcement. I'd say I got back here at six, give or take a few minutes."

This lined up with what Jessamine had told us when Joan and I returned to the medical bay, a little before six. She'd said that Payton had left about twenty minutes earlier. So far, so good. I turned to Nicole.

"Did you ever come back to the room during that time?" I asked her. "Maybe just to rest?"

Nicole shook her head. "I was in the medical bay all night. First with Gideon, who left after an hour or two."

"More than paying his dues as an ex-husband," noted Payton.

"Then I sat up on my own until I started to feel ill."

Joan nodded. "She went from visitor to patient around midnight."

"So we know the necklace must have been stolen sometime between dinner last night, which started at seven, and six o'clock this morning."

"But the room was locked the whole time!" exclaimed Payton. "I'm sure we locked it when we went to dinner. And I know it was locked when I came back this morning. It took me a hot second to get my key out of my pocket, and I tried opening the door on the off-chance I didn't have to fish for it."

I turned to the captain.

"I assume each room has a distinct key?"

She nodded.

"Are there duplicates? Or just the one copy for each room?"

"Just the one. Other than my master key."

Aha; a master key. That was interesting.

"Do you keep your master key on you at all times?"

She nodded. "It's protocol," she said—the way a scientist might say: *It's physics*.

"So we still don't know *how* they got in, but at least we know *when* it happened," I said. "And I'm beginning to think the *when* is critical."

"What do you mean?" asked Joan, though I could tell by the excitement in her voice that she had an idea where I was going with this.

I took a deep breath.

"What if everything that happened last night at dinner, and afterward, was just a ruse? What if it was a way to make sure this room stayed empty long enough to steal the necklace? A necklace worth potentially tens of millions of dollars to someone who was probably willing to pay a lot of money to get it back? Think about it. If no one had gotten sick and there hadn't been such an uproar, whoever stole the necklace would have had to do it *during* dinner, when their absence would have been obvious. But this way, they were able to guarantee no one would be in Room 101 at a time when everybody's whereabouts were all over the place."

"So you mean"—Payton paused to regroup—"Jackson may have been *accidentally* killed for the sake of a crypto bro douchebag necklace?"

I nodded.

She erupted with laughter. To be fair to her, in the last twelve hours she'd suffered a public humiliation, a medical emergency, the prospect of financial ruin, a second medical emergency for her wife, and a sleepless night. There was an argument to be made that delirious and inappropriate laughter was not only understandable at this point, but inevitable.

* * *

The captain instituted a search for the necklace, instructing everyone via the PA system to return to their cabins and remain there until further notice. Fortunately, everyone had eaten breakfast by then, and I personally welcomed the downtime. When I went back to my cabin, I had every intention of resting, though what happened instead was a whole lot of brooding and obsessing.

I couldn't stop thinking about that guilty look Jackson had given Payton in the dining room. On an instinctual level (call it "feminine intuition" and I will cut you), I felt certain he was implicated somehow in the series of events that culminated in his death. It wasn't likely, but there was a chance Jackson had been the one to tamper with the salads at Table 1 for purposes of stealing the necklace. He would have had plenty of time to get to Room 101 after Payton had been removed from the dining room, and before he fell ill. I had no idea how he'd gotten into the locked room, but that wasn't a Jackson-specific problem. If he really was the thief, the necklace would turn up somewhere in his cabin, and as Joan had already said, his death would be deemed the ultimate poetic justice.

But *why?* Why would Jackson steal the necklace? He had his own family money; he presumably didn't need either the money the necklace would fetch on a black market for stolen goods, or whatever retainer the crypto bro douchebag in question might have paid a person to steal the necklace on his behalf. Could either Gideon Pereira or Pierre Gasçoigne *be* the crypto bro douchebag? I dismissed this theory as soon as I raised it. They were both public figures with well-documented pasts. The crypto bro was more likely to have lured an anonymous passenger to do his bidding. As Theresa had pointed out at breakfast, technically *anyone* aboard could have been involved. Sure, a boat is a "closed circle" setting, but at nearly three hundred souls, this closed circle was unusually—and unhelpfully—large.

Payton and Nicole could have always stolen the necklace themselves—an old trick. There was no question they had a large insurance payment coming their way if it had truly disappeared, and maybe Payton wasn't thriving in her career as she claimed to be. It would have been easy for either or both of them to stage the theft before going up to dinner yesterday. Or for Payton to do it this morning, in the hour or so she had alone. In that case, they would have to hide the necklace somewhere during the search, which was why I'd pulled the captain aside and asked her to search Jackson's room immediately, lest they stash it there and pretend Jackson had stolen it himself.

There was still so much I didn't understand. My brain was like a laundry dryer stuck on "tumble," so to switch to a quieter mode I used the coping mechanism I developed for myself when I was seven years old, and turned to a book. Back then it would have been *The Boxcar Children* or *The Famous Five*, but on this morning I chose a story I'd never read before—one I was fairly certain no one had read, other than its creator. That's right: I did what I had vowed not to do, and began reading Helen's book.

Two hours later I came up for air, more than halfway through the manuscript. I felt let down on two counts. First, a part of me had been hoping that Helen's mystery would turn out to be set on a boat, featuring the death by digitalis of an obnoxious male assistant. Alas, her story had nothing to do with the real-life intrigue surrounding us. Second, it was outrageously good. I'm not going to tell you its title or anything about it, because you're sure to read it someday and I'd hate to sully the clean slate every book deserves—especially a mystery. I'll note that it had nothing to do with her pregnant sleuth, which was a third disappointment, as this meant she was brimful of ideas and had a flourishing career ahead of her as a mystery novelist—a career that would impose on mine, since we were going to share agents. (I'd already e-mailed Rhonda that I had someone for her to read. I did this without responding to her frantic texts and e-mails asking if I was okay on the #murderboat. I knew my e-mail would both assuage her fears and annoy her, a win-win.) My only hope was that Helen Sanchez would turn out to be Jackson's killer, somehow—not that convicted murderers haven't become bestselling mystery novelists. . . . But it would at least slow her roll a little.

I was just getting to the part where the action was ramping up in a sustained way, hurtling toward a conclusion I'd no doubt find satisfying and revelatory, when there was a knock on the door. With a sigh, I put the manuscript aside. "Who is it?" I called out.

"Captain McDwight here, ma'am."

Ma'am? Captain Marcie all over again. I was lucky she wasn't calling me "sir."

I opened the door, ushering her in along with Sandra Gutierrez.

"This is Sandra," said the captain. "She's assisting me with the search, though I'll be present for the duration of the procedure. We'll start with your effects and then move on to your person. We will not be asking you to remove any clothing, but we will be enacting a pat-down procedure similar to those conducted by the Transportation Security Administration in the course of domestic air travel. Sandra worked for the TSA for a number of years, which is why I've chosen her to help me."

If Captain Marcie wasn't in her element now, she was in more of a comfort zone. Unlike the investigation into Jackson's death, the search for the necklace was a concrete, finite task. In addition to her spiel and her minion, she had a literal checklist in the form of a diagrammed map of the third and fourth decks, which she'd attached to a clipboard she was currently clutching to her chest.

Sandra had already begun rifling through my socks. "Did you find anything in Jackson's room?" I asked the captain in a low voice.

She shook her head. "Nothing."

I learned while Sandra sifted efficiently through my belongings that after searching Jackson's cabin, they'd gone to the hallway on the fifth deck and searched the ship's crew and the cleaning/kitchen staff, who had been instructed to remain in their rooms along with the regular passengers. Then they searched all the public and utility spaces on the first, second, and fifth decks, and now they were moving as quickly as possible through the regular passengers.

"I've been meaning to ask you, did you visit Flora's room this morning to ask her about what happened?"

"I did," said the captain. "Per Payton's request."

"Payton is very hard to say no to, isn't she?" I said this lightly, in an attempt to wrangle some conversation out of her. "You never told me what she was like when you were growing up, I'm so curious!"

"I don't like to think about my childhood. It wasn't happy."

Was that an undercurrent of vitriol I detected beneath her matter-of-fact delivery? Maybe I was imagining things. Maybe I just wanted it to be there.

"Okay, well, I assume when Payton spoke to you, she told you about the foxglove?"

The captain nodded.

"And while you were talking to Flora, you passed along that information? About the foxglove leaves?"

"The chain of command starts with me," she said. "If Payton—"

"It's okay," I assured her. "I just wanted to make sure Flora found out about the foxglove from you."

"I told her, yes."

Point Flora Fortescue—a big one, and I have no problem admitting I was relieved.

"Has everyone been where they were supposed to be during the search?"

"All except one."

Because the captain had no aptitude for drama or suspense, she clarified immediately.

"Gideon Pereira."

This was interesting. "He wasn't in his room?"

She shook her head. "We knocked three times, according to—"

"Protocol, yes. I know. And you haven't seen him since?"

"No."

I wondered where Gideon was, and what he could be up to.

Sandra was good. She went over every item in my room, stripping and remaking the bed in record time. She even rifled through the pages of Helen's manuscript to make sure I wasn't hiding anything in there.

She found nothing, of course.

"All right." The captain drew a pair of vinyl gloves from her pocket and handed them to Sandra. "As I mentiond, this will be just like what the TSA does at the airport."

"Except I won't be running late for a flight."

Neither of them laughed. Sandra began running the backs of her fingers up and down my limbs with a practiced, professional air.

"I wish we could figure out how someone was able to get into the room to take the necklace." This was nervous chatter on my part, but it's hard not to chatter nervously when someone is patting you down. "You're sure no one else had a master key other than you?"

"No one," said the captain.

Sandra's hand froze below my knee. When I looked down to see what was the matter, she was staring at both of us with an expression somewhere between disbelief and contempt.

"We *all* have master keys," she said.

"Excuse me?" I thought I must have misunderstood her.

Sandra shifted onto her haunches, putting one hand on her hip (which is hard to do without toppling over). "How the hell do you think we get into your rooms to clean them?"

"Oh," I replied, feeling like an idiot.

"I forgot about that," admitted the captain.

If the social hierarchy of a ship was like that of a country estate a hundred years ago, then we'd committed one of the worst errors a person within that hierarchy can make—especially in the context of a murder investigation.

We'd underestimated the help.

"Who has a master key?" I asked her.

"I do," she said. "And Fiorella, and Lucy, and Raquel, and Kendall." Sandra resumed her pat-down, which was nearly finished anyway. "She's clear," she said a minute later, sitting back and snapping off her gloves.

The *gloves*. . . . I thought I'd been so clever about the gloves, but I'd missed a crucial detail, and it was pure luck my attention was directed to them now, in the wake of what Sandra had just told us. *Of course.*

I raced for the door.

"You're not supposed to—"

I have no idea what Captain Marcie said because I was already gone, racing down the corridor and for once not getting lost because I had to get there as quickly as possible and not a moment later, the urgency of the situation kicking the geospatial sector of my brain into a higher gear than normal. I took the stairs rather than the elevator, catapulting down them two at a time, three at a time—maintaining a death grip on the railing to keep from falling. Within seconds I was on the fifth deck and hurtling down one fluorescent-lit corridor and then another, running headfirst into Room 4 without pausing to think whether or not it would be locked. Fortunately for my cranium, it wasn't, the door swinging inward, revealing the fact that its two occupants were absent. Sandra Gutierrez was of course busy at work one deck above. But the reason Kendall Monteague wasn't here was that she was no longer anywhere.

Her *body* was still very much here. I stood staring at it now, trying to look anywhere other than the obvious place. Trying, and failing.

The best I could do was hope that wherever she was, Kendall Monteague would forgive me for focusing on the obvious and hideous fact that a crochet hook was sticking out of what used to be her left eye.

Part Four
Third Murder

CHAPTER 27

Another day, another corpse (technically it was two corpses in a day), but for the first time I was the one to have discovered it, and I was alone. This was the moment in which I was meant to drop whatever I was holding—a breakfast tray, a croquet mallet, a leather-bound book—and scream. But I was holding nothing, and I didn't come close to screaming. My instinct when an emotion overcomes me is to pounce on it, to do what I can to smother it into oblivion rather than let it express itself and thereby betray something fundamental about me. For this reason, all the scream-worthy scenarios of life (roller coasters, scary movies, orgasms) fail to induce an audible response in me. And to this list I could now add the solo discovery of a dead body.

Good to know.

But *was* she dead? As an animal attuned to the presence of other animals in its vicinity, I felt certain the compact, muscular body I'd compared to a bird's so many times before may as well have been an actual bird that had smacked itself against a window and fallen dead. Because the difference between a human body and a bird body is negligible, once life has departed them. Nevertheless, I took out my phone and texted a professional, who happened to be the one person whose company I craved.

Emergency in crew room 4 on deck 5 COME NOW!

To my relief, Joan wrote back seconds later.

on my way

I crouched down, picking up a wrist at random. It was still warm, but I couldn't feel a pulse or anything else. Now that I was closer, I could see significant bruising on her neck. Whoever did this must have held her down while they drove that metal hook into her eye. . . .

Without meaning to, I caught sight of the hook up close. No question it was Jessamine's: the "JL" carved into the instrument's handle looked like Cyrillic letters upside-down, but they were unmistakable. Upon closer examination, I realized the hook hadn't gone squarely *into* the eyeball but *around* it, on the outside of the socket—so deeply, a portion of the wooden handle had entered the cavity as well, uprooting and squeezing the eye itself. Suddenly I was in danger of vomiting. I scrabbled away on my hands and knees, not stopping till I was outside that horrible, stuffy room in that horrible, stuffy hallway, which was where Joan found me.

"What happened? Are you okay?"

I pointed wordlessly into the room.

She was in there almost no time at all, but what was there for her to do? When she came back into the hallway, she was ending a call.

"The captain's on her way," she said, pocketing her phone. "She told me you went running out of your cabin a few minutes ago."

I nodded. I was sitting with my back against the wall, arms

wrapped around my drawn-up legs. All I needed to complete the picture of "trauma victim" was one of those scratchy blankets the police hand out in the aftermath of a calamity.

Joan got down on the floor beside me.

"I was too late," I said.

"But how did you know she was in danger?"

It had been right there in my account of the day leading up to the murder. Once I realized what I'd missed, I couldn't believe I hadn't seen it before. But that's always the way of these things.

"Her hands," I said. "It wasn't just that she was wearing gloves at dinner. They were red, earlier in the day. I noticed them at lunchtime, when Flora and I were in the lounge."

When Kendall had taken away Flora's plate and then handed me her drink, I'd been too preoccupied by Flora's nonsense to make more than a passing note of it, but I *had* noted it. This meant that Kendall must have exposed her hands to the foxglove much earlier than she claimed, which meant the story she told us was a lie. And that meant she was covering for whoever was behind Jackson's death: the person who had not only relied on her to add poisonous leaves to the salads she served at Table 1, but who had used her master key to gain access to Room 101 and steal Nicole Root's necklace from the safe there. The same person who had now killed her, too.

I explained all this to Joan in a low voice, mindful of the fact that the rooms lining the hallway were filled with crew members sheltering in place, just like the passengers. To be honest, a low voice suited me just fine. Even while I was talking, Kendall's words at the end of our interview came back to me: *My daughter—I'm all she has. I can't get into any trouble.* What was going to happen to Kendall's daughter now?

"It makes so much more sense that she would have touched the leaves earlier in the day. In the morning probably," I said. "And that the irritation would have been gradual. It was always a little hard to believe her hands could have been instantly irritated like that, you know?"

"I suppose," said Joan. "Though like I said, people react differently."

"If I'd remembered about her hands at lunch when we were talking to her," I said, "I would've called her out for lying, and she would be alive now."

"I don't know about that. She probably would have just denied it. This is *not* your fault," declared Joan. "It's the fault of whoever coerced her into doing their dirty work, I'm guessing with the help of a ton of money. And even though some people might hate me for saying this, it's Kendall's fault too. She had to know she was playing with fire."

Joan was right. I knew she was right. And yet I still felt like crap.

"I could just as easily say it was *my* fault," she went on. "If I'd been in the medical bay like I usually am, that knitting needle wouldn't have been sitting there unattended, ripe for the taking." She pressed the heels of her hands into her eyes, raking them across her face and using them to massage her temples. The skin around her eyes was red and raw-looking. "I could've at least brought it with me when I went up to my room," she muttered.

"Did you get any sleep?" I asked her. She looked so tired.

"A little," she said. "Enough for my body to realize how rundown it is."

"I woke you up, didn't I?"

"Yes, how dare you disturb my beauty sleep with the discovery of a second murder victim?"

She leaned over—like the little teapot when it's about to be poured out—and butted shoulders with me. I almost started crying, she was being so nice. I suppose I was exhausted too.

"You know, it was actually a crochet hook, not a knitting needle," I said.

"Oh, fuck you."

We were still in the throes of stifled, giddy laughter when the captain and Sandra appeared.

"She's in there." Joan pointed to Room 4, the door to which she'd closed.

The captain disappeared inside, leaving Sandra looking down on us uncomfortably.

"Do you want to sit?" Joan patted the floor beside her.

She shook her head. We stood up, as it seemed the only polite thing to do.

"Did—did the captain tell you what—"

"She's dead in there? Kendall?"

"I'm afraid so," said Joan.

"How?"

"She was . . . stabbed."

Sandra crossed herself, muttering a prayer I couldn't hear properly because she barely needed to say it aloud to invoke it.

"You were her roommate, weren't you?" I asked.

She nodded. "Not going back in there now."

"Of course not," said Joan. "I'm sure we can get someone to move your things into another room. You'd only met her a few days ago, is that right?"

"Yeah. She was a quiet one. Not that I minded. Some people like to get real chummy on jobs like this. It can be a lot."

"I'm sure. Tell me, was she acting—strange at all? Today or yesterday?"

"Hard to say. Everyone's acting strange, you know? But when she found out about that man dying, it shook her up. No question. She kinda . . . froze up."

"When did this happen?"

"While we were doing breakfast. We were in the kitchen and word about what happened just sorta got around. Like all of a sudden, everybody was talking about it."

"And what did Kendall do?"

"Nothing." Sandra smiled out of the side of her mouth. "That was the problem. It's a busy job, making sure all the serving trays stay full, cleaning up all the spills. Gimme a self-serve buffet, I'll give you a mess. Rather just do the serving my-self. So we were running all over the place but when she found out, she just kinda went into a corner, over by the dishwashers? I told her to finish her shift early, get some rest. I didn't think she'd take me up on it, cuz she wasn't the type to take favors from anyone, you know what I mean? But she did."

"That was nice of you," I offered.

She shrugged. "It was the decent thing to do."

"Did you see her at all after that?" asked Joan.

"Not till the search. We're both on housekeeping here too, the work's nonstop. Bananas."

"So we gather," said Joan. "How was she when you were searching her?"

"Fine. Not nervous, if that's what you mean." She paused. "If anything, she was too calm. Almost like . . . removed."

"Probably in a state of shock," said Joan, more to herself than either of us. "And then you went on with your search, which you've been doing ever since. Is that right?"

"Yeah."

At which point anyone could have slipped out of their room, run down to the fifth deck, grabbed the crochet hook from the medical bay, and paid Kendall a visit. At the end of her message over the PA system announcing the search for the necklace, the captain had asked for Sandra Gutierrez to report to the bridge, effectively putting the entire ship on notice that Sandra would be conducting the search along with the captain. This meant the murderer must have known Kendall would be alone in her room. . . .

"Gideon Pereira wasn't in his cabin when you went to search him, is that right?" I asked.

Sandra nodded.

"Was anyone else missing when you looked for them?"

"No, just him."

Joan and I exchanged a look.

"Tell me," said Joan. "Have you and the captain been together the entire time you've been conducting the search so far? Was there ever a period of time you were apart?"

Sandra hesitated. She was smart enough to know it was in her interests to answer this question in the negative. Because in that case, she and the captain were each other's alibi, and neither of them could have killed Kendall. But it was also in her interests to answer truthfully every question put to her. No one wants to be caught lying in a murder investigation—even one conducted on the fly by a doctor and her sidekick writer.

"There was, like, ten minutes when the captain said she had an errand to run."

"Was this before or after you searched Kendall?"

"After," she said reluctantly.

"Do you know what the errand was?"

"No idea."

"And what did you do for the ten minutes?"

"Ate something," she said. "I hadn't eaten since five in the morning, I was starving. Actually, do you mind if I go to the bathroom?"

Joan assured her we didn't mind. As Sandra retreated down the hallway, I turned to her excitedly.

"When I asked the captain about her childhood before, it seemed like there was something painful there, something she didn't want to talk about. Payton admitted herself that she wasn't very nice to her."

"I don't know," said Joan. "So now we're saying it's the captain who accidentally killed Jackson because she meant to off Payton for being mean to her in middle school?"

"It's just a theory." I gave her a wounded look. "Gideon is fair game too."

"Look at you, throwing your boyfriend under the bus. Oh please," she added, as my wounded look deepened into one of horror. "Everyone knows you two are hooking up, and good for you. The funny thing is that if we weren't on a ship almost exclusively full of women, I would have said *that*"—she pointed again to Room 4—"was the work of a man. Not to stereotype, but it takes a lot of force to stab someone in the eye like that."

I shuddered involuntarily.

"And violent acts like that are almost always committed by men."

I told her for the first time what Gideon had shared with me about his ongoing custody battle. We were still reckoning with the implication of this when the captain finally came out of Room 4, having been in there for several minutes. She looked dazed, which for Captain Marcie was saying something.

"It's bad, huh?" said Joan.

The captain nodded, standing there without saying a word. Was she . . . swaying? Joan and I exchanged glances.

"Right. Here's what we're going to do," said Joan. "*You* are going to call the police, yet again, and go through the same procedure you did for Jackson."

At the word "procedure," the captain stirred, as though waking from a dream. Down the hallway, Sandra came out of the bathroom, wiping her hands on her shirt.

"*We* are going to the galley to see about finding some cold storage space for the two bodies we've got on our hands now. I know we're not supposed to disturb the scene of the crime—*scenes* of the *crimes*, I should say. But we also can't risk creating a health hazard."

The captain nodded eagerly, and I imagined the phrase "health hazard" rising out of the abyss: a life preserver for her to grab on to. There was a protocol for the avoidance of health hazards, a list of prearranged guidelines to follow.

Down the hallway, Sandra came out of the bathroom, wiping her hands on her shirt.

"By the way, Sandra says you had to run an errand earlier, while you were conducting your search," said Joan. "For ten or so minutes. What were you doing?"

I thought the captain might mind being questioned in so direct a manner, but she answered without hesitating.

"I went to my room to enter a series of notes in my log. It's vital to keep a contemporaneous record of events whenever anything unusual occurs."

She sounded like she was quoting from a manual or lecture again. I didn't doubt her, but I also wished she'd been with someone else—someone who could have corroborated her story.

"Got it," said Joan. "Well, good luck with the police. And wish us luck with cold storage."

We left her and hurried down the corridor, past Sandra.

"And if during our trip to the galley we should just so happen to interview the first of the two men on this ship," Joan added to me in an undertone, "so be it."

CHAPTER 28

Up till then I'd caught the galley only in glimpses through the swinging doors of the dining room, as the waitstaff went to and fro. I got my first good look at it now, mid-to-late morning—a time of day when there would have been a lull anyway. Due to the search, the space was absolutely deserted when we got there.

"Oh, fudge. I was hoping we'd get to meet the chef." With her toe, Joan lifted a corner of the thick black mat covering the floor, considering what to do next. I knew the mat was meant to prevent slips and also to provide padding for those who were forced to be on their feet for hours at a time, but I wondered how people managed not to trip on it. "Let's stick around a few minutes, maybe we'll get lucky. He's got to start prepping dinner soon."

We began to wander through the space. Along the back wall was a row of metal sinks, their deep, rectangular wells gleaming and empty except for the odd water stain and scrap of food. The faucets were the detachable kind with a nozzle connected to a hose that had a coiled spring around it. You could extend the hose to reach every corner of the sink: perfect for washing pots, pans, vats, serving trays, and other outsize dishware. I turned one of them on and coaxed a stubborn remnant of burnt cheese down the drain, enjoying the thrum of water pounding on metal.

"Did you say 'fudge' just now?" I asked, turning the water off.

"You try living with a four-year-old, see what it does to your vocabulary."

"No thank you," I replied, filing this away as Reason #492 not to have children.

"I can't stop thinking about Kendall's daughter, actually," said Joan.

"Me either," I admitted. "Do we know how old she is?"

"Nine." I could hear the wince in Joan's voice. (She had her head stuck inside one of the kitchen's two massive refrigerators at the time.) "I can't imagine. I don't *want* to imagine."

I nodded, even though she couldn't see me. Above the sinks on a magnetic strip was an array of knives, cleavers, mallets, and tenderizers. If this had been a horror movie there would have been a space where one of these lethal instruments was missing, but the collection looked to be intact. Besides, with enough intention, even the most innocent-seeming tool can be used for violent ends, as Kendall's death had proved. At least these sharp and spiky objects were upfront about their hazardous nature.

In a far corner were two industrial dishwashers with an array of glassware hanging above them on racks, and a shelving unit to one side as big as a wardrobe holding plates, bowls, and other dishes and assorted cutlery.

There was a long and narrow island in the center of the room, presumably for prep work such as chopping, with two tiers of continuous chrome shelving built above the counter space. These shelves had no backing, making them accessible both to the people standing at the counter and to the servers on the other side. It was on these shelves the plates rested once they had food on them, before being brought out to the dining room.

Someone had taped little Post-its on both sides, with numbers in black Sharpie to indicate which area corresponded to which of the tables in the dining room. I looked instinctively for the "1." Here was where Kendall had *not* dropped the plates for Payton's table the night before, but instead, deliberately added poisonous foxglove leaves to the plates on her tray. Leaves that she must have handled earlier in the day when she was preparing them. . . .

"The police will at least be able to look into her financial records." I followed Joan through a side door to a well-ventilated interior room, where all the burners and ovens were. This was where Chef Gasçoigne would have been working in the hours leading up to dinner last night, out of sight of the main room where the salads had been sitting. Beyond this was a pantry and two cold-storage areas, one of which Joan was inspecting with the upper half of her body, not having actually walked into it. "Maybe they can see if Kendall made any big deposits recently."

"Eh." Joan closed the door to the freezer, which *thunk*ed as the seal around it hit the frame. Together we walked back into the main room. "Whoever paid her probably did it in cash. It looks like there's one unit back there that isn't being used, even though it's still being kept cold. Super wasteful."

"Don't tell Gideon."

"Well, we'll put it to good use."

Just then the chef walked in. I knew it was the chef because he was a man, and I hadn't seen him before, so by process of elimination, he had to be Pierre Gasçoigne. If not for this technicality, I would never have taken him to be who he was. I only realized this once I was looking at him, but with a name like his and an occupation in the world of haute cuisine, my subconscious expectation was that he looked something like the animated chef in *The Little Mermaid*. You know, the one who runs around trying to hack up Sebastian the crab while singing: "*Les poissons! Les poissons!* Hee hee hee! Hongh hongh hongh!" (Has anyone apologized to the French people for this?) But Pierre Gasçoigne was nothing like the stereotypical French chef. He had no puffy hat, no mustache, no belly.

To be blunt: he was extremely hot.

Hot in a hipster way, I should add. He could have been a model for one of those chic-casual clothing brands with a laid-back, beachy vibe—Faherty Brand and the like. This isn't my preferred type, and yet even I could appreciate his scruffy charm: the thick beard that somehow accentuated his enviable jawline, the silky blond hair scraped to one side. I didn't even mind that his hair was long enough to pull into a messy bun at the nape of his neck. And I definitely didn't mind the lightly muscled arms, which were on full display in a white V-neck undershirt, a mosaic of tattoos covering almost every inch of available skin.

You know who also didn't mind? Joan Chen, MD. I saw her cheeks flush as she took him in, and despite the circumstances— or perhaps because of them, since emotion breeds any and all emotion, regardless of type—I had to stop myself from laughing.

"I can help you?" he asked.

His English was adequate, but he spoke it with an accent and cadence many Americans were sure to find adorable. In fact, I half suspected he was Frenchifying his English strategically (if so, he wouldn't be the first). In this way he was both attractive *and* approachable. I could see why he was so successful in the world of reality TV.

We introduced ourselves, explaining that we were investigating what had happened at dinner the night before.

"I know nothing about zees . . . 'ow do you say . . . fox-cloth?"

"Foxglove," said Joan. "We have reason to believe it was Kendall Monteague who put the foxglove in the salad before serving it."

"Kendall?" He said her name with an emphasis on the second syllable: *Ken-DAHL.* "I cannot believe this, she is the best worker I 'ave."

Oof.

"You never noticed her doing anything strange?" asked Joan.

He shook his head. "Never. But I am zere." He pointed to the inner room. "I see nothing. I prepare the salad here"—he gestured to the long and narrow island countertop—"and when they are ready, I return to my cave for ze main course. I work on this boat, so very 'ard. It is like when I am a boy, and I peel ze potatoes. Before I go to the cooking school."

He was smiling as he said this, making light of his travails as the Get Lit Cruise's celebrity chef. But if the late Kendall Monteague was to be believed, his current display of bonhomie was for our benefit only.

"So you didn't interact with anyone last night other than the servers?" persisted Joan.

"Zere is one woman, she is very annoying. Always asking about ze food, what is in it, 'ow I make it. But nevair does she tell me after if she likes it."

"Would this be Talia Simmons?"

"*Précisément.*"

"How do you know Payton?" I asked.

He turned to me. "She appears on my show. She is charming, we become friends. And now she 'elps with les mémoires that I write."

Aha. So that was how Payton had managed to book such an expensive chef—no doubt at a steep discount, and with a skeleton staff supporting him. I suspected her "help" on his memoir was more substantial than general advice or copy edits. It seemed I wasn't the only ghostwriter on board.

"So if you knew Payton, you must have known Jackson as well?"

He shrugged. (No one shrugs like the French.) "*Oui.*"

"You don't seem like his biggest fan," I observed.

"I am sorry 'e is dead. No one deserves this."

"Did you interact with him at all?" asked Joan.

His lips were thin, but extremely mobile, and they curled upward now in a smirk.

"He wanted to . . . I believe ''ook up' is the expression? I was not interested."

"Did he make you uncomfortable?" asked Joan. "Or feel unsafe?"

"No, no. Me, I am pansexual, I do not care who makes ze propositions. Maybe anothair time, I would have said yes. But here I must concentrate. Here, I am too busy. And tired."

"I see."

Was that a hint of disappointment I detected in Joan's voice?

"Please," he said. "I must start dinner now."

"What's on the menu?" she asked.

"Seafood bouillabaisse."

"That's a specialty of yours, isn't it?"

He nodded, looking at her for the first time with interest. "You have watched me before? Or per'aps eaten at my restaurant?"

"I'm a fan," she admitted.

"Yeah you are," I murmured—just loud enough for her to hear.

It was clear we would get nothing from Pierre Gascoigne. Less clear? Whether he was hiding anything behind that adorable French accent of his.

CHAPTER 29

"I'm not getting a killer vibe from Pierre Gasçoigne," said Joan.

We were on our way back to the elevator on the second deck.

"And *don't* say it's because I have a thing for him."

"All right, all right. Take it easy." She'd already chastised me for teasing her in his presence. "If anything, he had a good motive to keep Payton alive, if she's helping him with his book. I can't see him putting poisoned leaves in a salad she was going to eat, even if he meant to kill Jackson or one of the others."

"It's too bad Talia Simmons wasn't sitting at Table 1. I'm sure he wouldn't have minded killing *her*."

"That's the thing," I said. "He's one of the few people who wouldn't have needed Kendall's help to poison the salads. His access negates her access. But we know from her hands that she must have been the one dealing with the foxglove. So I guess he's off the hook."

"Wish we could say the same for Kendall. I'm sorry, that was tasteless."

"Don't worry about it," I said. "Puns are like demons. You have to exorcise them once they take up residence in your head."

"You know," she said, "you're a lot nicer than you pretend to be."

I replied with some self-effacing remark, but really, I was preoccupied by the thought that Theresa had been right. Something was telling me this entire case would come down to access. . . .

"I guess that's a point in Talia's favor too," said Joan. "She wouldn't have needed to hang around the kitchen if Kendall was doing her dirty work."

"Unless she had control issues," I argued. "I've always thought it was a stretch to imagine one of the passengers waltzing into the kitchen and slipping some foxglove into the salads sitting there. Dressing up like a waitress is something people pull off in crime fiction, but I have no problem believing someone like Talia Simmons would pay Kendall to do the crime for her, and then hang around like a mother hen to make sure it was being done properly. People are much less slick in real life."

"Talia Simmons certainly isn't slick," observed Joan.

We arrived at the elevator. I reached out, pressing the "down" button, the door opening instantly. It was late morning by then; if it had been a normal day, the elevator would have been in constant use. But everyone was still in their rooms, submitting to a search, or else cowering in fear. Today, the *Merman Rivera* felt like a ghost ship, and I shivered as we passed inside the elevator's metal cage, its doors slamming shut behind us.

"So we keep Talia Simmons on our list and take Pierre Gasçoigne off it," said Joan happily. "*Shut your mouth,*" she added in response to my grin.

I clamped one hand over my mouth, pressing the button for "3" with the other.

"You know what's pathetic?" Joan didn't wait for an answer.

"I haven't dated anyone since my ex, which was almost ten years ago. I'm a black hole of dating experience."

"Soul sisters unite."

"That fucker did a number on me." She reached out, depressing the button for "4" much harder than necessary.

"I figured we were going to Payton and Nicole's?"

"Nuh-uh. We have another interview first. Or at least, you do."

The dread filled me: bottomless sink that I am when it comes to such emotions. "Who?"

"Our second and final male specimen. A man whose wife left him for another woman, and who, according to you, wishes he didn't have to share custody of his kids with her. Also, the only person thus far whose whereabouts during the ship-wide search for the necklace are unaccounted for."

The elevator stopped on Deck 3, its doors dinging open. We stood there, waiting for it to close again.

"I'd say it's time we heard from Gideon Pereira, wouldn't you?"

"Sure," I said. "Let's do it."

"Not us. *You* already have a relationship with him." She offered me up the same grin I'd given her. "And then some, right?"

"Do you really think he could have done it?" I asked. "You think he wants to kill the mother of his children?"

The elevator stopped again and we got off, entering the fourth deck's labyrinth of hallways.

"If he did it, I don't think that was the reason. I think people underestimate the frailty of the male ego. Take it from one who knows," she added with a chuckle. "My ex tried to blame his cheating on me. He said I didn't 'tend' to him enough. Lovely." A cloud passed over her face. "I think when Payton left him for a woman, he was humiliated in a way that only a man can be humiliated."

"He's not like that," I insisted.

"Look who's advocating for her boyfriend now," teased Joan.

"Please," I begged her. "Don't make me do this alone."

Joan stopped walking. I stopped with her. "Why? Do you feel unsafe?"

This wasn't the reason, reader. The truth is, I didn't want the responsibility of questioning Gideon to rest on my shoulders alone. I guess I really am a sidekick. But I nodded, pretending (God help me) to feel unsafe.

"Okay," she said. "Then I'll go with you. No sweat."

"Thank you," I replied in a small voice I was by no means putting on.

It wasn't till then that I realized we'd stopped because we were in front of Gideon's cabin door. Had I led us here unknowingly? Or maybe Joan knew where his room was because she was the kind of person who knew everything. She reached out with one hand to knock, while with the other she found my hand hanging at my side, and squeezed it.

I didn't deserve her.

The door flew open.

"Ah, enter the sleuths. I was wondering when you would grace me with your presence; I was beginning to feel left out. Come in, come in."

I saw immediately that Joan was right. If I'd come alone, I could have pretended I was seeing him at least partially as a person seeking the comfort and counsel of the man she'd slept with two times in as many days. But coming as a pair like this, we'd raised his hackles from the start.

Gideon remained standing, looking very *Rebel Without a Cause* with his back and one foot against the wall. I let Joan take the armchair, and sat on the end of the bed—the same bed I'd lounged in, post-coitally, less than twenty-four hours earlier. Had it really been less than twenty-four hours ago? This day had been such a long one. And it wasn't nearly over yet.

"Where were you during the search?" I asked him. "The captain came to your room, but you weren't here."

"I went up to the top deck, did a little birding. I've never been so far north in the Atlantic, and I figured I might as well get something out of this shit show. I saw an Atlantic puffin, believe it or not."

"Would it be okay if the captain came back later to conduct the search everyone else has submitted to?" I asked.

He laughed—an ugly laugh. He'd gotten a little too much sun up on the observation deck, and his pale face was now an unbecoming shade of pink.

"I suppose I can . . . submit. If I have to."

That's the thing about men: they're not used to submitting, or to subjugation of any kind. He was outraged at having his integrity questioned, whereas the rest of the women on board had simply gone along with it. I wasn't sure whether I felt sorrier for him, or us.

"Maybe someone is targeting the men on this ship," he said. "Have you thought about that? I could be next. Or Chef, God forbid. Then we'd all starve."

It was obvious he was mocking us.

"How did you know Payton had been taken ill?" I asked him. "At dinner last night?"

This question had been nagging at the back of my head ever since he showed up, breathless, in the medical bay just a few minutes after we'd gotten there.

"What do you mean? I went to the dining room and it was in an uproar. Someone told me what happened, and I ran down to see what was going on."

"But you told me you were going to wait to eat till after everyone else did."

"Did I?" he said carelessly. "I guess I got hungry."

Or he couldn't stay away, knowing what was about to happen. . . . He must have realized what I was thinking, because his eyes narrowed, and when he opened his mouth I knew I wasn't going to like whatever came out of those plump lips of his.

"Fuck you," he snarled. "That's the truth, and I don't care if you don't believe me."

"You know," said Joan, trying valiantly to reset the conversation, "My fiancé left me."

"Yes?" He sounded supremely uninterested.

"It was the worst thing that ever happened to me. It couldn't have been easy when Payton left you for Nicole."

Oh, dear. This line of questioning was never going to work on him. This was all my fault; I'd been the one to insist she accompany me.

He looked my way.

"You really don't kiss and tell, do you?"

He turned back to Joan.

"As I mentioned to esteemed mystery novelist Belle Currer here, during our most recent bout of pillow talk, I was *grateful* to Nic for letting me off the hook where Payton was concerned."

Thrilled, grateful, relieved: Nicole was his savior, blah blah blah. What if he was simply saying the opposite of the truth? It was a reliable method practiced by liars the world over.

"But you were having custody issues with her, weren't you?" asked Joan.

He looked at me again.

"I take it back. Blabbermouth." He turned once more to Joan. "You're right, it makes perfect sense that I'd be so concerned about the welfare of my children that I would *murder their mother in cold blood.*"

"You obviously don't think much of her as a mother."

Gideon stared at Joan, his fists balled up—so tight, they were shaking. I marveled yet again at how thin-skinned he was compared to everyone else we'd questioned. Even Flora Fortescue was stronger than this.

"You have a child, Dr. Chen, don't you?" he asked after a lengthy pause.

"I do."

"So would *you* willingly kill the father of your child?"

"Maybe. I have no idea who the father of my child is. He was an anonymous sperm donor."

"You're being deliberately obtuse!"

"I suppose I am," she said, taking pity on him.

He sprang off the wall, advancing on her. I half rose from my perch on the bed.

"Then fucking stop it!" he shouted in her face.

Joan looked at me. We didn't need words to exchange the thought that had occurred to both of us. It was the only thought we could have had, given the display we'd just witnessed.

Well, he doesn't seem capable of violence at all.

CHAPTER 30

In our absence, Room 101 had been transformed.

The captain was there, and it was obvious she'd already told Payton and Nicole about Kendall's death: obvious, because Payton was in the process of drawing up a chart on a whiteboard-on-wheels I suspected was the same one I'd (barely) used in my black box theater. The chart looked like this:

		Suspects					
		Gideon	Pierre	Talia	Jessamine		
Victims	Jackson						
	Kendall						

It wasn't corkboard, and there were no photos or red string attached, but as murder boards go, it was a start. The chart was blocking the big-screen TV in the sitting area off to the side of the room, and the captain and Nicole were sitting on the sofa, contemplating it. Payton had just finished writing Jessamine's name when we walked in. She whirled round on us.

"Perfect timing!"

Payton capped the marker with a flourish. There was a glit-

244 / KEMPER DONOVAN

ter to her eyes I took to be both a vestige of tears and a sign that she was *not* fucking around. She was in "get stuff done" mode: a more dangerous mode for Payton Garrett than most others.

"Let's get started!"

"Aren't you forgetting someone?" I asked.

"We're excluding present company."

"No—what about Flora?"

"Ah, so then you haven't heard." She gestured for the captain to speak.

"My first mate has been keeping watch of Flora Fortescue since early this morning, when we discovered the body of Jackson Richards. She's confirmed that Flora could not have killed Kendall Monteague."

"And your first mate is to be trusted?" asked Joan.

The image of the efficient Nordic woman who welcomed us into dinner the first night wearing her First Mate badge came back to me.

"Yes," said the captain.

"Well, this is an interesting development," said Joan.

"Sure is," said Payton, who must have been mortified when she first learned of Flora's alibi. I guessed it was what galvanized her into the manic action she was taking now. She scribbled Flora's name after Jessamine's, and put a big "X" in the box for Kendall.

"Happy?" she asked me.

"So happy," I replied.

Nicole got up from the sofa. She was dressed now—in a lemon jumpsuit that looked like something Amelia Earhart would have worn, if Amelia Earhart had been a fashion icon. She easily looked the best of us, but even on her, the fatigue and worry were beginning to show.

"I still say if the real reason for the poisoning at dinner was to steal my necklace, then it could have been anyone on the boat."

"Nah, babe, I call bullshit on the whole necklace angle. Especially since it hasn't turned up." Payton turned to the captain. "The search is almost over, right?"

"We still have a handful of passengers to search on the fourth deck, ma'am."

Payton waved this away. "Do we really think someone poisoned a whole tableful of people just for the right moment to steal a necklace? If they were that willing to put people in harm's way, why not just break into our room in the middle of the night, kill me and Nicole, and be done with it?"

Nicole sat down again, looking stricken. I took the seat beside her.

"There's something just . . . *off* about the whole foxglove thing," said Payton.

"You're suggesting there's something strange about the poisoning of at least three people on a literary cruise?" I joked.

She pointed her finger at me like I was a witch or other deviant to be denounced. "*Stop.* We don't have time."

She was angry. Very angry. Not at me, but at whoever had done this—to Jackson and to Kendall. And to her cruise.

"I think the necklace was stolen to distract us, and I refuse to be distracted. Also, apparently there's a theory floating around that I was cheating on my wife, and that maybe Jackson was blackmailing me about it?"

Payton glared at me and Joan. Oops; maybe she *was* angry at me. When I turned toward Nicole, she refused to look my way. As I'd suspected, she must have overheard us in the medical bay when we thought she was sleeping.

"I just want to say, even though I shouldn't have to, that there is *zero* truth to this. Understood?"

I nodded, feeling like a miscreant who'd been hauled into the headmistress's office for a dressing-down. Partly in an effort to worm my way back into her good graces, I brought her and the assembled company up to speed regarding my realization that Kendall's story about dropping the salad plates must have been a lie, and how someone must have paid her to tamper with the salads she served to Table 1.

"There *has* to be some good reason we're not seeing, for why someone would poison the four people sitting at that table," said Payton. "And we're going to figure it out." She stared at each of us in turn. "Right now."

"Well," I said slowly, "you'll be happy to know Joan and I just interviewed your first two suspects."

Payton professed herself delighted to hear this, and I made short shrift of Pierre Gascoigne for all the reasons Joan and I had already discussed.

"It's true that I'm ghosting his memoir," she said. "No shame, right?"

As someone who had built her career as a ghostwriter, I decided not to take offense at this, and merely nodded.

"If anything, it'd be Nicole he'd want to get rid of. She almost talked me out of the arrangement with him and he was *not* pleased. Remember, babe?"

"It's not that I thought ghostwriting was *beneath* her," Nicole explained hastily. "She just had so many other projects on her plate, I thought she was taking on too much."

"You know, since Flora's out of the picture now, we shouldn't assume I was the intended target of the poisoning. But we also shouldn't assume it was Jackson. It could have been anyone at that table. It really *could* have been you, Nic, or Jessamine LaBouchère. I don't see where that gets us, though."

"I don't either." Joan turned to Nicole. "It's a strange question, but can you think of any motives anyone might have to kill you?"

"Besides jealousy?" said Payton gallantly, which was the first time she'd sounded like herself since we came into the room.

"I'm a poet. I don't have enough money for anyone to kill me over. Especially now that my necklace is missing." Nicole looked at Payton. "Plus we changed our wills a few months ago. Most of our estates go to charity now."

Joan turned to Payton. "You changed your will recently? What's the breakdown? If you don't mind my asking."

"Please, if there were ever a situation to be forthcoming about the breakdown of your will, I think it's this one. The wifey here gets a quarter, my kids get another quarter, and the other half goes to a few different charities."

"Would one of the charities be Read It and Reap?" I asked, trying to keep my voice from trembling.

"Yes! They're the main beneficiary, actually. How did you know that?"

"Because Jessamine was telling me about it. You're on the board together, right? She's obviously very passionate about it. Does she know you changed your will?"

"She does, actually. I knew how happy it would make her, so I made a point of saying something. But you don't think . . . ?"

I thought back to how passionate Jessamine had seemed—zealous, even—when she talked about her pet charity. I couldn't picture her killing for her own sake. But for the sake of others she'd pledged to help? It was possible. Maybe even probable.

"Holy fuck," exhaled Joan.

"It never made sense to me that she agreed to go on this cruise. No offense," I added to Payton.

"All taken," she snarked.

"It's just, it must have put such a dent in her output."

"And then there's that crochet hook," said Joan. "Which she so conveniently left in open view in a public space. So technically, anyone could have seen it and taken it, but in reality, how many people were aware it was down there? It's almost like reverse psychology to use a weapon that would be associated with you. Sort of a brilliant ploy."

"She *is* brilliant," said Payton.

I nodded my head in agreement.

"Okay, this is fantastic," said Joan. "Let's keep going through everyone we've got, and then we can do follow-ups at the end."

We moved on to Gideon Pereira, which went less swimmingly than Jessamine.

"Gideon would never do anything to me," said Payton, maddeningly matter-of-fact about it. "Or anyone else."

"I agree," said Nicole. "He's obviously an ex-husband, and that's provocative, but he's a father first."

I wondered, though, as she turned to fluff the pillow she was sitting against, whether Nicole believed in Gideon's innocence as fervently as Payton did.

"I don't think you realize how angry he is," I said.

Payton narrowed her eyes at me. "I know you think you know him better than I do, now that you've fucked him, what, twice?"

"Hey now," said Joan.

"Believe me, he is *not* a killer. Next!"

To my surprise, it was Nicole who comforted me, reaching out and putting a hand on the small of my back—a minor gesture, but a significant one. I felt the tears threaten to spill over, and realized how tired I was. How tired we all were.

Next up was Talia Simmons.

"Do you know how much money Talia makes?" asked Payton. "There's barely a week her name isn't on at least one of the NYT bestseller lists for YA; she makes *bank*. And she wouldn't gain anything from my death whatsoever."

"But she might gain something from Jackson's." I reminded them of that weird interaction between Talia and Jackson at dinner, before everything went to hell, when she accepted a manuscript from him that she'd promised to read.

"I'm surprised she agreed to read it, but it makes sense he gave it to her," said Payton. "The protagonist's a teenager. I've read parts of it. More than once." She grimaced. "It was . . .

not good. To be honest, it was becoming kind of an issue between us. I could tell he was getting impatient with the assistant gig and wanted to move on. But he kept getting rejected by agents, and it was like he expected me to strong-arm someone into representing him, which was never going to happen. It just wasn't good enough," she said brutally. "There wasn't anything to salvage."

"Maybe she was just being nice," I said. "But it felt like something else was going on. They didn't know each other very well, did they?"

Payton considered the question. "Not really. Talia and I did a little Euro tour last year, because we were both anthologized in some collection from a fancy publisher who had money to burn. Jackson came with, so they definitely met. But I never remember them hitting it off. Or *not* hitting it off."

"Sounds like we all have some follow-up to do," said Joan. She turned to me. "What do you say you and I pay Jessamine and then Talia a visit—"

"I'd like to go, if you don't mind," said Payton.

Joan gave her a tight expression. It wasn't quite a smile—more as if her lips had been sewn together crookedly. She was annoyed with Payton again: a doctor contending with an unruly patient.

"I do mind," she said. "You still need to rest, or at the very least stay in one place. I'd be a bad doctor if I didn't insist."

"And I'd be a bad cruise ship director if I listened to you," said Payton. "Okay, let's compromise. Jessamine will come to me, and Nicole and I will interview her. And you and Belle here can go interview Talia. Deal?"

Oh, how I loved that Joan checked with me before answering. I gave her a nod.

"Deal," she said.

"Aren't we forgetting someone?" I asked.

"I said present company was excluded."

I shook my head. "Not present company. Helen Sanchez."

Payton rolled her eyes. "Oh my God, I'm so sorry she broke into your room because she was so desperate for you to read her manuscript. That doesn't make her a killer. You know you could have just read it and solved your problem."

"I *have* read it," I shot back.

"And?"

"It's really good."

"Well, there you go." She smirked. "You're welcome. Now how could she *possibly* have anything to do with this?"

I told them my pet theory—how she was so obsessive about her writing, I wouldn't put it past her to have orchestrated a murder mystery to make her next novel that much better.

In my defense, it didn't sound nearly as ridiculous in my head.

"Oooookay," said Payton, after a lengthy silence to indicate her disbelief. "If you really want to stand by *that* theory, I'm happy to put her down."

She added Helen as a sixth suspect on the chart. The grid was now full, which pleased me.

The captain, whose presence I'd nearly forgotten, got up from the armchair and headed for the door. Joan laid a hand on her arm. "There's some freezer storage in a back room in the galley you can use. For the bodies."

The captain retracted her arm. "I'll make arrangements. After I finish searching the final passengers on the list."

She tapped the clipboard she was still holding, and made her exit.

"All right." Payton took out her phone. "I'll call up Jess while you two"—she pointed at me and Joan—"go interview Talia in her cabin."

Payton scrolled through what I assumed was a list of room numbers on her screen.

"Room 182," she said. "Let's report back here in, say, a half hour, see what we've got. We can do this!"

I was tempted to grunt: *Break!* I'd always found Payton's "group speak" cringeworthy, not to mention disingenuous. No matter what she did, or with whom, there was no question who the star of the show was from her point of view.

Bossy, mouthed Joan when I looked at her.

CHAPTER 31

As you can imagine, we had a lot to discuss on our way to Talia's cabin.

"So Payton was all about excluding present company, and I get how it would be awkward to do this in front of them," I said, "but we really *should* be considering her and Nicole as suspects."

"Believe me," said Joan, "I am."

"It's easy for her to stand there and shout about not having cheated on Nicole."

"The lady doth protest too much."

"Methinks. *Exactly*. Although they certainly *seem* happy enough."

"You probably haven't heard this before, so prepare for your mind to be blown, but"—Joan took a deep breath— "appearances can be deceiving."

I laughed, releasing a knot of tension from between my shoulder blades I hadn't realized I was holding in.

"There's also the fact that Nicole gets a fair amount of money from Payton if Payton dies," I said. "Did you catch that?"

"I certainly did," said Joan. "Because while Nicole has a solid career as a poet, she obviously makes nowhere near as much as Payton."

"Money is so often the root of evil, isn't it?" I asked.

"We are, as always, on the same wavelength, m'lady."

We walked in silence for a bit. Talia was on the same floor as Payton, but on the opposite end of the ship, so it took a while to get there. Luckily, Joan and her superior sense of direction were leading the way.

"You know," said Joan carefully, and I noticed she wasn't looking at me. "If we're going to include Payton and Nicole as suspects, there are two more people we should include, just to be fair."

"Who?" I asked.

Joan didn't stop walking; if anything, she quickened her pace.

"Us," she said. "We're just as fair game as they are."

"Oh, but, well," I spluttered, "you don't have any sort of a motive. You've never met any of these people before, right? And it's not like you're from the writing world."

"That's true," she said lightly.

And then I saw what she was getting at. *I* was an incredibly robust suspect. Think about it: I hated Payton (even though I also loved her), and I was a weird/secretive person. Was it so out of the realm of possibility to suppose I'd poisoned Table 1 out of jealousy, for instance? I mean, *I* knew I hadn't done it. But Joan didn't. Or anyone else. I remembered those two blank spaces on Payton's chart. Had she been about to put down *my* name? Was I—was I a prime suspect?

Without realizing it, I'd stopped walking. Joan was standing in front of me with her hand on my arm, and it was dark as ever in that labyrinth of hallways. But with her there, the darkness didn't bother me. She looked me full in the eyes.

"I know you had nothing to do with this. *I know you.* Even though I don't know you. If you know what I mean."

I did. It was the most comforting thing anyone had ever said to me.

She put her arm through mine, just like the first time we met. Together we walked onward, to Talia's cabin.

For the first time in my experience of her, Talia Simmons wasn't wearing a scarf. Her hair was so blond, it was nearly as white as Jessamine's. Without the head-covering or her signature lipstick, she looked old and washed-out. Not that I was judging anyone for their appearance at this point. She too was in a state of nervous agitation, though not for the reason I expected.

"Everyone is so worked up about what's happening!" she wailed. "I asked the captain to turn off the Wi-Fi, but she said no."

"I have to think that would be a safety issue," said Joan.

"That may be, but all the TikToking and YouTubing is a safety issue to *me*."

She was wearing a pajama set—matching silk shorts and shirt—and when she threw herself onto her unmade nest of sheets, the not unpleasant aroma of "bed" filled my nostrils.

"Now it looks like I'm holding back because I haven't posted anything. Like Payton asked! But my readers aren't liking it. I've been getting all sorts of messages asking me to weigh in, spill the tea. And my publicist is unreachable, on some remote island in the South Pacific for the next five days since we figured I wouldn't need him while I was on this godforsaken cruise. Disaster!"

"Why don't you say the situation is still developing, and out of concern for the safety of everyone on board, you can't say anything till matters are resolved?" *Otherwise known as the truth*, I thought.

"Yeah, I'm working on it. But I like that. The safety angle." She typed something into her Notes app.

"It must be hard having to be so online for your job," said Joan.

Talia looked up. "We already talked about this," she said sharply. "It is what it is."

"Still, I'd imagine it would be easy for someone to threaten or coerce you with an online scandal, if they wanted to?"

This got her to put down her phone. She hadn't offered us a place to sit, so we were standing on either side of the bed, looming over her.

"What are you suggesting?" she asked coolly.

"We all saw Jackson Richards give you his YA manuscript on a thumb drive last night."

"I know you did. I told you about it at the time. Of my own free will." She was downright icy now.

"There has to be some reason you agreed to help him. If you did that for everyone, you'd be reading unpublished manuscripts all day."

"That's the truth," she muttered.

"So how about sticking with the truth for a second? Cm'on, Talia. Did Jackson . . . encourage your help in some way?"

She was silent, but she was wavering; I could see it. I guessed that it would be a relief to tell someone. Joan guessed it too, pursuing her quarry like a dog sniffing out a bone. A very sly dog. . . .

"Just tell us," she said softly. "It'll be so much easier. Otherwise we'll have to start digging for ourselves, and who knows what we'll find?"

"Okay. And just to be clear, you're not—"

"For the love of God, we're not recording this!" I exclaimed.

"Thank you. So, I went on this publisher junket with Payton and Jackson last year? And there was one dinner where I let loose more than I normally do. There was . . . a *lot* of alcohol involved. I don't usually drink, and it really affected me. You have to understand how boring these events can be."

"I've been to my share of medical conferences," said Joan darkly. "I understand."

"Payton left early, but I stayed later than I should have. Jackson was egging me on, getting me to drink more and more. Eventually, he got me to talk about how much I love certain authors. Roald Dahl, Enid Blyton, J. M. Barrie."

She stopped.

"And?" Joan prompted her.

"Don't you see? He got me to say I didn't care if they're canceled now for their outdated opinions. I said it wasn't fair to judge them for what were commonly held beliefs in their time."

"Okay?"

"You really don't get it? If that video got out on social media I'd be pilloried for it. And I wouldn't be able to say it was a fake, because there were other people who heard me say it, even though Jackson was the only one recording. I've built my brand on being inclusive, and progressive. I actually *am* those things, don't get me wrong, it's just . . . these issues are complicated. But tell that to the kids on Twitter," she said bitterly. "To them the world is black and white. Oh!" She threw up her hands in frustration (not a ring or bracelet on them). "Listen to me, I sound like a—" She lowered her voice. "Like I support *him*. I'm telling you, my ratings would plummet on Goodreads. Eventually it would affect my sales."

"So you agreed to 'help' Jackson with his manuscript," I said, my tone indicating the air quotes around "help."

"Yes," said Talia. "I was rewriting it for him."

Was every writer on this ship entangled in a ghostwriting scheme *except* for me?

"What was to stop him from doing the same thing on the next book?" asked Joan.

"His self-respect, I was hoping."

We looked at her skeptically. I crossed my arms for maximum effect.

"Flora Fortescue never hit you, did she?" I asked her quietly.

Talia fiddled with her pillow, plumping it. "She accosted me."

"But she didn't hit you." I wasn't asking now. "Was that supposed to be a warning shot to Flora? Not to involve you in her beef with Payton? It got swallowed up in what happened at dinner last night, so you never had to bring it up again."

Talia shrugged. "Flora Fortescue is crazy."

But so was fabricating an assault for purposes of one's career. It was almost as crazy as killing a person for the exact same reason. . . . Crazy, but by no means impossible.

Chapter 32

While we were hurrying back to Room 101, we came across a familiar trio of passengers, who approached us from the opposite end of a long hallway.

"Not again," said Joan under her breath.

As I watched June, Phyllis, and Theresa draw near, I realized Phyllis was using a wheelchair powered by electricity, the kind with a remote-control joystick built in to one of the armrests.

"What happened?" I asked her as they drew close.

"What do you mean?" she replied.

"Did you have an accident?"

"No. Remember when I said at breakfast my back was acting up? Nothing like anxiety to make it go from bad to worse. I use my wheelchair when walking becomes too painful."

"Just don't call her wheelchair-bound," said June. "I learned that the hard way."

"Well, I'm not bound or confined by it, am I? It empowers me to get around."

"We can all use as much empowerment as we can possibly get right now," Theresa noted.

"You're not sleuthing, are you?" asked Joan.

"Are you kidding, doll? We're fun-loving, not suicidal."

"What do you mean?" I asked.

"Now that that poor waitress is dead," continued June, "it's only a matter of time before there's a third victim."

"Oh God," I said. "I hope not."

"Plenty of murder cases feature just one death." Theresa adjusted her glasses, squinting at us in the half-light of those globular sconces. "But whenever there's a second death, a third one is usually around the corner."

My eyes strayed involuntarily to the dark corner beyond them, which lay along our route back to Room 101.

"Not necessarily," I said with more confidence than I was feeling. "And anyway, why should murder be an exception to the way expectations fail to live up to reality? Everyone knows the real thing is always less exciting than the fictional one."

"Usually, doll. Usually it is."

June came a step closer, her cane thumping on the thinly carpeted floor.

"But sometimes?"

"Yes?" I asked her breathlessly.

"Sometimes life can be very, very exciting."

She winked at me, and I couldn't help smiling at her.

"Now that we've all been searched, we're going to barricade ourselves in Phyllis's digs. She's got a hot plate!"

"And we aren't coming out for anyone," declared Theresa.

Phyllis pushed her joystick forward, Joan and I parting for them as they passed between us.

The captain had already knocked on the door of Room 101 and announced her presence when we came up behind her. To my surprise, it was Gideon who opened the door.

". . . just like Van Gogh," he was saying, though he stopped abruptly upon seeing us.

"What's just like Van Gogh?" I asked.

"The mess we're all in," he answered shortly.

Payton and Nicole were sitting on top of the bedspread with their backs against the headboard, busily tapping away at their laptops. They both started at the sight of us: not that they actually jumped, but I could tell they were surprised—and flustered—to see us there.

It was strange.

I glanced at the whiteboard, which didn't look to have been touched since we left, with one glaring exception. Someone had written the word "AFFAIR?!?!" to the side of the chart Payton had made. They'd also underlined and circled it, just in case it weren't drawing enough attention to itself.

"What's that about?" I gestured to the word.

"That was me," said Gideon airily. "Payton was telling me about a pet theory of someone's. About how maybe she was cheating on Nic? I pointed out the best possible twist would be that *I* was the third point of the love triangle, and our separation was a sham. I'm not sure why we'd want to hoodwink Nic that way, but I'm still workshopping the possibilities."

"Shut up, Gid," said Payton.

The way she said this, it sounded like a warning. Something weird was going on here. Joan and I exchanged a glance. Why was Gideon even there?

"Sorry," he said. "But you ladies can't expect to have *all* the gumshoe fun."

I wouldn't have let this go, except that now was the moment the captain decided to drop a bombshell.

"I have news."

"Why am I a hundred percent sure it isn't good news?" sighed Payton. "All right, lay it on me."

The captain hesitated, her eyes darting toward Gideon.

"You can trust him," growled Payton. "Say what you need to say."

"One of the last people we searched was a passenger named . . ."

She looked down at her clipboard. I had one of those searing moments of clairvoyance in which I knew the name she was going to say before she said it. For this reason it felt as though I willed it into existence when she looked up and said:

"Geraldine Forrest."

"She goes by Gerry." Everyone looked at me.

"One of your students?" asked Payton.

"No, but we met when we first came on the boat."

"Does she have my necklace?" Nicole asked impatiently.

"No, the necklace still hasn't been found," said the captain. "But she does have a gun."

The word sat there among us: such a tiny word, a word as short and simple as the so-called "snap words" children are taught to recognize on sight so that they don't have to sound them out. But this means it's impossible to take such words apart—to break them down or do anything with them other than accept their implacable presence.

And suffer the consequences.

"Did she have it on her?" asked Payton.

The captain shook her head. "It was in her chest of drawers, underneath some socks."

"Did she admit it was hers?" asked Nicole.

The captain nodded. "Right away. She was very . . . cheerful about it."

"That's what she's like. Cheerful. I liked that about her." I paused. "At first."

Payton snorted, and the two of us made eye contact, micro-bonding in the way old friends can do—years' worth of experience compressed into a single look.

"She's nice, but odd." I told them about my strange interaction with Gerry outside my cabin, after Payton had been sick.

"Do you think she could have been hired by the man who wants my necklace back?" asked Nicole.

"I don't think so," I said. "She's too kooky. I don't get a criminal vibe from her at all."

"By all means let's operate on the authority of whatever vibes do or don't come to you," sneered Gideon.

"I assume you confiscated the gun?" asked Joan, ignoring Gideon's outburst.

The captain shook her head. "She had a license for it," she explained.

"She had a license?" Payton surveyed us doubtfully. "Then I guess that's okay?"

"What are the concealed carry laws in international waters?" asked Joan.

From the doorway, someone cleared her throat.

"In international waters, you follow the laws of the country where the boat is registered. So if her license is recognized under U.S. federal law, she's okay to have it on board the ship. Unfortunately."

Jessamine LaBouchère smiled at us grimly. I guess it's important to keep yourself well informed on the laws surrounding guns when you're doing everything you can to curtail the presence of these stubbornly ubiquitous weapons.

"I'm sorry it's taken me so long to get here. I was writing, and if the long years have taught me anything, it's that the muse must be attended to when she pays a visit. And crises like this tend to make one *more* rather than less productive, don't you find?"

We decided that while Payton, Nicole, and Gideon spoke with Jessamine and the captain transported those two bodies to cold storage, I would seek out Gerry, to get to the bottom of whatever was going on with her. Initially, Payton had suggested that Joan and I go together, but Joan pushed back on this, pointing out that I was the one who had the relationship. I think she just liked pushing back on Payton as a general proposition, but given what a disaster our interview with Gideon had been, I agreed immediately to do this one on my own.

CHAPTER 33

Gerry had told the captain she needed "to breathe some fresh air," so I knew I'd find her on the top deck. I took the stairs, reluctant to get there too quickly, lingering in front of the compass spray-painted on the wall, as though it were a work of art in a gallery. Upon closer viewing, I realized it wasn't a compass at all, but an astrolabe.

What else had I failed to see properly on this ship?

When I came out into the open air, I saw to my surprise that it was early afternoon—the height of the day. I experienced the same disorientation one does upon leaving a matinée show, when the daylight feels shocking, or at least inappropriate. (The nuclear version of this is extracting oneself from the dungeon of a Las Vegas casino and emerging into the hot desert sun . . . which I do not recommend.) It was a wonderfully pleasant day—sunny, with a few puffy clouds brightening rather than dimming the sky. And it was as warm as it had ever been, probably in the low fifties. The fact that no one was here was proof of the extremity of our situation. If not for all the murdering, there would have been a cacophony of voices emanating from under the canopy now. But no one was "getting lit" up here. As far as I could see, the space was empty.

I walked toward the bow of the ship, where Jessamine and I

had watched those two giddy women the day before. No one was here, either. I looked out on the ocean, which was as smooth as ice today. Aside from the condition of the water's surface, the view hadn't changed for days, and when I found myself willing something, anything, to appear—another ship, an iceberg, an airplane crashing into the sea—I realized how frustrated I was by the stasis that had settled over all of us, the hours ticking by and the answers failing to appear.

Who had done the awful things that had happened on this ship? And why?

I headed for the stern, climbing the short flight of stairs to the platformed deck, which was where Gerry and I had met and where I'd known all along she'd be. Sure enough, upon clearing the stairs I saw her: leaning against the railing, looking out at the ocean. I went over to her.

"Do you know the technical term for this deck?"

If she was startled by my presence, she didn't show it. I sidled next to her and she turned to me slowly, a big smile on her face.

"I don't. Please, tell me!"

"The poop deck."

She let loose a great whoop of a laugh, and I told her about how when I was a kid, there was a lot of giggling over Lucy, Edmund, and Eustace from *The Voyage of the Dawn Treader* out on "the poop."

"Oh, that's too funny! You know, I never could get into *The Chronicles of Narnia*. Too Jesus-y. Being Jewish, it always felt like it was on the precipice of being anti-Semitic. If you know what I mean."

I assured her I did, even though I treasure those books—including all the sexism and weird Christian stuff. Unlike Talia, I don't care who knows it.

"My son was a fan of them though. I remember it was one of

the first books he read alone, rather than me reading to him. Since I refused."

Did she not realize she'd done it again? I could hear the blood pumping in my ears, and I had to close my eyes to keep from getting dizzy. *Here goes*, I thought.

"See, that's what I wanted to talk to you about, Gerry. When we first met—"

"Right here!" She struck the railing with her knuckles.

"Yes, true. But this was a little later, when we were going down to find our rooms?"

"Yes?"

"I asked you whether you were with anyone, and you said you were 'footloose and fancy-free.' You said you didn't have a spouse or children. But . . . you just referenced your son. You did it last night too."

Gerry put her hand to her mouth. "How embarrassing. This is why I would make a terrible criminal. I'm glad I stopped before I tried!"

Huh? My look must have said as much, because she laughed. "I'm sorry, I'm being confusing, aren't I? I can see this is going to require a bit of explanation."

"That's okay," I said.

Explanations were in short supply aboard the *Merman Rivera*.

"You see, I was and I wasn't lying when I said I didn't have a partner or children. I *did* have a husband. Had him for forty-three years! And they were mainly happy years too, which is more than most people can say!"

She wasn't going to get an argument from me there.

"The only wrinkle was that his name was *also* Jerry, if you can believe it. With a *J* though. You'd have thought when we got together he'd start going by Jason, or I'd go by Geraldine, but we both thought it was hysterical. Oh, we had fun together."

If you say so, I thought.

"Jerry and I had a son."

"You didn't . . . ?"

She cawed with laughter again. "Of course not! We named him Stephen. Though I always called him Stevie-boy. Much to his annoyance, the older he got. Anyway, I knew from the time he was three that Stevie-boy was gay. Maybe it's problematic of me to say so, but it's true. I always knew and I didn't care. But Stevie-boy was such a sensitive soul. I just hoped he wouldn't get hurt. I lived in fear of hate crimes, homophobes, you name it."

She paused, staring out at the water.

"He got hurt. Badly. But not in the way I imagined." She turned to me. "It was Jackson Richards. He met Stevie-boy in San Francisco. We lived close by, in the Bay Area, but Stevie-boy moved to the city the first chance he got. After graduating from Berkeley, that is."

It was touching the way she could still brag about her son having gone to Berkeley, even in the course of what was obviously a tragic story.

"The two of them dated for nearly a year. Or at least, that's what Stevie-boy said. Now that I know more about the way Jackson Richards operated, I doubt he was ever faithful. But Stevie-boy was sure they'd spend the rest of their lives together. That's how he was—he'd get so attached, he was such a loving person—"

She teared up, and for the first time I could see the anguish in her screwed-up face. But she recovered quickly.

"That year wasn't an easy one for me. Jerry was diagnosed with pancreatic cancer, and it progressed more quickly than we expected. When he passed away, I just fell apart. So did Stevie-boy. That was why Jackson broke up with him. He couldn't handle the tears, the grieving. He didn't want to deal with it." She sighed. "So he got rid of my boy like a piece of trash he had no use for anymore. Like he was disposable."

She leaned further over the railing, as if to get away from what came next.

"Stevie-boy went through months of depression. I didn't ignore it. I did everything you're supposed to do, I made him see a therapist—"

She was getting worked up again, and I rubbed her on the back—just as Nicole had done for me. It wasn't the sort of thing that came easily to me, but she seemed to appreciate it. She stood up straight again, taking deep breaths.

"He killed himself," she said quietly.

"I'm so sorry."

"Thank you. Sorry is the only thing *to* say. It was a tragedy." She paused again, collecting herself. "Even though there was nothing left to say, there was plenty to *do*. I became obsessed with the idea of retribution, I think because in Stevie-boy's case I could latch on to a villain, which I couldn't in Jerry's. I was a psychiatrist," she added. "Back when I was a normal person."

"Ah." This made sense.

"It was a relief to hate Jackson. I put my all into it."

"So what did you do?" I asked.

"Jackson wasn't a total monster. No one is, you know. He felt guilty about Stevie-boy, so he kept in touch with me and I pretended not to hate him. I subscribed to Payton's newsletter, even though I'm not a fan like I pretended to be. She's a little annoying, isn't she?"

I let this go without comment. But Gerry certainly wasn't the first person in the world to hate-read Payton's newsletter.

"When this cruise came up, I wrote to Jackson and asked him if he could get me a ticket as a favor. He did, even though he swore me to secrecy about it. He said he'd get in trouble with Payton if she knew."

"That's why the interaction you had in the dining room that first night was so quick. And why you lied to me about it."

She nodded. "You almost caught us there. We weren't supposed to interact in public, but he didn't take it as seriously as I would have liked. He didn't take *anything* seriously. Of course, the real reason I was so intent on pretending not to know him was that I was planning to kill him! It's why I brought a gun, as I'm sure you know by now."

"Is it . . . ?" I indicated her oversized shoulder bag, which she was carrying with her as she always did.

"Oh! No. It's in my room. I hate the thing."

"I knew you were lying when you said you and Jackson were talking about Sally Rooney. Jackson didn't strike me as a Rooney fan."

"That was half a lie. I was carrying her first book when I checked in, and he told me his mother loved it even more than the second book, the one everyone's read. That was the moment I realized I couldn't go through with it. I'm not trash. Just like Stevie-boy wasn't trash. But Jackson Richards wasn't trash, either. Was I going to put his mother through the hell I'd barely survived?"

She smiled: the ecstatic smile of a believer.

"And then the strangest thing happened. Once I'd made that decision, right here, standing by the railing, standing next to *you*, it felt like a weight had been lifted off me. For the first time since losing my boys I felt like *me* again. I felt *free*—and not just of the anger. In the best of ways I felt free of them, too. Finally, I was able to let them go. It's why I told you I had no one in my life. It's how I felt, and I was celebrating. It felt glorious!"

As strange as her story was, it tracked. She'd been in a manic state when I met her, the euphoria of her epiphany fresh in her mind.

"I have to ask," I said. "What was going on when you were snooping outside my room? The night Payton was taken ill?"

"Oh, that." She swatted the air between us. "I was still so

keyed up. When Payton became ill, I couldn't see who it was in all the commotion, and for a moment I thought it was Jackson. It was almost as though I had—like I had manifested it or something. I was desperate for more information. I'm sorry I violated your privacy like that."

It was my turn to swat the air. "Did you tell anyone about the gun?"

"I told that strange writer girl, Helen Sanchez. She was asking me all sorts of questions about myself. For research, she said. I figured why not? But she was the only one, before my room was searched."

We stood leaning against the railing. The afternoon had peaked, and something had shifted, the sun deepening in hue from blinding white to ever-so-slightly golden.

"The point is," continued Gerry, "I didn't do a thing. I hope you believe me. I had nothing to do with Jackson's death, despite what brought me here."

She reached into her bag now, producing the reusable metal water bottle I always knew she had in there.

"But! I believe I know who *did* do something." She unscrewed the cap from the bottle, her eyes cast downward—slyly demure.

"Please tell me," I begged her.

She raised the water bottle in the air, taking an extended gulp, milking this moment for all it was worth.

Really, though, would I be able to believe whatever she told me? She was hardly an innocent or unbiased observer. Here at long last was the ironclad motive we'd been looking for. Mothers had killed for much less.

And yet I believed her; I believed Gerry before she divulged whatever it was she knew. And as it turned out, everyone else would believe her too. Or they would have believed her, if she'd been able to get the words out.

It happened while she was drinking. A shot rang out from

below—from Lovers' Point, that horseshoe-shaped platform beneath the raised deck, where Gideon and I had canoodled on the first night. Gerry fell to the floor along with her reusable water bottle, which clattered noisily on the wooden planks. But not as noisily as the shrieks that erupted from my throat. For once I was having an audible reaction to a scream-worthy scenario, and though I'm aware the "poop" in "poop deck" comes from the French word "*poupe*," for "stern," I was about to give the official derivation of this word an etymological run for its money.

Because Gerry Forrest had been shot dead, and I was officially losing my shit.

Part Five
Return

Chapter 34

No one had prepared me for what it was like to have a gun go off in close range. Despite the ringing it produced in my ears, the bang was more low-key than I expected; it really did resemble a firecracker, or a car backfiring, or a cork popping out of a champagne bottle. But the smell was much stronger than I anticipated—mainly because I hadn't been anticipating one at all. It smelled like the Zamboni ambling round the ice-skating rink I haunted when I was a kid, desperate to beat the Arizona heat. The fog machine we used for high school plays had a similarly acrid, sulfuric odor. Before now, I never associated the scent of sulfur with evil the way others did (fire and brimstone, etc.). If anything, I associated the smell with pitchy singing and the chewing of scenery. But from this moment on, I knew I'd always think of poor Gerry.

The bullet had entered through the back of her skull, following an upward trajectory, exiting just below the crown of her head. All the blood and brain matter had sprayed away from me, or else I would have been drenched in gory spatter. I don't know how much time passed. Ten seconds? Fifty? I reached out to check for a pulse or other bodily movement, just as I'd done with Kendall, equally certain she was gone.

Nothing. There was nothing.

I found myself racing down the stairs and onto Lovers' Point. I could pretend to you it was bravery that impelled me, or righteous anger. But I had to get away from all those bits of brain. Also, I was curious—determined to see who the culprit was.

I rounded the bend of the horseshoe-shaped platform, passing the bench where, in another life, Gideon and I had cuddled. As I came to the area where I knew the shooter must have been standing, I barreled forward before I could think better of it, coming face to face with—

Flora Fortescue holding a smoking gun.

And to be clear, I do mean that literally.

Flora dropped the gun. I jumped about three feet in the air, expecting it to go off.

"I didn't do it," she said.

"Didn't do what?"

"Shoot it! Was—was anyone hurt?"

"Yes," I said shortly. "Give me your shawl."

Her shawl was navy blue and made of a cashmere so soft, I nearly remarked on it when she handed it over. Wrapping one end of it around my hand, I picked up the gun as gingerly as possible, placing it on top of the shawl's other end. Freeing my hand, I then wrapped the hard black object in fold after fold of softest blue, till I had a neat little package.

"Come on."

I walked toward the main staircase, bypassing the murder scene. Flora followed, and as we made our way to Room 101, she told me her version of events.

"I'd just come up to the top deck. You know, to have a calm moment away from all this madness. Especially since I was on my own, finally. You know there's this woman who's been watching me ever since I saw you this morning? She refused to talk to me. Bitch had AirPods in her ears the whole time, it was so dehumanizing."

"You owe her your freedom," I said. "Otherwise everyone would've assumed you killed Kendall, just like they assumed you killed Jackson."

"I'm aware," she said coldly.

It was then that I realized the trajectory of suspicion as it applied to Flora had followed a familiar path. To begin with, she was the most likely suspect. And then, when the first mate had kept an eye on her, it had been proven she couldn't have done it. But now here she was, on the scene of the third crime and positioned perfectly to have pulled the trigger. This was ye olde double bluff, the oldest trick in the book. All it required to pull off was for Flora to have worked with someone *in addition to* Kendall, a third person who could have killed Kendall while Flora remained under surveillance. I went through all the people who were in Room 101 when the captain told us about the gun: Gideon, Nicole, Jessamine, Joan, Payton, and of course the captain herself. And Helen Sanchez had learned about the weapon directly from Gerry. In other words, every major suspect except Talia Simmons could have told Flora about the gun after I left Room 101, giving Flora plenty of time to run to Gerry's cabin, retrieve the weapon, and nip up to the observation deck. Maybe Flora and Helen had been working together this whole time? I could see it: the two ambitious writers, teaming up for wildly different reasons. . . .

"I heard the shot and came running," Flora was saying. "And when I saw the gun, I just picked it up without thinking. I know it was stupid."

"Why did you run in the direction of the shot? Most people run *away* from a shot."

"Well, why did you?"

"To see who did it."

"Same," she responded unconvincingly.

"You're sure you didn't see anyone else?"

She shook her head. "I feel like I may have heard footsteps

running down the stairs. But maybe I'm Mandela effect-ing them." She looked at me. "That's *it*. I swear."

If the death of Kendall Monteague rocked the *Merman Rivera*, the death of Gerry Forrest capsized it. I informed the occupants of Room 101 (Payton, Nicole, Joan) what had happened, including everything Gerry had told me about her son and Jackson, and her plan to kill the latter. By the time I left Payton and Nicole's cabin, everyone seemed to know about Gerry's death (Flora had been busy), and the fear I'd felt when the three "weird sisters" had prophesied a third murder now pervaded the ship. Everyone more or less barricaded themselves inside their rooms, including me. I was done with Payton's whiteboard, done with being Joan's sidekick, done, period, with sleuthing. I felt disoriented and confused, and I hope you won't think less of me, but when I returned to the safety of my room I began furiously writing notes to myself. Because I knew I had my next mystery.

If only I could survive to the end of it.

Someone knocked on my door.

"Who is it?" I asked warily. Or do I mean wearily? (I mean both.)

"It's Helen."

Oh, Lord.

"Do you have any dangerous weapons on you?"

"No," said Helen.

I opened the door.

The green contact lenses were back in, and today she was wearing orange suspenders that matched her hair perfectly, and which I hoped were a deliberate homage to Milla Jovovich's iconic outfit in *The Fifth Element*. When I was younger, and being noticed by strangers was not just a possibility but a frequent enough occurrence to be considered a nuisance, I made an effort not to stand out. In this way, I preserved my writerly ability to observe others unimpeded. I felt certain that if I critiqued Helen Sanchez for making a spectacle of herself, she and her contemporaries would chide me for my old-fashioned thinking and insist that one could—nay, must—have it both ways. So I said nothing, and pretended she didn't look crazy.

Despite the ridiculous lenses, I could see in her eyes that she was hoping I'd read her damn manuscript. Here we were, three murders deep, and she'd come to harass me about her novel—risking her very life for her art. *Ugh, fine.* I suppose she'd earned a little validation.

"I'm two-thirds of the way through your manuscript, which I only stopped reading because of the *actual* murders happening around us. I love it. You're very talented. I've already told my agent about you. However, if you ask me any follow-up questions now, I'll deny myself the pleasure of finishing it, and my inclination to help you will become much . . . less inclined than it currently is."

She opened her mouth. I could tell by her intake of breath she was about to ask me a question.

"Uh-uh-uh!" I waggled a finger at her.

Her shoulders sagged. "Thank you."

"You're welcome."

She turned to go.

"Hold on a second!" I cried. "I didn't say anything about *me* asking *you* a few questions."

She turned back eagerly. It was obvious she thought I was going to ask her about her writing. Foolish child.

"Before she was killed, Gerry told me that you and she talked about her gun."

"Oh. Yes, that's right."

"How did it come up?"

"I do surveys when I come across people I find interesting.

So that I can refer to them later. She seemed interesting, so I asked her some questions. One of them was, 'Tell me a secret.' She said she had a gun in her cabin, but she wouldn't say why."

Huh. I suppose this was one way to make a spectacle of yourself and continue to observe the finer details of those around you.

"Did you tell anyone about the gun?"

"No." She paused. "But Talia Simmons heard us talking about it. We were in the lounge."

Seriously? Talia was the one suspect I'd thought I could eliminate. Maybe the whole ruse about Flora hitting her was meant to hide the fact they were in cahoots the whole time. *Cahoots?* Enough: I was hanging up my fedora. No more investigating. For real this time.

"She was sitting nearby," continued Helen, "and she asked me about it afterward."

"Uh-huh."

"I never went looking for it," she added. "Or saw it myself. You can't think I had anything to do with her death?"

I gave her a small, sad smile. "If I'm not mistaken, that was a question. Better get out of here if you want me to finish your book."

About a half hour later, the PA system came on.

"Attention, all passengers."

Payton again. No more *Hey ladies*, I noted. We were well beyond such playfulness.

"The boat is due back in New York in approximately fifteen hours."

I looked at my phone. It was nearly four o'clock in the afternoon. This meant we'd be docking early Wednesday morning. The Get Lit Cruise had entered its countdown phase.

"We understand that convening for meals is something some of you may want to do."

The groans of protest I heard through the walls indicated otherwise.

"We'll be serving dinner tonight and breakfast tomorrow in the dining room, but upon your request, we can bring them to your rooms. Free of charge, of course."

It had better be free of charge, I thought. I wondered how many of the cruise's passengers would end up suing Payton. (As it would turn out: twenty-eight of them. And there's still a class action pending.)

"For those of you who might want to get out of your rooms but not for an entire meal, there's an event in Theater 1 in half an hour, where I'll be giving a short talk applying some mindfulness principles, to try to make sense of everything that's happened here over the last few days."

Good luck with that, I thought.

"Obviously you should only come if you want. And if you do, you are assuming the risk inherent in leaving your rooms. The same goes with coming out to eat. I am not *recommending* that you leave your rooms, merely inviting you to do so if you wish. Again, this talk will start in one half hour."

I'd just finished telling myself there was no way in hell I was leaving my room for any of this, when yet another knock came through my door.

"If that's you, Helen, I've got a flaming match I'm *itching* to drop on your book. Just say the word."

"Nice! Can I watch?"

It was Joan. I opened the door.

We stared at each other.

"Well?" she asked finally. "Are you ready?"

"I'm not going to Payton's dumb talk."

"Yes, you are. *I'm* going. So you have to go."

"Because I'm your sidekick?"

"Because you're my friend." She pulled me through the door frame, forcibly intertwining our arms. (She was stronger than she looked.) "This is where the touchy-feely music gets piped in and the studio audience goes: 'Awwwwwwwww.'"

I laughed, allowing her to lead me down the hallway.

"Where were you in high school?" I asked. "I might have actually had a social life if you'd been around."

"Back in high school I was as bad as you."

"Well, at least one of us got better."

Joan insisted on going up to the observation deck first, since we had some time. I didn't want to, given what had happened there the last time I went outside, but she told me I had to face my fears rather than give in to them, and by then someone had covered the entire poop deck with a drop cloth anyway. Not that we went anywhere near it.

"Is she still . . . ?"

"Her body is down in cold storage with the other two," Joan said softly.

I shook my head. "It's unbelievable."

"I know," she replied. "And just like with Kendall, anyone could have done it. When you left Room 101 to come up here to meet with Gerry, the captain and I left right after you did, going our separate ways. And from what I understand, the interview with Jessamine was quick and uneventful. She and Gideon both went back to their respective cabins, leaving Payton and Nicole by themselves. It's pretty clear *those* two would vouch for each other, no matter what. Personally, I've got my eye on Jessamine. That woman knows more about guns than anyone else, and there's also—"

"Could we not?" I begged her. "Could we just . . . look at the sunset?"

"Sure," she replied, switching gears immediately. "Sunset it is."

I hadn't realized how late it had gotten, though at that time of year—late January—the sun began setting around 4:30. Yesterday's sunset had been cloudless: a roiling, fiery ball. Today it was as if that ball of fire had exploded, leaving streaks and trails of brilliance all around the sky. The handful of puffy clouds from middle afternoon had given way to a series of high, wispy formations, which were able to absorb and reflect a surprising array of colors: the usual oranges and reds, but yellows and purples too, even a few shades that came close to green. Heedless of the death and decay below it, the sky was alive with color.

The two of us threw our heads back, gawking at all this glory.

"You can't say it hasn't been a memorable trip," murmured Joan.

That I could not. So I said nothing, and we stood there in silence watching the sky grow darker, until finally it was time to go inside.

CHAPTER 35

This was the first and last time that I visited Theater 1, which was the largest auditorium aboard the *Merman Rivera*. It had a ground level and a balcony, with proper bucket seats bolted to the ground. There was a traditional proscenium arch over the stage, and from the ceiling dangled a teenage version of the ballroom's elaborate chandelier. Joan and I scored good seats down in the stalls, considering there wasn't much room. The theater seated one hundred, and it was nearly full—which was a lot more people than I'd been expecting.

Even in the midst of a murderous rampage, Payton Garrett was a draw.

Nicole was there, of course, taking in the scene with her keen eye. (Could she have tried to murder Payton for the money that would come to her?) Beside her sat Gideon, phone in hand. (Did he hate his ex-wife so much, or was he so desperate to have his children to himself that he would kill her over it?) I twisted around, looking up at the balcony. In the front row was Helen Sanchez, her trusty notebook and pen in hand. (She was undeniably a crazy writer: crazy enough to murder for purposes of honing her craft?) A few seats away from her sat Flora Fortescue, who waved down at me when she saw me looking. (Had her revenge campaign against her former best

friend spun wildly out of control?) Making a point of not waving back, I turned around in my seat. Three rows ahead of us,
near the front of the stage, Jessamine LaBouchère and Talia
Simmons were deep in conversation. *About what?* I wondered. (Had Jessamine committed an "altruistic murder" for
the sake of a pet charity? Or had Talia murdered the man
who was threatening to jeopardize her career?) All the way to
the right, at the edge of the orchestra section, Captain Marcie
sat slumped in her aisle seat looking spent. (Could everything
that had happened on this boat, *her* boat, be tied to a childhood grudge?)

So much for hanging up my fedora. Old habits die hard.

Payton was five minutes late by now—and counting. The
diffuse hum of chatter grew into a buzz, threatening to grow
into a roar as the seconds ticked by. Infected by this nervous,
fidgety energy, I twisted around in my seat again, spying a familiar trio shuffling into the back of the theater, taking up a
space in the back row where there was room for a wheelchair.
Despite their declaration that they wouldn't budge from the
safety of a locked cabin, June, Phyllis, and Theresa hadn't been
able to stay away. Theresa and I nodded at each other, and I
faced forward again.

The only people who were missing were Pierre Gasçoigne,
who I guessed was in the kitchen putting the finishing touches
on his seafood bouillabaisse, and Sandra Gutierrez, who was
probably helping him amid a million other food-related and
housekeeping chores. Kendall Monteague's death had rendered a short-staffed situation significantly shorter.

"Payton's late," I observed.

"The better to make her grand entrance, my dear," said Joan,
and indeed, when Payton Garrett walked out a minute or two
later, there was an immediate hush.

She was dressed in straight-leg chinos and a scoop-neck
shirt, both black. She looked to me like a well-heeled tech ex-

ecutive (though she was wearing loafers, not heels). Maybe that's because she had on one of those fancy headsets with a microphone built into it. Also, she was carrying a tall bottle of Smartwater with its cap already removed, which she placed on a lone barstool standing in the very center of the stage.

I watched her press the palms of her hands together, and for one horrible second I thought she was going to say *namaste*.

"Welcome."

The microphone volume was adjusted perfectly to the room. It felt like we were attending a TED Talk. And in a way, I suppose we were.

A TED Talk on murder.

"A lot has happened since we embarked on this journey."

Her voice was deeper than in regular conversation, and she was enunciating more carefully. She was in podcast-host mode.

"We began it with such high hopes at our drinks Sunday night. When the brilliant poet, Nicole Root, graced us with her words."

Payton gestured to her wife, who blew her a kiss—but in an appropriately solemn manner.

"And what a day we had on Monday. I was so heartened by the thoughtfulness my students brought to both our sessions. And from all I heard from my colleagues, I know they would say the same." She walked to the edge of the stage. "Do you know why I brought you all here?"

"To make money?" Joan whispered in my ear.

I threw her a warning look. If she kept this up, there was no question I'd start laughing. I always get the giggles when I'm nervous.

"Because I knew that together, we would be stronger. That we would go further than we ever could on our own. This is the power of bringing people together. And in particular, of bringing *women* together."

She paused to let this sink in, the room perfectly silent.

"But contrary to what men have been telling us since the first woman was forced to sit down, shut up, and listen to the first man, we women are *not* angels. We are as flawed as our male counterparts, because we're human too. It's crazy that we have to remind ourselves of that. But we do."

She paused again, and this time the silence was punctuated by the repositioning of numerous bodies. Not in a restless way, but in an effort to settle in, to get comfortable.

"And so, things took a turn for the worse on Monday night." She placed a hand on her chest. "At dinner, in front of all of you, I projectile-vomited!"

She opened her eyes wide, eyebrows lifted, forming an "O" with her mouth: a caricature of surprise.

"A horrifying experience, worthy of one of those stress dreams we all have every now and then. You know, where you're naked in public or you haven't studied all year for a final exam." She shook her head, and began pacing along the front edge of the stage. "Oh, how we *love* to torture ourselves. In one way, the real thing was nowhere near as bad as what I imagined, because there was no room for embarrassment. I was too scared to be embarrassed." She stopped again, looking out on all of us. "It's important to acknowledge that. I was scared when I threw up and my body began to hurt. I thought I was dying. And I'm not going to stand here and chastise myself for that fear. It was an understandable emotion. But the downside to my fear is that it kept me from thinking clearly. That's what fear does. I've talked about this before. Fear is the enemy of objectivity. It robs us of the clarity we need to assess whatever problems are thrown our way."

The people around Joan and me were all nodding their heads.

"It took me a long time, much longer than I would have liked, to see what was happening here on this ship. To see it for what it *really* is. And now for the mea culpa. For a long time, I focused on the easy answer. I was convinced the person who boarded this ship to make my life more difficult *had* to have been behind everything that went wrong. I thought she poisoned me and my unfortunate dining companions at Table 1 because she wanted me to suffer."

Payton stopped, pointing with her index finger up at the balcony. Everyone turned to see the object of her gaze, which was Flora, of course. (Flora was so perfectly positioned in the front row for this moment, I wondered if they'd worked it out together, beforehand.) And then Payton turned her hand over, palm-side up, and stretched out the rest of her fingers so that what had started as an accusatory gesture became a joyous one.

"I'm sorry, Flora, that I wasn't a better friend to you. I will always argue for an artist's right to create whatever she feels driven to create, as long as it doesn't constitute plagiarism. And I stand by the fact that my book was *not* plagiarism. But I could have chosen to do something different, out of consideration to you as my friend. I chose not to. I chose my art over my friendship, and that makes me a bad friend. I own that. And I apologize for it. I know this doesn't erase the pain I've caused you, but I hope it can help you move forward."

I saw Flora's face crumple, and turned away because I can't bear watching other people cry—especially people I know. Payton retracted her hand and took a few steps backward, toward the stool in the middle of the stage.

"And moving forward is *so* important. For all of us. Because it allows us to solve the problems we're confronted with every day. The big ones and the not-so-big ones. And here's a biggie for you. Who the heck is behind all the horrible things that have been happening on this boat? Whodunit, am I right?"

She paused to take a sizable gulp of water.

"This denouement is brought to you by Smartwater," Joan whispered—just loudly enough to ape the tone and cadence of an announcer.

This time, I'm afraid I let loose a titter or two. But I stifled them quickly.

"Unfortunately, my obsession with what Flora was or wasn't doing distracted me from a more important question surrounding her." She put down the water. "How on earth did she get on this cruise? Like all of you, she'd signed up for my newsletter under her own name, but given what was happening between us, an invite never would have gone out to her. *And it didn't*. But she says she got one, and you know what? I believe her. So that means someone who got one of the invites we sent in the mail slapped a fresh label on it with Flora's name and address, and mailed it to her."

This information generated more than a few murmurs in the audience. Many of these women had benefited from the sharing of invitations among friends. But the notion of *re*-mailing an invitation to a person who hadn't been invited was a new one.

"I know, pretty crazy, right? Flora herself admitted using a fake name to sign up, which brings us to the moment she boarded the ship. As you're all aware, it was my assistant, Jackson, who checked in the passengers. And when I confronted him after Flora's dramatic entrance, he claimed he didn't recognize her when she came onto the ship because she must have been wearing some sort of disguise."

Payton thrust her chin up, shading her eyes with one hand—even though there was no light shining in them.

"Tell me, Flora. Were you in disguise when you boarded the ship?"

"I wore sunglasses and a straw hat!" Flora shouted down.

I already knew that, I thought.

"But it's not like you couldn't have recognized me," she continued, clearly enjoying this bonus moment in which everyone was looking at her again. "I was surprised when Jackson didn't say anything."

Payton put her hand down. "Thank you. It's clear to me that Jackson Richards was prompted by someone to let Flora onto the ship without raising an alarm, and to pretend later that he didn't know anything about it. This was the same person who sent Flora the invite, and who murdered three people in the last twenty-four hours: first Jackson himself, and then, to cover up that murder, Kendall Monteague, and finally, Geraldine Forrest."

Payton put her hands together, letting them rest in front of her.

"When I learned that my assistant Jackson had died, the first thing I did was to call his mother."

No, I thought, *the first thing you did was to freak out about how much money you were going to lose.*

"And when I spoke to her, do you know what she asked me?"

Payton paused, letting this question hang in the air.

"She asked: 'Was it a hate crime?' "

This time the muttering was so loud, Payton had to quiet her audience using her hands.

"How tragic, but how understandable, that that's where a mother's mind would go concerning the fate of her son who identified as a gay man. And while Jackson's death was *not* a hate crime in the way we've come to use that phrase, it very much *was* a crime of hate."

She began pacing the stage again, Gideon tracking her with his phone's camera. I felt certain he would have made an audio-only recording if he were acting independently, and guessed she'd asked him to videotape her.

"I of course assumed this was all about me. But, ladies, it was never about me. These murders had *nothing* to do with me." She lifted her arms, opening them wide on either side of her and giving them a little pump with each word she now bellowed: "*It. Is. Not. About. Me!*"

"Oh, dear," murmured Joan.

My thoughts exactly.

Payton let her arms fall. "There's a lesson here. About the perils of privilege. And the power of humility. I'll have a *lot* more to say about that real soon, I promise you." She began walking again. "But so long as I continued to suffer from main character syndrome, I couldn't see anything clearly. So when Flora Fortescue was proven beyond a doubt to have had nothing to do with the murder of Kendall Monteague, I was lost. Especially when I realized that if Flora hadn't done it, *anyone on the boat* could have been guilty.

"By that point we knew Kendall had poisoned the salads at Table 1, and that someone must have paid her to do it. Easy enough. But at the time Kendall was killed, we were all in our cabins, submitting to a boat-wide search for the necklace someone stole from my wife. And yes, the person who stole the necklace was also the person who committed the murders."

She stopped, throwing out her hands in an imploring gesture.

"Ladies, it isn't true that anyone could have done it, and I'll tell you why. We were all made to believe that everything started with the poisoning of those salads. But it didn't. Because let's go ahead and exercise our left-brain, rational thinking for a second: Does it make any sense that after I ate a few foxglove leaves I more or less *spontaneously* threw them up and started having heart palpitations? And that Jackson, who was fit and young, would have died a few hours later from those same leaves? Yes, he indulged in some recreational drugs—frankly, who hasn't—but that doesn't account for how quickly the foxglove killed him. The only reaction that made sense was my wife Nicole's. She got fairly sick a number of hours later, and then she got better."

Payton crossed over to the bar stool again.

"It takes *time* for these poisons to work. They aren't instantaneous. So if I hadn't been consumed by fear, if I'd been thinking straight, I would have realized what was obvious. That Jackson and I were both poisoned *before* dinner."

290 / KEMPER DONOVAN

While a ripple of disbelief ran audibly through the crowd, Payton took a quick sip of water.

"Do you have any idea where she's going with this?" I whispered to Joan.

Joan shook her head: *no.*

"I had a drink yesterday when the afternoon session ended, at four o'clock. It was my usual virgin strawberry daiquiri, but it tasted strange to me. So much so that at dinner, I asked for something different. I'm now convinced my first dose of digitalis was in that daiquiri, at lunch. It was in reaction to *this* drink that I threw up a little over three hours later, at dinner. As for Jackson—"

She put down the water and began walking again—prowling, really. An animal on the scent of a solution.

"He'd been getting regular doses of digitalis for days by that point. Four days, to be exact. Ever since we first got on the ship in New Jersey, *three days* before the cruise began. The digitalis must have been administered in small doses so as not to debilitate him. But over time, it began to build up so that by the night of the welcome drinks, I wasn't the only one to notice his dilated pupils, and the way he was sweating profusely. When he called my frozen strawberry daiquiri, which was very obviously red in color, a lemon daiquiri, I joked that he was blind. This was insensitive of me, and not just for my internalized ableism. Minutes later he called Flora 'Little Miss Sunshine,' and I thought he was being sarcastic." Payton stopped walking and looked up, putting her hands over her eyes again. "No offense, Flora, but you weren't exactly . . . congenial when you first made your presence known."

"None taken!" shouted Flora.

At least someone in the audience was enjoying herself.

"But what if she *looked* like sunshine to him? If I'd been paying attention, I would have realized Jackson was suffering from a condition known as xanthopsia, which makes everything, or most things, look yellow. And what is the most common cause of xanthopsia, ladies? You guessed it. An excess of digitalis."

Did you know that some people believe the artist Vincent van Gogh suffered from xanthopsia, as a result of being prescribed digitalis for his epilepsy? Apparently Gideon Pereira did! Hence the mismatched pupils in at least one of Van Gogh's self-portraits, and the haze around the stars in his famous *Starry Night* painting. And all the yellow in his "yellow period," overall. There's even a portrait of his doctor with what looks like foxglove in the foreground. . . . I'm much more knowledgeable about xanthopsia now than I was then.

"The foxglove in the salad on Monday was nothing more than window dressing. Which means the only people who could have been responsible for the death of Jackson Richards had to have been on the boat before any of the regular passengers set foot on it. Not three hundred people, but just over a dozen."

If this had been the last ten minutes of a mystery show on BritBox or PBS, Payton would have run through the shortened list of suspects while each protested their innocence in turn. She didn't do this, however. The majority of these suspects weren't even inside the theater. They were workers, like Sandra, crew members needed for the running of the ship.

"Once I was able to whittle down the list and take a closer look at who was left, it didn't take me long to zero in on the culprit."

She walked to the edge of the stage again, exactly in the center. "Okay. It's time to talk about Geraldine Forrest, or Gerry, as her friends called her. The woman who lost her life a short while ago."

I stiffened in my seat, resisting the urge to flee. I didn't want to hear what Payton had to say about Gerry. I didn't want to think about Gerry at all.

"Gerry had a son, who had been in a relationship with Jackson Richards. Now I don't want to get into the nitty-gritty of it all, because Jackson isn't here to defend himself and it's not my story to tell. But suffice to say that when they broke up, it was at Jackson's instigation, and Gerry's son took it badly. So badly that a number of months later, he died by suicide."

Gasps and murmurs from the crowd. I was pretty sure it was June who croaked, "Poor fellow," from the back of the theater.

"Gerry asked Jackson for a spot on this cruise and, unbeknownst to me, he gave her one. I'm sure he felt guilty about what happened. The irony is that by going out of his way for her, he put himself in great danger. Gerry brought a gun on board, and her plan was to kill him."

Greater gasps. Longer murmurs.

"But, and I'm very proud of this, from the moment Gerry set foot on this cruise she felt the possibility, the power of different choices. *Better* choices." Payton unleashed a beatific smile on us. "She couldn't go through with it. Which makes it even more tragic that she was killed by the very gun she brought on board. You see, she was in the process of telling someone—"

Here Payton turned to *me*, and I had to forcibly fight the urge to sink down in my seat.

"—about having recognized another person on the ship. I believe I know what she was about to say, and I'm prepared to say it now."

Payton was still looking at me. She gave me an encouraging smile, which I returned uneasily. What did she want from me?

"It was a person she recognized as being wrapped up in the tangled web of Jackson's love life. A person who Jackson himself hadn't recognized, which should give you a sense of just how tangled that web was. Come on." She beckoned me with her hand. "It's time to come clean."

What the hell? She didn't seriously think *I* was the murderer, did she? I was nowhere near the boat till the day it left the port in New Jersey. She had to know that.

And yet she was still staring at me.

"It's time."

Holy crap, I was seriously in danger of passing out, what was her—

"Don't you agree, Doctor?"

Oh, never mind. She'd been looking at Joan, not me.

CHAPTER 36

Joan turned to me with an expression of outraged astonishment I could feel mirrored on my face. Had Payton lost her mind? I had just enough brain power left over to process the fact that Nicole was turning around in her seat and now recording Joan on her phone, which allowed Gideon to maintain his hold on Payton. They had planned this out beforehand. . . .

Payton let out a sigh. "Looks like you're not quite ready. Okay."

She moved stage right and began pacing again—slowly, from one side of the stage to the other.

"It was Dr. Joan Chen who got an invitation as one of my subscribers, but never used it. Instead, she contacted me and was hired as the ship's locum physician. This was how she invited Flora along, for purposes of distraction. As a member of the staff, she was on the boat three days before it set sail—with me, Jackson, and the rest of our staff, giving her plenty of time to befriend her victim. She made sure the nurse who was supposed to accompany her got sick just before the boat was set to leave, so that we couldn't hire a replacement in time. This gave her free rein, and meant she would be the only medical authority on board. She had all the opportunity in the world to approach her fellow staff member, Kendall Monteague, and offer her money in exchange for help, for what I suspect she told Kendall was a harmless prank. Kendall took her up on her offer because she needed the cash. Not just for her, but for her daughter. After that dramatic episode at dinner, it was Dr. Chen who kept pushing the idea of the foxglove leaves having such a quick reaction. It was one of the first things I asked her: Wasn't my reaction strangely fast? When she said that different people react differently, I took her at her word, since she's a doctor. And I was willing to listen to her when she kept telling me I couldn't get out of bed, or leave my cabin, or do much of anything. Time and again, it was the good doctor who held me back while *she* went everywhere. She herself admitted that on the night everyone at Table 1 fell ill, she went around to the cabins of passengers who thought they might have been poisoned. So what was stopping her from going to Jackson's cabin? My guess is she gave him something she said would make him feel better, which was the final dose of digitalis that did him in.

"When it came time to silence Kendall Monteague, who played such a key role in her scheme, she used a crochet hook that Jessamine LaBouchère had left in the medical bay. What was easier than picking it up and popping down the hall to Kendall's room to use it? Later, after Kendall's body was discovered, it was Dr. Chen who propagated the fallacy that such a violent act was more likely to have been committed by a man. Regressive much? I've said it before, and I'll say it again. We women can do *anything*. I'm not going to pretend this is a banner day for women's lib, but it's a lesson worth taking to heart."

Payton spread her arms wide.

"In other words, Joan Chen had *all* the access. Not just the access to poisons and drugs that came with being a doctor, but the access that came with being on this boat for three days before the cruise began."

"Oh my God," I heard someone exclaim from the back of the theater, and this time I was sure it was Phyllis.

The importance of access was *my* lesson. How dare Payton appropriate it like this? Sure, if Joan Chen had had time to organize jokey pools about how long it would take passengers to reenact *Titanic,* she had enough time to plan a murder. But *why*? It still made no sense.

Payton stopped pacing. She let her arms fall gently to her sides.

"But why, right? That's the big question. Why commit all this murder? For what?" She looked at Joan again. "Are you *sure* you don't want to tell this part yourself?"

This time I didn't look at Joan. I couldn't. But I could see out of my peripheral vision that in addition to not speaking, she wasn't moving. Eventually Payton had to say something.

"Up till now, I haven't offered you any evidence for any of this. Maybe that's why the doctor is reluctant to speak out. She must have been careful not to communicate with Jackson or Kendall by phone, and I'm sure she swore them both to secrecy. But there was one thing about Jackson the doctor forgot to take into account."

Payton paused. The silence in the theater was exquisite. If she'd been delivering a Shakespearean monologue, her command over us couldn't have been abler. . . .

"Jackson Richards was a writer. He made a habit of jotting thoughts down on his Notes app, which saved automatically to the cloud. A cloud that *we* shared as coworkers, which means I have access to everything he wrote. He must have been thinking his adventures with the doctor would make a good story, because he took *a lot* of notes. In detail." She turned again to Joan. "So please. Tell us in your own words. Once the lawyers get involved, you might never get another chance."

I could sense Joan shifting at my side. Her mouth must have been dry, because I could hear her lips unsticking from each other as she opened her mouth. Finally, Dr. Joan Chen, MD, was ready to speak.

"Jackson Richards was a fuckboy. A few years back, in San Francisco, he had sex with my fiancé, which put an end to my engagement. None of you will understand this, but I'd managed to find a man I respected who fit my parents' *extremely* specific requirements. I'd done the impossible, inserting the thread of self-actualization inside the needle's eye of filial duty. And Jackson Richards destroyed all that work in a matter of hours because of his libido. The sad thing, *ladies*, is that all this murder and intrigue comes down to one man's lust for another man."

I thought back to the word that had been circled on the whiteboard in Room 101: *AFFAIR?!*

"Thank you." Payton did her namaste pose again, pointing her pressed-together hands at Joan. "Once I zeroed in on the people who were on the boat before we set sail, I remembered you talking about your ex-fiancé. And I stopped being such a heteronormative dinosaur. Though my wife had a little to do with that as well."

She nodded at Nicole, as a few audience members tittered.

I was in no danger of giggling now.

"A quick look back at the engagement announcements for the *San Francisco Chronicle* gave me your ex-fiancé's name," she continued to Joan, "and I e-mailed him. He told me about the whole thing. He takes full blame for it, by the way."

"I know," said Joan. "He's lovely."

I felt like an idiot for having assumed her ex-fiancé's affair was with another woman—I guess because he'd gone on to marry another woman? Back in the '90s, bisexuality seemed like a half measure designed for people who couldn't quite

298 / KEMPER DONOVAN

commit to homosexuality yet. Especially the men. I thought I'd moved on from such antiquated thinking. I guess I hadn't.

This whole time I'd thought I was the sidekick to Joan. But it turned out I wasn't even the sidekick. *Payton* was the detective.

I was just a dupe.

Odds and ends floated into my consciousness now, like so much flotsam and jetsam:

—Joan telling Kendall at dinner that first night, "You're as much my concern as any of the paying passengers. Remember that."

—The way I'd pawed through Jackson's things, laughing along with his murderer. . . .

—Joan "texting" with her colleague while we were in the dining room examining the remains of the salad, laying the groundwork for her argument about how quickly foxglove acted on the body.

—The way she'd gestured for me to knock on Kendall's cabin door so that Kendall would see *me* first, rather than her conspirator, and know not to say anything that could incriminate either of them.

—Kendall pleading in the conversation the three of us went on to have: "I would never do anything other than what I was hired to do. All I want is to get paid, and go home." And later in that same interview, Joan name-checking Kendall's young daughter. . . .

—Joan's obvious fatigue in the aftermath of finding Kendall's body.

—My realization minutes before we came to this very theater that Joan was stronger than she looked.

"This is a sad, sad story," Payton was saying. "I wish it were a different story. But it's the truth."

Were we done? We couldn't be done. As much as I hated everything about the time I'd spent thus far in Theater 1, I prayed against hope there was more. Because what came after this? I didn't want to think about it. I couldn't.

"Wait!" cried a voice from the audience. "What about my necklace?"

It was Nicole. Payton gestured for Joan to take this one, if she would.

"Right," said Joan. "That was just another smoke screen, I'm sorry to say. I threw it overboard."

Nicole let out a groan.

"Just like Rose," she continued mischievously. "Though I didn't do it in my nightgown, and I didn't make that annoying little 'ope!' sound she does. I'm pretty sure it's lost forever. Sorry." She looked at Payton. "I feel like you want me to spill my guts here, but all this"—she waved her hands in front of her—"is not my scene. I'm sorry for having terrorized you all. And for Kendall and Gerry. I'm not sorry for Jackson, though. If that makes me a monster, then so be it. He was a monster too. And a dumb one. At least I have some depth to me. After all, you know what they say."

And now, for the first time since confessing, she looked down at me. I knew suddenly what she was going to say, and I shook my head, pleading with her not to do it. But she shook hers back at me. Determined. Ruthless.

"A woman's heart is a deep ocean of secrets."

CHAPTER 37

Joan went willingly with the captain. When they exited the theater, there was a palpable sense of relief—not so much a collective sigh as a collective slumping: shoulders sinking, backs curving, the diffuse chatter that had preceded Payton's performance making a turbocharged reappearance. Gideon and Nicole had stopped recording, and even though Payton was still on the stage, she was no longer in speechifying mode. I noticed how tired she looked. When she moved to one side, the audience quieted down again, I suppose expecting her to bestow on them one final pearl of wisdom. She sensed the expectation and stopped, throwing up her hands helplessly.

"That's all, folks!"

People laughed. To my left, two women began complaining to each other about how hungry they were. I could picture them so easily in the dining room at their Hogwarts tables, slurping down their seafood bouillabaisse as they reviewed each gory detail. . . .

For the most part, however, the people around me hadn't moved yet, and I knew why. They were too busy on their phones, dishing to the world about what they'd just witnessed. This was the calm before the storm: a reverse hurricane that would grow in strength as soon as we left the water and moved onto dry land.

I rose, shuffling past the people in my row, trying not to step on anyone's feet. (I'd already done enough damage aboard the *Merman Rivera*.) As I made my way down the aisle, I willed myself not to look at the three "weird sisters," though I couldn't call them that anymore. That had been Joan's name for them.

Naturally I looked up at the last minute, making direct contact with Theresa, whose eyes conveyed nothing harsher than pity. And yet her pity wounded me much more than her contempt would have, laying waste to whatever tatters of pride I'd drawn around me.

I reached the lobby area on the second deck in record time, catching sight of Joan and the captain as they entered the stairwell. I waited till they'd gone down half a flight before entering it myself, so that I could keep tabs on them without announcing my presence. They exited one floor down, so I ran after them, following at a discreet distance as they wended their way down a number of hallways within the labyrinth. Eventually, they stopped at a cabin and disappeared inside.

I waited exactly two minutes (I used my phone timer) before knocking.

The captain came to the door.

"Is this your room?" I asked her.

She nodded. "I didn't know where else to put her."

"Do you mind if I talk to her for a few minutes? Alone?"

She nodded; I think she was relieved. And though Captain Marcie had proven herself less than capable at knowing what to do in various social settings, this time I couldn't blame her for being at a loss.

Also, I wasn't exactly in a position to judge anyone else for, well, anything.

The captain slipped out, and I slipped in. The cabin was the same size as mine, and the layout was almost identical. Joan was sitting on the bed.

In hindsight I'm surprised at myself for not being afraid she might do something to me when we were alone. She was a triply murderous sociopath, after all. But I was in such pain, the threat of more pain didn't bother me.

I settled into the small, hard chair that went with the desk. We regarded each other wordlessly. The strangest thing about seeing her like this was that after a murderer confesses, she's basically supposed to stop existing. I think this is why in so many murder mysteries, the culprit dies at the end—either by way of suicide, or due to some other machination of the plot. It's a tidy ending that dispenses with having to worry about life after confession. But here she was.

And here I was.

"I'm sorry," she said finally. "I know I'm the worst."

Another violation of the genre: Wasn't she supposed to turn into a gibbering psychopath upon being unmasked? There were even comedy sketches sending up the way these villains' voices, and faces, changed mid-denouement. But Joan was still very much herself.

"I'm sure you want to know why I did this. The *real* reason why. I'll tell you, and only you. It's the least I can do for what I put you through."

"Thank you," I said—because heaven forbid this serial killer not like me. What would I ever do?

"It's not that I lied up there. I *did* do it for revenge. But it wasn't revenge for the death of my marriage. It was revenge for—as cheesy and overblown as this is going to sound—the death of my dreams."

She looked away from me, fixing her eyes on a patch of wall.

"Ever since I was a teenager I wanted to be a writer. But pursuing it in college, or at grad school, was never an option. I had to do something practical. It's just what was expected of me. So I took my pre-med courses and went to med school. But that whole time I wrote on the side whenever I could— which wasn't much. And at med school I met this wonderful guy, who was the first, and only, person I shared my writing with. And he was so supportive. And when he proposed to me, he talked about how I could take time off after school, or maybe after my residency, before we had kids. And I would write my little heart out, give it a real go. He was so great about it. So supportive in a way no one else ever was. But then Jackson came along and derailed all that, and I had to go back to supporting myself. So I did my residency, and started working as a doctor. Do you want to know the real reason I had a kid?"

I nodded. I mean, I didn't *want* to. But I had to.

"For the time off. To get to write. I even had a night nurse, the whole shebang. I thought I was all set, all ready to concentrate on my craft, full steam ahead." She laughed: a hollow, mirthless noise, nothing like the lively sounds I was used to hearing issue from her mouth. "You can guess how that went. I got nothing done. Zip. And there was even less time after the maternity leave ended, which happened in the blink of an eye."

"How could you kill another mother like that?"

"I've never really identified as a mother," she replied. "I know that sounds awful, but then I *am* pretty awful, aren't I?"

"Not identifying as a mother doesn't make you awful. Killing three people does."

"Fair," she said. "Listen, I want to be totally upfront about having used you. But I also want you to know all the friend stuff? Which I think you felt too? It was real." She laughed again, and this time she sounded like herself. "I'm basically the protagonist in a romantic comedy who starts protesting late in the second act—or is it at the top of the third act?—that what started as an artificial relationship for whatever dumb reason turned genuine. And now there's nothing I can do to prove it, but that doesn't change the fact that the feelings are real. Do you know what I mean?"

I nodded, because I always knew what Joan meant. Therein lay the problem.

"Remember when I said murder is stupid?" she continued. "I stand by that. It *is* stupid. *I'm* stupid. I don't think I'd ever have fallen into the rut that led to . . . all of this, if I'd had a friend like you."

Was she trying to have a *moment* with me?

"Did you have a plan for how you were going to use me?" I asked sullenly, refusing to play along.

"No. For all the planning I did, there was a lot I had to figure out on the fly. I had a lot of good luck, but I had just as much bad luck. Take that drink of Payton's on Monday afternoon, the one that had the digitalis in it. She drank that at four. The idea was that she'd get sick soon *after* she ate the salad at dinner. I figured around nine or so, and that she'd get sicker than the others since she'd had the drink *plus* the foxglove in the salad. And she did get sick after eating the salad, but only just. And that became the weakest part of the plot—that the foxglove from dinner would have kicked in so quickly. So that was bad luck. But what would have happened if she'd gotten sick twenty minutes earlier? *Before* she ate the salad? Then there would have been no question she'd been poisoned before dinner, and the whole thing would've fallen apart much quicker than it did. So that was good luck."

The words were flowing out of her. It was helping her to tell me all this, and while I wasn't particularly interested in helping Joan the murderer, her confession was helping me, too. I needed to know everything. Also, I'd been recording our conversation since entering the room. So I sat there, letting her talk as much as she liked.

"I never knew Flora liked gardening. That was a happy coincidence. Sorry, 'happy' is a poor choice of words. And all that nonsense about Jessamine maybe wanting to kill Payton, I had no idea about all that beforehand. I did know about Jackson having dirt on Talia Simmons, because he told me all about it. I was the one who encouraged him to ask her for help on his manuscript. And I figured there was tension between Payton and Gideon, how could there not be? God, the whole thing was exhausting to pull off. Not that I did, did I? It all went off the rails much faster than I expected, like a crash in real time. Kendall was a big mistake. Big. Huge! But I had to rely on *someone* to put the foxglove in the salad, and I didn't think she'd fall apart the way she did. I was the one who came up with that story about dropping the salad plates, after she came crying to me about the state of her hands. What a mess. I also thought I'd get a lot more out of everyone assuming Payton was the intended victim. The key was not looking too closely at Jackson, and to get everyone to assume he was collateral damage. But that assumption never really took hold. I guess that's the hazard of killing someone on a boat full of readers."

"How did you think it up?" I asked, goading her to continue.

"Well, I subscribed to Payton's newsletter for the same reason Gerry did. One of many ways I kept tabs on Jackson, which I'd been doing ever since the affair. By the way, I personally can't *stand* her writing, I think you're *much* better than she is."

"Aw, shucks. Make sure you tell that to all your new friends. Think how huge I'll be with all the violent offenders in federal prison."

It was shocking how easy it was to fall back into this bantering rhythm with her.

"Will do. And then I got that invitation. I mean, talk about luck! If I hadn't been one of the five hundred subscribers to get that invitation, I never would have been able to do any of this. But when I saw that disclaimer about no surveillance, no security presence, how could I resist? What better place to carry out a murder, right? Especially with all the intrigue I knew Flora Fortescue would provide. And especially when all those news stories came out about how people were sharing their QR codes. I knew if I sent mine to Flora it would never be traced back to me." She paused. "There were a few details Payton got wrong. I took my address label off, for one. I never would have risked slapping Flora's address over mine. And I actually hand-delivered the invitation to her apartment in New York. I put it in the slot of her mailbox myself, with a hoodie over my face in case someone caught me on the building's surveillance camera. I felt like a spy or something. But I couldn't leave it up to the USPS, you know?"

I nodded.

"I worried beforehand Flora might notice the stamp hadn't been canceled by the post office, but then I started noticing the post office forgets to cancel stamps a lot, so I figured that wouldn't matter. . . . You can see the obsessiveness that went into all this. But I knew a murder on a boat would be easier than a murder on dry land. This might be the most obvious thing anyone's ever said, but figuring out how to kill someone without getting caught is really, *really* hard. Especially since you can't hire a hitman. I'm sorry, but that's not really a thing. Any hitman a regular person can find online is a cop in disguise, everyone knows that."

"But you did hire a hitman," I said. "Or hit-woman. That's essentially what Kendall was, wasn't she?"

"Yeah, and look how that turned out. I gave the foxglove to her on Monday morning. Up till then I had it in a grow bag filled with dirt that I put in my suitcase. I could barely bring any clothes with me, it took up so much room. I *told* her to use gloves when she cut off the leaves and washed them."

"Did she know the leaves were strong enough to kill someone?"

"Well, they weren't really, were they? As Payton so bitchily explained. I told Kendall it was a prank, but I honestly think she would've done anything for the thousand bucks I gave her."

"How did you—"

"Crypto. Untraceable."

I nodded again.

"You know the rest. The idiot forgot to use gloves and got sap and oils all over her hands. That's why they were red on Monday afternoon when you saw her at lunchtime. By that night they were a disaster."

"If only I'd remembered about her red hands when we were interviewing her," I lamented. "I could have saved her."

"Actually, if you'd put two and two together in the moment, I was prepared to kill *both* of you and make it look like Kendall did you in and then died herself, from wounds you'd inflicted. So it's a good thing you didn't. *Please* don't beat yourself up. You don't deserve it."

Yes, I did.

"In a perfect world I'd have been able to make it look like Kendall killed herself, even when I killed her solo. But I didn't know about Gerry's gun at that point, and without a gun it's almost impossible to stage a suicide," she explained. "So I really should have killed you. That plus the danger you posed generally, curious cat that you are. The fact that I didn't shows how much I like you. See, there's your proof!"

"Aw, how sweet," I cooed. "My therapist's been encouraging me to make connections with people. I can't wait to tell her about my new friend who likes me so much, she didn't murder me in cold blood."

I don't actually have a therapist. But Joan guffawed, as I knew she would.

"You know," I continued, "you made another mistake, which I should have called you on. But I didn't realize it till now."

"Oh? What was that?"

"You said you told Kendall not to touch anything on Table 1 after Payton had thrown up there. But there was no time for you to have said anything to her after that happened. I was there when you ran over to Payton and then helped her to the

308 / KEMPER DONOVAN

elevator. You never interacted with Kendall. You were refer-
ring to one of your secret meetings with her, *before* the fact."

"You know, I never realized that but you're absolutely right.
Wow. I really should have killed you."

"Flattery will get you nowhere. I have one more. Mistake,
that is."

"Bring it."

"Helen Sanchez was able to leave her manuscript in my
room because the door was unlocked. I assume you had something to do with that?"

She nodded. "I had Kendall's master key, of course. I used it
to slip into your room during Monday's afternoon session, just
to try to get a better sense of you. I was in such a rush, I forgot
to lock the door on my way out."

"What were you doing in there?"

She shrugged. "Just my due diligence. Not that I found anything useful. You had your phone with you, and your laptop
was password-protected. It's not like I'm a cryptographer."
She smirked. "Not like Captain Ellen McDwight. I should've
left well enough alone. That key was only useful when I gave it
to Jackson to get into Room 101, to steal the necklace from the
safe. Payton was wrong about that too. I didn't steal the necklace. He did."

"How did you get Jackson to go along with everything?" I
asked wonderingly. "Letting Flora onboard, poisoning Payton,
stealing the necklace?"

It was no wonder he'd looked guilty when Payton had gotten sick at dinner. . . .

"I got him to do it because I was supplying him with drugs.
Payton glossed over this in her little lecture upstairs, but he
was a massive addict. I wasn't making that up. I promised I'd
keep supplying him with drugs, and I think he would've done
anything to keep the good times rolling. He thought my whole
purpose was to get the necklace. I told him I was working for

the original owner, who was desperate to get it back. I admitted I was behind Flora getting on the ship for purposes of a distraction, and I told him we were going to make Payton sick for the same reason, so that he could go and steal the necklace after dinner. He thought it was all pretty exciting. He was into it. I'm sure he figured he could blackmail me for years to come. What a fucker that guy was. Total trash."

The word "trash" reminded me of what Gerry had said—about how Jackson had treated her son. But Gerry had come to the conclusion that *nobody* was trash, including Jackson.

"How did Gerry know who you were?" I asked.

Joan rolled her eyes. "Her son, Stephen, was *obsessed* with all of Jackson's exes, even before Jackson dumped him. I'm sure he told mommy about me and my ex. He actually looked me up after he and Jackson split. I think he was looking for sympathy."

"He was in unbelievable pain."

"Yeah, well, so was I. I didn't realize his mother was on board till you waved to her at the welcome drinks. I avoided her after that. Until I couldn't anymore." She sighed. "The fact that she was able to piece together who I was, whereas Jackson had no idea, tells you everything you need to know about him. Luckily Gerry didn't figure it out till after he died, or if she did, she failed to enlighten him. Did I mention he was trash?"

"I don't know," I said. "I'll never forget the look on his face when he saw how sick Payton was at dinner."

"Sheesh, that's like your favorite thing, to talk about how guilty Jackson looked after Payton puked. What a guy, be still my heart."

"It wasn't just that," I said. "When I ran into him before dinner that night, he was the one who referenced Payton's daiquiri that afternoon not being to her liking. Even though *he* was the one who poisoned it. It's like he wanted to be caught."

"Eh, maybe. You know he came to me about his yellow-tinted eyesight? I told him to lay off the drugs. I knew he wouldn't. I almost lost my shit when he made that comment about Payton's cocktail at the welcome drinks. I thought for sure someone would realize what was going on."

"Yes, I can't imagine why the word 'xanthopsia' didn't roll off my tongue in that moment," I replied sarcastically.

"I made sure there were trace amounts of digitalis in the drugs left over in his room, by the way. They would have explained away the high concentration in his bloodstream when the autopsy was performed. Death of a junkie who already had elevated digitalis in his system due to impure drugs. People die every day ingesting fentanyl and other opioids unknowingly. Finding digitalis in recreational pills would be odd, but not out of the question. You can find practically anything in street drugs these days."

"Did you visit him that night? After the dinner?"

"The night he died? Sure. I went in while I was making my rounds to the other passengers who thought they were poisoned, which is when I collected the master key and the necklace. I could see he was near the end. But I gave him one last dose, right in the arm. And then there was no question he was going to die. I told him everything, you know. As he lay there helpless, receding into a coma."

I suppressed a shudder. "You did?"

She nodded. "*Very* satisfying. He died knowing he'd been tricked. And since I'm telling you every dirty detail, apparently, I may as well share the one I'm most ashamed of, which is that after I knew the crew rooms had been searched, I went to the medical bay and rubbed some hydrogen peroxide in my eyes to irritate them. Then I grabbed that crochet hook and visited Kendall. I said the foxglove had done something to my eyes, irritated them. Thanks to her hands and the power of suggestion, it wasn't long before her eyes were hurting, too. So I had her lean her head back for me to examine them. I steadied myself like so"—she gently laid a hand on her neck—"and then—"

"Please—stop. You don't have to paint me a picture."

"People are so trusting of doctors. They shouldn't be."

"What about Gerry?" I asked. "Aren't you ashamed of killing her?"

"I am," she admitted. "Another mother sacrificed. But at least her child is dead already. And honestly? It was such a rush pulling that one off. I had to *book* it out of Room 101 after you left, and then pray she'd left her gun in her room. Once I had that, I could take my time a little, since I knew it'd take her a while to work up to the part where she said who I was, if she ever did. I was obviously hoping she wouldn't! But I was down on that ledge, listening. And there was no question she was going to name me."

I pictured her crouching there, listening intently while we chatted above her, clueless. . . .

"The shot was easy. I was lucky no one was up on the top deck. But then everyone was more or less hiding in their cabins at that point."

"Except Flora," I pointed out.

"Except Flora. More luck, since she didn't see me, *and* she managed to cast suspicion on herself." Joan chuckled. "Poor Flora."

Was she seriously *chuckling*? She obviously had no remorse. I needed to vacate the room, to get away from this monster. No—not a monster. As Gerry herself had pointed out, no one was a total monster. But that didn't change the fact that I wanted nothing more to do with her.

I got up from my chair and walked to the door before turning around again.

"You know, you can blame your parents, who it sounds like did their best for you, or your ex-fiancé, who was probably looking for an excuse to move on, or your child, whose existence you find so annoying. You can blame all of them for your not having become a writer. But do you know what all writers have in common?"

She shook her head.

"They write. No matter what. Also?" I held up my phone, ending the voice memo I'd created. "If you think everything you told me was between us girlfriends, then you're about as dumb as you thought Jackson was. Goodbye forever."

I'd like to say I never saw Joan Chen again. But her criminal trial is ongoing, and it doesn't look to be ending anytime soon. As you can imagine, I'm a key witness in the proceedings.

CHAPTER 38

By the time I left Joan, dinner was long over, and most of the passengers who'd ventured out had gone to bed. I'd expected people to emerge from their hiding places as word spread that Payton had captured the killer. But I suppose the passengers had had enough, and who could blame them? I didn't mind, because this meant I was free to roam the empty ship as though I were one of the people Joan had murdered—a ghost revisiting the scene of my demise. . . . This was an excellent way to review the events of the past few days, and to record as much of my impressions as possible while I still had access to the place where it happened. In a matter of hours I'd be leaving the *Merman Rivera*, and even in the unlikely event that I revisited it, the ambiance wouldn't be the same.

Around midnight I found myself up on the observation deck, whispering like a ghost into another voice memo file so that I didn't have to take off my gloves and attempt to type with frozen fingers. It was literally freezing, the temperature well south of the 30s, and I was bundled up, standing at the railing that looked toward the bow of the ship. It was overcast, which was just as well. I had no time or inclination on this final night for oohing and aahing at the stars.

"Isn't this where we first met?"

It was Gideon.

"We'd met a hundred times before this boat," I reminded him.

"True. But we *really* met here."

"Actually, we met on the poop deck." I tilted my head toward the stern of the ship. "But I'm avoiding that area since it still has Gerry Forrest's brain matter splattered all over it."

"I'm sorry for being an asshole to you."

"You mean when I was assisting the murderer in our interrogation of you? Yeah, I think we're good."

We stared out at the black ocean. I wondered how deep it was, and tried imagining my body floating in its limitless depths. What a comfort it would be to know that no one could ever look at me again. . . .

"You must think I'm so stupid," I said softly.

"Not at all. You know it was Payton who figured it out? I was just the accidental trigger, I happened to have read—"

"I don't really want to hear it," I said. "If you don't mind."

"Not at all," he said again.

We resumed our staring.

"You cold?"

I shook my head. There would be no cuddling tonight.

"I know this isn't the time or place, but I'd really like to take you out sometime. In the city."

I almost laughed. Then I almost cried, because the only person I wanted to tell about Gideon Pereira asking me out after everything that had happened was Joan.

"I don't think so," I said—not cruelly. Or at least, I hope not.

"Why?"

"I just don't think it's a good idea."

"Well, there's a nonanswer." He smiled at me sadly, his red lips easily the brightest objects in my field of vision. "Can we at least be friends?"

I thought about what Joan had said: about how maybe if she'd had friends, she wouldn't have become the kind of person capable of doing what she did. This was nonsense. But it was time I started cultivating friends. *Real* friends. And though I had zero confidence that Gideon Pereira and I would ever sustain a meaningful relationship in a platonic sense, I figured I may as well leave the door open.

"I'd like that," I said.

He left soon afterward, to get some sleep before the boat docked. I felt sure I was too wired for sleep myself, but when I went down to my cabin around one in the morning to thaw my frozen body, I passed out much as I had the night before: in my clothes on top of the bedspread. Mercifully, my sleep was dreamless.

I woke up in a state of alarm, convinced before I opened my eyes that I'd overslept. But then I saw by the darkness of the sky outside my porthole that the sun hadn't risen yet. It was just past five, which meant I had plenty of time to take a shower, brush my teeth, comb my hair, and put on a clean set of clothes. I knew from past experience how much the simple act of readying myself for the day would strengthen my mental resolve, and yet I was surprised anew by the efficacy of this routine.

I packed my suitcase, leaving it on its hind legs by the door—ready and waiting to be wheeled out once the boat reached New York. On went my coat and winter accessories again. I returned to the top level, intent on watching the sunrise.

This time I sought the shelter of the middle part of the deck, where the canvas would cover me. It was windy today, with little whitecaps on the water's surface. The space heaters were going full blast and they felt glorious—so much so that I let out a little sigh of contentment.

"I agree, these heaters are *fabulous*. Such an indulgence."

Jessamine LaBouchère sat down beside me. "Fancy meeting you here. You're looking well. Did you sleep?"

I nodded. "You?"

"Barely. But I must admit, it was more sleep than I was expecting to get!"

She pulled out some gray yarn and another crochet hook. It had the same wooden handle with the engraved initials on it, though the metal hook was slightly smaller: the next size down in her set, I guessed.

"Another gun cozy?" I asked.

"Booties this time. For my great-nephew."

"There's something I wanted to ask you."

"Ask away."

"What was the real reason you didn't eat the foxglove at dinner?"

She put down her crocheting. "I was wondering if anyone would ask me about that, now that we're on the other side of things. I was hoping it might get lost in the hubbub."

"You don't have to—"

She held up a hand. "I don't mind. Because you're absolutely right. I was lying to you. You're very clever, you know. Even though you didn't solve the crime. I hope you can appreciate that."

I couldn't.

She picked up her crocheting again, and began working the needle through the small patch of yarn in her lap. "Sometimes I get these . . . senses about things. You could call it a sixth sense, if you like. Or a premonition, if you want to be bombastic about it. The simple truth is that with no evidence at all, I knew those leaves were trouble and that I shouldn't eat them."

"But then why didn't you tell everyone else?"

"Because I had no evidence! There was no earthly reason I knew those fuzzy leaves to be harmful." When her eye caught mine, it twinkled at me. "I'm already an aged and prolific romance novelist. Add any more kook to the mix, and people will take less seriously than they already do." Her voice grew quieter, though without any softness in it. If anything, it was harder than before. "No one likes being reduced to a stereotype."

I thought about Jackson Richards, who I had typecast as venal and heartless the moment I met him. Maybe if more people had given him a chance, he wouldn't have fallen prey to the likes of Joan Chen. Maybe if I had given him—and others—a chance, I wouldn't have fallen prey to Joan Chen.

It was so obvious to me now that I should have latched on to Jessamine rather than Joan. The sun peeked over the horizon, suffusing the gray sky with a bouquet of orange and red blossoms. I turned to her. There was still time.

"Do you think we could be friends?"

She didn't answer right away, her hook wiggling busily.

"The easy thing for me to do would be to say yes. But I'll grant you the rare courtesy of an honest response." Again, she put down her work. "I have enough friends. And at my age, I don't have room for more. Not in a meaningful way. And I know that's what you're after. I commend you for that."

I tried to hide my embarrassment—my crushing humiliation.

"Don't be embarrassed," she continued. "You should be the opposite. Truly. Besides, you already have a friend to tend to."

"I hope you don't mean Joan."

"Good heavens, no. Let that one rot. No, you've known this person a long time, and it's obvious you feel deeply for one another. The timing couldn't be better. And on that note—"

I looked across the deck, to where she was looking. Payton had just emerged from the main stairwell into the open air. She waved at us.

"Go talk to her." Jessamine waved back. "Go on. Before she comes over here and the conversation becomes trite like almost all conversations do, no matter who's conducting them. Go on! You don't have much time."

* * *

"It's the woman of the hour," I cried out.

"I don't know about *that.*" Payton simpered, and I had to will myself to continue walking toward her rather than running in the opposite direction. "Have you seen the blowback I'm getting on social media for reappropriating the phrase 'hate crime'?" She shook her head. "Major misstep."

"Do you want to watch the sunrise?"

"Please!"

We went to Lovers' Point, at the stern of the ship. Even though the poop deck was above us, we couldn't see it, and it was easier than I expected to pretend we weren't so close to the scene of Gerry's demise.

We sat down on the outermost bench—the same bench I'd sat on with her ex-husband the first night of the cruise.

"Other than the hate crime thing, how's the response been?" I asked.

"*Amazing.* There are all these TikTok mash-ups of me and, like, Columbo and Vera Stanhope? Doing their final summations at the end of their cases?"

"Denouements."

"Day-noo-whats?"

"The denouement. It's the summation at the end of a mystery."

"Ahhhh. I knew I hired the right person as my mystery expert."

"Not really," I said. "Thanks for not humiliating me, by the way. During your denouement. You easily could have."

"I would never do that," she said seriously. "Do you know how much trauma you've been through? Way more than anyone else on this boat. I'm amazed you're still stringing sentences together. I'm in awe of you. I mean that."

"I enabled a murderer. I can't believe how dumb I was—"

"You weren't dumb," said Payton. "Never call yourself dumb. Maybe a little more easily manipulated than your average per-

son, which has nothing to do with intelligence and everything
to do with—"

She hesitated.

"With what?" I asked. "Just say it. If you don't tell me, I'll
go crazy wondering."

"With being so unavailable. Flora and I used to talk about it
all the time. How . . . *closed off* you are. I mean, what's the first
thing they do in a cult? Cut you off from anyone outside it."

"So now I'm in a cult?"

"Kind of. Your own weird, one-person cult. But forget all
that." She waved this away with her gloved fingers. "Take it
from me, the dam's got to break sometime, girl. That tide's got
to rise."

Ugh, was she going to try to sell me a copy of her book? But
why did I hate so hard on her? I was always trying to catch her
out at not being true to her public persona, but can't you be
two things at once? Can't you be perky and supportive to your
readers and fans—the people you don't know very well, and
on whom your livelihood depends? Isn't this what people who
work in retail do? Did I fault the cashier at a clothing store for
smiling at me when she didn't feel like it? There's nothing
wrong with a little duplicity. The trick is knowing where the
line lies—across from which you became Joan Chen. There
was no question Payton was on the right side of it.

And so was I. The shock of this washed over me as the sun
grew brighter, and began warming my frozen nose. Maybe
there wasn't as much wrong with me as I'd grown accustomed
to thinking there was. Maybe I'd been using my warped sense
of self-perception as a crutch.

I put my hand—my glove, I should say—on her arm. Still,
the intimacy of this gesture was unprecedented between us.
And yet she didn't draw back.

"I had an older sister," I told her. "She killed herself when
she was twenty-one and I was seventeen. And even though I

wasn't legally responsible for it—morally, I was. I truly believe that. Till my dying day, I'll believe I was the reason she died. Or the main reason, anyway. It's why I never talk about my family. I don't ever talk to my parents. It's like they're dead, too."

"Oh, honey," she began—but I cut her off.

"The name you know me by is as fake as 'Belle Currer.' I gave it to myself when I was eighteen, after what happened. Legally, it's my real name now, but it's never felt real. It never did me any good. I still think about her every day. So you may as well call me Belle now, if you don't mind."

"Okay."

"I've never been honest with you. But I'd like to try."

"I'd like that too."

She'd said it instantly, without hesitating. I couldn't believe her warmth, her openness. Except I could, of course. This was the kind of person Payton Garrett was.

I still hadn't taken my glove off her arm, and when she placed her glove on top of mine, it would have been rude to move it. So we sat like this on the bench, looking out at the ocean, which had calmed considerably since earlier in the morning.

"You know," she said after a while, "I was totally bluffing about Jackson having written anything down."

"*Really?*"

She nodded. "Whatever, it's not like I'm the police, right? I just wanted to get her to confess."

"She confessed a bunch to me too."

"I assume you recorded it?"

"What do you take me for?"

"See, that's what I love about you. You always seal the deal in the end. New York State has jurisdiction out here, which means all you need is one-party consent, so all of that should be admissible." (It was. And is.) "Anyway, Jackson didn't write shit. He wasn't a real writer. He *wanted* to be, which is why it took him years to write that crappy YA novel. But it wasn't in his bones. *I've* been taking notes like crazy." She gave me a sideways glance. "I'll bet you have too."

I confirmed her suspicion, and for a while we compared notes, literally, till someone interrupted us.

"Room for one more?"

It was Nicole. The bench sat three easily, and together we continued watching the sky grow brighter. I closed my eyes: a strategy I've developed for taking in an otherwise overwhelming sensory experience. Removing the visual element allows me to zero in on what else is happening, and so I sat there, basking in the surprising warmth of the January sun; listening to the water rush against the sides of the swiftly moving boat; feeling the wind on my face, light as a kiss; appreciating the muted presence of the light swimming across my inner darkness—a darkness that was a lot less dark than usual.

When I opened my eyes, Nicole Root was watching me.

"I never got a chance to prove you wrong about poetry," she said. "Maybe we can pick up that conversation some time in New York?"

I nodded.

"Lunch, then?" said Payton. "Yes?"

I nodded again.

"Great! And I don't mean that in the usual it'll-never-happen way." She pulled out her phone. "How's next Tuesday at one, at Pastis?"

"Okay."

"Don't you need to check your calendar?"

"No," I retorted. "I don't have a social life. But thanks for forcing me to admit that aloud."

"Ha, fine." She plugged it into her phone. "Okay, I just e-mailed you a reminder."

Annoying. Did she think I wouldn't remember on my own?

* * *

Nicole and Payton returned to Room 101 to pack up their things. It was now fully morning, and the land mass of the Eastern Seaboard was just making itself visible. I realized we were in about the same place as when the journey had been starting and I was going down to my room with Gerry, urging myself to appreciate the beginning of things, knowing how quickly the end would come. . . .

Once again, time had sucker-punched me. And like a chump, I'd fallen for it. Maybe one of these days I'll learn to appreciate the beginnings.

But I'm not counting on it.

CHAPTER 39

The *Merman Rivera* docked in Staten Island at ten in the morning, well over an hour ahead of its amended schedule, and four days earlier than originally planned. The crowd I'd been hoping for when we departed had materialized for our arrival: a throng of concerned family and friends, journalists, and general lookie-loos. It reminded me of the way people used to wait for the next installment of serialized novels back in Victorian times—works of suspense like *The Woman in White*, by Wilkie Collins.

It was a reference Joan Chen would have appreciated.

I walked off the ship as inconspicuously as I could, shaking my head whenever someone asked me for a comment. I spied the captain as I was leaving—patting the side of the ship the way a proud and affectionate horsewoman would touch the rump of her steed. I trust that Captain Ellen McDwight has a long career ahead of her, and the ill-fated voyage of the *Merman Rivera* turns out to be a blip, a rare blemish on an otherwise spotless career.

It was difficult to board another boat immediately after this one, but the only way to get from Staten Island to Manhattan is by ferry. It was at least a short ride, and blessedly uneventful. From there it was but a few subway stops to my beloved studio apartment on the Upper West Side.

Everything was just as I had left it. I threw open the two large windows in my living room, and the tiny window in the wall opposite, above my kitchen sink. It smelled *ever* so slightly of mildew, which happens whenever I have to shut up the place for days on end. The diffuse hum of traffic and humanity drifted upward from the street, and I stopped to listen, savoring the distance—six whole stories—between me and the rest of the world. After three days sandwiched alongside three hundred bodies, I was *ecstatic* to be alone.

Ecstasy is not built to last, however. And thank goodness for that, because I had a murder mystery to write. By the time I was lunching with Payton and Nicole at Pastis, my agent, Rhonda, had negotiated an advance fee with my publisher that was three times what I'd earned for my labors on the Get Lit Cruise. Payton made me drink an extra glass of champagne in celebration. I see her regularly now, with Nicole making frequent appearances. (Occasionally Nicole and I hang out just the two of us as well.) I don't see anyone as frequently as I do my therapist, however. Don't worry—I won't become one of those tiresome people who can't shut up about therapy, now that they've *finally* succumbed. Just know that I *have* succumbed, and it seems to be helping. I never would have found myself, for instance, celebrating the near-completion of this very manuscript by pulling up a contact on my phone labeled "The Bodyguard," and sitting with my finger poised over the call button.

My finger darted sideways, pressing the edit button instead. I relabeled the contact "Denny Peters," because he deserved a real name. Also, I was stalling. Denny was the only man in recent memory I'd liked: a man I'd met during my first adventure up in Maine, who I found attractive (and then some), and with whom I could imagine a relationship beyond the physical realm. I'd already imagined it, actually. We'd spent ages together, if only in my head.

I pressed the call button. And as the phone rang, my mind darted to the one image that's endured from my time aboard the *Merman Rivera*. Somewhat to my surprise, it's Nicole's necklace, which was never recovered. It must have settled somewhere on the bottom of the northern Atlantic, out of view of all but the very deepest ocean dwellers. It tickles me to think of this necklace getting more or less valuable according to the whims of the economy on any given day, like some radioactive Heart of the Ocean. Personally, I can't think of a truer reflection of the dizzying, disorienting experience of being human. And I don't mean that in a cynical or hopeless way. Truly. We're so afraid of change. But in the end, change is our only means of salvation.

The line clicked over. He'd answered.

Say something, you idiot.

And so I did.

Acknowledgments

The frustrating thing about acknowledgments is that you have to write them before so much of the work is done—in particular, the crucial work of book promotion, and the myriad little miracles a good publisher performs on behalf of a book as it emerges into the world. Kensington Books is not just a good publisher, but a great publisher, and now that I am publishing my second book with them, I get the opportunity to shower a bevy of well-deserved accolades on the many people who've helped the Ghostwriter and company come into being, both in *The Busy Body* and *Loose Lips*.

John Scognamiglio makes my work better every time he interacts with it. And while this is all I could ask for in an editor, he *also* has impeccable taste in classic movies, including an ocean-deep knowledge of obscure noir films. Please keep those recommendations coming, John.

Larissa Ackerman is an absolute genius when it comes to book promotion. Most importantly, she is a kind and attentive person who always answers my questions, no matter how stupid and/or neurotic they are.

Lauren Jernigan helps me make sense of what to do on the Internet as an author. She is also the best book club moderator in the business. I could chat with her for hours, and with any luck, I will.

Kris Noble has designed two outstanding covers that get tons of compliments wherever I go; I cannot wait to see what she does the third time around. (No pressure!)

Huge and hearty thanks also to Jackie Dinas, Vida Engstrand, Matt Johnson, Robin Cook, Sarah Beck, and Kait Johnson. I am so lucky to work with this outstanding team of lovely and industrious people.

My agent, Abby Saul, is simply the best. Abby, thank you for your generous and productive presence, and for shattering every negative stereotype in existence when it comes to being a successful agent.

Eva Kaminsky is the voice of the Ghostwriter on the audio-book version of these novels, and I hear as much raving about her as I do about the cover art. Thank you, Eva, for instinctively understanding who the Ghostwriter is, and inhabiting her so effectively. I am in awe of what you do.

Where worldwide rights are concerned, Dorie Simmonds has connected me with some fabulous publishers. Thank you, Dorie, for all your hard work, and thanks also to Krystyna Green at Little, Brown in the UK, and to Rebecca Saunders at Hachette in Australia for bringing the Ghostwriter overseas. (And she didn't even have to get on a boat to make the journey!)

Thank you to Kathryn Harkup, author of *A is for Arsenic: The Poisons of Agatha Christie*, for crucial information about the workings of a certain poison. Any errors I've made are my own.

I shamelessly stole the name "Get Lit" from a Los Angeles-based non-profit that bears no resemblance to my fictional cruise. There is nothing frivolous about the real Get Lit, which is a thoroughly worthy organization devoted to student engagement and literacy.

Thank you to my eternal mystery inspiration, Dame Agatha Christie, and to all the listeners of the *All About Agatha* podcast, who have been so supportive of my literary endeavors. Special thanks to my former podcasting partner, the late Catherine Brobeck, who will never be forgotten.

I was so heartened to hear from as many readers of *The Busy Body* as I did, both virtually and in person. The act of writing is a solitary pursuit, but the act of publishing is anything but, and

I'd like to thank these readers for their interest and engagement. My conversations with you have been both joyous and instructive.

While I was writing this book, I had the pleasure of reading *The Voyage of the Dawn Treader* by C. S. Lewis with my oldest daughter, Angelica. While the book provided me with some nautical inspiration, Angelica continues to provide me with a much deeper and more enduring inspiration. And for the record, she never once giggled about the "poop deck," because she is already much more sophisticated than her daddy.

My youngest daughter, Maeve, has a ways to go in the sophistication department. But therein lies the glory of a two-year-old, whose curiosity and joie de vivre know no bounds. (I'm looking forward to the introduction of a bound or two in future, to be honest.)

Thank you always and forever to my husband, Adam Milch. For everything.